Praise for

Thank You for Smoking

"Is it even remotely possible that a novelist could have the skill, to say nothing of the wit, to write a book about a tobacco lobbyist and have the reader actually rooting for the scoundrel in its final pages? If Christopher Buckley made some sort of bar bet that he could, in fact, pull off such a trick, then Mr. Buckley can take the money off the bar. By writing *Thank You for Smoking*, he's won. . . . A hilarious novel."
—*The New York Times Book Review*

"Buckley takes aim at political correctness and incorrectness alike in this gleefully venomous send-up of Washington's 'sin lobbyists.'"
—*The New Yorker*

"In crazy scene after crazy scene, the author urges you to turn on the film projector in your head, to watch and listen to his characters as they act out his satiric script."
—*Los Angeles Times*

"As a political satirist, Christopher Buckley can count among his chief assets a penchant for creating unique comedic vehicles and a sense of timing that borders on a karmic gift. . . . He has a fine ear for comic dialogue and one-liners."
—*The Boston Globe*

"In this tale of a newsman-turned-tobacco-flack, Buckley shows himself to have an unmatched eye for the culture of Washington politics, media, and media manipulators."
—*The Washington Monthly*

"Buckley is a smoother, funnier and more refined heir apparent to Art Buchwald's throne."
—*Publishers Weekly* (starred review)

"Exquisitely vicious satire. . . . Buckley is comfortable walking the tightrope between the absurd and the absurdly real."
—*The Washington Post Book World*

"A hilarious, cleverly observed novel. . . . The book takes no prisoners along the Potomac River: greedy amoral lobbyists, scheming reporters, sanctimonious health experts and old-time Tarheel tobacco bosses."
—*USA Today*

"Read Buckley's novel in a designated area, because your guffaws will waft around like second-hand smoke. . . . Buckley is a superb writer of politically incorrect satire."
—*Entertainment Weekly*

Thank You for Smoking

THANK YOU

YOU

for

SMOKING

A Novel

Christopher Buckley

Random House Trade Paperbacks

New York

2006 Random House Trade Paperback Edition

Published in the United States by Random House Trade Paperbacks, an imprint of
The Random House Publishing Group, a division of Random House, Inc., New York.

RANDOM HOUSE TRADE PAPERBACKS and colophon are
trademarks of Random House, Inc.

Originally published in hardcover in the United States by Random House,
an imprint of The Random House Publishing Group,
a division of Random House, Inc., in 1994.

LIBRARY OF CONGRESS CATALOGING-IN-PUBLICATION DATA
Buckley, Christopher
Thank you for smoking / Christopher Buckley.
p. cm.
ISBN 0-8129-7652-5
1. Public relations—Tobacco industry—United States—Fiction. 2. Tobacco industry—
United States—Employees—Fiction. 3. Smoking—United States—Fiction. I. Title.

PS3552.U3394T48   1994
813'.54—dc20   93–45485

Printed in the United States of America

www.atrandom.com

8 9 7

Book design by Lilly Langotsky

FOR JOHN TIERNEY
LF

Author's Note

Some real people appear here under their own names,
but this is fiction.

Thank You for Smoking

Prologue

Nick Naylor had been called many things since becoming chief spokesman for the Academy of Tobacco Studies, but until now no one had actually compared him to Satan. The conference speaker, himself the recipient of munificent government grants for his unyielding holy war against the industry that supplied the coughing remnant of fifty-five million American smokers with their cherished guilty pleasure, was now pointing at the image projected onto the wall of the cavernous hotel ballroom. There were no horns or tail; he had a normal haircut, and looked like someone you might pass in the hallway, but his skin was bright red, as if he'd just gone swimming in nuclear reactor water; and the eyes—the eyes were bright, alive, vibrantly pimpy. The caption was done in the distinctive cigarette-pack typeface, "Hysterica Bold," they called it at the office. It said, WARNING: SOME PEOPLE WILL SAY ANYTHING TO SELL CIGARETTES.

The audience—consisting of 2,500 "health professionals," thought Nick, who leafing through the list of participants, counted few actual M.D.s—purred at the slide. Nick knew this purr well. He caught the whiff of catnip in the air, imagined them sharpening their claws on the sides of their chairs. "I'm certain that our next . . . panelist," the speaker hesitated, the word just too neutral to describe a man who earned his living by killing 1,200 human beings a day. Twelve hundred people—two jumbo jet planeloads a day of men, women, and children. Yes, innocent children, denied their bright futures, those happy moments of scoring the winning touchdowns, of high school and college graduations, marriage, parenthood, professional fulfillment, breakthroughs in engineering, medicine, economics, who knows *how* many Nobel Prize winners? Lambs, slaughtered by Nicholas Naylor and the tobacco industry fiends he so slickly represented. More than 400,000 a year! And approaching the half-million mark. Genocide, that's what it was, enough to make you weep, if you had a heart, the thought of so many of these . . . victims, their lives stubbed out upon the ashtray of corporate greed by this tall, trim, nicely tailored forty-year-old yuppie executioner who, of course, "needs . . . no . . . introduction."

Not much point in trying to soften up this crowd with the usual insincere humor that in Washington passed for genuine self-deprecation. Safer to try insincere earnestness. "Believe it or not," he began, fidgeting with his silk tie now to show that he was nervous when in fact he was not, "I'm delighted to be here at the Clean Lungs 2000 symposium." With the twentieth century fast whimpering and banging its way to a conclusion, every conference in sight was calling itself Blah Blah 2000 so as to confer on itself a sense of millennial urgency that would not be lost on the relevant congressional appropriations committees, or "tits" as they were privately called by the special interest groups who made their livelihood by suckling at them. Nick wondered if this had been true of conferences back in the 1890s. Had there been a federally subsidized Buggy Whips 1900 symposium?

The audience did not respond to Nick's introductory outpouring of earnestness. But they weren't hissing at him. He glanced down at the nearest table, a roundtable of dedicated haters. The haters usually took the closest seats, scribbling furiously on their conference pads—paid for by U.S. taxpayers—which they'd found inside their pseudo-suede attachés, also paid for by amber waves of taxpayers, neatly embossed with the conference's logo, CLEAN LUNGS 2000. They would take those home with them and give them to their kids, saving the price of a gift T-shirt. *My folks went to Washington and all I got was this dippy attaché.* The haters, whipped by the previous speakers into ecstasies of Neo-Puritanical fervor, were by now in an advanced state of buttlock. They glowered up at him.

"Because," Nick continued, already exhausted by the whole dreary futility of it, "it is my closely held belief that what we need is not more confron*tation,* but more consul*tation.*" A direct steal from the Jesse Jackson School of Meaningless but Rhymed Oratory, but it worked. "And I'm especially grateful to the Clean Lungs 2000 leadership for . . ." a note of wry amusement to let them know that he knew that the Clean Lungs 2000 leadership had fought like marines on Mount Suribachi to keep him out of the conference ". . . finally agreeing to make this a *conference* in the fullest sense of that word. It's always been my closely held belief that with an issue as complex as ours, what we need is not more talking *about* each other, but more talking *to* each other." He paused a beat to let their brains process his subtle substituting of "issue" for "the cigarette industry's right to slaughter half a million Americans a year."

So far so good. No one stood up and shouted, "Mass murderer!" Difficult to get back on track after being compared to Hitler, Stalin, or Pol Pot.

But then it happened, during the Q and A. Some woman about halfway back got up, said that Nick "seemed like a nice young man," prompting guffaws; said she wanted "to share a recent experience" with him. Nick braced. For him, no "shared experience" with anyone in this crowd could possibly bode well. She launched into a graphic account of a dear departed's "courageous battle" with lung cancer. Then, more in sadness than in anger, she asked Nick, "How can you sleep at night?"

No stranger to these occasions, Nick nodded sympathetically as Uncle Harry's heroic last hours were luridly recounted. "I appreciate your sharing that with us all, ma'am, and I think I speak for all of us in this room when I say that we regret your tragic loss, but I think the issue here before us today is whether we as Americans want to abide by such documents as the Declaration of Independence, the Constitution, and the Bill of Rights. If the answer is yes, then I think our course is clear. And I think your uncle, who was I'm sure a very *fine* man, were he here today, might just agree that if we go tampering with the bedrock principles that our Founding Fathers laid down, many of whom, you'll recall, were themselves tobacco farmers, just for the sake of indulging a lot of frankly unscientific speculation, then we're placing at risk not only our own freedoms, but those of our children, and our children's children." It was crucial not to pause here to let the stunning non sequitur embed itself in their neural processors. "Anti-tobacco hysteria is not exactly new. You remember, of course, Murad the Fourth, the Turkish sultan." Of course no one had the faintest notion who on earth Murad the Fourth was, but people like a little intellectual flattery. "Murad, remember, got it into his head that people shouldn't smoke, so he outlawed it, and he would go out at night dressed up like a regular Turk and wander the streets of Istanbul pretending to have a nicotine fit and begging people to sell him some tobacco. And if someone took pity on him and gave him something to smoke—*whammo!*—Murad would behead him on the spot. And leave the body right there in the street to rot. WARNING: SELLING TOBACCO TO MURAD IV CAN BE DANGEROUS TO YOUR HEALTH." Nick moved quickly to the kill: "Myself, I'd like to think that we as a nation have progressed beyond the days of summary executions for the crime of pursuing our own definition of happiness." Thus, having compared the modern American anti-smoking movement to the depredations of a bloodthirsty seventeenth-century Ottoman, Nick could depart, satisfied that he had temporarily beaten back the horde a few inches. Not a lot of ground, but in this war, it was practically a major victory.

1

There was a thick stack of WHILE YOU WERE OUTs when he got back to the Academy's office in one of the more interesting buildings on K Street, hollowed out in the middle with a ten-story atrium with balconies dripping with ivy. The overall effect was that of an inside-out corporate Hanging Gardens of Babylon. A huge neo-deco-classical fountain on the ground floor provided a continuous and soothing flow of splashing white noise. The Academy of Tobacco Studies occupied the top three floors. As a senior vice president for communications at ATS, or "the Academy" as BR insisted it be called by staff, Nick was entitled to an outside corner office, but he chose an interior corner office because he liked the sound of running water. Also, he could leave his door open and the smoke would waft out into the atrium. Even smokers care about proper ventilation.

He flipped through the stack of pink slips waiting for him at the receptionist's stand. "CBS needs react to SG's call for ban on billboard ads." ABC, NBC, CNN, etc., etc., they all wanted the same, except for *USA Today,* which needed a react to tomorrow's story in *The New England Journal of Medicine* announcing medical science's conclusion that smoking also leads to something called Buerger's disease, a circulatory ailment that requires having all your extremities amputated. Just once, Nick thought, it would be nice to get back to the office to something other than blame for ghastly new health problems.

"Your mother called," said Maureen, the receptionist, handing him one last slip. "Good morning," she said chirpily into her headset, exhaling a stream of smoke. She began to cough. No dainty little throat-clearer, either, but a deep, pulmonary bulldozer. "Academy of"—*hargg*—"Tobacco"—*kuhhh*—"Studies."

Nick wondered if having a receptionist who couldn't get through "hello" without a broncospasm was a plus.

He liked Maureen. He wondered if he should tell her not to cough if BR walked by. Enough heads had rolled in the last six months. Murad IV was in charge now.

Back in his office, Nick took off his new Paul Stuart sports jacket and hung it on the back of the door. One advantage to the change in Academy leadership was the new dress code. One of the first things BR had done had been to call in all the smokesmen—that is, the Academy's PR people, the ones who went in front of the cameras—and told them he didn't want them looking like a bunch of K Street dorks. Part of tobacco's problem, he said, was that the sex had gone out of it. He wanted them, he said, to look like the people in the fashion ads, and not the ones for JC Penney's Presidents' Day sale. Then he gave them each a five-thousand-dollar clothing allowance. Everyone walked out of the meeting thinking, *What a great boss!* Half of them got back to their desks to find memos saying they'd been fired.

Nick looked at his desk and frowned. It was very annoying. He was not an anal person, he could cope with a certain amount of clutter, but he did not like being the depository for other people's clutter. He had explained this to Jeannette, and she had said, in that earnest way of hers, that she completely understood, and yet she continued to use his desk as a compost heap. The problem was that though Jeannette was technically under Nick in communications, BR had brought her with him from Allied Vending and they obviously had this rapport. The odd thing was how she acted as if Nick were her real boss, with rights of high, middle, and low justice over her.

She had dumped five piles of EPA reports on secondhand smoke on his desk, all of them marked URGENT. Nick collected knives. She had carefully placed his leather-sheathed Masai pigsticker on top of one of the piles. Was this insolence masquerading as neatness?

Gazelle, his secretary, buzzed to say that BR had left word he wanted to see him as soon as he got back from Clean Lungs. Nick decided he would not report to BR immediately. He would make a few calls and *then* go and make his report to BR. There. He felt much better, indeed swollen with independence.

"BR said soon as you got back, Nick," Gazelle buzzed him a few moments later, as if reading his thoughts. Gazelle, a pretty black single mother in her early thirties, was very bossy with Nick, for Nick, having been largely raised in a household dominated by a black housekeeper of the old school, was powerless before the remonstrations of black women.

"*Yes*, Gazelle," he said tartly, even this stretching the limits of his ability to protest. Nick knew what was going on in Gazelle's intuitive head: she knew that Jeannette had her beady eyes on his job title, and that her own job depended on Nick's keeping his.

Still, he would not be ruled by his secretary. He had had a harrowing morning and he would take his time. The silver-framed picture of Joey, age twelve, looked up at him. It used to face the couch opposite his desk, until one day when a woman reporter from *American Health* magazine—now *there* was an interview likely to result in favorable publicity; yet you had to grant the bastards the interview or they'd just say that the tobacco lobby had refused to speak to them—spotted it and said pleasantly, "Oh, is that your son?" Nick beamed like any proud dad and said yes, whereupon she hit him with the follow-up, "And how does *he* feel about your efforts to promote smoking among underage children?" Ever since, Joey's picture had faced in, away from the couch.

Nick had given some thought to the psy-decor of his office. Above his desk was a quote in large type that said, "Smoking is the nation's leading cause of statistics." He'd heard it from one of the lawyers at Smoot, Hawking, the Omaha law firm that handled most of the tobacco liability cases brought by people who had chain-smoked all their lives and now that they were dying of lung cancer felt that they were entitled to compensation.

Above the couch were the originals of two old cigarette magazine ads from the forties and fifties. The first showed an old-fashioned doctor, the kind who used to make house calls and even drive through snowdrifts to deliver babies. He was smilingly offering up a pack of Luckies like it was a pack of lifesaving erythromycin. "20,679* Physicians say 'Luckies are *less irritating*' " The asterisk indicated that an

9

actual accounting firm had actually counted them. How much easier it had been when medical science was on their side.

The second ad demonstrated how Camels helped you to digest your Thanksgiving dinner, course by course. "Off to a good start—with hot spiced tomato soup. And then—for digestion's sake—smoke a Camel right after the soup." You were then supposed to smoke another before your second helping of turkey. Why? Because "Camels ease tension. Speed up the flow of digestive fluids. Increase alkalinity." Then it was another before the Waldorf salad. Another after the Waldorf salad. "This double pause clears the palate—and sets the stage for dessert." Then one *with* the plum pudding—"for the final touch of comfort and good cheer." It amounted to five, and that was just during dinner. Once coffee was served, you were urged to take out that pack and really go to town. "For digestion's sake."

BR, on his one slumming expedition to Nick's office so far, had stared at it as if trying to make up his mind whether it was the sort of thing his senior VP for communications should have in his office. His predecessor, J. J. Hollister, who had hired Nick after the unpleasantness—now *there* was a tobacco man of the old school, a man who in his day would have put away ten Camels with the Thanksgiving turkey, a man born with tar in his blood. A lovely man, kind, thoughtful, loved to sit around in his office after work over highballs and tell stories about the early days of slugging it out with Luther Terry, who had issued the catastrophic Surgeon General's Report back in 1964. Nick's favorite JJ story was—

"Nick, he said right away."

Really, it was intolerable. And he would not put up with it. "I *know*, Gazelle." To hell with it, he thought, flipping through his pink message slips like an unruly hand of poker; let Gazelle *and* BR wait. He would do his job.

He called the networks and issued his standard challenge to appear "anytime, anywhere" to debate with the surgeon general on the subject of cigarette billboard advertising or indeed on any topic. The surgeon general, for her part, had been refusing all Nick's invitations on the grounds that she would not debase her office by sharing a public platform with a spokesman for "the death industry." Nick went on issuing his invitations nonetheless. They made for better

sound bites than explaining why the tobacco companies had the constitutional right to aim their billboard messages at little ghetto kids.

Now for Buerger's disease. This was trickier. Nick thought for a
few minutes before calling Bill Albright at *USA Today*. He didn't like
getting into disease specifics and he didn't particularly want his name
attached to quotes containing the word "amputation."

"Well," he began, more in sadness than in anger, "why *not* blame
us for Buerger's disease? We're taking the rap for everything these
days. I read somewhere a week ago that cigarettes are widening the
ozone hole, so why not Buerger's? What's next? Dolphins? The way
things are going, we'll be reading next week that dolphins, arguably
the most majestic of the smaller pelagic mammals, are choking on
filters that people on cruise ships toss overboard."

Actually, Nick had not read that cigarettes were widening the
ozone hole, but since Bill was a friend, he felt that he could in good
conscience lie to him. He heard the soft clacking of the keyboard at
the other end. Bill was taking it down. They were each playing their
assigned roles.

"Nick," Bill said, "this report was in *The New England Journal of
Medicine*."

"For which I have the highest respect. But can I just ask one question?"

"Yeah."

"Where are the data?"

"What do you mean, where are the data? It's *The New England
Journal of Medicine*. It's *all* data, for Chrissake."

"This was a double-blind study?"

". . . Sure."

Fatal hesitation. Attack! "And how big was the control group?"

"Come on, Nick."

"Was this a prospective study?"

"You want to be in the story, or not?"

"Of course."

"You want me to go with 'Where's the data?' "

" 'Where *are* the data.' Please, I don't mind your making me out to
be a soulless, corporate lickspittle, but at least don't make me sound
like an ignorant, soulless, corporate lickspittle."

"So your comment is *The New England Journal of Medicine* doesn't know what it's talking about?"

"My comment is . . ." What was the comment? Nick looked up at the Luckies doctor for inspiration. "Buerger's disease has only recently been diagnosed. It has a complex, indeed, *extremely* complex pathology. One of the more complex pathologies in the field of circulatory medicine." He hoped. "With all respect, I think further study is warranted before science goes looking, noose in hand, to lynch the usual subjects."

From the other end came the soft clack of Bill's keyboard. "Can I ask you something?" Bill was frisky today. Usually he just wrote it down and put it in and moved on to the next story.

"What?" Nick said suspiciously.

"It sounds like you actually believe this stuff."

"It pays the mortgage," Nick said. He had offered this rationalization so many times now that it was starting to take on the ring of a Nuremberg defense: *I vas only paying ze mortgage. . . .*

"He just called, Nick. He *wants* to see you. *Now.*"

Tempted as he was to make his other calls, there was the matter of the mortgage, and also, somewhere underneath Jeannette's landfill of papers, the tuition bill for Joey's next semester at Saint Euthanasius—$11,742 a year. How did they arrive at such sums? What was the forty-two dollars for? What did they teach twelve-year-olds that it cost $11,742? Subatomic physics?

Nick walked pensively down the corridor to BR's office. It was lined with posters of opera and symphony and museum exhibitions that the Academy had underwritten. In JJ's day there had been glorious color posters of drying tobacco plants, the sun shining luminously through the bright leaf.

Sondra, BR's secretary, looked up at him unsmilingly and nodded him in. Also into health. No ashtray on *her* desk.

It was a large, woody, masculine corner suite, richly paneled in Circassian walnut that reminded Nick of the inside of a cigar humidor. So far, BR had not ripped out all of JJ's lovely wood and replaced it with brushed steel.

Budd Rohrabacher raised his eyebrows in greeting. He was leaning back in his big chair reading *Morbidity and Mortality Weekly Report,* standard reading matter around the Academy. BR was forty-nine years old, but exuded the energy of a younger man. His eyes, light green, intense and joyless and looking at life as a spreadsheet, might strike some as belonging to an older man who had been fundamentally disappointed early on and who had therefore decided to make life unpleasant for those around him. He was rumored to play squash at five A.M. every morning, not an encouraging habit in a boss, who would therefore arrive at the office at six-thirty, all pumped up and aerobicated and ready to eat the day, and any less-than-1000-percent-committed staffers along with it. Nick suspected he wore shirts one size too small to make his upper body bulge more, though it was true that twice a week he lunched on V-8 juice while lifting weights at a health club. He was tall, six-four, and he had a tendency to throw his height around in little, subtle ways, like holding the door open for you while waving you through under the archway formed by his arm. It gratified Nick to notice, when he did this to him once at the end of a day, a whiff of B.O. It is always consoling to discover humiliating bodily imperfections in those who dominate our lives. He had begun his tobacco career working in the grubby, rough-and-tumble—and not always strictly legit—arena of cigarette vending machines. He was known to have an inferiority thing about it, so staffers tended to avoid references to vending machines, unless it was unavoidable. Since taking over the Academy, BR had flexed a number of executive muscles and made some impressive gains for the industry. He had worked closely with the U.S. trade representative to make Asian countries allow U.S. cigarette manufacturers to advertise during children's morning TV programming. (In Japan alone, teenage smoking of U.S. cigarettes was up almost 20 percent.) He had fought off two congressional print-advertising bans here at home, gotten three southern state legislatures to declare "Tobacco Pride" weeks, and had brilliantly maneuvered the Los Angeles City Council into including a provision in their smoking ban ordinance that permitted smoking in the bar section of restaurants, a coup for which he had been lavishly congratulated by the chairman of the board of the Academy of Tobacco Studies, the legendary Doak Boykin. BR had what Napoleon's favorite generals had—luck. Since coming aboard, three of the people who had been suing the tobacco industry because they'd gotten cancer from smoking had died from smoking in their beds, causing their heirs and assigns to drop the suits; out of sheer embarrassment, as one lawyer at Smoot, Hawking had put it.

"Hey, Nick," BR said. Nick was tempted to say "Hey" back. "How were the lungs?"

"Clean," Nick said.

"Get any face time?"

Nick replied that he had jumped in front of every TV camera in sight in order to emphasize the industry's concern for responsible advertising, health, and underage smoking, but that he doubted that his face would be prominently featured, if at all, in the newscasts. Face time for tobacco smokesmen was a disappearing electronic commodity, more dismal handwriting on the wall. Not so long ago, TV producers would routinely send a camera crew over to the Academy to get an official industry rebuttal, only a five- or ten-second bite casting the usual aspersions on the integrity of the medical research that showed that American cigarette companies were doing the work of four Hiroshima bombs a year. But recently there had been fewer and fewer of these dutiful little opposing-viewpoint cabooses. More likely, the reporter would just close with "Needless to say, the tobacco industry *disputes* the NIH's report and claims that there is no—and I quote—'scientific evidence that heavy smoking by pregnant mothers is harmful to unborn fetuses.' "

"Did you bring the Kraut along with you?" BR asked, his eyes going back to his *MMWR,* a slightly distracting habit—in truth, a maddeningly rude but managerially effective habit—that he had acquired at Stanford Biz. Keeps underlings on their toes. By "Kraut" he meant G—for Graf—Erhardt von Gruppen-Mundt, the Academy's "scientist-in-residence." Erhardt had a degree in Forensic Pathology from the University of Steingarten, perhaps not Germany's leading academic center, but it made him sound smart. JJ had brought him onboard back in the seventies and had built a "research facility" around him out in Reston, Virginia, called the Institute for Lifestyle Health, consisting mostly of thousands of pampered white rats who never developed F344 tumors no matter how much tar they were painted with. The mainstream media hadn't taken Erhardt seriously in years. Mainly he testified in the endless tobacco liability trials, trying to confuse juries with erudite, Kissingerian-accented, epidemiological juju about selection bias and multivariable regressions. The decision to have him appear in court during the Luminotti trial wearing his white lab coat had not been well received by the judge.

"Yes," Nick said. "NHK—Japanese TV—did an interview with him. He was very good on secondhand smoke. He's really got that down cold. He'll get face time in Tokyo. I'm certain."

"That won't do us a whole lot of good in Peoria."

"Well . . ." So Erhardt was next. Twenty years of devoted service to science and *auf Wiedersehen,* you're history, Fritz.

"I think we ought to get ourselves a black scientist," BR said. "They'd *have* to cover a black scientist, wouldn't they?"

"That's got heavy backfire potential."

"*I* like it."

Well, in that case . . .

"Sit down, Nick." Nick sat, craving a cigarette, and yet here, in the office of the man in charge of the entire tobacco lobby, there were no ashtrays. "We need to talk."

"Okay," Nick said. Joey could always go to public school.

BR sighed. "Let's do a three-sixty. This guy"—he hooked a thumb in the direction of the White House, a few blocks away—"is calling for a four-buck-a-pack excise tax, his wife is calling for free nicotine patches for anyone who wants them, the SG is pushing through an outright advertising ban, Bob Smoot tells me we're going to lose the Heffernan case, and lose it big, which is going to mean hundreds, maybe thousands more liability cases a year, the EPA's slapped us with a Class A carcinogen classification, Pete Larue tells me NIH has some horror story about to come out about smoking and *blindness,* for Chrissake, Lou Willis tells me he's having problems with the Ag Committee with next year's crop insurance appropriations. There is zero good news on our horizon."

"Fun, ain't it, tobacco," Nick said companionably.

"I like a challenge as much as the next guy. *More* than the next guy, if you want the honest truth."

Yes, BR, I *want* the honest truth.

"Which is what I told the Captain when he begged me to take this on." BR stood up, perhaps to remind Nick that he was taller than him, and looked out his window onto K Street. "He gave me carte *15* blanche, you know. Said, 'Do what you have to do, whatever it takes, just *turn it around*.' "

BR was being elliptical this morning.

"How much are we paying you, Nick?"

"One-oh-five," Nick said. He added, "Before tax."

"Uh-huh," BR said, "well, you tell me. Are we getting our money's worth?"

It made for a nice fantasy: Nick coming over BR's desk with his World War I trench knife. Unfortunately, it was followed by a quick-fade to a different fantasy, Nick trying to get a second mortgage on the house.

"I don't know, BR. You tell me. Are you getting your money's worth?"

"Let's be professional about this. I'm not packing a heavy agenda. I'm putting it to you straight, guy-to-guy: how are we *doing* out there? I get this sense of . . . defeatism from your shop. All I see is white flags."

Nick strained to cool his rapidly boiling blood. "White *flags*?"

"Yeah, like that stupid proposal you floated last month suggesting we admit that there's a health problem. What was *that* all about, for Chrissake?"

"Actually," Nick said, "I still think it was a pretty bold proposal. Let's face it, BR, no one appears to be buying into our contention that smoking isn't bad for you. So why *not* come out and say, 'All right, in some cases, sure, smoking's bad for you. So's driving a car for some people. Or drinking, or flying in airplanes, or crossing the street, or eating too much dairy product. But it's a legitimate, pleasurable activity that, done moderately, probably isn't that much more danger-ous than . . . I don't know . . . life itself.' I think a lot of people would think, 'Hey, they're not such liars after all.' "

"Stupidest idea I ever heard," BR said with asperity. "Stupid *and* expensive. I had to have every copy of that memo burned. Can you imagine what would happen if it turned up in one of these goddamn liability trials? An internal document admitting that we know smok-ing is bad for you? Jesus Christ on a toasted bagel—do you have any *idea* what a disaster that would be?"

"Okay," Nick shrugged, "let's go on pretending there's no proof that it's bad for you. Since that's working so well . . ."

"See what I mean," BR shook his head, "defeatism."

Nick sighed. "BR, I'm putting in the hours. This is the first time in six years that my dedication has been called into question."

"Maybe you're burned out. Happens."

Jeannette walked in without knocking. "Whoops," she said, "sorry to interrupt. Here's that Nexis search you wanted on 'sick building syndrome.' "

She was attractive, all right, though a tad severe-looking for Nick's taste, business suit and clickety-click heels, icy blond hair pulled back into a tight bun, plucked eyebrows, high cheekbones, eager-beaver black eyes, and dimples that managed to make her even more menacing, somehow, though dimples weren't supposed to do that. She apparently went horseback riding in Virginia on weekends. This made perfect sense to Nick. Put a riding crop in her hand and she was the very picture of a yuppie dominatrix.

"Thanks," BR said. Jeannette walked out, shutting the door behind her with a firm *click*.

"Since we're talking 'guy-to-guy,' " Nick said, picking up where they'd left off, "you want to just give it to me straight?"

"Okay," said BR, tapping a pencil on his desk. "For one-oh-five a year, I think we could do better."

"I don't think I'm going to end up talking the surgeon general into deciding that smoking is good for you. I think we're past that point, frankly, BR."

"That's your whole problem! Don't think about what you *can't* do. Think about what you *can* do. You're spending your whole time stamping out wastebasket fires when you ought to be out there setting forest fires."

Forest fires?

"You're stuck in a reactive mode. You need to think proactive. Don't just sit behind your desk waiting for your phone to ring every time someone out there spits up some lung. You're supposed to be our communications guy. Communicate. Come up with a plan. Today's what?"

"Friday," Nick said glumly.

"Okay, Monday. Let me see something Monday." BR looked at his appointment book. "Whaddya know?" he grinned. It was the first time Nick had seen him do this. "My six-thirty A.M. slot is *wide* open." *17*

2

Here Nick could be himself. Here he was among his own.

The Mod Squad met for lunch at Bert's every Wednesday, or Friday, or Tuesday, or whenever. In their line of work, things—disasters, generally—tended to come up at the last minute, so planning ahead presented a problem. But if they went much longer than a week without a lunch or dinner together, they would get nervous. They needed each other the way people in support groups do: between them there were no illusions. They could count on each other.

The name Mod Squad was not a reference to the 1960s TV show about a trio of hip, racially and sexually integrated undercover cops, but an acronym for "Merchants of Death." Since they consisted of the chief spokespeople for the tobacco, alcohol, and firearms industries, it seemed to fit. Nick said that they might as well call themselves that since it was surely the name the press would give them if they ever got wind of their little circle.

They were: Nick, Bobby Jay, and Polly. Besides having in common the fact that they all worked for despised organizations, they were also at that age in life—late thirties, early forties—where the thrill of having a high-profile job has worn off and the challenge of keeping it has set in.

Bobby Jay Bliss worked for SAFETY, the Society for the Advancement of Firearms and Effective Training of Youth, formerly NRBAC, the National Right to Bear Arms Committee.

Bobby Jay was a soft-speaking, curly-headed 220-pounder from

Loober, Mississippi, population 235, where his father had been sheriff, mayor, and the principal collector of tax revenue by virtue of arresting every third driver who went through Loober, regardless of how fast he was going. He kept a variety of speed-limit signs, which could be changed on the spot as required. Bobby Jay, whom he had first deputized at age eight, instilling in his son a lifelong regard for law enforcement (and handguns), would hide in the bushes and change the signs depending on how fast the person had been going while his father pulled him over and berated him for driving so recklessly through downtown, despite the fact that there really was no downtown, per se, in Loober, Mississippi.

Following the Kent State shootings, Bobby Jay, then seventeen, hitchhiked all the way into Meridian in order to sign up for the National Guard, in order that he too could shoot college students; but the National Guard recruiter was out to lunch and the Army recruiter next door, recognizing a good thing when he saw one, offered to pay for his college education. So Bobby Jay ended up shooting at Vietnamese instead, which was almost as good as college students except that they shot back. Still, he enjoyed his two tours in Southeast Asia and would have signed up for a third, only the tail-rotor of a helicopter blade got the better of his left arm up to the elbow during a hasty evacuation of a red-hot LZ. He was one of the few Vietnam-era soldiers to receive a welcoming parade on his return home, though the parade, attended by all the residents of Loober, could not truthfully be called a huge one. Still, parades being rare in those troubled times, it made the papers and caught the attention of Stockton Drum, the legendary head of SAFETY. Drum had taken a run-down gun-owners' organization and turned it into the equivalent of the world's largest standing army, thirty million strong and nothing if not vocal, as any senator and congressman could tell you. With his colorful Southerner's way and steely left hook, Bobby Jay was a natural spokesman for the cause of gun ownership in America, and he prospered, rising to become SAFETY's chief spokesman. Along the way he repented of his sinful ways and became a born-again Christian, and not at an easy time, either, what with all the television evangelists going to jail for unevangelical behavior. He carpooled in from suburban Virginia with a group of fellow SAFETY born-agains, and on his way home to his wife and four children, they would stop at a firing range and discharge the tensions accumulated during the day by blasting away at paper-target silhouettes of vaguely ethnic attackers.

The Moderation Council, formerly the National Association for Alcoholic Beverages, represented the nation's distilled spirits, wine, and beer industries, and it had made a smart choice when it promoted Polly Bailey as its chief spokesperson. Faced with a rising tide of neo-puritanism, neo-prohibitionism, and disastrous volumetric decline, they resolved that a new approach was needed. So as beer commercials switched from bikini blondes and bibulous dogs to oil-coated baby seals being heroically rescued, as wine promotions began to emphasize its cholesterol-reducing qualities, and as liquor ads turned from ice-cold, dry martinis to earnest pleas for responsible driving, their trade association turned not to the traditional tough-talking, middle-aged white guy in a business suit, but to a talking head that could turn heads. Pretty, dark, a petite size-six, with lively, challenging blue eyes and (naturally) long eyelashes, Polly would not have looked out of place in a soap commercial; so when you saw her on the TV screen challenging the latest government report on alcohol-related car crashes or fetal alcohol syndrome, instead of talking about how she only used Ivory soap, the effect was downright arresting. It was her genius, Nick had noted, to wear her hair long, well down over her shoulders, suggesting youth and vitality, instead of the usual dutifully professional style that women feel they must adopt in order to show that they are willing to suppress natural beauty for the sake of gender assimilation, if that's what it takes to make partner, senior VP, or cabinet secretary.

Polly smoked—chain-smoked, in fact—which gave her voice a nice husky rasp, so that her flawless equivocations on the subject of blood alcohol content, phenolics, and excise taxes sounded down-right sexy, as if she were sharing them with you in bed, with the sheets rumpled, jazz on the stereo, the candle flickering, smoke curling toward the ceiling. She was a stylish dresser too—unusual in Washington, where stylishness in women is suspect—favoring Donna Karan black and white suits, especially the ones with the oversized collars that manage to impart a touch of the schoolgirl while also announcing that it would be very foolish to take this woman lightly. All in all, an effective voice in Washington for ethanol.

The liquor industry had been using women to sell its stuff since time began, rubbing them up against phallic bottles, displaying their gams while they cooed about how the new boyfriend drank their brand of scotch; why, Nick wondered, had it only recently occurred to them to use a good-looking lady while pitching public policy? Weren't congressmen and senators who decided on health warning labels and excise taxes as susceptible as anyone else to sex? Indeed, Nick himself was now in the midst of justifying his own traditional white-male self to his own boss, who seemed increasingly eager to replace him with the telegenic Jeannette.

Polly had come from southern California and gone to Georgetown University with thoughts of entering the foreign service, flunked the foreign service exam, gone to work on Capitol Hill, where she spent a good deal of time running from congressmen who had more than cloture on their minds.

She ended up as assistant staff director for the House Agricultural Committee, her member being the ranking majority member. He was from northern California, whose vineyards at the time were being virtually wiped out by the phylloxera parasite; it was Polly who brilliantly maneuvered an alliance of convenience between her member and the member from the citrus region, screwing the members from the avocado and artichoke regions out of their subsidies in the process, but all's fair in love and appropriations. Her member rewarded her hard work and diligence by passing her over and appointing someone else staff director, so when the genuinely grateful head of Wines at the Moderation Council called to congratulate her on her brilliant victory and mention in passing how he wished he had someone like her on his staff, she leapt.

While still in her twenties, Polly had married a fellow Hill rat named Hector, a smart, attractive, and ambitious young man who seemed destined for some kind of big role eventually in someone's presidential administration; but after attending a lecture by Paul Ehrlich, the overpopulation guru, he became a devotee to the cause, and quit his job on the Hill and went to work for a nonprofit organization that distributed birth control—condoms, mainly: three hundred million a year—free throughout the Third World. He spent four-fifths of his time in the Third World. The remaining fifth he spent back home in Washington looking for cures for various exotic tropical and infectious diseases, some of which made it unpleasant to be around him. Hector was passionate about overpopulation, Nick gathered from Polly's accounts, to the point where it was pretty much all he talked about.

Returning from a long trip to West Africa, however, he announced to Polly, in rather an unromantic, businesslike way, that he wanted to start having children, lots of them, and right away. This took Polly by surprise. Whether it was guilt over all those billions and billions of thwarted Third World sperm, or simply the desire to populate his own little corner of the world, Polly could not say; at this point all she did know was that she had, in a moment of weakness brought on by being chased around desks by too many congressmen, married a total loser.

Hector, meanwhile, became more and more adamant. By this time his skin had turned greenish from some suspect malaria pills dispensed by the local apothecary in Brazzaville. This, combined with his monomaniacal procreative fervor, had a calamitous effect on Polly's libido. He presented her with an ultimatum, and when she refused, he announced that it was all over and he was taking his fertility stick elsewhere. The divorce would become final in the fall. He was now living in Lagos, Nigeria, organizing a massive airdrop of condoms on the crowds expected to attend the pope's mass on his upcoming visit.

Discreet as the Mod Squad was, from time to time they invited other spokespeople to lunch to promote camaraderie among the despised. Their guests had come from such groups as the Society for the Humane Treatment of Calves, representing the veal industry, the Friends of Dolphins, formerly the Pacific Tuna Fishermen's Association, the American Highway Safety Association, representing the triple-trailer truckers, the Land Enrichment Foundation, formerly the Coalition for the Responsible Disposal of Radioactive Waste; others. Sometimes they had foreign guests. The chief spokesman for the Brazilian Cattlemen's Association had come by recently to share with them his views on rainforest management, and had entertained them with his imitation of a flock of cockatiels fleeing from bulldozers.

Their regular table was in the smoking section of Bert's, next to a fireplace with a fake electric fire that gave off a cozy, if ersatz, glow. Nick ordered his usual Cobb salad, which at Bert's came with about a quart of gloppy blue cheese dressing on top of enough bacon and chopped egg to clog an artery the size of the Holland Tunnel, and iced black coffee to wash it down and zap the thalamus for an afternoon of jousting with the media.

Bobby Jay ordered his usual: batter-fried shrimp with tasso mayonnaise. Polly, after briefly contemplating calamari, went for a trimming tossed green salad, French dressing on the side, and a glass of the house chenin blanc, crisp with a nice finish and not overpriced at $3.75 a glass.

Polly noticed that Nick was staring morosely into his iced coffee.

"So," she said, "how're we doing?" This was the traditional Mod Squad gambit. The answer was always *awful,* for it was unlikely that medical science had discovered that smoking prolonged life, or that the handgun murder rate had declined, or that somewhere out there some promising young life had been saved, instead of tragically snuffed out by a teenager with a blood alcohol content of .24 percent.

"How did your Lungs thing go?" Polly said, dragging deeply on a long low-tar cigarette. Nick had told her not to bother with the low-tars, since research showed you only smoked more of them to get the same amount of nicotine, a point nowhere to be found in the voluminous literature of the Academy of Tobacco Studies.

"Oh," Nick said, "it was all right. She called for a total advertising ban. *Big* surprise."

"I caught a bit of you on C-SPAN. Liked the Murad bit."

"Uh-huh."

"You all right?"

Nick explained about his meeting with BR and how he had until six-thirty A.M. on Monday to come up with a plan that would reverse forty years of antismoking trends. Polly cut directly to the heart of the matter. "He wants to put Jeannette in. *That's* what this is about." She promised to try to think of something by Monday.

She changed the subject back to the surgeon general. "You know she's going after us next. Never met an excise tax she didn't love. It has *nothing* to do with financing national health. She just doesn't want anyone to drink. Period. I've got my beer wholesalers coming into town for their annual convention next week and they're ready to kill. They're threatening to drive all their trucks onto the Mall."

"That would be an interesting visual," Nick said, rallying slightly   *23* from his depression. "The Washington Monument, surrounded by Budweiser trucks."

"They're pissed off. Sixty-four cents on a six-pack? They're trying to erase the deficit on the backs of the beer industry, and they don't think that's exactly fair." The Mod Squad in ways resembled the gatherings of Hollywood comedy writers who met over coffee to bounce new jokes off one another. Only here it was sound bites de-emphasizing the lethality of their products.

Until now Bobby Jay had not joined in on the conversation, as his cellular telephone was pressed to his ear. He was in the midst of a "developing news story," which for people in their business tended to be a bad news story. Another "disgruntled postal worker," those Bad News Bears of the gun industry, had been up to the usual shenanigans again. This one had gone as usual to Sunday church in Carburetor City, Texas, and halfway through a sermon on the theme of "The Almighty's Far-Reaching Tentacles of Love" had stood up and blasted the minister clear out of the pulpit, and then trained withering fire on the choir. Here he had departed from the usual text, for he did not then, as the newspapers put it, "turn the gun on himself." He was disgruntled, but not so disgruntled as to part with his *own* life. He was now the object of the most massive manhunt in Texas history. Bobby Jay told them that SAFETY was logging over two thousand calls a day.

"Pro or con?" Nick said. Bobby Jay did not rise to the bait.

"Do you know how many 'disgruntled postal workers' have pulled this sort of stunt in the last twenty years?" Bobby Jay said through a large forkful of shrimp. "Seven. Do you know what I want to know? I want to know what are they so disgruntled about? *We're* the ones whose mail never comes."

"Assault rifle?" Polly asked professionally.

Bobby Jay ripped off a shrimp tail with his front teeth. "Under the circumstances I'm tempted to say, probably, yeah. 'Course, nine times out of ten what they call an 'assault rifle' isn't. But try explaining that to our friends"—he hooked a greasy thumb in the direction of the *Washington Sun* building—"over there. To them, my ten-year-old's BB gun is an 'assault rifle.' " He held up his fork. "To them, *this* could be an 'assault' weapon. What are we going to do, start outlawing forks?"

"Forks?" Nick said.

"Forks Don't Kill People, People Kill People," Polly said. "I don't know. Needs work."

"It was a Commando Mark forty-five. You could, technically, consider it a semiautomatic assault rifle."

"With a name like that, yeah," Polly said. "Maybe you should ask the manufacturers to give them less awful names? Like, 'Gentle Persuader,' or 'Housewife's Companion'?"

"What I don't get is, the son of a gun was using hollow-point Hydra-Shok loads."

"Ouch," Nick said.

"That's a military load. They use those on, on terrorists. They blow up inside you." Bobby demonstrated with his hand the action of a Hydra-Shok bullet inside the human body.

"Please," Polly said.

"What was he expecting?" asked Bobby Jay rhetorically. "That the minister and the choir were wearing Kevlar bulletproof vests underneath their robes? What gets *into* people?"

"Good question," Nick said.

"So, what are you doing?" Polly asked.

"And why is it every time some . . . nutcase postal worker shoots up a church, they come rope in hand, to hang *us*? Did we give him the piece and tell him, 'Go forth, massacre a whole congregation'? Redekamp"—a reporter for the *Sun*—"calls me up and I can *hear* him gloating. He loves massacres. Thrives on massacres, Godless swine. I said to him, 'When a plane crashes on account of pilot error do you blame the Boeing Corporation?' "

"That's good," Nick said.

"When some booze-besotten drunk goes and runs someone down, do you go banging on the door of General Motors and shout, *'J'accuse!'* "

"You didn't tell him that?" Polly winced.

"Okay," Nick said, "but how are you handling the situation?"

Bobby Jay wiped a gob of tasso mayonnaise from his lips. A glint came into his eye. "The *Lord* is handling it."

Nick knew Bobby Jay to be an upright, car-prayer-pooling citizen, who occasionally salted his language with biblical phrases like so-and-so had "sold himself for a mess of porridge, like Esau's brother," but he was not a nut. You could have a normal, secular conversation with him. But this suggestion that the Lord himself was engaged in spin control made Nick wonder if Bobby Jay was crossing the line over into the Casualties column. He stared. "What?"

Bobby Jay looked over his shoulder and leaned in toward them. He said, "It had to be. Opportunities like this can only come from above. And they happen only to the righteous."

"Bobby Jay," Polly said, looking alarmed, "are you all right?"

"Listen, O ye of little faith, then tell me if you don't think the Lord was looking out for old Bobby Jay. I'm in the car driving to work—"

"With Commuters for Christ?"

"No, Polly, and I don't see the humor in that. It was just me. I'm listening to Gordon Liddy's call-in show—"

"Figures," Polly said.

"Gordon happens to be a friend of mine. Anyway, he's yakkety-yak-yakking about the shooting, his lines are lit up, and suddenly he says, 'Carburetor City, you're on the air,' and there's this woman's voice saying, 'I was *in* that church and I want to tell that last person you had on that he is just *wrong*.' I practically drove right off the road. She was saying, 'I own a pistol, but because the law in Texas says you cannot carry it on your person, you can only keep it in your car, I left it in the glove compartment. And if I had had that handgun with me there inside the church, that choir would still be singing 'Walk with Me, Jesus.' "

Nick felt a pang of jealousy. No one had ever called while he was being flayed alive on a radio talk show to say, *If I hadn't smoked five packs of cigarettes every day for forty years, I'd be dead by now.*

Bobby Jay, eyes bulging, went on. "Gordon was in seventh heaven. He kept her on the line for must have been fifteen minutes. She went on and on about how what a tragedy it was she didn't have her little S & W .38 airweight with her in that pew, how the whole misery could have been avoided. She was *this far* away from him! She couldn't have missed him! A clean head shot." Bobby held out his arm in combat shooting stance and aimed at a person at the next table. *"Bam!"*

"You're scaring the other patrons."

"So what did you do?" Nick asked.

26   "What did I *do*?" Bobby Jay bubbled. "What did I *do*? I'll tell you what I did. I put the pedal to the metal and went straight to National Airport and got on the next plane to Carburetor City. There *is* no 'next plane to Carburetor City.' You got to go through Dallas. But I was in that little lady's living room before six o'clock that afternoon."

" 'Little lady's'?" Polly said. "You're such a trog."

"Five-foot-four," Bobby Jay shot back. "In heels. And every inch a lady. A simple descriptive sentence, so may I continue, Ms. Sty-nem? I had our camera crew there by noon the next day. It is as we speak being edited into the sweetest little old video you ever saw." He spread his hands apart like a director framing the scene. "We open with . . . 'Carburetor City, Texas. A mentally unbalanced federal bureaucrat—' "

"Nice," Nick said.

"Gets better: '. . . attacks a church minister and choir . . .' Footage of ambulances, people on stretchers, people gnashing their teeth and rending their hair—"

"How," Polly said, "do people rend their hair?"

"Everywhere a scene of carnage," Bobby Jay continued, "a scene of devastation. Red chaos!"

"Red chaos?" Polly said.

"Shut up, Polly," Nick said.

"Voice-over. And guess whose?" Bobby Jay asked coyly.

"Charlton Heston?"

"No sir," Bobby said, all tickly and beaming. "Guess again."

"David Duke," Polly said.

'Jack Taggardy,' Bobby Jay said triumphantly.

"Nice," Nick said.

"Didn't he have his hips replaced? I read that in *People.*"

"What do his *hips* have to do with anything?" Bobby Jay said.

"Is he in a walker, or what?"

"No he's not in a any damn walker!"

"Go on," Nick said.

Bobby reframed the scene. "So Taggardy's voice-over: 'Could this awful human tragedy have been avoided?' "

"Question," Nick said. "Why 'human'?"

"Why not 'human'? They're humans."

"I would have thought, 'inhuman tragedy'?"

"He's got a point," Polly said.

"Look, we can edit. Do you want to hear this?"

"Yes," Nick said, "very much."

"Now we cut to my little lady. She's sitting in a chair, all prim and pretty. Darling girl. I had her hairdresser come over. She wanted to do her makeup but I wouldn't hear of it. I wanted her eyes red from crying. We dabbed a little onion under the eyelids, nothing wrong with that, just to get her in the mood, get those ducts opened up."

"Onion?"

"Didn't even need it. Soon as she saw those color police photos I was holding up for her off camera she started bawlin' like a baby. She's going on about how awful it was, and then she gets to the part about how she had to leave her pistol in the glove compartment. *Then* she looks right into the camera, right in your face, and dabs the corner of her eye—and that was *not* in the script—and says, 'Why won't our elected lawmakers just let us *protect ourselves*? Is that too much to ask?' Fade to black. Then Taggardy's voice comes back on and there's no mistaking that voice, like bourbon over sandpaper: 'The Second Amendment says the right of the people to keep and bear arms shall not be infringed. Does *your* elected lawmaker support the Bill of Rights? Or are they selling you a Bill of Goods?' " Bobby Jay leaned back in his chair. "What do you think?"

"Transcendent," Nick said. "A deft manipulation of post-traumatic stress."

Bobby Jay grinned. "Sweeter than honeysuckle in moonlight."

"Congratulations," Polly said. "Really masterful."

"By this afternoon, every member of the Texas congressional delegation and the state legislature will have a copy. By tomorrow, every sinner in the Congress will have one. We may even air it nationally. Mr. Drum hasn't signed off on that yet, but I am most strongly recommending that we do."

Bobby Jay's boss was one of the few in Washington who insisted on the *mister*. It was part of his aura, and he did cast a large aura. When he had taken over the leadership of the troubled SAFETY years back, there had been only fifty million guns circulating in America. There were now over 200 million. He was a physically imposing man with a trademark bald head. Redekamp of the *Sun* had dug up the fact that at the age of sixteen he had shot to death a seventeen-year-old in a dispute over the ownership of a box turtle. The conviction was later overturned on the grounds that the box turtle, having subsequently died, probably of stress, had never been introduced as evidence. Ever since, the anti-SAFETY Washington press, comprising all of the press except for the conservative *Washington Moon,* included a reference to this unfortunate incident in every mention of him.

Coffee arrived. Nick asked Polly, "What's happening at Moderation?"

"We actually got some great news yesterday." This was a stunner. Nick could not recall such words ever having been spoken over one of their lunches. "The Michigan Supreme Court ruled that sobriety roadblocks were unconstitutional," she said.

"Party *down,*" Nick said.

"The U.S. Supreme Court has ruled that they are constitutional, so for now they're constitutional everywhere except Michigan."

Bobby Jay said, "Don't you *see?*"

"See what?" Nick asked.

"The pattern. First they disarm us, then they start throwing up roadblocks. It's all happening on schedule."

"Whose schedule?"

"Do you know how to beat a Breathalyzer?" Bobby Jay said. "Activated charcoal tablets."

"Maybe we could use that in our new Designated Driver campaign," Polly said. " 'If You Must Drive Drunk, Please, Suck Charcoal.' "

"You get them in pet stores. They purify the air that goes through the little pump. I don't know why they bother, all my kids' fish went belly-up within a day. You keep it under your tongue. Breaks down the ethanol molecules."

"Don't the police wonder how come you've got a charcoal briquet in your mouth?"

"There's no law against charcoal," Bobby Jay said.

"Yet," they chimed in unison. It was understood among them that at any given moment, somewhere, someone in the "vast federal bureaucracy" was issuing regulations against them. They were the Cavaliers of Consumption aligned on the field of battle against the Roundheads of Neo-Puritanism.

Polly said, "My beer wholesalers convention next week. I'm worried."

29

"Why?" Nick asked.

"I'm scheduled to debate with Craighead in front of two thousand of them." Gordon R. Craighead was the chief "unelected bureaucrat" in charge of the Office of Substance Abuse Prevention at the Department of Health and Human Services, "Helpless, Hopeless, and Stupid" to those in the alcohol and tobacco industries. Craighead's office dispensed about $300 million a year to anti-smoking and anti-drunk-driving groups. Though it had been calculated that the tobacco industry spends $2.5 billion a year, or $4,000 per second, promoting smoking, Nick nonetheless railed against OSAP's "runaway budgets."

"Oh, you can handle Craighead."

"I'm not worried about that. It's my beer wholesalers. These are not subtle people. Most of them started out driving their own trucks. I'm worried that if Craighead starts talking about raising their excise taxes again, or if he gets into the recycling deposit, they'll start throwing things at him. They'll get abusive. That's not going to help anyone."

"Are you doing Q and A?" Polly said yes, there would be a question and answer after the debate.

"Make them write down the questions. We did a panel once with Mothers Against Smoking at a vending-machine owners' convention. We took spoken questions. A nightmare. The vendors were wrestling the microphone away from each other, shouting at the mothers, 'You're stealing bread outa my kid's mouth and you call yourself a mother!' I was a little surprised. I always thought the mafia was traditionally more respectful of mothers. Now I can't get Mothers Against Smoking even to return my calls. After that I made it a policy, only written questions. Have you got a slogan for the meeting?"

" 'We're Part of the Solution,' " she said. "What do you think?" Nick considered. "I like it."

"We had a hard time with it," Polly said. "They wanted something more aggressive. They're very feisty, the wholesalers."

"I've got a slogan for you," Bobby Jay said. "I saw it on a T-shirt. 'A Day Without a Buzz Is a Day That Never Wuz.' "

"Our first choice," Polly continued, ignoring him, "was 'In the Spirit of Cooperation,' but they said it sounded too much like 'spirits.' I spend half my time keeping my beer people from killing my spirits people, and my wine people from trying to kill the other two. The whole idea behind the Moderation Council was strength through unity at a time of volumetric decline, but it's like trying to unify Yugoslavia." She sipped her iced cappuccino. "It's tribal."

Polly lit a cigarette. Nick appreciated a woman who smoked sexily. She leaned back and tucked her left arm under her breasts to support her right elbow, the arm going straight up, cigarette pointing at the ceiling. She took long, deep drags, tilted her head back, and let the smoke out in long, slow, elegant exhalations, with a little lung-clearing shot at the end. A beautiful smoker. Nick's own mother, in her day, had been a beautiful smoker. He remembered her by the pool, summers in the fifties, all long legs and short pants, pointy sunglasses and broad straw hats and lipstick that left bright, sticky smudges on the butts that he filched and coughingly relit behind the garage.

Nick was rousted from the reverie by the shrill cricketing of Bobby Jay's cellular phone. Bobby Jay flipped it open with practiced cool, like it was a switchblade. "Bliss. Yeah?" Bobby said. *"Great."* He said to Nick and Polly, "The postal worker. They got him. Uh-huh . . . uh-huh . . . Missouri . . . uh-huh . . . uh-huh . . . *what?"* His brow beetled. "Well how the hell does CNN know? It was *on* him? FBI . . . what did, you didn't say anything to them, did you? Look, did you check with Membership?" Nick watched Bobby's face sag and thought, *This face is in freefall.* "Sustaining? Was he paid up? Well, *yes,* check, right away, before you do anything. No, *don't* call CNN or the FBI back. I don't care. I'll be there in three minutes."

Bobby Jay folded up his phone. Nick and Polly stared, awaiting explication.

"I got to go," Bobby Jay said, tossing a twenty onto the table. It landed like a fall leaf in a little puddle of melting ice.

"Do we have to find out what happened from CNN?"

Bobby Jay looked like he was about to break a sweat. "Take deep breaths," Nick suggested.

"The son of a bitch was a member," Bobby Jay said. "Not just a member, but a sustaining life member."

"How did CNN find out?"

"He had his membership card with him. CNN got a shot of it lying with the rest of his wallet. In a pool of blood."

"Hm," Nick said, no longer jealous about Bobby Jay's incredible   *31* good luck. At least with tobacco the casualties were tucked away in hospital wards.

"I'm on SAFETY!" Polly said, doing a take on the famous SAFETY ads showing macho, if slightly fading, actors standing on skeet ranges, holding expensive, engraved shotguns.

"Polly," Nick rebuked her. She was so cynical, Polly. Sometimes Nick wanted to spank her. She made a *big-deal* gesture. Bobby Jay was oblivious, staring at the center of the table. Polly waved a hand back and forth in front of his face and said to Nick, "I think he's going into shock."

"Oh my Lord," Bobby Jay said quietly, *"the video."*

"You probably want to recall it," Nick said, but Bobby Jay was already out the door, on his way, it appeared, to a long afternoon of certain buttlock.

3

WHILE YOU WERE OUT a producer for the *Oprah Winfrey* show had called to ask if Nick would go on the show in Chicago on Monday afternoon. The SG's call for an outright ad ban was getting a lot of play, and Oprah wanted a show on smoking right away. Nick called back immediately to say that, yes, he'd be available. This was face time, major face time. Millions and millions of women—tobacco's most important customers—watched Oprah. He was tempted to pick up the phone and tell BR, but decided to play it cool and conduct a little experiment. He called Jeannette and, in the course of asking her about some routine stuff, slipped it in. "Oh, I almost forgot, I have to do the Oprah show on Monday, so can you get me everything we have on the ineffectiveness of advertising?"

He set the timer on his watch. Four minutes later BR was on the line wanting to know what the deal with the Oprah show was. Nick laid it on a bit about how he'd been "cultivating" one of the producers for a long time and it had finally paid off.

"I was thinking maybe we should send Jeannette," BR said.

Nick ground his jaw muscles. "It's going to be a pretty splashy show. Top people. They made it pretty clear that they want the *chief* spokesman for the tobacco industry." Not your office squeeze.

BR said with an edge, "All right," and hung up.

His mother called to remind him that he and Joey had not been by for Sunday supper in over a month. Nick reminded her that the last time he had, his father had called him a "prostitute" at the table.

"I think it says how much he respects you that he feels he can speak *33* to you so frankly," she said. "Oh, by the way, Betsy Edgeworth called this morning to say she saw you on C-SPAN talking about some Turkish sultan. She said, 'Nick's so *attractive*. It's such a shame he didn't *stay* in journalism. He might have had his own show by now.' "

"I've got to go," Nick said.

"I want you to bring Joey for supper on Sunday."

"Can't. Sunday's bad."

"How can *Sunday* be bad, Nick?"

"I have to cram for the Oprah show on Monday afternoon."

Pause. "You're doing the *Oprah Winfrey* show?"

"Yes."

"Well. You'd better get her autograph for Sarah. Sarah loves Oprah Winfrey." Sarah was the housekeeper, the reason Nick was incapable of standing up to his own secretary. "Does Oprah smoke?"

"I doubt it."

"Maybe you'd better get her autograph *before* the show. Just in case everyone gets angry, the way they did when you were on with Regis and Kathy Lee."

He was late. He hurried down to the basement garage and drove aggressively through the Friday afternoon traffic, and pulled up in front of Saint Euthanasius a good half hour late. Joey, in his uniform, was sitting on the curb outside the main building looking miserable. Nick screeched to a stop and bolted out of the car as if he were part of a SWAT team operation. "I'm late!" he shouted, loudly belaboring the obvious. Joey cast him a withering glance.

"Ah, Mr. Naylor." Uh-oh. Griggs, the headmaster.

"Reverend," Nick said with what forced delight he could muster. Griggs had never quite forgiven him for putting down under "Father's Occupation" on Joey's school application form, "Vice President of Major Manufacturers' Trade Association." Little had he realized that Nick was a senior vice president of Genocide, Inc., until one night when he caught Nick on *Nightline* duking it out with the head of the flight attendants' union over the effects of secondhand smoke in airplanes. But by then Joey was safely enrolled at this, the most prestigious boys' school in Washington. Griggs glanced at his watch to indicate that it was not lost on him that Nick was half an hour late.

"How are you," Nick said, thrusting out his hand. He decided to dispense with mendacious banter about the congestion of Friday afternoon traffic in D.C. "Good to see you," he said mendaciously. He didn't especially enjoy being singled out for silent contempt by the headmaster of a school whose parents included Persian Gulf emirs and members of Congress. For $11,742 a year, the Reverend Josiah Griggs could park his attitude in his narthex.

"The traffic was awful," Nick said.

"Yes." Griggs nodded slowly and ponderously, as though Nick had just proposed major changes in the Book of Common Prayer. "Fridays . . . of course."

"We're going fishing this weekend," Nick said, changing the subject. "Aren't we, Joe?"

Joey said nothing.

"I wonder if you might stop by sometime next week," Griggs said in that assured, headmasterly way. Nick was seized with alarm. He looked over at Joey, who provided no clue as to this summons.

"Of course," Nick said. "I'm away on business the beginning of the week." It crossed Nick's mind: did Griggs watch Oprah? Surely not.

"End of the week, then? Friday? You could come by to pick up Joseph a little . . . early?" A thin smile played over his narrow face.

"Fine," Nick said.

"Splendid," Griggs said, brightening. "What are you fishing for?"

"Catfish."

"Ah!" Griggs nodded. "Ellie, our housekeeper, loves catfish. Of course, I can't get past their looks. Those *fearsome* whiskers." He walked off to the deanery with his hands clasped behind his back.

Safely inside the car, Nick said, "What did you do?"

"Nothing," Joey said.

"How come he wants to see me?"

"*I* don't know," said Joey. Twelve was not the most communicative age. Conversations consisted of games of Twenty Questions.

Great, Nick thought, I get to go into a principal conference totally blind.

"I'm offering total and unconditional amnesty. Whatever you did, it's all right. Just tell me: why does Griggs want to see me?"

"I said I don't *know.*"

"Okay." Nick drove. "How'd the game go?"

"Sucked."

"Well, you know what Yogi Berra said. 'Ninety percent of baseball is half-mental.' "

Joey thought about this. "That's forty-five percent."

"It's a joke." And, having nothing to do with revolting bodily functions, not likely to split the sides of a twelve-year-old. He extracted from Joey the score of the game: 9–1.

"The important thing is," he ventured consolingly, "is . . ." What *was* the important thing? Having himself been brought up in the Vince Lombardi School of Child-Raising, where his father shoutingly questioned his manhood from the stands every time he missed a grounder, Nick had resolved on a more tolerant approach for his own son's education. ". . . is to feel tired at the end of the day." Aristotle might not have constructed an entire philosophy on it, but it would do. True, Hitler and Stalin had probably felt tired at the end of their days. But theirs would not have been a *good* tired.

Joey registered no opinion of this Grand Unified Theory of Being, except to point out that Nick had just driven past Blockbuster Video and would now have to try a U-turn in busy traffic.

They went through their usual ritual, Joey proposing one unsuitable video after another, usually ones with covers showing a half-naked blond actress with ice picks, or the various steroid-swollen European bodybuilders-turned-actors in the act of decapitating people with chainsaws. Nick countering with Doris Day and Cary Grant movies from the fifties, Joey sticking his finger down his throat to indicate where he stood on the Grant-Day oeuvre. Nick was generally able to reach a compromise with World War II movies. Violent, yes, but tasteful by modern standards, without the super-slow-mo exit wounds pioneered by Peckinpah. "*Here's* one we haven't seen," he enthused, "*The Sands of Iwo Jima*. John Wayne. Cool." Joey showed no great zeal for the exploits of the Duke, John Agar, and Forrest Tucker as they fought their way up Mount Suribachi, but said he'd go along if they could also rent *Animal House* for the seventeenth time.

Nick lived in a one-bedroom off Dupont Circle that looked out onto a street where there had been eight muggings so far this year, though only two of them had been fatal. Most of his one-oh-five went to servicing the mortgage on the house a few miles up Connecticut Avenue in the leafy neighborhood of Cleveland Park, where Joey lived with his mother. On alternate weekends, Joey got to go get down and urban with Dad.

Together they ate a nourishing dinner of triple pepperoni pizza and cookie dough ice cream. Cookie dough ice cream. And society fretted about cigarettes?

The Sands of Iwo Jima was a little dated, but it was a good, big-hearted movie. And there was this . . . transfiguring moment where Wayne, having brought his men through hell to victory, exults, "I never felt so good in my life. How about a cigarette?" And just as he's offering the pack around to his men, a Jap sniper drills him, dead. Without realizing it, Nick took out a cigarette and lit up.

"Da-ad," Joey said.

Obediently, Nick went outside on the balcony.

4

BR did not offer Nick coffee from his pot, despite the fact that it was six-thirty on a Monday morning. He did not bother with "Good morning," only "I really hope you've got something for us, Nick. A lot depends on it."

"Good morning," Nick said, anyway.

"I'm listening." BR was signing things, or pretending to sign things.

"Could I get some coffee?"

"I'm *listening*," BR said.

Better skip the coffee. Nick sat, took a deep breath. "Movies."

"I don't have time for Socratic dialogue, Nick. Get to the point."

"That *is* the point."

BR looked up slowly. "What?"

"I think movies are the answer to our problem."

"How?"

"Do you want the reasoning behind it? I could put it in a memo."

"Just *tell* me."

"In 1910," Nick said, "the U.S. was producing ten billion cigarettes a year. By 1930, we were producing one hundred twenty-three billion a year. What happened in between? Three things. World War I, dieting, and talking pictures."

BR was listening.

"During the war, it was hard for soldiers to carry pipes or cigars on the battlefield, so they were given cigarettes. And they caught on so much that General Pershing sent a cable to Washington in 1917 that said, 'Tobacco is as indispensable as the daily ration. We must have thousands of tons of it without delay.' " Nick left out the detail that it was in 1919, just after the war, that the first cases of an up-to-then nearly unheard of illness called lung cancer began to show up. The chairman of a medical school in St. Louis invited his students to watch him do the autopsy on a former doughboy because, he told them, they'd probably never see another case of it again.

"So now the men are smoking cigarettes. In 1925, Liggett and Myers ran the Chesterfield ad showing a woman saying to a man who's lighting up, 'Blow some my way.' It broke the gender taboo. But it wasn't until a few years later that we *really* gave women a reason to want to smoke. George Washington Hill, who's just inherited the American Tobacco Company from his father, is driving in New York City. He's stopped at a light and he notices a fat woman standing on the corner gobbling chocolate, cramming it down. A taxi pulls up and he sees this elegant woman sitting in the back and what is she doing? She's smoking a cigarette, probably one of Liggett and Myers' Chesterfields. He goes back to the office and orders up an ad campaign and the slogan is born, 'Reach for a Lucky instead of a sweet.' And suddenly the women are lighting up. And they've been puffing away ever since. As you know, they're about to become our most important customers. By the mid-nineties, for the first time in history, there will be more women smokers than men."

BR shifted in his chair.

"What else is happening around then? The talkies. Talking pictures—1927, Al Jolson. Why was this significant? Because now directors had a problem. They had to give actors something to do while they talked. So they put cigarettes in their hands. Audiences see their idols—Cary Grant, Carole Lombard—lighting up. Bette Davis—a chimney. That scene where Paul Henreid lights both cigarettes for them in his mouth at the end of *Now, Voyager*? Pioneered the whole field of cigarette sex. And Bogart. Bogart! Do you remember the first line Lauren Bacall says to him in *To Have and Have Not,* their first picture together?"

BR stared.

"She sort of shimmies in through the doorway, nineteen years old, pure sex, and that voice. She says, 'Anybody got a match?' And Bogie throws the matches at her. And she catches them. The greatest screen

39

romance of the twentieth century, and how does it begin? With a match. Do you know how many times they lit up in that movie? Twenty-one times. They went through two packs in that movie."

"Now she's hawking nicotine patches," BR said. "Where is this all leading?"

"Do you go to the movies, BR?"

"I don't have *time* for movies."

"Perfectly understandable. With your schedule. Point is, these days when someone smokes in a movie, it's usually a psychopathic cop with a death wish, and then by the end he's given it up because he's adopted some cute six-year-old orphan who tells him it's bad for him. Sometimes, rarely, you get a situation where the smokers are cool or sexy, like in that TV show, *Twin Peaks*. But it's never mainstream. It's always"—Nick made quote marks with his fingers—" 'arty.' But nine times out of ten, they're deviants, losers, nutcases, convicts, and weirdos with bad haircuts. The message that Hollywood is sending out is that smoking is uncool. But movies are where people get their role models. So . . ."

"So?"

"Why don't we see if we can't do something about that?"

"Like what?" BR said.

"Get the directors to put the cigarettes back in the actors' hands. We're spending, what, two-point-five billion a year on promotion. Two-point-five billion dollars at least ought to buy lunch out there."

BR leaned back and looked at Nick skeptically. He sighed. Long and soulfully. "Is that *it*, Nick?"

"Yes," Nick said. "That is it."

"I'll be frank with you. I'm not blown away. I was hoping, for your sake, to be blown away. But," BR sighed for effect, "I'm still on two legs, standing."

Sitting, actually. It was Nick who was being blown—or swept—away. Pity, too. He thought the Hollywood idea had possibilities.

BR said, "I think we need to rethink your position here."

So, there it was, the handwriting on the wall, in large, blinking neon letters: YOU'RE HISTORY, PAL.

"I see," Nick said. "Do you want me to clear out my desk before lunch, or do I have until five?"

"No no," BR said. "Nothing has to happen today. Jeannette will need you to show her where everything is. Why don't you go ahead and do the Oprah show."

Nick wondered if he was supposed to thank BR for being so magnanimous. "Oh," BR said, "if you see an opening, you can go ahead and announce that we've committed five hundred grand to an antiunderage smoking campaign."

"Five hundred . . . thousand?"

"I thought you'd be pleased," BR gloated. "It *was* your idea. It wasn't an easy sell in Winston-Salem. The Captain called it 'economic suicide,' but I told him you thought we needed a little earnest money so people will know that we care about kids smoking."

"Five hundred thousand dollars isn't going to impress anyone. That'll buy you a couple of subway posters."

"It's the idea that counts." BR smiled. "Better hurry or you'll miss your plane."

On the way out it occurred to Nick to buy some flight insurance in case BR had already canceled his benefits.

5

Nick just had time for a quick jog along Lake Michigan.

If you represented death, you had to look your best. One of the first smokesmen to get the axe was Tom Bailey. Poor Tom. Nice guy, didn't even smoke, until he'd boasted about that one time too many to a reporter, who put it in her lead. JJ had called him in on the carpet, handed him a pack of cigarettes, told him that as of now he was a smoker. So Tom had started to smoke. But he had not kept up at the gym. A couple of months later JJ saw him on C-SPAN wheezing and pale and flabby, and that was the beginning of the end for Tom. So Nick kept up: jogging, weights, and every now and then a tanning salon where he would lie inside a machine that looked like it had been designed to toast gigantic grilled-cheese sandwiches.

"*You* look good," Oprah said backstage before the show. She was very cheery and chatty. "You look like a lifeguard."

"Not as good as you." Nick was pleased to see that she had put back on some of those seventy-five pounds that she'd lost. As long as there were overweight women in the world, there was hope for the cigarette industry.

"We tried to get the surgeon general to come on, but she said she wouldn't come on with a death merchant." Oprah laughed. "That's what she called you. A death merchant."

"It's a living." Nick grinned.

"I can't understand what that woman is saying half the time with that accent of hers." Oprah looked at him. "Why *do* you do this?

You're young, good-looking, white. Weren't you . . . you look familiar, somehow."

"I'm on cable a lot."

"Well why *do* you do this?"

"It's a challenge," Nick said. "It's the hardest job there is."

She didn't seem to buy that. Better get on her good side before the show. "You really want to know?"

"Yeah."

Nick whispered, "Population control."

She made a face. "You're bad. I wish you'd say that on the show." She left him in the care of the makeup woman.

Nick studied the sheet listing the other panelists, and he was not happy about it. There had been changes since Friday.

It showed: the head of Mothers Against Smoking—swell—an "advertising specialist" from New York, the head of the National Teachers' Association, one of Craighead's deputies from the Office of Substance Abuse Prevention. It irked Nick to be up against someone's deputy. What was Craighead doing today that was more important than trying to scrape a few inches of hide off the chief spokesman for the tobacco industry? Dispensing taxpayers' dollars to dweebish do-gooders? There was not much preshow banter between them as they sat in their makeup chairs.

They were taken onstage to be miked. Nick found himself being ushered to a chair next to another guest, a bald teenage kid. Who, Nick wondered, was he?

"Hello," Nick said.

"Hello," said the kid, friendly enough.

Now why would a bald teenage kid—bald, with no eyebrows—be on this particular panel? A technician wearing large earphones called out, "One minute!" Nick waved over a supervising producer, who rushed over to inform him that it was too late to go to the bathroom. A lot of first-timers were stricken with nervous bladders at the last minute and ended up sitting through the entire hour in damp underwear.

"I, uh," Nick said. "I'm fine." He whispered, *"Who's the kid?"*

"Robin Williger," the producer whispered back.

"Why is he on?"

"He's got cancer."

"Tell Oprah I need to speak to her *right now*."

"Too late."

Nick pinched the little alligator clip on his lapel mike and un-clamped it from his Hermès necktie, the orange one with the giraffe motif. "Then she's doing this show without me."

The producer bolted. Oprah came hurrying, her admirable bosom jiggling under blue silk.

"What's the problem?"

Nick said, "I don't like surprises."

"He was a last-minute substitution."

"For who? Anne Frank? Well, he can substitute for me."

"Nick," she hissed, "you know we can't do the show without you!"

"Yes, I do."

"Fifteen seconds!" a technician shouted.

"What do you want me to do? Kick him off the set?"

"Not my problem."

But she did nothing. Nick's instinct told him to get out of there. Quick! But there she was, this black woman, commanding him to sit there and finish his supper and he couldn't move.

She wheeled around with her wireless hand mike and bared her gleaming pearlies at the camera with the little red light.

Get up! Flee!

Too late! They were live! Maybe he could just slip quietly away.

Headline: CIGARETTE FLACK FLEES CANCER KID.

To complete the humiliation, he would trip on an electrical cable and bring a klieg light crashing down. The audience would laugh as he lay there, dazed on the studio floor. They would laugh across America, all the housewives hooting, pointing at him. BR would not laugh.

Cancer Kid would not laugh. No, only the merest, thinnest smile of triumph would play over his lips, tinged with sadness at the tragedy that was so personally his. Nick felt the hot trickle of sweat above his hairline, little beads of molten lava, nothing between them and his eyebrows but smooth, tanning-saloned forehead. And didn't *that* al-ways look good on TV, having to mop your forehead while you sat next to some dying National Merit Scholar—surely he was one, oh yes, surely he was the president of the student council and debating society and ran the soup kitchen in his spare time when he wasn't tutoring young inner-city kids. His only imperfection had been to smoke that one cigarette—yes, just one, that was all, one; proof that nicotine can be fatal in even minute doses—and it had been forced on him, against his better instincts, by the tobacco companies, and by those . . . fucking . . . saxophone-playing camels with the phallic noses; and by him, by Nick Naylor, senior vice president for communications, Academy of Tobacco Studies, Merchant of Death.

And he could not move. She had epoxied him to his seat. The perfidious bitch had outmaneuvered him!

In such moments—not that he had experienced this extreme before—he imagined himself at the controls of a plane. Pilots always managed to remain so calm, even when all their engines were on fire and the landing gear was stuck and the Arabic-looking passenger in 17B had just pulled the pin on his grenade.

He sucked in a lungful of air and let it out slowly, slowly, slowly. That's it. Breathing exercise. He remembered it from Lamaze classes. Still, his heart was going kaboom-kaboom ka-boom in his chest. Would the necktie microphone pick that up? How suave that would be, having his thumping heartbeat broadcast into everyone's living room.

Maybe he should offer some small sign of comradeship to Cancer Kid. He needed an opening line. *So, how long do they give you?*

Oprah was doing her introduction.

"Last year, RJR Nabisco, the company that makes Camel cigarettes, launched a new seventy-five-million-dollar ad campaign. The star of the campaign is Old Joe, a camel. But this is no ordinary ruminant quadruped." Shots of Old Joe were shown: playing the sax, playing bass, hanging out at the beach, checking out the chicks, being cool, the old coffin nail hanging jauntily from his mouth, or foreskin, depending on your phallic suggestibility. "He's become very popular, especially among children. According to a recent poll, over ninety percent of six-year olds . . . *six*-year-olds, not only recognized Old Joe, but knew what he stood for. He is almost as well-known as Mickey Mouse.

"Before Old Joe began showing up on billboards and magazine pages everywhere, Camel's share of the illegal children's cigarette market was less than one percent. It is now . . . thirty-two percent—thirty-two point eight percent, to be precise. That amounts to four hundred seventy-six million dollars a year in revenues.

"The surgeon general of the United States has called on RJR to withdraw this ad campaign. Even *Advertising Age,* the top advertising industry trade magazine, has come out against the Old Joe campaign. But the company refuses to withdraw them.

"Then last Friday she called for a *total* ban on advertising for cigarettes. Magazines, billboards, everything. This is bound to be controversial. A lot of money is at stake.

"I want you to meet Sue Maclean, head of the National Organization of Mothers Against Smoking. Sue began organizing NOMAS after her daughter fell asleep in bed while smoking and burned down her dormitory at college. Fortunately, no one was hurt. Sue tells me that her daughter quit smoking right after that."

Laughter in the studio. Heartwarming.

"Her daughter is now a mother herself, and a very active member of NOMAS."

The audience cooed.

Nick, synapses overheating, tried to coordinate his facial features into an appropriate expression, something between waiting for a bus that was very late and being lowered headfirst into a tank full of electric eels.

"Frances Gyverson is executive director of the National Teachers' Association in Washington. She is in charge of the NTA's health issues program, which instructs teachers in how to relay the dangers of smoking to their students.

"Ron Goode is deputy director of the Office of Substance Abuse Prevention at the Department of Health and Human Services in Washington, D.C. OSAP is the command center in the nation's war against cigarettes, so that would make you, what, Ron, a colonel?"

"Just a footsoldier, Oprah."

Where, Nick wondered, was *this* gorgeous self-effacement coming from? Goode was one of the more pompous, self-important assholes in the entire federal government.

Oprah smiled. A warm and fuzzy murmur went through the studio audience. *He has so much power, and yet look at him, he's so humble!* She turned toward Cancer Kid.

THANK YOU FOR SMOKING

"Robin Williger is a high school senior from Racine, Wisconsin. He likes studying history and he is on the swimming team." Momentarily, Nick's heart leapt. Perhaps it had all been a dream. Perhaps he didn't have cancer. Weren't swimmers always shaving their heads for speed? And didn't the weird ones also shave their eyebrows?

"He was looking forward to continuing his education at college. But then something happened. Recently, Robin was diagnosed with cancer, a very tough kind of cancer. He is currently undergoing chemotherapy treatment. We wish him all the luck in the world." The audience and other guests burst into applause. Nick joined in, wanly.

"The reason we asked him to be on this show with us is that he started smoking Camel cigarettes when he was fifteen. Because, he told me, he wanted to be quote cool like Old Joe. He also tells me he's quit smoking Camels since learning about the cancer. And that he no longer thinks smoking is quote cool." Thunderous applause.

Nick yearned for a cyanide capsule. But now Oprah turned to face Nick.

"Nick Naylor is a vice president of the Academy of Tobacco Studies. You might think with a name like that that they're some sort of scientific institution. But they are the tobacco industry's main lobby in Washington, D.C., and Mr. Naylor is their chief spokesman. Thank you for coming, Mr. Naylor."

"Pleasure," Nick croaked, though what he was experiencing was far from pleasure. The audience glared hatefully at him. So this is how the Nazis felt on opening day at the Nuremberg trials. And Nick unable to avail himself of their defense. No, it fell to him to declare with a straight face that ze Führer had never invaded Poland. *Vere are ze data?*

"Who'd like to start?" Oprah said.

Nick raised his hand. Oprah and his fellow panelists looked at him uncertainly. "Is it all right," he said, "if I smoke?"

The audience gasped. Even Oprah was taken aback.

"You want to *smoke?*"

"Well, it's traditional at firing squads to offer the condemned a last cigarette."

There was a stunned silence for a few seconds, and then someone in the audience laughed. Then other people laughed. Pretty soon the whole audience was laughing.

"I'm sorry, but I don't think that's funny," Mrs. Maclean said.

"No," said the National Teachers' Association lady. "I don't either. I think it's in extremely poor taste."

"I have to agree," Goode said. "I don't see the humor in it. And I suspect Mr. Williger doesn't either." But Cancer Kid was laughing. God *bless* him, he was laughing! Nick was seized with love. He wanted to adopt this young man, take him back to Washington, cure him of his cancer, give him a high-paying job, a car—a luxury car—a house, a pool, a big one so he could keep up with his swimming. Nick would buy him a wig, too, and get him eyebrow hair transplants. Anything he wanted. He felt so badly about the cancer. Maybe, with radiation . . .

Forget the kid! He's history! Press the attack! Attack! Attack!

"Oh why don't you leave him alone," Nick wheeled on Goode. "And stop trying to tell him how he ought to feel." He turned to Oprah. "If I may say so, Oprah, that is typical of the attitude of the federal government. 'We know how you should feel.' It's this same attitude that brought us Prohibition, Vietnam, and fifty years of living on the brink of nuclear destruction." Where was *this* going? And how had nuclear deterrence gotten in? *Never mind! Attack!* "If Mr. Goode wants to score cheap points off this young man's suffering just so he can get his budget increased so he can tell more people what to do, well I just think that's really, really sad. But for a member of the federal government to come on this show and lecture about cancer, when that same government for nearly fifty years has been producing atomic bombs, twenty-five thousand of them, as long as we're throwing numbers around, Mis-ter Sta-tistics, bombs capable of giving every single person on this planet, man, woman, and child, cancers so awful, so ghastly and untreatable, so, so, so *incurable,* that medical science doesn't even have a name for them yet . . . is"—*Quick, get to the point! What is the point?*—". . . is just beneath contempt. And frankly, Oprah, I'd like to know how a man like . . . *this* comes to occupy a position of such power within the federal bureaucracy. The answer is—he doesn't *have* to get elected. Oh no. *He* doesn't have to participate in democracy. He's *above* all that. Elections? Consent of the governed? Pah! Of the very people who pay his salary? Oh no. Not for Ron Goode. *He* just wants to cash in on people like poor Robin Williger. Well, let me tell you something, Oprah, and let me share something with the fine, concerned people in the audience today. It's not pleasant, but you, and they, need to hear it. The Ron Goodes of this world *want* the Robin Willigers to die. Awful, but true. I'm sorry, but it's a fact. And do you know why? I'll tell you why. So that their . . . *budgets*"—he spat out the distasteful word—"will go up. This is nothing less than trafficking in human misery, and you, sir, ought to be *ashamed* of yourself."

Ron Goode never recovered. For the next hour, he could only scream at Nick, in violation of every McLuhanesque injunction against putting out heat in a cool medium. Even Oprah strained to calm him down.

For his part, Nick assumed a serene mask of righteous serenity and merely nodded or shook his head, more in sadness than in anger, as if to say that his outburst only validated everything he had said. "All well and fine, Ron, but you haven't answered the question," or, "Come on, Ron, why don't you stop pretending you didn't hear me," or, "And what about all those people you irradiated during those nuclear test blasts in New Mexico? Want to talk about *their* cancers?"

During one of the commercials Ron Goode had to be physically restrained by a technician.

The head of NOMAS and the representative of the teachers' organization did what they could to come to the aid of their federal benefactor, but every time they ventured a comment, Nick cut them off with "Look, we're all on the same side, here," a statement so dazzling that it left them mute. When they finally rejoined that they could not find one square inch of common ground between their humanitarianism and the fiendish endeavors of the tobacco industry, Nick saw his opening and pounced. No one, he said, was more concerned about the problem of underage smoking than the tobacco companies. Not, of course, that there was a shred of scientific evidence linking smoking with disease, but the companies, being socially responsible members of the community, certainly did not condone underage smoking—or drinking and driving, for that matter—for the simple reason that it was *against the law.* Here was the ideal moment to unveil their new anti-underage smoking campaign.

"As a matter of fact, we're about to launch a five-million-dollar campaign aimed at persuading kids not to smoke," Nick said, "so I think *our* money is on the table."

6

Nick heard the urgent chirruping on his cellular telephone inside his briefcase when he retrieved it from the greenroom in Oprah's studio, but ignored it. He continued to ignore it on the drive to the airport. The cab driver, half-curious, half-annoyed, finally asked him if he was going to answer it. It pleased Nick to know that BR was going through significant agonies on the other end, so he did not pick up. In the waiting lounge at O'Hare, he did, more because people were staring than because he wanted to put BR out of his misery.

"Five million dollars?" It was BR, all right. Nick put his blood pressure at about 180 over 120. "Are you out of your *mind*?"

"Probably. It's been a very stressful period for me. But I'm feeling much better now."

"Where in the name of God are we supposed to get five million for, for *anti*-smoking ads?"

"It's not all that much when you think about it. RJR is spending seventy-five million a year on those stupid dick-nosed camels. You'll probably get a lot of good press out of this."

BR was fulminating, making legal threats, saying they were going to put out the story that he was having a nervous breakdown. On and on. It was very satisfying. In the middle of it, Nick heard BR say to someone, "Who? Oh, Jesus." Then he said to Nick, "It's the Captain on line two."

"Give him my regards."

"Stay on the line." Nick stayed on, not because BR had asked him, but to see what the reaction would be from the most powerful man in

Tobacco to the news that an upstart executive VP had just committed his industry to spending some serious money to alienate potential customers.

He waited for over ten minutes. They called his flight, but the people at the gate wouldn't let him on while he was using his cellular telephone.

BR came back on. His voice had changed from open bellowing to ice water squirted through clenched teeth. "He wants to see you."

"He does?" Nick said. "What about?"

"How the hell should I know," said BR, hanging up with an emphatic *klump*.

There were no direct flights to Winston-Salem from Chicago, so he had to fly to Raleigh. On the way there the woman sitting next to him, heavyset, in her late fifties, with hair of a color not found in nature, kept staring at him as he read, out of habit, from his clipping file, an article in *Science* magazine entitled "Scientific Standards in Epidemiologic Studies of the Menace of Daily Life."

"I *know* you," she said accusingly, as if her inability to identify Nick were his fault.

"You do?"

"Uh-*huuh*. You're on the television."

Nick heard a stirring from the seat behind. What's this? Celebrity in their midst? "Who is it?" "I knew I'd seen him." "It's whatsisname, from *America's Funniest Home Videos*." "What would he be doing going to Raleigh? Anyway, he'd be sitting in First Class." "I'm telling you . . ."

This happened to Nick fairly often.

"Yes," he said quietly to the lady.

"I knew it!" She slapped the issue of *Lear's* magazine onto her lap. "*Studs*."

"Yes. That's right."

"Oh! You must have been so humiliated when she said that you kissed like a fish."

"I was," Nick said. "It was hard."

Taking pity on Nick, she shared her own disappointments in love, in particular those pertaining to her second marriage which was apparently failing. Nick was not good at disengaging himself in these situations. After an hour of sympathetic listening, his neck muscles had hypercontracted into steely knots of tension. He would need a session with Dr. Wheat when he got back. He found himself yearning for a terrorist incident. Fortunately, what the pilot announced as a "severe thunderstorm system" moved in and things got so turbulent inside the cabin that the woman forgot her problems of heart, and left deep fingernail impressions on Nick's left forearm. By the time he checked into the hotel it had been a long day and he was too tired to do anything but drink two beers and eat about four hundred dollars' worth of nuts and pretzels from the minibar.

His room service breakfast arrived and with it the morning paper, the *Winston-Salem Tar-Intelligencer*. He flipped it open and to his surprise saw his picture on the front page, in color, beneath the fold. The headline read:

FIGHTING BACK: TOBACCO SPOKEMAN
RIPS GOVERNMENT "HEALTH" OFFICIAL
FOR MANIPULATING HUMAN TRAGEDY

The article fairly glowed with praise for his "courage" and "willingness to cut through the cant." They'd even managed to get a sympathetic quote from Robin Williger in which he absolved Nick of personal responsibility for his cancer and said that people ought to take more responsibility for their own lives.

The phone rang, and a businesslike woman's voice announced, "Mr. Naylor? Please hold for Mr. Doak Boykin."

The Captain. Nick sat up. But how did they know where he was staying? There were many hotels in Winston-Salem. He waited. Finally a thin voice came on the line.

"Mister Naylor?"

"Yes sir," Nick said tentatively.

"Ah just wanted personally to say, *thank you.*"

"You did?"

"I thought that government fellow was going to have himself a myocardial infarction right there on national television. Splendidly done, sir, splendid. Are you here in town, do I gather?"

It was a sign of the really powerful that they had no idea where they had reached you on the phone. "Would you lunch with me? They do a tolerable lunch at the Club. Is noon convenient? Wonderful," he said, as if Nick, many levels below him on their food chain, had just given him a reason to go on living. They fought a war over slavery, and yet they were so courteous, southerners.

He bought *USA Today* in the lobby on his way out. He found it in the "Money" section, front page, below the fold:

TOBACCO COMPANIES PLAN TO SPEND $5 MILLION
ON *ANTI*-SMOKING CAMPAIGN, SPOKESMAN SAYS

He read. BR flailed in a vortex of neither-confirming-nor-denying. While many details remained to be worked out, yes, the Academy had always been "in the front" of concern about underage smoking and was prepared to spend "significant sums" on a public-service campaign. Yadda, yadda. Jeannette was quoted saying that Mr. Naylor, who had made the remarkable assertion on the *Oprah Winfrey* show, was unavailable for comment: "We're not sure exactly where he is at this point in time." She made it sound like he was in a bar somewhere.

In the cab on the way to the Tobacco Club, Nick reviewed what he knew about Doak Boykin, which wasn't much. Doak—he was said to have changed the spelling from the more plebeian Doke—Boykin was one of the last great men of tobacco, a legend. Self-made, he had started from nothing and ended with everything. Except, evidently, a son. He had seven daughters: Andy, Tommie, Bobbie, Chris, Donnie, Scotty, and Dave, upon whom the burden of her father's frustrated desire for a male heir had perhaps fallen hardest. It was Doak Boykin who had introduced the whole concept of filters after the first articles started to appear in *Reader's Digest* with titles like "Cancer by the Carton." (The asbestos filter was a particular brainstorm of his, which was now causing Smoot, Hawking many thousands of billable hours in the liability courts.) As the articles proliferated and the industry found itself in need of a little more presence in Washington, he had founded the Academy of Tobacco Studies to serve, as its charter stated, as "a clearinghouse of scientific information and an impartial and always honest mediator between the concerns and needs of the American public and the tobacco companies."

The Captain's health was in some question. Rumors abounded. He had collapsed at the Bohemian Grove in California, and had been taken to the hospital in nearby Santa Rosa, where he was rushed into surgery. The young cardiology resident, having been told who his patient was, told the groggy Captain, as he was wheeling him into the OR, that the doctors' nickname for this particular operating room was "Marlboro Country," this being where they usually did the lung cancer surgery. The Captain, convinced he was in the hands of an assassin, tried frantically to signal someone, but the Valium drip had rendered him incapable of coherent speech, and so he was left to flail helplessly and mutely as he was wheeled into the gleaming steel prairies of Marlboro Country. It did not help when he woke up in the recovery room to the news that an anticipated double-bypass had instead required a quadruple-bypass, and that, to boot, an additional discovery of mitral deterioration had required the insertion of a fetal pig's valve into his heart. The Captain, it was said, had left the hospital a rattled man, and had made arrangements that in the event of any further medical problems, he was to be immediately medevacked to Winston-Salem's own Bowman-Gray Medical Center, which had been built entirely with tobacco money. Here he would be safe from further surgical sabotage at the hands of the *St. Elsewhere* generation.

Nick arrived for lunch at the Tobacco Club a half hour early. It was a massive Greek Revival affair that had been built by the tobacco barons in the 1890s so that they would have a place to get away from their wives. Nick was shown into a small, well-appointed waiting room. The walls were decorated with expensively framed original artwork for various brands of American cigarettes long since gone up in smoke. There was Crocodile, Turkey Red, Duke of Durham, Red Kamel, Mecca, Oasis, Murad—sweet revenge on the old beheader—Yankee Girl, Ramrod ("Mild as a Summer Breeze!"), Cookie Jar ("Mellow, Modern, Mild"), Sweet Caporal, Dog's Head, Hed Kleer ("The Original Eucalyptus Smoke"). What history was here!

Nick sat and smoked in a heavy leather armchair and listened to the tick-tock of the giant grandfather clock.

At one minute to noon the crystal glass swing doors opened and a man of obvious importance walked in, creating a bow-wave of commotion. He was a trim, elegant man in his late sixties, with a David Niven mustache and wavy white hair that suggested a brief, long-ago flirtation with bohemianism. He was not a tall man, but the erect way he carried himself seemed to add several inches. He was gorgeously tailored in a tropical-weight, double-breasted, dark blue pinstripe suit that looked as though it had been sewn onto him at one of those London places like Huntsman or Gieves & Hawkes where you need a social reference from three dukes and a viscount just to get in the door. Pinned to the lapel, Nick noted, was a brightly colored military rosette. The man radiated authority. Porters rushed to relieve him of his hat and silver-tipped cane—did it conceal a sword?—with such solicitude as to suggest that these objects were insupportable burdens. Another porter materialized with a small whisk and began gently to brush the shoulders of the suit. Disencumbered and dusted, this gentleman looked in the direction of the waiting room as a porter inclined to whisper into his ear and to point in Nick's direction.

He turned and strode, smiling, toward Nick with outstretched hand.

"Mister *Naylor*," he said with delight and a sense of moment, "I am Doak Boykin and I am *extremely* pleased to meet you."

Faced with such grandeur, Nick mumbled, "Hello, Mr. Boykin."

"Please," the old man said, "call me Captain." Taking Nick's elbow he steered him to the table in the corner.

"Punctuality," he grinned, "is the courtesy of *kings*. Not many northerners appreciate that." One servant pulled his chair out for him as another swiftly removed the starched white napkin from its place setting and in one graceful motion snapped it open and eased it down onto the Captain's lap.

"Will you join me in a refreshment?" He did not wait for Nick's response. Nothing was said to the waiter, who merely nodded while another momentarily appeared with a tray with two silver cups beaded with condensation and overflowing with crushed ice and fresh sprigs of mint.

"Mud," the Captain said. He sipped, closed his eyes, and let out a little *ah*.

"Do you know the secret to a *really* good julep? Crush the mint down onto the ice with your thumb and grind it in. Releases the menthol." He chuckled softly. "Do you know who taught me that?" Nick did not, but he supposed some descendant of Robert E. Lee. "Ferdinand Marcos, president of the Philippines."

Nick waited for elaboration; none came. Another prerogative of the really rich.

"What year were you born, Mister Naylor?" Should he tell him, Call me Nick?

"Nineteen fifty-two, sir."

The Captain smiled and shook his head. "Nineteen fifty-two! Good Lord. Nineteen fifty-two." He took another sip of his julep, crunched down on a chunk of ice, bared his teeth, which were white. "I was in Korea shooting Chinese in nineteen-fifty-two."

"Really," Nick said, unable to think what else to say.

"Today, the Chinese are my best customers. There's the twentieth century for you."

"Seventy percent of adult Chinese males smoke," Nick observed.

"That is correct," the Captain said. "Next time we won't have to *shoot* so many of 'em, will we?"

He sat back in his chair, chuckling. "Will you join me in another?" Another tray appeared with more drinks. What was the protocol? Should Nick drain his first one? He did, spilling ice chunks onto his lap.

"Nineteen fifty-two was a significant year for our business," the Captain continued. "Do you remember what Mr. Churchill said?" The Captain did a growly imitation: " 'It is not the end, or even the beginning of the end. But I believe that it may be the end of the beginning.' Nineteen fifty-two being of course the year the *Reader's Digest* published that article about the health . . . aspect." Tobacco executives avoided certain words, like "cancer." "That was, you might say, the end of our beginning."

Lunch was served, much to Nick's relief as he was now woozy with mentholated bourbon. The Captain talked about what the new leadership in Korea meant for the industry. They began with chilled spiced shrimp and moved on to filet mignon and baked potatoes with globs of sour cream. The Captain told the maître d' that he must never reveal to Mrs. Boykin what he had eaten or, he warned direly, "she'll skin both of us alive." Rich men delight in displaying an exaggerated fear of their wives. They think it humanizes them.

"Yes *sir,* Captain!" the waiter said, enjoying his part in the conspiracy of silence.

"May I?" Nick said, taking out his pack when the plates were cleared.

"Please, thank you. I'm always so *grateful* when members of the younger generation smoke." He seemed wistful. "I would join you, but since my recent . . . experience Mrs. Boykin has become quite vehement on the subject, so I will forgo and forbear, for the sake of domestic tranquillity. My eldest daughter asked me the other day what, at my age, I enjoy, and I told her, 'Voting Republican and being left alone by your mother.' "

Coffee was served. Other club members stopped by their table to pay court to the Captain, who graciously introduced Nick to them.

"*The* Nick Naylor?" one said, grasping Nick's hand. "Well, I *am* pleased to meet you, sir. Fine job, fine job!" They made quite a fuss over him. It was all very gratifying. Yes, indeed, this was most pleasant. Nick could see living in Winston-Salem, lunching at the Tobacco Club, not having to apologize or justify his existence all the time. "Tobacco takes care of its own," went the saying. Yes it did, it certainly did.

"I'd say you've made a splendid impression, Nick," the Captain glowed as the last of Nick's admirers had receded. "May I call you Nick? I do not usually engage in diminutives, but in this case I would like to. You remind me just a little bit of myself when I was your age."

"Please," Nick said, embarrassed, "by all means."

"You were a television reporter, before?"

Nick flushed. Well, there was no escaping it. It would be in his obituary. *It was Naylor who, as a local Washington TV reporter, announced on live television that the President had choked on a piece of meat at a military base and died, causing the stock market to drop 180 points and lose $3 billion worth of value before the White House produced the President, alive.* The best he could hope for was to accomplish something else in life that would relegate that to the second paragraph.

"That was a long time ago," Nick said.

The Captain held up his hand. "You don't have to explain it to me. In your shoes I probably would have done the same thing. One does have to *seize* the day. JJ told me all about it. That's why he hired you. Knew exactly what he was doing."

57

"He did?"

"Damn right. Whatever else JJ was, and I regret that I had to let him go, he was a student of the human condition. He said to me, 'That boy is going to work his *behind* off putting this thing behind him, making a new name for himself.' "

"Other than the Three Billion Dollar Man."

"He said something else. He said, 'That boy is going to be one *angry* young man.' I didn't realize just how angry until I watched you yesterday on that colored woman's show, Obrah. Son, you were *magnificent*."

"Thank you."

"I was angry, too, when I got back from Korea. Do you know *why*, Mister Naylor?"

"No sir."

"Because I resolved that I would never—ever—again be put in a situation where I had to submit to the authority of *incompetent men*. I started in the flues and within five years I was a vice president, the youngest vice president in corporate tobacco history. That, sir, is what anger can do for you. Join me in a brandy, won't you."

Once again the drinks materialized out of air, borne on a silver tray. What a club! And the waiters didn't introduce themselves to you by their first name. They were everything waiters should be: subservient, efficient, taciturn.

"Do you *enjoy* your work, Nick?"

"Yes," Nick said. "It's challenging. As we say around the office, 'If you can do tobacco, you can do anything.' "

The Captain snorted into his snifter. "You know, your generation of tobacco men—and women, I'm always forgetting to add 'and women'—think they have it harder than any generation who came before. You think it *all* began in nineteen fifty-two. Well, puh!"

Puh?

"It's been going on for almost five hundred years. Does the name Rodrigo de Jerez mean anything to you?" Nick shook his head. "No, I suppose it doesn't. I suppose they don't teach history in the schools anymore, just attitude. Well, for your information, sir, Rodrigo de Jerez went ashore with Christopher Columbus. And he watched the natives 'drink smoke,' as he put it, with their pipes. He brought to-bacco back to the Old World with him. Sang its praises high to the frescoed ceilings. Do you know what happened to him? The Spanish Inquisition put him in jail for it. They said it was a 'devilish habit.' You think you have it bad having to deal with the Federal Trade Commission? How would you like to have to state your case before the Spanish Inquisition?"

"Well . . ."

"You bet you would not. Remember that name, Rodrigo de Jerez. You're walking in his footsteps. He was the first tobacco spokesman. I suppose he, too, found it 'challenging.' "

"Uh. . . ."

"Does the name Edwin Proon mean anything to you?"

"Prune?"

"God in heaven, the billions of dollars we *throw* at the public schools. Edwin Proon lived in the Massachusetts Colony in the early 1600s when the Puritan fathers were going around nailing up the first no-smoking signs in the New World. You think you're the first to have to deal with building restrictions and public ordinances? No sir, I do not reckon that you are. Edwin Proon was fighting that battle long ago. They passed a law saying you couldn't smoke in public and 'public' meant anywhere more than one person was present. They put *him* in the stocks. And when they caught him smoking in the stocks they clamped an iron hood over his face. Do you suppose Edwin Proon found it 'challenging'?"

Fasten your seat belts, Nick thought, we have four hundred more years to go. In detail, the Captain reminded him that America had waged outright war against the "pernicious practice"—in the 1790s, the 1850s, the 1880s. He reminded him that Horace Greeley had called a cigar "a fire at one end and a fool at the other," that Thomas Edison had refused to hire smokers, that in this very century, Americans—and not just women—had actually been arrested for the act of lighting a cigarette. On and on it went until little beads of perspiration appeared on the Captain's forehead, like julep sweat. Finally he stopped and patted his brow with his handkerchief.

"Forgive me. I seem to have this tendency since the operation to get . . . exercised. By the way, never get sick in California. Least nothing that requires surgery. They don't know the first *thing* about surgery. There was nothing wrong with me that a little bicarbonate of soda would not have rectified."

59

They discussed the hypocrisy and villainy of Region 11 politicians. Almost all the anti-smoking ordinances came out of Region 11, California, Reichland of the Health Nazis. What justice was possible when Californians were allowed to determine national health standards?

"You know who Lucy Page Gaston was?" the Captain asked with one of his penetrating, interrogatory stares.

No, Nick did not know who Lucy Page Gaston was.

"She came out of the Temperance Union movement in the 1890s looking for more souls to save. She had six hundred cigarette vendors in Chicago arrested for selling to minors. Founded the Anti-Cigarette League. In 1913 she and some doctor started a clinic where they dragged in poor newspaper boys off the street and swabbed their throats with silver nitrate and told 'em to chew on gentian root whenever they got the urge. Now we got these damned patches. In 1919 she wrote Queen Mary and President Harding and asked them to stop smoking. What crust! Announced she was running for President. In 1924 she was struck down by a streetcar in Chicago coming out of an anti-cigarette meeting. She survived. She died eight months later. Do you know *what* she died of, Nick?"

"No, sir."

The Captain smiled. "Throat cancer. Do you know what that proves, Nick? It proves that there is a God."

Outside the Club the Captain declared that since it was such a fine spring day he felt like strolling. So they strolled, with the Captain's car following slowly along.

"Tell me," he asked, "what is your *opinion* of BR?" He added, "Just 'tween us girls."

Suddenly the sidewalk was strewn with large banana peels. "BR," said Nick, "is . . . my boss."

The Captain gave a little bemused grunt. "Well, I like to think that *I'm* your boss, son."

Son?

"But I do admire loyalty in a man. I *esteem* loyalty. I can forgive almost anything in a man if he's loyal." They walked along. He stopped to examine some vines. "We should have the wisteria in three weeks. There's no smell like it. I imagine heaven smells like wisteria. BR's got this notion we ought to start bribing producers in

Hollywood to make their actors smoke. Interesting notion. Year from now we may have a total advertising ban. He thinks this is the way around it. Cheaper, too, probably. We're spending almost a billion dollars a year in advertising now as it is. What do you think?"

"Interesting notion," Nick said simmeringly.

"Yes, I like it *quite* a bit. Smart man, BR."

"Oh yes. And loyal."

"Glad to hear it. He comes from vending machines, you know. Rough part of our business. You need someone like BR these days. He's good with the Japs. *Tough*. The Far East is going to be increasingly important to us in the years ahead. That's why I made him an offer would've made Croesus blush. Not that anyone in corporate America has the capacity to blush these days. I *did* hate to let old JJ go. But, he's got his condominium down in Tarpon Springs right on the eighteenth hole. I suppose they'll be putting *me* out to stud soon enough. On the other hand," he grunted, "when you own twenty-eight percent of the stock you have the luxury of setting your *own* timetable. Still, I'm not getting any younger. Sometimes I feel like a *Tyrannosaurus rex* stumbling through the swamp one step ahead of the glaciers. Do you know," he said with an air of incredulity, "that the scientists are now saying that the dinosaurs died on account of their own *flatulence*?"

"No," Nick said.

"They're saying all those dinosaur farts going up into the atmosphere created a kind of global warming effect that caused the ice cap to melt." He shook his head. "How do they *know* such things?"

"Where are the data?"

"That's right. That's right! Do you remember what Finisterre said?"

"Wake up, boys, it's Good Friday, let's go have a few beers?"

"Not that Finisterre. Romulus K. Finisterre. The president. You do remember *him*? He said, 'The torch is passed to a new generation.' He was talking about my generation. And now the time is coming to pass it to your generation. Are you ready to accept the torch, Nick?"

"Torch?"

"It won't be easy. It's a hostile world out there. I look around and all I see is muzzle flashes. What's more, I see muzzle flashes coming from where our *friends* sit. I had Jordan in to see me the other day.

That old *whore,* we put so much money into his campaigns over the years he put his children through college on the surplus. Hell, I couldn't even use my own corporate jet during his last campaign he was so busy using it. And what does he have the crust to tell me, in my own office, if you please? That he has to go along with this excise tax or the White House is going to shut down LaGroan Air Force Base."

Nick had to agree: it was a sorry situation indeed when the Honorable Gentleman from North Carolina, Chairman of the Senate Agriculture Committee, was casting his vote in favor of a two-dollar-a-pack cigarette tax.

"Sometimes I feel like a Colombian *drug* dealer. The other day, my seven-year-old granddaughter, flesh of flesh of my own loins, says to me, 'Granddaddy, is it true cigarettes are *bad* for you?' My own granddaughter, whose private education, and horse and everything else is being *handsomely* provided for by cigarette money!"

The Captain stopped and said, "We got to do something. Something big, smart, and fast. This Hollywood project of BR's. I want you to work on it. And report to me, directly."

"It *was* BR's idea," Nick said. "I wouldn't want to offend him by taking over his brainstorm."

"Don't you worry about that. I'll handle BR. He seemed to think this gal Jeannette was the person to do it. Thinks the sun rises and sets on her. But I think you're our man." He put his hand on Nick's shoulder. "And I am *seldom* wrong."

He signaled his driver. They got in. "HQ, Elmore," the Captain told him. "Then take Mr. Naylor here to the airport."

"I need to pick up my bags at the hotel."

"That's already been taken care of, sir," Elmore said. The Captain smiled. "Tobacco takes care of its own."

They pulled up in front of Agglomerated Tobacco. There had been no mention of Nick's five-million-dollar monkey wrench. Nick asked him about it.

The Captain nodded to himself thoughtfully. "That's a significant amount of money, of course. I must say that you do seem to have a penchant for causing extremely *large* sums of money to be spent." His face darkened, as if a severe emotional system were moving in over it, and for a moment or two Nick thought all bets might be off and he was headed for the unemployment line after all. But then the thunderclouds headed off. The old man chuckled, "Well I don't suppose five million dollars is going to *bankrupt* us. However, I do not expect to be swept off my feet by the persuasiveness of this particular advertising campaign." He extended his hand. "Thank you for taking the time to visit with me. I will be in touch."

At the airport a chain-link fence automatically parted at the car's approach. The plane, a sleek Gulfstream 5, was waiting, engines whining, with a *Sports Illustrated* swimsuit issue–quality stewardess smiling at the foot of the stairs. No wonder the chairman of the Senate Finance Committee had developed a thing for it. *"Hello,"* the stewardess said, "pleasure to have you aboahd!" Nick climbed up. His feet sank softly into lush carpeting. There were oil paintings on the bulkheads, the overhead was quilted, the chairs were enormous, like BarcaLoungers, upholstered in creamy leather that absorbed Nick as he sat down. "The Captain says that's his *favorite* chair in the whole world," said the stewardess. There was fresh fruit on the table next to it, five newspapers that looked like they'd been ironed, and a heavy-stock card that said, WELCOME ABOARD, MR. NICK NAYLOR OF ATS, and gave the flight time to Washington along with the airspeed, planned altitude, weather conditions, the temperature in Washington. She leaned over, affording Nick an unavoidable peek into the soft crevasse between her creamy bosoms, from which wafted the most delicate perfume. "If there's anything I can do to make your flight more pleasant, you be *sure* to let me know, now."

7

"Flight okay?" BR asked.

"Fine," Nick said.

"What flight *were* you on? The four-fifteen doesn't get in until five-twenty, and it's only five."

"Actually, I came up on the plane."

"Of course you came up on a *plane,* for Chrissakes."

"The Captain's plane." He hadn't really decided how to handle his new status, but he felt like a spotted owl flitting about the office of the head of the Weyerhaeuser lumber company—protected.

BR stared. "That was certainly . . . gracious of him."

"Yes," Nick said, enjoying himself. "That's quite some plane, isn't it?"

"I wouldn't know."

"Oh?"

"Yet. I was on the old one. I practically lived on it. The Captain's invited me on the new one a dozen times, but I just haven't been able to fit it in."

"Well, with your schedule. I can certainly see why Senator Jordan likes it. Ashley, the stewardess—very nice person—told me it's quite an improvement over the G-4, in terms of range."

"Um-huh. What did he say about your five-million-dollar anti-smoking campaign?"

"Said do it. But he doesn't want to be blown away."

BR's face fell. It was visible, like a glacier melting, only faster. Funny thing, life, thought Nick: thirty-six hours ago he was sitting here in this same office being denied caffeine and told he was finished. Now it was BR whose jaw muscles were twitching and looked like he needed a session with Dr. Wheat. Maybe he should give BR Dr. Wheat's card. DR. WHEAT, D.O. OSTEOPATHIC MANIPULATION. Relax . . . *crrrrack.*

"I thought I'd give it to BMG, that new firm I told you about out in Minneapolis. Unless you have any objection."

"No. Whatever."

"By the way, BR, the Captain *really* liked your idea about trying to get movie actors to smoke more."

BR blushed. "That was your idea. He must have gotten it mixed up."

"Of course. With all he has on his mind."

"At his age." Nick could almost see the thought-bubble rising above BR's head. *He won't be around much longer, Naylor, and ten seconds after they pronounce him DOA, your ass is mine.*

"Yes," Nick said, "but he seems incredibly sharp. Doesn't miss a thing, does he?"

"He directed," BR slid a piece of paper across his desk, "that you get this."

It was a Salary Increase form. At first Nick thought it must be a typo. From one-oh-five to . . . two-oh-oh?

"Well," Nick said, "thank you."

"Don't," BR said sincerely, "thank me."

People he passed in the hallways didn't know whether to greet him as a leper or a hero. The air was thick with rumors. Nick was out. But here was Nick with this radioactive smile, so how out could he be? He must be in.

"Hey, Nick, great going on Oprah."

"I thought Goode was going to strangle you."

"Nick, we really spending five mil on anti-kidsmoking?"

Gazelle was waiting for him, looking vastly relieved over having a boss who still had a job. The boards from BMG had arrived, which was timely. Not a moment to lose there.

"Let's have a look."

She propped them up on his couch as Nick studied them. People started to gather around his open door, peering in. What's happening? What's Nick up to? Palpable buzz. Suddenly Nick's office was the red-hot center of things at the Academy. And here came Jeannette, smiling like a cobra in a very fetching suit and tie.

"Nick," she said, making her entrance, "you were *fabulous* on Oprah. We're getting amazing feedback."

"You seen these death threats?" Gazelle said, holding up a fistful of WHILE YOU WERE OUT.

"You wrote death threats down on message slips?"

"I wouldn't pay any attention to those," Jeannette said, brushing Gazelle aside. "Give them to Carlton." Carlton handled the Academy's security.

"Excuse me?" Gazelle said.

"Nick wouldn't be doing his job if he didn't draw out the wackos," said Jeannette dismissively. She turned to Nick and said, "Really, you were *amazing*."

"Do you want to read what some of these people had to say?" Gazelle picked one out of her hand like a playing card. " 'I'm going to pour hot tar down your throat, you rotten scumbag. See how you like it.' 'You're a slick dick aren't you, Nick Naylor? I own a high-powered rifle could drop a sack of shit like you at 250 yards, so watch your ass.' "

"I just wanted to say how terrific you were," Jeannette said, giving Nick's elbow a little squeeze. She turned to the small crowd gathered in the doorway. "Wasn't he?" They applauded.

Gazelle all but slammed the door on Jeannette's caboose as she walked out. "Can't *stand* that bitch."

"I don't know," Nick said, "looked like she was waving the white flag."

"Oh? Yesterday she was in here with color swatches, redecorating. Now she's in here kissing your ass. And you liking it."

Nick looked at the boards and frowned. "Would you get me Sven Gland in Minneapolis. That is, if you're finished critiquing?" He flipped through his phone messages. Sammy Najeeb, Larry King's producer. Well well . . . "Who's Heather Holloway?"

"*Washington Moon* reporter," Gazelle snapped.

"What does she want?"

"To interview you."

66   "What *about*?"

Gazelle put her hands on her hips. "What do you *think* she wants to interview you *about*? Peace in the Middle East?"

"Well why do you take down every word these, these drooling maniacs with high-powered rifles tell you, and you don't bother to take down what a reporter says? And why are you so *surly* today? What's the deal here, anyway?"

"Do you want me to get you Sven Gland on the phone, or what?"

"Yes, *please*," he said through gritted teeth. "And coffee," though he didn't want any; that was just for punishment.

"It's five-thirty, what do you want coffee for? You won't be able to sleep." She walked out. What a smart decision *that* had been, to go to bed with Gazelle that night after they'd been working late and they went out afterward to Bert's for a few pops. One thing had led to another—it always does—and before he knew it he was booking a room at the Madison Hotel from a smartass night clerk. No, no reservation. No, no luggage. Yes, for two people. No, *not* two single beds. Riding up in the elevator with the porter, who insisted on showing him how the minibar worked, the heat, the A/C, the TV, Christ, he was about to explain about the dry cleaning procedures when Nick shoved him out the door with a ten-dollar bill. Then the next day they had to go through the whole office awkwardness. Good morning, Miss Tully. Good morning, Mr. Naylor. Coffee? Yes, *please,* Miss Tully. Then the first time she got something wrong and he said something to her, boom, kettledrums, the evil eye, and a lecture about sexual attitude. And every time they'd worked late since and he'd said what about a few pops at Bert's it was, No, it's late, and I've got to pick up Jerome at my sister's, leaving Nick in the role of Caucasian sexual paranoid, to wonder if he had somehow . . . failed in what he seemed, anyway, to recall of that sweaty evening as a perfectly honorable performance. Series of performances. It was true what they said about black women, every word—they *were* insatiable. No wonder black men fled their homes in droves. They needed sleep.

Nick turned his attention to the boards. They were compelling, brilliant, arresting. He was right to have fired the Academy's dull ad agency and gone to Buda/Munganaro/Gland, the hot-hot new, small-is-beautiful agency in Minneapolis that had taken a second-rate

Swedish vodka with an aftertaste of herring scales and turned it into the number-one selling liquor in the country. He sighed.

"Sven," he said into the speakerphone, "it's dazzling. I'm totally blown away."

"I know," Sven said. "So are we."

"That's the problem. It's a good news/bad news situation. The bad news is we've got to make it a turkey. It's going to have to gobble, or my people aren't going to go for it. The good news is, they're willing to spend five million dollars on this campaign." Between fees and commissions, BMG stood to make northward of $750,000.

"Sven? You there?"

"You want it to *gobble*?"

"Yes. It must gobble."

"That's not really what we do, Nick."

"No, you convince millions of people to think they're hip because they drink vodka that tastes like any other vodka, only worse. I heard no one in Sweden in his right mind drinks that stuff. It tastes like fish. They must be rolling in the snow in Stockholm, laughing. So you want to tell me that for massive amounts of money you can't produce a dull anti-smoking campaign aimed at underage kids."

Pause. "We could do that."

"Then what's the problem?"

"No problem."

Nick said he would need something to show the grown-ups by Friday because they were already getting heat from the Advertising Council, which was getting heat from the gasper groups, who sniffed a large, hairy rat.

He called Sammy Najeeb. The secretary of Health and Human Services was calling for Nick's resignation. "I'm always the last to know," Nick said. Larry wanted him on the show tomorrow. As soon as Nick hung up, Jeannette stuck her head in his office to tell him that Secretary Furioso of Helpless, Hopeless, and Stupid (above) was calling for his resignation, and Nick was able to say that he'd just heard this from Larry King's executive producer. When you're hot, you're hot.

BR called him five minutes later. Talk about an attitude implant. His whole tone had changed. He'd heard about the Larry King invite.

A definite score, nice going. Now this Furioso thing, how should they play it? Tobacco Fighting Back, that was good, that was fine. Nick was definitely earning his two-oh-oh. But she's a cabinet secretary and we don't want you too out-front. Right?

Right. They agreed. Nick would be unyielding on the points, but respectful. He'd push the theme of we're-on-the-same-side-here, to the extent that was possible. Furioso was a tough old buzzardess. BR paid him a compliment. Amazing. He said, "You better put your five-million-dollar baby on display. May turn out to be the best money we ever spent." We! Team Tobacco!

The planets were in harmonious alignment. Polly was having a good day, a really good day. In fact, it was possible that she might never ever have such a day again. For several years now, the Neo-Prohibitionists within the federal government had been using a phrase that drove the liquor, beer, and wine lobbies crazy: "alcohol and other drugs." The Moderation Council had spent millions in trying to get Uncle Sam's roundheads to stop using it in all their communications. To no avail. And now the pope had publicly said that wine should not be considered a drug. True, he was talking about sacramental wine, and wine used in moderation, at the family dinner table, preferably while working up to a little connubial and reproductive sex. Nonetheless, Polly was running with His Holiness's pontification in a big way, issuing a blizzard of paper. Her wine people were beside themselves. Her beer people were passing peach pits. The head of Gutmeister-Melch had spent thirty minutes reaming her out for not having "gotten him" to say the same thing about beer.

"I told him it wasn't us who did it. It was the Italian producers. They saw the plummeting U.S. consumption figures and worked it through one of the cardinals."

"It's hard to see what the pope could say good about *beer*," Bobby Jay said. "It's not like the Good Lord changed water into beer at Cana. And they weren't hardly drinking beer in the upper room at the Last Supper."

"Then my distilled spirits people called to bitch."

"What do they expect," Nick said, "that he's going to come out for scotch?"

"No, they just—it's a zero-sum game. We're in declining volumetrics, and they're all totally paranoid. They see anything good happen to wine or beer and they think, Less for us. I spend over half my time keeping them from killing each other, when they should be protecting each other's backs."

"Well, cheers anyway," Nick said, raising his glass. "Nicely done, even if you didn't have anything to do with it. Say, do either of you guys know a Heather Holloway, works for the *Moon*? She wants to do a piece on me."

"Heather Holloway? Oh yeah," Bobby Jay said. "Irish type, reddish hair, big green eyes, great skin. *Amazing* tits."

"Tits?" Polly said. "Why are her *tits* relevant?"

"Humh," Bobby Jay said through his food. "World-class honkers on a reporter interviewing a male of the species are *relevant,* believe you me."

"I thought Jesus freaks didn't talk locker-room."

"I am not a 'Jesus freak.' I do not accost strangers on street corners. I do not play the guitar. I am a born-again Christian. And I shoot," Bobby Jay said, "to kill."

"You're going to end up just like that guy in Waco. Praising the Lord, passing the ammo, and shooting ATF agents. I get very nervous around guns and religion."

Nick said, "Is there anything *else* you can tell me about her, aside from what size bra she wears?"

Bobby Jay said that Heather Holloway had come to one of SAFETY's press conferences, in which Mr. Drum called for building more jails. It was part of SAFETY's offensive strategy: instead of sitting still and being a punching bag for liberals who didn't want criminals to have guns, they went after liberals for releasing people who had shot people in the first place. Heather had charmed the socks off Drum, and had written a more or less antigun-control piece—the *Moon* being a conservative paper—but she had taken issue with Drum for insisting that a prior history of mental illness ought not to disqualify a person from buying a handgun. So Drum suspected her of liberal tendencies.

"What's the focus of her piece?" Polly asked. "Tobacco fighting back?"

"She says it's for a series on the New Puritanism. Maybe the *Moon*'s looking for some tobacco advertising."

"You be careful," Bobby Jay said. "Just pretend it's some ugly old harelip interviewing you."

"Bobby, I think I can handle a good-looking girl reporter."

"Seen it happen again and again. They come in, bat their pretty eyes at you, cross their legs a few times, and before you know, it's 'I shouldn't really be telling you this' and 'Would you like to see our confidential files?' Beware of Jezebels with tape recorders."

"Bobby Jay, you've got to lay off the breakfast prayer groups. You're getting kind of weird."

"All I'm saying is that most men, confronted with a babe reporter, talk too much."

"Well thanks for the advice."

"Hundred bucks says you end up spilling the company beans all over the floor so bad you need a Wet-Vac to clean up. You in for a piece of the action, Ms. Steinem?"

"I think Nick can manage."

"A hundred each says he commits at least one major indiscretion."

"You're on," Nick said.

"Done," Polly said. "Damnit," she said, "I've got a two-thirty meeting. *Prime Time Live* is doing a segment on fetal alcohol syndrome next Thursday."

"Um," Nick said, sipping coffee, "that's a tough one."

"We're going to get creamed."

"I saw this piece on CNN about a woman who drank a gallon of vodka every day in her third trimester. Oddly, her child has problems."

"Got any ideas for me?"

Nick thought. "I don't know. Deformed kids are tough. I'm lucky. My product only makes them bald before it kills them."

"That's a big help."

"Challenge their data. Demand to see the mothers' medical histories. Her mother's m.h., her mother's mother's m.h. Say, 'Look, where's the *science* here? This is just anecdotal.' "

"Maybe you could hug the kids," Bobby Jay said, "like Mrs. Bush and the AIDS baby."

"They're not going to let me *hug* the kids, for Christsake, Bobby."

"Who's doing the segment? Donaldson or Sawyer?"

"Sawyer, I think. They're being cagey about it, but the producer we're dealing with is one of hers, so I'm pretty sure."

"That is tough."

"Why?"

"'Cause *she's* going to hug them. Look, if it looks like, if you see her reaching to hug one, try to get in a hug first."

"God, I'm really not looking forward to this."

"Set up a fund," Bobby Jay suggested. "The Fetal Alcohol Syndrome Foundation. F-A-S-F. Fasfuff."

"Right, I can just see Arnie Melch's face, or Peck Gibson's or Gino Grenachi's faces, when I tell him I want money for the kids of drunken mothers. And we're going to have the words 'Fetal' and 'Alcohol' in the name. That's a brilliant goddamn idea. But excuse me. I forget I was talking to the master spin doctor of the Carburetor City Church Choir Massacre."

"Why not? It would show compassion, generosity of heart."

"Do you set up funds for people who get shot?" Polly said testily. "No, because you'd go broke."

"Guns don't kill people, Polly."

"Oh, *yeah*."

"No, he's right," Nick said. "Bullets kill people."

"I've got to go," Polly sighed heavily. "Jesus, this is going to be just *awful*."

Nick walked with her part of the way back to the Moderation Council. It was a beautiful Washington spring day—the hideous Washington summers are Nature's revenge for the loveliness of Washington's springs—and the magnolia tree on the corner of Rhode Island and Seventeenth was blooming. Nick noticed that Polly was wearing white stockings with a bit of silver sparkle in them that gave her long legs a shimmer of frost as they disappeared up into her pleated blue skirt. He found himself looking down at her legs. All that talk about Heather Holloway's tits, Gazelle at the Madison Hotel, the spring weather, it had Nick thinking. The white stockings, boy they were nice, reminded him of the night ten, no, twelve years ago, after he'd first come to Washington, in the summer, and he and Amanda had put away two bottles of crisp, cold Sancerre between them and strolled on down to the Lincoln Memorial. It was one of those steamy Washington July evenings. She was wearing this cotton, floral print dress that with all the humidity clung to her and, well, he couldn't say about Heather Holloway, but Amanda's body had no apologies to make, the way, um, and she was wearing white stockings, thigh-highs, the kind that didn't need garters, but allowed easy access to the dreamy area above, and um, yes, well, Nick had a definite thing about white thigh-highs. They went around to the back of the Lincoln, where it looks out onto Arlington Cemetery, and Amanda was leaning up against one of the massive granite columns, giggling about how the ridges were digging into her back. Nick was down on his knees, which wasn't so comfortable on the marble but he wasn't thinking about his knees, and lifting the floral print dress slowly, slowly, planting kisses until the cool thighs appeared, then a triangle of white—white again!—silk panties and . . .

"Do you want to have a drink tonight later, after the King show?" Nick asked.

Polly looked at him. "A drink?"

"The studio's down on Mass and whatever, Third or something. We could go to Il Peccatore." Senator Finisterre, nephew of the slain president, had recently made it famous when a waitress walked into the private back room with the food and found the senator filibustering a young female aide on the table. The incident made print and ever since the tour buses had been stopping there next to the sidewalk in front, where Il Peccatore's outside tables were set up and the tour guides would say over the loudspeakers, "That's where the incident involving Senator Finisterre took place," and people from Indiana would take their pictures while Il Peccatore's sidewalk patrons tried to eat their arugula and calamari without feeling that they were background in some live sex act show.

"I . . ."

"Aw, come on."

"I better not."

"Why?"

"I've got a Designated Driver Committee dinner."

"After the dinner, then. How late can a Designated Driver Committee dinner go?"

For a second there it looked like she was going to say yes, yes I will, yes. Then she said, "I really can't. Maybe some other time."

8

Sammy Najeeb, Larry King's producer and a force of nature, six-foot-something, big, hearty, came to fetch him in the reception area and take him to makeup. "I used to smoke like a chimney," she said.

"It's never too late to take it back up again. By the way, who's on the second segment?"

"You don't want to know," Sammy said.

Nick stopped. "Not the cancer kid?"

"No. This isn't Oprah. But you're in the right ballpark."

"Who?"

"Trust me, you won't have to be in the same room at the same time, I promise. It's all fixed. I gave instructions."

"*Who?*"

"It's Lorne Lutch."

"I'm on with the Tumbleweed Man? Are you *nuts?*"

"You're not on with anyone. It's two completely different segments. Look, it's not a setup, Larry wanted *you* on, then Atlanta said he had to put someone else from the other side on after, for balance."

"Balance," Nick muttered.

"It's gonna be fine. Larry *loved* what you did on Oprah. He's a fan. He used to smoke three packs a day."

"Hi there," said the makeup lady.

Fuming, Nick took his seat. "I take Innocent Bisque?"

"I'm out of Innocent," she said. "But Indigo is close."

"All right. And Tawny Blush highlight."

Jesus, the Tumbleweed Man. For over twenty years the very symbol of America's smoking manhood in the saddle, his rugged, granite face on the back cover of every magazine, on billboards, on TV, in those happy bygone days. Now he was breathing through a hole in his throat and with every breath he had left—which was not many, thank God, according to Gomez O'Neal, the head of the Academy's intelligence unit—paving his way to the Pearly Gate by warning everyone about the evils of smoking. Ironically, it was Nick who had talked Total Tobacco Company management out of suing him for breach of faith, on the grounds that it would do no good to the industry's image to sue a dying man with three kids and twelve grandchildren, especially since his croaky pleas to the nation's youth had made him a media darling (at least with the broadcast media since they couldn't accept cigarette ads anyway). Maybe, thought Nick, he could trot out this pathetic little detail in his defense tonight.

Sammy was hovering, as if she didn't trust him not to flee down the fire stairs with his makeup bib still on.

Larry King was very welcoming. "Good to see you. Thanks for coming."

"Pleasure," Nick said tightly. His trapezius muscles were hypercontracting. He was going to need a session with Dr. Wheat soon. He could use a session with Dr. Wheat right now.

"I used to smoke three packs a day," Larry said. "And you know something, I still miss it. We're gonna have a good show tonight. Lot of calls. Very emotional issue."

"I understand Lorne Lutch is on the second segment," Nick said.

Larry shrugged. "What can you do? I'll tell you something, though."

"What's that?"

"He's a nice guy."

"Yes, that's what we hear."

"By the way, you know what that hole is called? The one in the throat. Stoma. Must be Greek, right?"

"Undoubtedly." Nick screwed in his earpiece.

"Good evening everyone. My first guest tonight is Nick Naylor, chief spokesman for the tobacco lobby here in Washington, D.C. Good evening, Nick."

"Good evening, Larry."

"A couple of days ago you were on the *Oprah* show and stirred up quite a fuss, right?"

"Apparently, Larry."

"And now the secretary of Health and Human Services and the surgeon general are calling for you to be fired, I understand. Kind of rare, isn't it?"

"Well, those two aren't exactly unbiased when it comes to tobacco. Actually, I would have thought that they would have been pleased by our announcement that our industry is prepared to spend five million dollars on a very high-level campaign to keep underage kids from smoking. But I guess politics got in the way. Too bad."

"Lot of money, five million."

"You bet it is, Larry."

"Let me ask you something, Nick. Smoking's bad for you, right? I mean . . ."

"No, Larry, actually that's not really true."

"I used to smoke a lot and I had three heart attacks and bypass surgery. My doctor told me I could either go on smoking or die."

"I wouldn't be comfortable discussing your medical history, Larry. I don't know what the incidence of heart disease is in the King family. I'm certainly happy that you're feeling better. But if I could steer us a little away from the anecdotal and toward the more scientific, the fact is that ninety-six percent of heavy smokers never get seriously ill."

"Isn't that a little hard to believe?"

"They get colds and, you know, headaches and the normal sort of things, bunions"—*Bunions?*—"but they don't get seriously ill."

"Where does that figure come from?"

"From the National Institutes of Health, right here in Bethesda, Maryland." Let NIH deny it tomorrow; tomorrow people would be on to the next thing—Bosnia, tax increases, Sharon Stone's new movie, Patti Davis's latest novel about what a bitch her mother was. As long as he was at it, he threw in: "And from the Centers for Disease Control, in Atlanta, Georgia."

"That *is* news." Larry shrugged. Larry was basically too polite to accuse his guests of being shameless liars. It was probably why Ross Perot liked him so much. With any luck, no one from NIH or CDC would be watching.

"Of course," Nick said, "neither Secretary Furioso nor the surgeon general, both of whom continue to refuse to debate with me on the issues, want you to know that or their budgets will go down. Sad, but true."

"Interesting."

"There are a lot of things," Nick sighed, "that the government doesn't want people to know about tobacco. Such as . . ."— *What?*—". . . the indisputable scientific fact that it retards the onset of Parkinson's disease."

"So we should wait till we're sixty-five and then start smoking like crazy?"

"Well, Larry, we don't advocate that anyone should take up smoking. We're just here to provide the scientific facts. Like the report that just came out showing that tobacco smoke is replenishing the ozone that has been lost due to chlorofluorocarbons."

"Really?" Larry said. "Well, maybe I should take it up again, do my part for the ozone hole. I better check with my doctor first."

"Doctors tend to have their own agendas. I'd also like to call to your attention the report last week that smokers who are clerical workers tend to get less carpal tunnel syndrome, you know, the wrist thing, because they take more breaks. There's something else the quote medical science establishment unquote doesn't want you to know about."

"We're going to take some calls. Spokane, Washington, you're on the air.

"Hello?"

"You're on *Larry King Live.*"

"Oh. Uh, yes, hello."

"Do you have a question?"

"Yes. I would like to ask your guest how he can live with himself."

"I take it you don't approve of what he does."

"I think he's a criminal, Larry. He should be locked up. Or worse. There should be a death penalty for what he does."

"Nick, care to comment?"

"Not really, Larry."

"Blue Hill, Maine, you're on the air."

"Yes, I smoked for many, many, *many* years. And then I developed   *77* these like, lumps?" Uh-oh. "And the doctor said it was from smoking, so I gave it up, but the lumps still didn't go away, so I'm thinking about taking it up again."

"Uh-huh," Larry said. "And your question?"

"The doctor who told me that was a young fellah and I think he just told me that to get me to give up. I don't think the lumps had anything to do with smoking."

"Okay, Milwaukee, Wisconsin, you're on the air."

"I smoke and it hasn't made me sick. I'll tell you what made me sick is drinking Milwaukee public water. I thought I was going to die."

"Thanks. No one has a question tonight?" Larry looked over at Sammy in the booth who gestured to say that the callers had *said* they had questions.

"Okay, we need a question. Atlanta, Georgia"—Nick's gut went into Condition Red—"you're on the air."

"Thank you, Larry. I work at the Centers for Disease Control and I would like to try to correct the *extraordinary* misimpression that this . . . individual is trying to create. While it may be true that as many as ninety-six percent of smokers never gets seriously ill, it simply does not follow that smoking is not dangerous. It is extremely dangerous. It is the number-one preventable killer in the United States. There have been so far over sixty thousand studies since the 1940s showing the link between smoking and disease. For this guy to claim that we're saying it's all right to smoke is just beyond immorality. It's grotesque."

"Nick?"

Nick cleared his throat. "If this gentleman wants to debate the *science,* I'm all for it. Our attitude has always been . . . bring on the data."

"He's lying through his teeth, Larry. That guy is lower than whalecrap."

"Well," Nick said, "it's a little difficult to carry on a rational discussion while being verbally abused. But abuse does seem to be the lot of the modern-day smoker." Oh yes, please, let's do shift this steaming pile away from ourselves. . . . "They're scorned, victimized, shunned—if they're *lucky* they're shunned, most of them are actively abused. They have to huddle in doorways in the dead of winter and shiver. I would like to ask the *gentleman* from the CDC, if that's really where he's from, about the recent rise in cases of pneumonia—"

"What rise in pneumonia? There's no rise in pneumonia."

"Hoh! Who's lying now? Larry, there has been an *extraordinary* increase in this ghastly, life-threatening disease, well documented by medical authorities, thank you very much, and it's happening because smokers are being forced out-of-doors in freezing temperatures. Let's face it, *sir,* you and your ilk have turned one-fifth of the population of the United States into lepers. Talk about your tyranny of the majority."

"I give up, Larry, I can't listen to this anymore, I'm going to get violent."

"Emotional issue," Larry said. "Herndon, Virginia."

"Yeess," said a man's voice with a nervous air to it, "I have a question for Mr. Naylor. I would like to ask him his opinion of these nicotine patches that so many people are wearing."

"Good question," Larry said.

"Yes it is. Frankly, sir, we at the Academy of Tobacco Studies are a little concerned about these things."

"Why?" said Larry. "They dispense nicotine into the system, same as cigarettes, and your position is that cigarettes aren't bad for you, right?"

"Well," Nick said, "your typical cigarette delivers a relatively minute amount of nicotine into your system, a very minute amount. Whereas just one of these deadly little Band-Aids—"

"Hold on," Larry said, "you said 'deadly'?"

"Oh, absolutely. People have been dropping dead all over as a result of these patches. Even our previous caller, Dr. Doom down there in Atlanta, would admit to that."

"I read that some people who kept on smoking after they starting wearing the patches had had heart attacks," said Larry. "But—"

"Well there you go. Heart attacks. I tell you something Larry, and Mr., sorry, I don't know your name, there in Herndon, I wouldn't let one of those things get *near* my skin."

"It's very interesting you say that," said the voice. "I will certainly be careful with them. Larry, has anyone ever announced that they're going to kill someone on your show before?"

"No," said Larry, "but we get a lot of angry calls."

"Then this is your lucky day, because I'm here to tell you that within a week, we're going to dispatch Mr. Naylor for all the pain and suffering he's caused in the world."

There was an awkward pause. "Wait a minute," Larry said, "are you threatening him?"

"Yes, Larry. I have really enjoyed talking with you. You have a very nice show." There was a click.

"Emotional issue," said Larry.

9

It was just a short item, in the "Reliable Source" section of the late edition of the *Sun,* slugged, CALLER TO KING SHOW THREATENS TO STUB OUT TOBACCO SMOKESMAN. Nick felt a little short-changed. The guy was obviously just some nut with too much free time on his hands, but where did the *Sun* get off making puns out of a death threat? In *this* crazy, mixed-up world?

He called the *Sun* on his car phone to complain. After explaining to the operator that he had a complaint and wanted to speak to an assistant managing editor, he was put through to a recording.

"You have reached the *Washington Sun*'s ombudsman desk. If you feel you have been inaccurately quoted, press one. If you spoke to a reporter off the record but were identified in the article, press two. If you spoke on deep background but were identified, press three. If you were quoted accurately but feel that the reporter missed the larger point, press four. If you are a confidential White House source and are calling to alert your reporter that the President is furious over leaks and has ordered a review of all outgoing calls in White House phone logs, press five. To speak to an editor, press six."

Exhausted, Nick hung up. His phone rang. It was Gazelle, concerned because Jeannette was going around breathlessly telling everyone in the office that five of the six major pharmaceutical companies that manufactured nicotine patches were threatening to sue unless Nick issued a retraction of his comments on the King show. The achievement of car phones is that your morning can now be ruined even before you get to the office.

People greeted him in the corridors.

"Hey, Nick, way to go!"

"You gonna be okay, Nick?"

"Jesus, Nick, who *was* that guy?"

Gazelle handed him coffee and told him that BR wanted to see him right away.

Jeannette was there when he walked in. She jumped up and went over to him and—hugged him. "Thank *God,*" she said.

"Nick," BR said, with this concerned, three-furrows-in-his-brow look, "are you all *right?*"

"Fine. What's the problem?"

"The problem," BR said, sounding a little surprised, "is that your life has been threatened."

Nick lit up a Camel. Nice, being able to smoke in BR's office now. "Oh, come on. Some nut."

"That's not how I see it. And that's not how the Captain sees it."

Nick exhaled. "The Captain?"

"I just got off the phone with him. He wants full security around you until this matter is . . . until we know exactly what we're dealing with here."

"That's crazy."

"Jeannette," BR said, "would you excuse us?" Jeannette left the room. "Nick, we got off to a bad start, and that was my fault, for which I hereby apologize. Sometimes I can be an asshole. It's . . . the world I come from, vending machines, it's a tough world. I have some edges. But never mind that. I've come to realize lately just how valuable you are to Team Tobacco. So," he smiled, "my concern for you isn't just warm and fuzzy feelings. Basically, I don't want to lose you. And certainly not to some nutcase."

Nick was quite overwhelmed. "Well," he stammered, "I appreciate that, BR."

"So it's settled. We're putting a security detail on you."

"Wait, I didn't agree to that."

"Nick, you want to tell this to the Captain?"

"But I get dozens, hundreds of threats. I've got a whole file labeled 'Threats.' It's under 'T.' One guy wrote that he was going to tar and feather me. He was going to collect an entire vat full of tar from those disposable cigarette-holder filters and cover me with it and then feather me. You can't take this stuff seriously."

"This is different. This was live, national—international—television. Even assuming the guy is just a crank, other people watching might get an idea. They're called copycat killers, I think. Anyway, we're just not prepared to take the chance."

"You're telling me," Nick said, "that I have to have a *bodyguard*?"

"Bodyguards, plural."

"Uh-uh. Not my style."

"Then *you* tell the Captain," BR said, holding out his phone. "Listen, in this town it's considered a sign of having arrived."

"I'll look like a drug lord, for crying out loud."

"Look, I don't want to sound like I'm capitalizing on a gruesome situation, but, how can I put this?—the fact that it's gotten to the deplorable point where a senior vice president for a major trade association, for God's sake, is reduced to needing security, in the nation's capital, to keep himself from being killed by a bunch of fanatic antismokers—"

"You're really getting into this, aren't you?"

"Nick, I *know* it's a sow's ear, but maybe there's a silk purse inside."

"Well, yeah, but . . ."

"All right, then. Aren't you having lunch with Heather Holloway of the *Moon* today?"

"Yes," Nick said, surprised at how well apprised BR was about his daily schedule. Jeannette.

"So, she's going to notice that you've got bodyguards and put that in her story. How bad can that be for our side?"

Nick left BR's office in a foul mood and went back to his office and called the Captain and asked him if this ridiculous order had come from him. In fact it had, and the Captain was adamant.

"Take it as a measure of our esteem for you, son. Can't go taking chances. I just got off the phone with Skip Billington and Lem Tutweiler and they want to put you in an armored personnel carrier." Billington and Tutweiler were heads of, respectively, Blue Leaf Tobacco, Inc., and Tarcom, two of the largest of the Big Six tobacco firms; by virtue of which they occupied seats—large ones—on the ATS board.

"I think," Nick said, "that we're overreacting to a crank call."

"You let us be the judge of that. Now what progress have you made on the Hollywood project?"

Nick fudged, the correct answer being none. The Captain, shrewd as he was, already knew. "I hope you'll be able to apply yourself to that as *soon* as possible. In fact, things being what they are, you being a ter'rist target . . ." This seemed to Nick a rather fraught way of looking at it, but paranoia rubs off and now he was getting sort of nervous. ". . . it might behoove you to get out of town for a few days and go out there and—don't they all hang out by pools, with their telephones and glamorous stars? That doesn't sound like such an unpleasant assignment," he chuckled. "On second thought, why don't you come down here and run the tobacco business and *I'll* go out to Hollywood and hang out by the pool with all the beautiful women." He added, "Don't tell Mrs. Boykin I told you that or she'll put a water moccasin in the toilet bowl."

In a serious tone of voice, he said, "Now you listen to the security people and don't you go taking any chances. By the way, did BR convey to you my expression of confidence?"

"Yes sir, he did," Nick said, embarrassed that he hadn't thanked the Captain for his extremely generous raise. "Thank you. It was extremely generous."

"Tobacco takes care of its own. Call me from the pool and tell me all about the women. I like that what's her name, blond gal, in that movie they have the ads for about those fellahs throw themselves off cliffs with rubber bands tied to their ankles. . . ."

"Fiona Fontaine."

"That's her. *Fine* specimen. Now if you could get *her* to light up, well, that would be something."

Nick went to see Carlton. Carlton was a former FBI agent who looked like anything but. More like a goofy friendly-faced ice cream vendor, thin, short, and mild, except that his eyes had this tendency to widen and widen as you talked to him, so that by the time you were finished he was looking at you like you were a serial axe murderer.

"Tell you the honest truth, Nicky"—security people had this tendency to use the diminutive in order to achieve instant intimacy—"I think we're overdoing this."

"Hey, *I* know that," Nick said.

"Big guy says you get security, so we're going to give you a detail."

"A detail? No one said anything about a detail."

"The big guy said a detail. It's expensive, let me tell you. Somebody up there must like you." Nick groaned. Carlton said, "Look at it this way—you'll save a fortune on cab fare."

"Oh no," Nick said. The company had given him use of a BMW, which Nick liked to drive. "I drive myself. They want to follow me, that's fine. But I drive myself, alone."

"Nicky, Nicky, Nicky."

"Carlton, could you please not call me that, okay?"

"Look," Nick said to Mike, head of his three-man detail, "could you not come into the restaurant with me? I'm meeting a reporter and I'm going to look like a total wimp if I walk in there with you guys."

"Can't do it, Nicky. Orders."

So Nick walked into Il Peccatore, trying to keep as far ahead of his three obvious bodyguards as he could. They had the little pigtail radio cords that came up the back of their collars and went into their ears. Though with whom were they supposed to be communicating? Nick suspected they wanted to be mistaken for Secret Service agents.

He scanned the room. Senator Finisterre was not there—he was pretty much avoiding Il Peccatore since the incident. But his nephew, Senator Ortolan K. Finisterre, was there, lunching with Alex Beam, the *Sun* columnist, no doubt telling him how he really wasn't interested in running for governor of Vermont when there was *so much work to do right here in the Congress yada yada yada.*

Heather Holloway was already there, at the corner table, looking over her interview notes.

Hm. Very nice indeed, bit of a cross between Maureen O'Hara and Bonnie Raitt, without the gray thing in the hair. Glasses. Nick found glasses sexy on a woman. The shrink he went to during the divorce said this was significant but wouldn't tell him why, wanted him to figure it out for himself. Nick told her, for seventy-five bucks an hour—fifty minutes—she could goddamn well tell *him,* but she wouldn't. Great skin, smattering of freckles. The figure, well, yes, Bobby Jay was right about that, it was a *very* attractive figure, rounded yet exercised, StairMaster voluptuous. And what was this peeking out beneath the table? Pale, ivory stockings? Whoa. She was in a short

85

green suit, open collar, and gold earrings. She smiled up at him through the glasses. Dimples. *Dimples!*

"Who are they?" she said after the introductions, pointing to Mike, Jeff, and Tommy, his bodyguards.

"Off the record?"

"No," she smiled, "on the record. I'm sure that you're good company, but this isn't a social lunch."

That was encouraging. Nick explained, emphasizing that they were unnecessary.

She said, "I have spoken to a number of people who don't . . . I wouldn't call them major fans of yours."

"Well, that's tobacco for you." He picked up a menu. "The sole *in flagrante* is good."

" '*In flagrante*'?"

"It's named after Senator Finisterre."

Heather stared.

"You remember, he was interrupted in the middle of . . . in the back room here? Maybe you read about it?" Maybe sexual jokes of questionable taste—or wit—within sixty seconds of having met were . . . not such a good idea? With all that red hair she might be Catholic. "Everything's good. Pasta. Veal chop Valdostana, very good. The trout is excellent. Lot of almonds, if you like almonds."

She ordered salad and San Pellegrino water, which made him feel like a spurned waiter. Nick, feeling trapped inside his own recommendation, ordered the trout, though he did not particularly like trout with a lot of almonds.

"So," he said, "how long have you been a *Moonie*? I mean, how long have you been with the *Moon*?" Very good, two gaffes in two minutes. Why not follow up with something suave like "Your breasts are really incredible. Are they real?"

"A year," she said. "Do you mind if I tape?"

"Please," Nick said magnanimously.

She put her tape recorder on the table between them. "I'm always convinced that I'll get back to the office and there'll be nothing but static on it."

"I know." Perfume. Dioressense? Krizia? Fracas? Fracas, definitely. "Is that Fracas you have on, by any chance?"

"No."

"Oh?"

"I interviewed Mick Jagger last year," she said, turning on the recorder, "when the Stones played at the Cap Center. When I got back all there was was hissing. I thought they were going to fire me. I had to reconstruct everything he said. I had to put it all in italics."

"Well," Nick said, "he's never *said* anything interesting." From the look Heather gave him he realized he was probably not going to score points with her by denigrating rock and roll's biggest icon. Not that being a Washington trade association spokesman wasn't incredibly sexy.... "I mean," he said, "I *am* a Stones fan. It's just . . ." Move *on,* Nick.

"So," he said, "what's the focus of your piece?" Yes, let's talk about me.

"You are."

"I suppose I should be flattered."

"I started out with the idea of writing about what I'm calling 'The New Puritanism.' "

"Oh yes. Lot of that going around. Olive?"

"No, thank you. I was going to talk to lobbyists for unpopular industries. Tobacco, guns, liquor, lead, asbestos, whaling, toxic waste dumpers, you know. . . ."

"Your basic planet- and human-race–despoiling swine."

"Not necessarily," said Heather, blushing. "Then I saw you on the Oprah show and thought . . . something interesting going on in there."

"The idea being to find out how I'm able to live with myself." Nick tore into a bit of oven-hot *bruschetta.*

"No," she smiled, "I don't imagine *that's* a problem. Any more than it was for . . ."

"Goebbels?"

"I wasn't thinking of him," Heather said delicately, "but that is an interesting analogy. Is that how you see yourself?"

LOBBYIST SEES HIMSELF AS A GUCCI GOEBBELS.

"Not at all. I see myself as a mediator between two sectors of society that are trying to reach an accommodation. I guess you could say I'm a facilitator."

"Or enabler?"

"Beg pardon?"

Heather flipped through some pages of her notebook. " 'Mass murderer,' 'profiteer,' 'pimp,' 'bloodsucker,' 'child killer,' 'yuppie Mephistopheles,' here it is, 'mass enabler.' "

"What is that you're reading from?"

"Interviews. In preparation for our meeting today."

"Who did you talk to? The head of the Lung Association?"

"Not yet."

"Well, frankly, this doesn't sound like a very balanced article you're writing."

"You tell me—who else should I talk to?"

"Fifty-five million American smokers, for starters. Or how about some tobacco farmers whose only crime is to be treated like cocaine producers when they're growing a perfectly legal product. They might have a different view, you know."

"I hurt your feelings. I'm sorry. Actually, I was going to talk to a tobacco farmer."

"I know a lot of them. Fine people. Salt of the earth. I'll give you some phone numbers."

"I guess what I'm trying to get at is, why do you do this? What motivates you, exactly?"

"I get asked that all the time. People expect me to answer, 'The challenge,' or, 'The chance to prove that the Constitution means what it says.' " He paused thoughtfully. "You want to know why I really do it?" Another thoughtful pause. "To pay the mortgage."

This manful statement appeared to make no impression on Heather Holloway, other than mild disappointment. "Someone told me that's probably what you'd say."

"*Did* they?"

"It's a kind of yuppie Nuremberg defense, isn't it?"

"What is it with the Y-word? That's a very eighties word. This is the nineties."

"Excuse me."

"And, I mean," he said, looking offended, "are you calling me a Nazi?"

"No. Actually, you're the one making Third Reich analogies."

"Well, it's one thing to call yourself a Nazi. That's self-deprecation. For someone else to call you one is deprecation. And it's not very nice."

"I apologize. But a mortgage isn't much of a life goal, is it?"

"Absolutely. Ninety-nine percent of everything that is done in the world, good and bad, is done to pay a mortgage. The world would be a much better place if everyone rented. Then there's tuition. Boy, has *that* been a force for evil in the modern world."

"You're married?"

"Divorced," Nick said a bit too quickly.

"Kids?"

"One son. But he's practically grown up."

"How old is he?"

"Twelve."

"He must be quite precocious. So how does he feel about what you do?"

"Frankly, twelve-year-olds don't care where the money comes from. I could be a vivisectionist and I don't think it would make a whole lot of difference as long as I keep him in Rollerblades and snowboards. Not that I equate vivisectionists and the tobacco industry. As a matter of fact, I feel very strongly about animals being, you know, used for dubious scientific purposes. The ones they torture out at NIH. My God, those poor little bunnies. It would break your heart to see them in their little cages, puffing away."

"Puffing?"

"Those smoking machines they attach to them. Criminal. Listen, if I had to smoke like seven thousand cigarettes a day, *I'd* get sick, probably. And I consider myself a heavy smoker."

"But doesn't it bother you being vilified like this? There *are* easier ways of paying mortage and tuition."

"If it makes other people happy to have me play the role of villain, when all I really do is provide information about a legal and, I might add, time-honored industry, fine, no problem. Whatever."

She flipped through her notepad, making Nick suspicious.

"You were a reporter at WRTK."

"Um-hum," Nick said, lighting up. "Do you mind if I smoke?"

Heather seemed to find this amusing. "No, please. Isn't their nickname W-Right To Know?"

"Um-hum."

"Is this an uncomfortable subject for you?"

"Not at all," Nick said, thoughtfully exhaling straight up so it   *89* wouldn't go in her face, though this made him feel like a metal dolphin in a fountain.

"I looked up the news clips," she said delicately, "but if you're agreeable, it would be better if you could tell me about it. So I get everything right."

"It's just kind of old news, is all. This is going to be a big part of your piece?"

"No. Not big. So this happened at Camp LaGroan . . . ?"

"Um-hum." Nick slowly stubbed out his cigarette. Thank *God* for cigarettes, they gave you time to get your act together, or at least to look philosophical. "You'll recall President Broadbent liked to spend time with the boys, being a former marine and all. And I was in our van, monitoring the radio. We'd gotten the base frequencies from, well, someone, which you probably already knew, since you know all this, anyway," he sighed, "so we had the frequency and I was monitoring it and there was this, suddenly there was all this radio traffic about Rover choking to death on a bone. Rover being President Broadbent's Secret Service code name, and the fact that at that very minute the President was in the mess hall having lunch with the boys, so I, you know . . ."

"Went with it?"

"Um-hum. And it turned out to be a different Rover that had choked to death."

"The commandant's dog?"

"Um-hum. A German shorthaired pointer. A six-year-old, sixty-seven pound German shorthaired pointer. On a chicken bone."

"And . . . ?"

"This was not a career-enhancing episode."

"It must have been awful . . . I'm sorry."

"I look on the positive side. How many people get to announce to the nation, 'The President is dead.' It's quite a feeling to say those words. Even if he wasn't dead."

"Yes," Heather said. "It must have been."

"Do you remember when Walter Cronkite said, 'We have just received this news flash. President Kennedy died at one o'clock, Eastern Standard Time.' You're probably too young. It was an amazing moment. I always used to get a chill when I thought about it. I still get it, except that it's immediately followed by the urge to vomit."

"What happened afterwards?"

"Walter Cronkite became the most respected newsman in history. I became a spokesman for cigarettes."

"It must have left you pretty damaged."

"On the contrary, I have extremely thick skin. It's practically like leather. I'd make a very comfortable Chesterfield. Couch, not cigarette."

"It didn't seem that way on the Oprah show," Heather said. "You really tore into that guy."

"That guy? *Please.* That guy is a dork. There are an awful lot of sanctimonious people out there who expect everyone else to canonize them because they're going around like hall monitors confiscating all the ashtrays. And once they've confiscated the last ashtray, do you think they're going to stop there? Oh no. They'll be slapping warning labels on kids' Popsicles. 'Warning, the surgeon general has determined that Popsicles make your tongue cold.' "

"Speaking of kids, what about this five-million-dollar program you announced on the Oprah show? Doesn't that indicate that your industry feels guilty about its product?"

"No," Nick said. "Not at all."

Heather appeared to be waiting for a better answer.

"I think it shows a remarkable sense of sensitivity."

"But isn't it hypocritical for the tobacco companies to mount an anti-smoking program for kids when they're spending millions in advertising to hook them in the first place? That absurd camel, Old Joe, with the nose like a penis and a saxophone. Honestly."

Nick shook his head. "Boy, you put up five million dollars to keep kids from smoking, and does anyone say, 'Thanks'?"

" 'Thanks'?" Heather laughed.

"Not that we're implying that smoking is harmful to their health. But you don't want to take any chances where children are concerned. I mean, they're the future, right?"

"Wow," Heather said.

" 'Wow'?" Nick said. It was her admiring tone that threw him off balance.

"I . . ." she flushed, "this is awkward for me."

"Please," Nick said, almost taking her hand, "tell me."

"It's a little embarrassing."

"You don't have to be. Really."

"I find this all very . . . stimulating."

"What do you find stimulating?"

"Your total absence of morality." She sounded excited. Her eyes looked dreamy behind the glasses; she was leaning in close to him. "I get the feeling you'd do *anything* to pay that mortgage."

"Well, within limits."

"I was raised Catholic. Maybe that's why I find evil so refreshing."

"Evil?" Nick said with a nervous laugh.

She reached over and with her thumb and forefinger started playing with his silk Hermès tie. "But rarely have I seen it so attractively packaged." Her eyes raised slowly from the tie to his. Dimples. "Sick, isn't it?"

"Oh," Nick shrugged, "I'm not much into judging."

"I've actually gone to shrinks about it. They say it's all bound up with my feelings about religion and authority. Some women are turned on by dirty talk. I'm turned on by moral degenerates."

"Well, I don't really see myself as—"

"Oh," she said huskily, "shut up and tell me again about your plans to get more children to smoke."

"Don't you have it backwards?"

"Oh no," Heather said, dipping into her zabaglione and putting a custardy finger into her mouth, "I don't think so."

"Off the record?"

Her chest swelled. "What about very . . . deep . . . background?"

"Check." Nick waved to the waiter.

10

A Thoroughly Modern Merchant of Death:
Nick Naylor, Tobacco's Chief "Smokesman"

An Evil Yuppie or Merely a Mass Enabler to 55 Million Smokers?
Claims He Is 'Proudest' of ATS's Anti-Underage Smoking Program

BY HEATHER HOLLOWAY
MOON CORRESPONDENT

Bobby Jay and Polly were waiting for him at their usual table by
the fake fire at Bert's. Bobby Jay was wearing a smirk the size of the
Trump Tower. Polly appeared not to have drawn a conclusion yet
about the full-page story in the *Moon*'s "Lifestyles" section, but she
looked at Nick as he sat down—late—with more than usual curiosity.

"You look tired," she said pointedly.

"Rough morning," Nick said. "Advertising-ban strategy session,
sick-building-syndrome position paper to get out, radio debate with
Craighead. Get this—Helpless, Hopeless, and Stupid is going to start
using the phrase 'tobacco and other drugs' in all its literature. So now
we're just like heroin. Or alcohol," he tweaked her.

Nick ordered a vodka negroni. It was nice, these Mod Squad
lunches. You could drink hard liquor in the middle of a school day
without people assuming you were an alcoholic underachiever.
Strange how in America in the 1950s, at the height of its industrial and
imperial power, men drank double-martinis for lunch. Now, in its

93

decline, they drank fizzy water. Somewhere something had gone terribly wrong.

"What's with him?" Nick said. Bobby Jay was poring over Heather's article, running his hook down the columns of ink as though he was looking for something crucial.

"I can't quite figure out if I won my hundred bucks," Bobby Jay said. " 'Merchant of Death,' huh? Well I guess she got that right."

"You didn't . . ." Polly said with a look of latent ferocity.

"Of course not. What do you take me for?"

"I'm not," she said, tapping loose her cigarette ash, "entirely sure."

Bobby Jay read aloud from the *Moon:*

" 'Morality is not the issue here,' Naylor told the *Moon.* 'Tobacco is a hundred percent legal product that nearly sixty million American adults enjoy, just as they do coffee, chocolate, chewing gum, or any number of other oral refreshments.' "

" 'Oral refreshments'?" Polly snorted. "*That's* new."

Nick winked. "Sounds like a breath mint, doesn't it?"

Bobby Jay continued:

"Even his adversaries, and there are many of them, admit that Naylor is a formidable opponent. 'He's very, very slick,' said Gordon R. Craighead, head of Health and Human Services' Office of Substance Abuse Prevention, the tobacco lobby's principal federal opponent, 'and very, very smart, and that makes him very, very dangerous. This is an industry that kills about half a million Americans a year, and this nicely dressed, smooth-talking, BMW-driving Joseph Goebbels manages to make it sound like we're against free speech.' "

"The BMW-driving bit *really* hurt," Nick grinned.

Fortunately, Dr. Wheat had had a cancellation and was able to see Nick after lunch. Though his delicious evenings with Heather went *far* toward stress reduction, and were a darn sight more fun than Prozac, the Larry King phone threat, plus having bodyguards, had gotten to him.

Nick had been going to Dr. Wheat for about a year. Dr. Wheat had a lot of clients in high-stress jobs. Occasionally, Nick's neck had a tendency to kink so that he couldn't swivel his head, and since part of his job involved being a "talking head" on television, it behooved him to have a head that swiveled. He'd tried neuromuscular massage, yoga, acupuncture, electronic relaxation machines that emitted bleeping noises and had pulsating red lights that supposedly persuaded your brain that you were relaxed, when in fact you were extremely alarmed; also Valium, Halcion, Atarax, and other state-of-the-art calmer-downers, some more controlled than others. Finally some-one—the chief spokesman for the Savings and Loan Association, who had herself been coping with stress—suggested that he go see her D.O., or osteopath, who, she assured Nick, were real doctors. So Nick went and Dr. Wheat, a pleasant young man—Nick noted with some chagrin that he was now not only older than most policemen, but also than many doctors—felt his neck, tsk-tsked, and performed a series of high-velocity, low-impact maneuvers on him, each of which resulted in a terrible *crrrack* of various bones, but which afterward allowed him to rotate his head almost like the girl in *The Exorcist*. Nick had become quite a fan of OMT, or osteopathic manipulative technique; in fact, he had even done some pro bono work for their trade association. It was he who had come up with the successful slogan for their ads: "D.O.s Are People Doctors."

Dr. Wheat felt Nick's trapezius muscles (anterior and posterior), the suboccipitals, and his sternocleidomastoid. By now he knew these muscles as well as suburban Arlington, which is on the whole much more complicated than the human anatomy.

"Boy," he said—he was very chipper, Dr. Wheat, midwestern and good-natured—"if I didn't know better, I'd say rigor mortis had set in. What have you been *doing* to yourself?" He did a few HVLIs, but was not satisfied with the result, and disappearing, returned pushing a disturbing-looking device on wheels. It looked like something that the Iraqi secret police would use on someone caught writing SADDAM SUCKS on a public wall; it had straps and electrodes. Dr. Wheat rubbed jelly on parts of Nick's chest, attached the electrodes, and said, "You may feel a slight burning."

It felt like he was being struck on the back with wooden mallets. He realized that he was in fact arching off the table with every jolt of current like a frog in a high school biology class experiment.

"H-how m-many v-volts?"

"We're at three-thirty already. Very impressive. I don't like to go much higher than four hundred. The smell of burning flesh alarms the other patients." Dr. Wheat was prone to black humor. He explained that this was DC current that was coursing through Nick's body, that being preferable to AC, which would have the effect of stopping his heart and cooking him. After fifteen minutes, he turned it off and tried to rotate Nick's neck, pronouncing himself still unsatisfied with the result.

"Have you ever considered a less stressful line of work?" he said, opening a cabinet and taking out a bottle of liquid and a hypodermic needle. "Like air traffic controller?"

"And abandon the fifty-five million people who are counting on me," said Nick, checking his chest for burn marks. "What is that?"

"This," Dr. Wheat said, filling the syringe, "is for the stubborn cases." He sank the needle into Nick's shoulder by the neck. It was not a good sensation going in, but . . . oooooooh what a delicious feeling suffused through all those hypercontracted muscle bands. Suddenly it felt as if his head were borne on clouds.

"Whoa," he said, rotating like a gyrocopter, "what *is* that?"

"Novocaine. We need to break a cycle here."

"Could I get a prescription for that?"

"I don't think so. I'm going to give you some Soma tablets. Four a day, no driving, and let's see you in two days."

Nick felt pretty great, humming down Route 50 toward Washington, trying to see if he could lose his bodyguards. Little game he'd developed, and good sport. He zoomed over the Roosevelt Bridge and turned hard right onto Rock Creek, left onto the Whitehurst and up Foxhall to Saint Euthanasius for his appointment with the Reverend Griggs.

His bodyguards pulled up in a pissed-off screech of tires as he was walking into the administration building, and came running over sweatily.

"Hi guys." The guys didn't look happy.

"Nicky, I really wish you wouldn't do that, or we're going to have one of us in the car with you."

"Re-lax, Mike." It's soo easy with one cc of novocaine in your traps. . . .

They waited inside for the Rev, who came after a few minutes and started at finding so much suited gristle in his quiet waiting room.

"Ah yes," he caught on, "these must be the gentlemen referred to in the newspaper article today. Terrible business." Nick told the boys that he was unlikely to be assaulted in the offices of the Rev and left them to peruse copies of *Anglican Digest* and *Modern Headmaster* while he went off to conduct whatever business it was the Rev had in mind.

"Thank you *so* much for coming," he said, ushering him toward a leather chair. His study looked as though it had been decorated in 1535: floor-to-ceiling Tudor wainscoting, mullioned windows, a threadbare Persian rug, and the faint smell of a hundred years of spilled dry sherry.

They had a little preliminary chin-wag about the recent controversial nomination of a female suffragan bishop. Being a lapsed Catholic, Nick had only a tenuous grasp of hierarchical Episcopalian nomenclature. In fact, he had no clue as to what a suffragan bishop was, except that it sounded like a bishop in distress. Eventually he grasped that it just meant the number-two bish. Since Joey's entire future lay in the hands of the Reverend Griggs, Nick feigned keen interest in the controversy, until even the Reverend Griggs seemed to lose interest and with a soft clearing of his long throat came to the much-awaited point.

"As you know, we hold an auction every year, to raise money for the scholarship students. I was wondering if your association might possibly be interested in participating? This recession has put everyone in a pinch. Even our more—" he smiled "—pecunious parentry."

Geez, Louise. For *this* Nick had been churning all week? So the Reverend Griggs could hit him up for some underwriting? And yet the Soma and the novocaine had him in a complaisant frame of mind. He reflected warmly and fuzzily that things really had not changed much since 1604. That was the year that James I, king of England, published (anonymously, pamphleteering not being seemly in monarchs) a "Counterblaste to Tobacco." He noted that two Indians from the Virginia colony had been brought to the Sceptered Isle in 1584 to demonstrate this newfangled thing called smoking. By the standards set by *Dances With Wolves* and *The Last of the Mohicans,* James not been very pc.

"What honor or policie," thundered His Royal Highness, "can move us to imitate the barbarous and beastly manner of the wilde, godlesse, and slavish Indian, especially in so vile and stinking a cus-

97

tome?" He allowed as how it had first been used as an antidote to the dreaded "pockes"—which had ruined the complexion of his relative Elizabeth I—but wrote that doctors now considered it a filthy, disgusting habit, providing in a way the first surgeon general's report, and a full 360 years before Luther Terry's in 1964.

As for himself, wrote His Grace, smoking was "a custome loathsome to the eye, hatefull to the nose, harmefull to the braine, dangerous to the lungs and in the blacke stinking fume thereof, nearest resembling the horrible, Stigian smoke of the pit that is bottomlesse."

By 1612, however, James I was having second thoughts. His exchequer was bursting at the bolts with the import duties on tobacco from the Virginia colony in the James River Valley. In fact, nothing further was heard from His Majesty ever again on the loathesome custome. And thus it has remained, in a way, even to the present day, as the U.S. government goes about like Captain Renaud in Rick's Café shouting, "I'm shocked—shocked!" while its trade representatives squeeze foreign governments—particularly Asian ones—to relax their own warning labels and tariffs and let in U.S. weed.

"Mind if I smoke?"

The Rev looked momentarily stricken. "No. Please, yes, by all means."

Nick lit up a Camel, but refrained from blowing one of his nice tight smoke rings, despite what a nice halo it would have made around the Rev's head. "Ashtray?"

"Of course, let's see," the Rev fumbled, looking helplessly around the study. "We must have an *ashtray,* somewhere." But there was nothing, and with Nick's cigarette already lit, the fuse was, so to speak, burning. Nick took deep drags, hastening the process.

"Margaret," the Rev said desperately into the phone, "do we have an *ashtray* anywhere? Anything, yes." He sat down.

"We're finding one."

Nick took in another deep drag. The cigarette hovered over the Persian rug. The door opened, Margaret bearing a chipped tea plate embossed with the coat of arms of Saint Euthanasius. "This was all I could find," she said in a voice somewhere between embarrassment and resentment that she had been called upon to play enabler to the blacke stinking fume.

"Yes, thank you, Margaret," said the Rev, nearly grabbing the plate and handing it over to Nick mere seconds before the ash fell onto the school motto: *Esto Excellens Inter Se*. ("Be Excellent to Each Other.")

"Mainly," Nick said, "we sponsor sports events. But we might be able to work something out."

"Wonderful," the Rev said.

"I'll have to run it by our Community Activities people. But we speak the same language."

"Marvelous," said the Rev, twisting in his Queen Anne chair. "I wonder, would it be necessary to . . . promulgate the . . . exact provenance of the underwriting?"

" 'Underwriting by the Academy of Tobacco Studies' on the programs?" Nick exhaled. "That is pretty standard."

"Yes, certainly. Yes. I was only wondering if perhaps there was some other . . . corporate entity that we could acknowledge. Generously, of course."

"Hm," Nick said. "Well, there is the Tobacco Research Council."

"Yes," the Rev said with disappointment, "I suppose." The TRC had been in the news recently because of the Benavides liability suit. It had come out that the TRC had been set up by the tobacco companies in the fifties as a front group, at a time when American smokers realized they were coughing more and enjoying it less, the idea being to persuade everyone that the tobacco industry, by gum, wanted to get to the bottom of these mysterious "health" issues, too. The TRC's first white paper blamed the rise of lung cancer and emphysema on a global surge in pollens. All this, apparently, the Rev knew.

"Are there by chance any *other* groups?"

Nick clasped his hands together and made a steeple. "We are affiliated with the Coalition for Health."

"Ah!" the Rev said, clapping his hands. *"Perfect!"*

The Rev walked Nick to his car. Nick asked, "By the way, how's Joey doing?"

"Joey?"

"My son. He's in your seventh grade."

"Ah! *Extremely* well," the Rev said. "*Bright* lad."

"So everything's okay?"

"Spiffing. Well then," he shook Nick's hand, "thank you for coming. And I'll look forward to hearing from"—he winked, the dog-collared son of a bitch actually winked—"the Coalition for Health."

11

The novocaine had worn off by now, but Nick still felt pretty good and loose as he roared out of the Saint Euthanasius parking lot ahead of his bodyguards, and after the way he'd handled the Rev, entitled to his sense of triumph. The Soma had crept in on its little cat feet and was now purring in his central nervous system, hissing away all bad thoughts. He lost Mike and the boys by executing a sudden left turn at a red light off Massachusetts Avenue, narrowly avoiding an oncoming dry cleaning van and almost flattening a group of Muslims returning from prayer at the mosque; at which point it occurred to him that Dr. Wheat had told him not even to drive, much less play Parnelli Jones in city traffic.

Jeannette reached him on the car phone to say that she needed to get with him on media planning for next week's Environmental Protection Agency's report on secondhand smoke. Yet another bit of good news on the tobacco horizon. Erhardt, their scientist in residence, was cranking up the report about tobacco retarding the onset of Parkinson's disease.

"I'll be there in ten minutes," Nick said, feeling a little tired at the prospect of another meeting. His whole life was meetings. Did they have this many meetings in the Middle Ages? In Ancient Rome and Greece? No wonder their civilizations died out, they probably figured decadence and the Visigoths were preferable to more meetings.

"I'm going to swing by Café Olé, pick up some cappuccino," he yawned, feeling a little Soma-tose. "You want some?"

"God, *please*."

He parked in the basement garage—no sight of Mike, Jeff, and Tom, he noted with satisfaction; some bodyguards—and made his was upstairs to the Atrium. There were a dozen food places here with names like Peking Gourmet (very low mein and chicken MSG), Pasta Pasta (sold by weight), RBY (Really Bodacious Yoghurt), and So What's Not To Like Bagel. There were tables around the fountain where people could eat. It was a nice place to eat lunch, especially during the Washington summers when no one wanted to venture out onto melting sidewalks.

Nick was standing in front of the counter at Café Olé waiting for his two double cappuccinos when he became aware of someone staring at him. He turned but didn't see anyone, except for a bum. Having been born in 1952, he still thought of them as "bums," rather than "the homeless," though he was careful never to call them that. In fact, he had tried to set up a program whereby the cigarette companies would distribute free cigarettes to homeless shelters, but the gaspers got wind of it and got HHS to stop it, so it was no free smokes for those who needed them most.

Nick recognized most of the bums who would pandhandle in the Atrium until Security chased them away, but not this one. Quite a specimen he was, a hulking, big figure, and talk about the Grunge Look—he was wearing the remnants of about a dozen overcoats. The hair hung down in greasy clumps over his face, which looked like it had last seen soap and water during the seventies. He approached.

"Gaaaquadder?" His eyes were clearer than most of these guys', which looked like bad egg yolks.

Nick gave him a dollar and asked him if he wanted a cigarette.

"Gaaaablessyoubruhh." Nick gave him the rest of the pack.

"Gaaaamash?" Nick gave him a disposable lighter. His cappuccinos were ready. He headed off for the escalator that led up to the lobby where the office elevators were. The homeless guy followed along. Nick wasn't looking for a relationship here, but being a lapsed Catholic, he would never be entirely sure, despite his certainty that it was all a crock, that one of these wretches wasn't the mufti Christ checking to see who was being charitable toward the least of his creatures, and who wasn't and was therefore going to have such a hot time in the eternal hereafter as to make a Washington summer seem Antarctic by comparison.

"What's your name?" Nick asked.

"Regggurg."

"Nick. You from around here?"

"Balmurrr."

"Nice town." They were on the escalator now. "Well," Nick said, "hang in there."

He felt something poke him in the middle of his back, like an umbrella tip. Then he heard a voice—it came from the bum but it was a whole new one—say, "Don't turn around. Don't move, don't speak. That's the muzzle of a nine millimeter, and if you don't do everything I tell you to, when I tell you to, you'll be on a slab at the morgue with a tag on your toe by the time that coffee cools."

As introductions went, it was attention-getting. They reached the top of the escalator. There were so many people all over the place Nick wanted to shout, *Help!* but the voice, the voice had been very emphatic that he not do that.

"See that limo over there?" said the bum. "Walk toward it very slowly. Do not run."

Nick did not run. The limo's windows were opaque-black. They had about fifty feet to go. Here he was, all these people—he was being kidnapped in broad daylight, in front of hundreds of people. And—why?

He paused about five feet from the car. The gun dug into his spine. "Keep moving."

He should be remembering details. *It was black. No, dark blue. Cadillac. No, Lincoln. No, Cadillac.* That would be a big help. So few limousines in Washington.

The rear door opened.

All those Beirut hostage news stories flashed before him. *He was last seen being forced into the trunk of a black sedan four years ago.* At least they weren't putting him in the trunk. . . .

Nick became aware of pain in his hands. He was holding his two cappuccinos in their Styrofoam cups. His heart was beating fast. No need for caffeine.

He turned round and threw the cappuccinos at the pistol-packing bum. They hit him on the chest and bounced off. The lids held. The cups fell to the ground and burst open, scalding his ankles with foamy cappuccino. How many times in his life had the plastic tops come off when they weren't supposed to, burning his hands, his lap, ruining the upholstery, making brown stains in the crotch of tan summer suit pants, usually before an important meeting. But no, now, the one time in his life it would have actually helped for the tops to come off, *they had held,* the insolent, mocking little plastic bastards.

The bum shoved him backward into the limousine. Nick's head took a whack on the door jamb on his way in. Hands pulled him in, and while the lights of the Milky Way pulsated through his optic nerve, a black silk hood went over his head and his hands were efficiently cinched behind him with what felt like garbage bag ties. The car took off, slowly, into the traffic.

"Hello, Neek. It's so good to meet you finally."

It was a strange accent, mittel-European, creepy and oleaginous.

"What's the deal, here?" Nick said.

"Can you breathe okay under de hood? It would be terrible if you couldn't *breathe,* wouldn't it?" A little cackle of laughter. It sounded familiar, like . . .

"Where are we going?" Nick asked.

"What an incredibly unrealistic question, Neek. You're expecting maybe an address?" That accent. That's it—Peter Lorre, the actor who played whatsisname, the greasy little hustler in *Casablanca,* Uguarté. Only Lorre, as far as Nick could recall, was long dead.

"Is this for ransom money?"

"It's for de *mortgage,* Neek." Laughter. Nick decided to dispense with further conversational ice-breakers.

After about half an hour, the car stopped, doors opened, hands pulled him out, doors opened and shut, muffled voices spoke, they went up a flight of steps, down a hall, another door opened and shut, he was pushed down onto a chair, his ankles were tied to its legs. None of this was reassuring. The hood stayed on. That was reassuring, assuming they didn't want him to see their faces. The tie binding his wrist was undone, and now came a part he really didn't like at all, not one bit: they started to remove his clothes.

"Excuse me. What's happening?"

"Don't worry, Neek, dere aren't any women here. You don't have to be embarrassed." That voice. It was creepy and unnerving. That was it for Peter Lorre movies, never mind that *Casablanca* was one of his favorites. "Oh, I'm so sorry, you must be dying for a cigarette."

In fact, a cigarette would be good right about now, yes.

"On the udder hand, if you wait a leetle while, you'll have all de nicotine you can handle." Laughter. And not a nourishing kind of laughter either, more what you'd expect from someone with severe psychological problems. Maybe he *should* try to keep up some conversation.

"Can we talk about this? Usually, they let you know why they're kidnapping you. Otherwise, like, what's the point?"

"You know why, Neek. We want you to stop killing people. So many people. More dan half a million people a year. And dat's just in the United States."

"There's no data to support that," Nick said, who perhaps could be forgiven, this once, for using the singular rather than plural verb form.

"Neek! Dat's not going to woork. You're not on de *Oprah Winfrey* show anymore."

"Well, it's nowhere near half a million. Even hardcore gaspers only claim as high as 435,000."

"Gaspers. I *like* dat, Neek. Is dat what you call people who want the tobacco companies to stop committing human sacrifice for the sake of their profits?"

Nick was down to his boxer shorts now. He heard the sound of cardboard boxes being opened. With a black hood over your head, you become very curious about noises. More ripping, like plastic wrapping.

A hand pressed against his chest over his heart. He leapt up in his chair, straining at his ankles and wrists. The hand came away and he felt something left behind on his chest, something sticky and clinging, like a bandage.

Another hand, or the same hand, clamped down on his skin next to the first spot and left another whatever it was. Again, again, again, till his entire chest was covered, then the arms, the back, the legs from below the boxers to the ankles.

Then his forehead and cheeks. Every square inch of him was covered. When he shifted in his chair, he felt like one adhesive mass, a Band-Aid mummy.

"Look, can we get a little dialogue going here?"

"Don't you remember, Neek, how I told you on de Larry King show dat we were going to dispatch you?"

Dispatch? Dis? Patch? Nick grasped, reluctantly, that this lunatic had just covered him head to toe in nicotine patches. Which meant that a massive, indeed, probably lethal amount of nicotine was at this moment being delivered, through his skin, into his bloodstream. Not that there was any scientific proof that nicotine was bad for you . . .

He made some calculations. Were there twenty-two milligrams in a patch? Something like that. And a cigarette contained about one milligram, so one patch was about one pack. . . . felt as though they'd plastered him with about forty of them . . . which made . . . forty packs . . . four *cartons*? Even by industry standards, that was a serious day's smoking.

"Let me read you something," Peter Lorre said. "Dis comes with the patches, in de boxes. Under 'Adverse Reactions.' Dis is my favorite part. I don't care so much about the incidence of tumors in the cheek pouches of hamsters and forestomachs of F344 rats. I don't even know what an F344 rat is. Anyway, dere are so *many* adverse reactions here, I don't hardly know where to begin. Why don't I read only de big ones?"

Nick was starting to feel a little queasy. And his pulse seemed . . . well, he was nervous, for sure, but it was starting to beat pretty fast.

"Look, I think it's perfectly legitimate that nonsmokers feel they're entitled to breathe smoke-free air. Our industry has been working hand in hand with citizens groups and the government to ensure that—"

"*Neek* . . . Just listen, okay? 'Erythema,' it says. Do you know what dat means? I had to look it up in a dictionary. All it means is redness of the skin, like from chemical poisoning or sunburn. I would say you are going to have *very* red skin, Nick. Maybe you can get a part in a movie playing an Indian. Heh heh. Oh, I'm sorry, Neek. Dat was in very poor taste."

"My industry does forty-eight billion a year in revenues. I think we're looking at an attractive opportunity situation here. I think everyone in this room is looking at early retirement in Saint Barth's, or wherever."

"Now dis I can understand. 'Abdominal pain, somnolence'—dat's sleeping, isn't it?—'skin rash, sweating. Back pain, constipation, dyspepsia, nausea, myalgia.' Here we go again with dese *words*. Ah, okay, 'dizziness, headache, insomnia.' I don't understand, they tell you sleepiness then they tell you insomnia. We'll just have to find out. You know, you could be making an incredible contribution to science. You could be written up in de *New England Journal of Medicine.* What else? 'Pharyngitis'? I think dat must mean when your pharynx is broken, don't you? 'Sinusitis and . . . dysmenorrhea.' I don't even *want* to know what dat means, it sounds so horrible. You can tell me about it later."

Burning. His skin *was* burning. "I would guess that you could *start* by asking for five million. And work your way up from there. I don't want to boast, but I'm an extremely important part of our overall media strategy, so—"

"But I don't *want* any money, Neek."

"Well, what do you want? I mean, I'm all ears, here." His heart. Whoa. *Ba-boom, ba-boom.*

"What does any of us want? A little financial security, de love of a good woman, not too big a mortgage, crisp bacon."

Nick's mouth was starting to go very dry and taste like it was wrapped in tinfoil. His head began to pound. His heart was going like a jackhammer. And something was brewing down there in his stomach that was going to come up . . . soon.

"Uuuh."

"By de way, did you see de story in *Lancet*? About dis incredible fact that in de next ten years 250 *million* people in the industrialized world are going to die from smoking? One in *five,* Neek. Isn't dat amazing? Dat's five times how many died in de last world *war.*"

Boomboomboomboom. "Urrrrrrrg."

"Dat's the entire population of de United States."

"I'll quit. I'll . . . work for the . . . Lung . . . Association."

"*Good,* Neek. Boys, don't you think Nick is making *excellent* progress?"

"Urrrrr."

"You don't sound so good, Neek."

"—rrrr—" *Bumbumbumbum.* His heart was knocking on his rib cage, saying *I want out.*

"Look at de bright side, Neek. After dis, I bet you're never going to want to smoke anodder cigarette again."

"—roop."

12

"You see that?" a U.S. park policeman said to his partner as they sat in their cruiser on Constitution Avenue near the Vietnam Veterans Memorial.

"Late for joggers," the other yawned.

"Better check it out." They got out and walked toward Constitution Gardens and shone their flashlights at the object of their curiosity. It was a male, Caucasian—though the skin had a strange, lifeless hue and texture to it—six feet, 170 pounds, brown hair, athletic build. He was stumbling at the edge of the lagoon. Doper, for sure.

"Sir. SIR. Stop and turn around, please."

"Did you see his face?"

"Yeah. Like a deer on speed. What's that all over his body?"

"Bandages?"

"Anything about any escapees from Saint E's?"

"Nothing. Son of a bitch is fast. Look at him go."

"Coke?"

"Nah, that's angel dust."

They cornered him on the small island in Constitution Gardens, where the preamble to the Declaration of Independence is carved into granite beneath your feet, along with the signers' names.

"Sir?"

"Get away from me! I don't even like your movies! I hated *Casablanca*!"

"What's he talking about?"

"Easy does it, buddy. No one's going to hurt you."

"Get me the surgeon general! I have *urgent information for the surgeon general!*"

"Okay, pal, we'll go see the surgeon general."

"No one must know but her!"

"*That's* right, buddy. What's that around your neck?"

"It's a sign."

" 'Executed for crimes against hominy.' "

" 'Humanity.' "

"What's that supposed to mean?"

"I don't know, but for someone who's been executed, he's moving pretty fast."

"He *looks* like he's been executed."

"Oh boy, stand back."

"That's okay, pal. Take a deep breath. I never saw anyone spew like *that*."

"He's on some dope. Better call the medics. Whup, stand back, there he goes again."

"What's the matter, pal, something you ate?"

"You know what they look like—those smokers' things, the patches."

"Joe Rinckhouse tried those things. He's still smoking."

"I bet he didn't put on that many. Hey buddy, you okay?"

"No, he's not okay. Look at him."

"Think we oughta do CPR on him."

"Be my guest."

"Uh-uh. It's *your* turn."

"Let's wait for the medics. I don't like this. It could be some new sex thing."

"Good thinking."

"Coming through!"

"What do we have?"

"John Doe, four plus agitated, vomiting, dry as a bone. BP two-forty over one-twenty. Vomiting, erythema. Pulse one-eighty and regular. Looks like PAT."

"Sir? Sir, can you hear me? SIR? Okay, let's get a Nipride drip going. Get up verapamil, ten milligrams IV push. *Today,* please."

"Coming."

"What are those things all over him?"

"Looks like nicotine patches, a lot of them."

"Maybe it's the new suicide of the nineties."

"Let's get them off him. Fast. There's enough here to kill a horse."

"Ouch, this poor guy is going to be sore."

"This guy is going to be dead. Sir? SIR? What is your name?"

"Uh-oh. V-fib!!"

"Okay, he's going to have to ride the lightning. Crank it up to max. Gimme the paddles. Ready? Stand back."

Vvvvvvvvvvump.

"Again. Clear."

Vvvvvvvvvvump.

"I like it! I like it! Back on sinus rhythm. Start the lidocaine drip."

Nick awoke to the sound of bleeping machines and a headache that made him wish that he had not survived. His mouth tasted like it had been filled with hot tar and pigeon droppings. His hands, feet, and nose were cold as ice. He was conscious of wires leading to his chest and tubes leading in and out of every bodily orifice but one, thank God.

He'd had this very strange dream. Dr. Wheat had gone bonkers while Nick was on the table hooked up to the DC current machine. He increased the voltage enough to power the Washington Metrorail system, while cackling maniacally to Nick that this was his big opportunity of getting into *The New England Journal of Medicine.*

"Ohhh," he groaned, alerting a nurse, who scurried off for a doctor. People in white came and hovered. There were hushed conversations. A voice addressed him.

"Mr. Naylor?"

"Urrr."

He heard dimly the word *morphine,* followed by a warm sensation in his arm, followed by . . . visions of a voluptuous red-haired woman, with glasses, naked, on a horse.

Horse?

Suits entered the room.

"Mr. Naylor? I'm Special Agent Monmaney, FBI. This is Special

Agent Allman. We've been assigned to your case. Can you tell us what happened?"

Nick peered through the druggy haze at the cavalry. Monmaney was tall, rangy, with intense, pale, timber wolf eyes. Graying at the temples. Good, a G-man with experience. Allman was stocky, built like a fireplug. Excellent. He could be the one to beat Peter Lorre's face into rennet custard. He had a ruddy, almost jovial sort of face that made him look like everyone's favorite high school teacher. Nick would have preferred him to look leaner and meaner, like Monmaney, but that was all right, as long as they functioned like a team and their guns were oiled. He saw Peter Lorre, on his knees, begging them for mercy as they emptied their 9mms into his chest.

A tsunami-sized wave of nausea rolled through him. Nick's eyes went groggily back to Monmaney, who was peering at him without sympathy. Yes, a real killer, this one, looked like he flossed with piano wire.

They asked questions. Many questions. The same questions, over and over and over. Nick told them what he knew, which was that he had been abducted and tortured by a dead Hungarian movie star. He told them about hurling his cappuccinos at the bum. Surely someone on K Street had witnessed that. His last memory? Feeling like his heart was trying very urgently to exit his body, along with everything he had eaten in the last two years. Speaking of which, boy was he hungry. Gazelle had brought him Double-Stuff Oreo cookies, the kind with extra cream filling inside, but the nurses took one look at it and carried the bag out of the room like it was toxic waste.

Agent Monmaney made him go over it again and again and again, until he was tempted to start making things up just out of sheer boredom. Agent Allman merely stood by, nodding pleasantly, looking jovial. A little sympathy would have been nice. But it was all detail, detail, detail. Nick became annoyed. He was tempted to ask them what was their last assignment, driving tanks in Waco?

Mercifully, Dr. Williams came in and they left. As soon as they were gone he started telling jokes about J. Edgar Hoover wearing pink tutus. Dr. Williams was Nick's new cardiologist, a very pleasant fellow in his early fifties with a hearing aid that was the result of having served as a navy doctor aboard destroyers during Vietnam.

The idea of being in the care of a cardiologist at only age forty alarmed Nick, but Dr. Williams set him at ease by explaining in a clear and friendly way exactly what had happened.

He had had a very close call. The massive dosage of nicotine had caused a condition called paroxysmal atrial tachycardia, which he likened to driving along at sixty miles per hour and suddenly shifting into first gear. The heart is asked to do things it wasn't made to do, namely pump at an insanely fast rate. In the Emergency Room, the PAT had degenerated into ventricular fibrillation, where the fibers of the heart muscles go wormy and stop pumping blood efficiently, thus depriving his brain of oxygen. The massive electrical charge administered, in microseconds, through the defibrillator paddles arrested all the heart's own electrical activity and permitted its own pacemaker to restore vital functions as a pump. Nick took it all in, struggling against great weariness. It occurred to him, during the portion of the lecture on defibrillation, that between Dr. Wheat and now this, he had spent a lot of his life being electrocuted. Dr. Williams said that, ironically, it was his smoking that had probably saved him. That many patches on a nonsmoker would almost certainly have brought about cardiac arrest sooner.

The second morning, a nurse came in to check on his wires and tubes and noticed that his chest had been smeared with nitroglycerin jelly, a precaution to offset the toxic effects of nicotine. She went pale, then looked angry as she wiped it away, muttering, *"Jesus Christ,"* which got Nick's attention. At first she was reluctant to say what the problem was. Finally she told him that NTG was *always* to go on the arms, *never, ever, ever* on the chest. Why? Because if his heart had gone wormy again in the middle of the night and they'd come running in with the cart and put the paddles on his chest where the nitroglycerin was . . . she made a *boom* gesture with her hands. She stormed off in search of the orderly, leaving Nick to wonder if he might be safer in his own bed at home.

He had many visitors. His mother brought Joey, who was technically fascinated by the story of how the orderly had turned his father into a human bomb, and peppered Nick with questions as to where he could buy nitroglycerin jelly and defibrillators.

Bobby Jay and Polly came with flowers and fruit baskets and illicit cheeseburgers and Bloody Marys, compliments of Bert. They also brought the fake fireplace from Bert's Grill, just to make him feel at home, a very thoughtful gesture, though the nurse forebade them to plug it in. Polly got all teary-eyed when she saw how pale he was; and blue, in parts, from where the vasoconstricting nicotine had shut off the blood to his extremities. Nick hadn't yet started entertaining sexual thoughts, but he hoped, how he hoped, that when he did, the shutoff of blood would not have had long-ranging effects on those particular extremities.

Jeannette came, twice, sometimes three times a day. She was very concerned, very caring about it all. Nick wondered if he hadn't misjudged her. It's tough being a woman in a man's world, so, clearly, some women get tough, but that doesn't mean they're dykes or dominatrixes. She brought truffles and strawberries from Sutton Place Gourmet and flowers, interesting flowers that, well, seemed rather sexual, frankly. Could she do anything for him? Check on his apartment? Pick up his dry cleaning? Clear his messages? Take Joey to his Little League games?

BR came by, acting like Patton on a surprise inspection, storming off to notify the hospital's chief administrator that this was one Very Important Patient in Room 608 and by God he expected Nick to be treated as such, even if she had to bring the bedpan in herself at four in the morning. He called Nick five times a day with a progress report. The Academy—the entire tobacco industry—was enraged by this and was calling in all its congressional chits, demanding that tobacco state members call on the White House to put pressure on the attorney general to put pressure on the FBI. (Perhaps that explained Agent Monmaney's brusque bedside manner.)

The Captain called regularly with his progress reports as he worked his way through his congressional Rolodex. He had spoken with Senator Jordan, the Gulfstream-hogging whore, informing him that he expected him personally to call the President and *instruct him* to tell the FBI to *get on the hump and nail these sons of bitches.* Or he'd had his last free ride on his G-5.

It was very gratifying. Nick was extremely touched. Tobacco takes care of its own.

Heather snuck in after visiting hours so that she wouldn't run into any Academy staffers. She and Nick had decided to keep their little thing between them, just for security's sake. He didn't want BR and everyone else to know he was sleeping with the enemy; not that she'd written an entirely unflattering piece, but in BR's book, *all* reporters were the enemy.

She sat at the foot of Nick's bed, wearing a light summer dress with her hair up in a Gibson girlish sort of way, strands of hair dribbling down her neck. She looked quite alluring. Nick, however, lacked the energy to talk amorally, her kind of verbal foreplay, so he just listened to her talk about how she'd gotten a job interview with Atherton Blair, the rather self-satisfied, bow-tie-wearing, Ivy League assistant managing editor of the *Sun,* Washington's legit paper. She was working on a story about the new image guy that the President had hired; she had information that he'd once done some consulting for a close relative of Erich Honecker, the former East German dictator who'd built the Berlin Wall.

Jeannette called the next day to say that she had "convinced" Katie Couric of the *Today* show to do a live remote interview from his hospital bed. Nice as Jeannette had been, Nick doubted she'd had to do much arm-twisting to bring about an interview. Nick was front-page, above-the-fold news, for crying out loud. They'd been *deluged* with interview requests.

"I don't want you to think that we're in any way capitalizing on this," she said, "but if you're feeling up to it, I don't think we should pass this up."

True enough, Nick's kidnapping had been a godsend, after a fashion. The gasper groups were falling all over themselves trying to distance themselves from the "nico-terrorists"—as the perpetrators had been dubbed by the tabloid press—and were busily denouncing this "deplorable," "extreme," "repellent," "intolerable" act. Even Nick's Oprah punching bag, Ron Goode, was quoted in *Newsweek* as saying that no matter what his personal opinion of Nick was, he certainly didn't deserve to be murdered for his views. Doubtless, he'd been coached, swine; and just as doubtless, it had killed him to say it.

"Thanks, Bryant. Four days ago, Nick Naylor, chief spokesman for the tobacco lobby, was abducted outside his office in Washington, D.C. He was found, later that night, with a sign around his neck that said he had been, and I quote, 'Executed for crimes against humanity.' His body was covered with a lethal number of nicotine patches, the kind prescribed for smokers who want to give up. According to doctors at George Washington University Hospital, he was near death when he was brought in. The FBI is investigating the case, which seems to indicate that at least one element of the anti-smoking movement has adopted the tactics of terrorists. Mr. Naylor joins us this morning from his bed at George Washington University hospital. Good morning."

"Good morning, Katie."

"I know this has been quite an ordeal for you. My first question to you—How *did* you survive? Reports are that you were literally covered with patches."

"Well, Katie, I guess you could say that smoking saved my life."

"How?"

"As a smoker, a pastime I happen to enjoy along with fifty-five million other adult Americans, I was able to absorb the dosage, though it did almost kill me. If those policeman hadn't found me when they did, I wouldn't be chatting with you today."

"We'll get back to the issue of smoking—"

"If I might point out, Katie, this just goes to prove what we've been saying for some time now, namely, don't mess with these nicotine patches. They're killers."

"But not if you use them as directed, surely."

"Katie, out of respect for your viewers, I won't go into what these things did to me, the nausea, the projectile vomiting, the paroxysmal atrial tachycardia, the cutting off of blood to the brain, the numbness and cold in your extremities, the horrible skin rash, the blurred vision and migrainous neuralgia. So I won't go into all that, except to say, If that's what a bunch of these patches can do, well, huh, I can only imagine what *just one* could do to a normal, healthy smoker. So put me down for a big resounding, Just say no."

"We understand that a note from the kidnappers was delivered to the *Washington Sun*."

"I'm not sure I'm supposed to comment on that, Katie."

"It's in today's edition."

"It is?"

"So it's already out there. Would you like to hear what it says?"

"Uh . . ."

"Quote, Nick Naylor is responsible for the deaths of billions—"

"Billions? Millions, surely."

"No, it says billions."

"Well, that's absurd. I've only been with the Academy for six years, so even if you accepted the 435,000-a-year figure, which of course is completely nonsense anyway, I would only have been quote responsible unquote for what, two-point-six million. So I don't know where this individual is getting 'billions' from? What am I, McDonald's?"

"Should I go on?"

"Please, yes, by all means, I'm fascinated."

"He was dispatched as a warning to the tobacco industry. If they don't stop making cigarettes right now, we will dispatch others."

"Was this by any chance written on the surgeon general's letterhead?"

"I beg your pardon?"

"I thought I recognized her style. No, of course, I'm kidding, Katie. Humor, you know. The best medicine. . . ."

"Do you have any idea who might have done this to you?"

"No, but if those people are listening, as I'm sure they are, being probably big fans of yours as I certainly am, I'd like to say to them, Come forward, turn yourselves in. I'm not going to press charges."

"You *won't*?"

"No, Katie, I think people who would do something like this need help, more than anything."

"That's a very tolerant point of view."

"Well, Katie, you can't spell tolerance without the *t* in *tobacco*. Our position all along has been, we understand there are people who care strongly about smoking. We're saying, Let's work together on this. Let's get some dialogue going. This is a big country, and there's plenty of room in it for smoking *and* nonsmoking areas."

The first call was from the Captain. "Brilliant, son, *brilliant*."

BR called. "I gotta hand it to you, Nick, you blew us all away. We're out of breath here."

Jeannette came on. "Nick, you give *great* talking head."

Polly called, laughing. "What was *that* all about?"

"It's not up to *me*," Nick said. "I just hope it turns out to be Virginia they took me to and not Maryland."

"Why?"

"Because," Nick said, "Virginia has the death penalty."

13

On Nick's first day back at work, BR gave him a welcome-back speech in front of the whole staff. He made it sound as though Nick had outwitted his captors and escaped. In fact, Nick still had no idea how he had ended up on the Mall, but he doubted that he had outwitted them as it's difficult to outwit while having a heart attack and projectile vomiting. The staff treated him like a returning war hero. All the attention was starting to make him a little squirmy, and now here was BR suddenly sounding like Henry V at the battle of Agincourt, exhorting his happy band of brothers. Then he quoted Churchill during Britain's darkest hour: "Never give in," he said. "Never. Never. *Never!*"

The staff stood up and applauded. Some had tears in their eyes. Well, he'd never seen anything like *this* at the Academy of Tobacco Studies. His kidnapping had had an amazing, morale-boosting effect. It was as if the long, uneasy truce between tobacco and the hostile world out there had finally broken down into open warfare, and by God, if this was war, then let it start here. They were ready. People who had never been inside a military base, much less on the business end of a gun, were walking around using phrases like *lock and load* and *incoming*. It was galvanizing, truly. Talk about esprit de corps. Nick was moved.

"Nick," said Gomez O'Neal, "a question." Gomez, tall, dark, pockmarked, with arms like bridge cable, was head of Issues Intelligence, the division in charge of coming up with personal information about the private lives of prominent gaspers and tobacco litigants. He'd been in some unspecified branch of the government, and did not invite questions about his past. For vacations, he went on one-man survival treks in places like Baffin Island and the Gobi Desert. BR seemed not to like Gomez, but then Gomez did not seem to care; he was not the sort of person one casually fired, any more than presidents had been able to get rid of J. Edgar Hoover.

"Shoot," Nick said, a figure of speech one used carefully around Gomez.

"You gonna quit smoking?"

There was nervous laughter. The truth of it was that Nick had not had a cigarette in over a week; the thought of putting any more nicotine into his system held little appeal. It occurred to him that this might even qualify him for workmen's comp.

They were all looking at him expectantly. He couldn't let them down. He was more than their spokesman now; he was their hero.

"Anyone got a smoke?" he said. Twenty people produced packs. He accepted a Camel, lit up, took just a little down into his lungs, and exhaled. It felt quite good, so he took another puff and let it out. People smiled approvingly.

Then spots appeared. Soon the whole Milky Way galaxy was pulsing through his optic nerve and he was in a cold sweat and the room and—oh no, not again, not in front of the whole staff. . . .

"Nick?" BR said.

"I'm fine," he said wobbly, putting the Camel down in an ashtray. The taste in his mouth. Uch.

"Take it slow at first," BR said.

"Maybe you should start with filters," someone said helpfully.

There was this awkward silence as Nick stood there in front of them, blinking, quietly reeling.

"Hey Nick," Jeff Tobias said. "Did you see the figures on female eighteen to twenty-ones?"

"Uh-uh." My kingdom for a wintergreen Life Saver. . . .

"Up twenty percent."

"Wonderful," Nick murmured.

BR added, "Wait until after Nick's anti-smoking campaign." Quite a few chuckles. "By the way, when do we get to see boards?" *119*

"I'm videoconferencing with Sven this afternoon," Nick said, noticing that his fingers had gone cold again. Should he call Dr. Williams? *You smoked a cigarette?*

"I'm sure we're all eager to see what he's come up with. Okay," BR said, "now I'd like to turn the meeting over to Carlton, who is going to brief us on some new security procedures."

Carlton warmed up his audience with a joke about two guys who go camping and a grizzly bear attacks them in the middle of the night and one guy puts on his sneakers and starts lacing them up. The other guys says, "Why are you putting on sneakers, you can't outrun a grizzly bear." And his friend tells him, "I don't have to outrun the bear, I only have to outrun you." The point, Carlton said, was that in anti-terrorism, a phrase that put everyone into buttlock, you win by making the terrorists pick on the other guy. People glanced uneasily at each other. *We few, we happy band of brothers.*

Warming to his message—and was Carlton ever in his element— he emphasized the importance of *not setting patterns.* Everyone should leave for work at a different time every day, take a different route every day, be alert to strangers, especially ones wearing uniforms. He passed out photocopied sheets entitled WHAT TO DO IF YOU FIND YOURSELF LOCKED IN A CAR TRUNK. People stared at it, hemorrhaging macho. *Locked . . . in a trunk?*

"Now let's talk about explosives." This part of his presentation went on for a full quarter-hour, during which he enumerated some three dozen types of bombs, including one that was attached to your windshield wiper blades. "Turn on the wipers and boom, eye-level, in the kisser." Betty O'Malley went pale.

BR interjected, "Now give us the good news." Carlton opened a case and passed out little black things that looked like beepers. They were electronic locator devices, like the ones in life rafts that send out emergency signals. If anyone was snatched, they should push the two little buttons together and the whole U.S. government would be alerted. Then he opened another case and gave everyone little canisters of pepper gas. These were to be spritzed into the faces of any suspicious individuals. But only after they'd made the first move. And only if it looked like they were about to kill you. Otherwise, do exactly what they said, even if they wanted you to get into that locked trunk.

Any questions? By now you could have heard a pin drop, and the floor was carpeted.

"I'm not sure I understand," said Charley Noble, from Legislative Affairs, "are we *all* targets?"

"I don't know the answer to that," BR said, "but I'm not prepared to take any chances. Carlton has arranged for everyone here, and I mean everyone, no exceptions—except of course for you, Nick—to spend next weekend at a facility in West Virginia where they train government people in anti-terrorist driving tactics."

There was intense murmuring. "You'll all receive instruction in— what *is* the drill, Carlton?"

"Examining a vehicle for bombs, evasive maneuvers, J-turns and bootleg turns, proper ramming technique, and surveillance detection."

"Bombs?" said Syd Berkowitz of the Coalition for Health. "Are there *bomb* threats?"

"Just a precaution. I assure you that the FBI is going to have these people in custody very, very soon. In the meantime, we've made arrangements with 1800 K Street to use their basement parking. For the time being, there'll be no parking in our own underground garage."

By now the murmuring was quite loud. BR had to raise his own voice to be heard. "People, people. This is just precautionary. There have been no bomb threats. Anyway, we're on a high floor here. And I'm certain everyone here could handle a little smoke inhalation."

Jeannette laughed. No one else did.

After the meeting, BR took Nick aside. He handed him a box of NicoStop patches. Nick held it as if BR had just handed him a fresh, steaming turd.

"Guess what?" BR said. "Sales of your 'deadly Band-Aids' are off *forty-five percent* since your gig on the *Today* show."

Nick handed him back the box with a shudder. No more nicotine for him.

"I feel awkward scoring points off this rotten business, but, God, talk about stepping in shit and coming out smelling like roses. *Look* at this press." He handed Nick a thick folder, a veritable media hero sandwich, clippings sticking out like bits of lettuce and ham. Nick had already seen most of them. He'd been on all the morning network *121* shows, all the cable shows. The Europeans and Asians, who were still puffing away happily, couldn't get enough of him. Nick had experienced the thrill of being simultaneously translated. The French interviewer, a very fetching and soulful-looking woman, had done a little medical research on vasoconstricting and had put it to him: had it affected his "romantic capabilities"? Nick blushed, said no, *pas du tout,* and broke out in cold sweat. He'd been on Slovakian TV, a very important appearance as Agglomerated Tobacco, the Captain's own company, was moving into the former Eastern Bloc in a big way, introducing a brand whose name translated as "Throat-Scraper." The Eastern Euros, who'd been brought up on cigarettes that tasted like burning nuclear waste, were old-fashioned about their smokes: they demanded more, not less tar. To them, lung cancer was proof of quality.

"Jeannette tells me that *Young Modern Man* wants to do a week-in-the-life story on you," BR said.

"Yeah," Nick said, again annoyed at the Jeannette-BR pipeline, "I'm inclined to pass on that one."

"Japan's very important to us, and they do reach two out of three Japanese men between the ages of sixteen and twenty-one." This was the age group known within the Academy as "entry-level."

"I just don't know if I want Japanese reporters hanging out in my office for a week. Or any reporters. I think maybe I'm getting a little overexposed."

"Two out of three, Nick. Millions and millions of young, modern Japanese. You're a hero to these people. That brings a certain responsibility."

"I'll get back to you." The nice thing was that Nick was now a certifiable, eight-hundred-pound gorilla, with I'll-get-back-to-you privileges.

"I spoke to the Captain earlier. He hopes you'll be able to do it." Agglomerated was moving into Japan, too, now that the U.S. trade rep had threatened to slap imported soy sauce with a 50 percent tariff unless they opened their ports and lungs to U.S. tobacco products.

"I'll get back to him, too." Nick was pushing the envelope a little here, but all BR could do was make a face that said, *All right, but I hope you know what you're doing.*

All this attention. And Sammy Najeeb had called this morning to ask—to insist—that he go back on the Larry King show. She and Larry were sure, knew in their bones, that the threatening caller would call in again, and could Nick *imagine* what kind of TV that would make?

"By the *way*," BR said, full of drama, "Penelope Bent is coming in next week and guess who she wants to meet?" Penelope, now Lady Bent, had recently signed a seven-figure-a-year deal with Bonsacker International, formerly Bonsacker Tobacco, Inc., to lend a little *clahss* to their board and annual shareholders' meetings. This was increasingly common among the Big Six tobacco companies, which were retaining a lot of substantive celebrities—Vietnam-era POWs, former presidents of prestigious universities; they'd even asked Mother Teresa—to shill for them under the guise of celebrating freedom of speech, or the Constitution. The former British PM was their latest acquisition.

"Oh?" Nick said.

"The Captain called me this morning. They're all still in awe of her and haven't been able to get in a word edgewise. She's quite a talker, apparently. Anyway, he thought you might take the opportunity to give her a little gospel so if she gets any hostile questions about the relationship, everyone will be singing off the same sheet of music. Stress diversity. Agglomerated isn't just tobacco, it's infant formula, frozen foods, industrial lubricants, air filters, bowling balls. You know the drill."

"Yes, I do," Nick said, miffed at being given advice on spin control. "I doubt that the Titanium Lady needs lessons on handling the press from me."

"She wants to meet you, Nick," BR said brightly. "You should be flattered."

"Okay, I'm flattered."

"Maybe you'll pick up some tips on how to deal with terrorists. Remember what she did to the IRA after they blew up her bulldogs?"

"Aren't I supposed to be going out to Hollywood?"

"We're working on setting up a meeting with Jeff Megall's people. It's like getting an appointment with God."

"The Jeff Megall?" Nick said.

"Himself. But the Captain says he wants you right here where the press can find you until they get tired of you. Frankly, if I'd known that a kidnapping would result in this kind of coverage, I'd have kidnapped you myself. Speaking of L.A., as long as you're going to be out there . . ."

"Uh-huh," Nick said suspiciously.

"Your friend Lorne Lutch."

"He's not my friend, BR. All I did was talk you people out of suing him. I ducked into a closet at the Larry King show to avoid running into him."

"He's been hitting us very hard lately," BR said. "Did you see the things he said about us last week? No, of course not, you were still in Intensive Care. Your pal Oprah had him on with the Silver-O's girl. You should have seen them, both talking through their voice boxes. A duet for two kazoos."

It was one Oprah appearance Nick was glad not to have been invited to share.

"It was pathetic. Her being a woman, I can forgive her. But him. The man has *no* sense of personal responsibility."

"He's dying, BR. We should probably cut the man some slack. If it was me, I'd slip him some money, help out with the expenses."

BR said, "I'm not sure that's the approach I'd take, but you and the Captain think alike on this one."

"Okay," Nick said to Sven, who was staring back at him on the video-phone, "does it gobble?"

Sven said, "I want to point out at the beginning that thrilled as we are to be on this account, and we're extremely thrilled, everyone here, what you asked us to produce was an ineffective message that will have no impact on the people it is targeted at."

Nick had the feeling he was being taped. It was like having a conversation in the Oval Office with Nixon at the height of Watergate.

"I just want it clear what our role is," Sven said.

Nick said, "Okay, you've established that your role is the tormented *artiste*. Can we proceed?" Honestly, these creative hothouse orchids. And in Minneapolis, no less. Nick still had frostbite from his visit there six months ago.

"What we did was to take the *'Some People Want You to Smoke. We Don't'* concept, which avoided the whole health issue, and instead tapped into the adolescent's innate fear of being manipulated by adults. You didn't like it."

"Right. Because it was effective."

"It's gone. So now we're going to be blunt, we want to speak to them with the voice of despised authority, nag them, tell them to go to their rooms, turn them completely off."

"I like it already," Nick said.

"Okay." Sven said. "Here we go. He pulled the board into video camera range. All it had on it was type. It said, "Everything Your Parents Told You About Smoking Is Right."

"Hmm," Nick said.

"You know what I love about it?" Sven said. "Its *dullness*."

"It *is* dull," Nick admitted.

"It's deadly. Kids are going to look at this and go, *'Puuke.'* "

That would probably be Joey's reaction, Nick mused.

"And yet," Sven said, "its *brilliance,* if I may say so, is in its deconstructability."

"How's that?"

"Say the last three words out loud."

" 'Smoking Is Right.' "

"Gobbles on the outside, grabs you on the inside. A Trojan turkey."

"I think," Nick said, "that I can sell this to my people."

Nick was looking forward to lunch, an hour or two of normalcy with Polly and Bobby Jay. As a Ph.D. in Spin Control, he could certainly understand why the Captain and BR were eager to suction every golden egg from the goose before it died, but fame has its price. As Fred Allen used to say, a celebrity is someone who works hard in order to become well-known and then has to wear dark glasses in order to avoid being recognized. On his way from the Academy to Bert's, he became aware of people staring at him as he passed, saw people nudge each other, whisper, "Isn't that *him*?" At the corner of K and Connecticut, while waiting for the light, he heard a woman murmur, "You *deserved* it."

He whirled but the woman kept going and he didn't feel like running after her to ask her if he'd heard correctly. It sent a chill up his spine. Nick was no wimp, he'd been called "mass murderer" and worse by entire crowds of people, often simultaneously; but that was heckling, and usually by card-carrying gaspers or "health professionals." But when pedestrians, total strangers, started coming up to you—at Washington's busiest intersection, in the middle of the day—and expressing solidarity with people who had kidnapped and tortured you, it could be taken as a sign that somewhere along your career path you had taken a wrong turn.

He ducked into the Trover Shop and bought some cheap sunglasses. He made it the rest of the way up Connecticut and down Rhode Island without anyone else wishing him dead.

Once inside Bert's he felt secure again. Bert came over and hugged him and made a big fuss; the regular waiters came over to shake his hand and congratulate him and tell him how well he looked. He was hearing that a lot these days: "You look *good,* Nick," despite the fact that he had lost ten pounds and his skin was fish gray.

Bert told him that lunch today was on the house and led him personally to his regular table by the fake fireplace, which was flickering away, casting its comforting acetate flames onto the chimney brick.

Bobby Jay and Polly were already there. They both got up to greet him, unsettling Nick. Here of all places he valued the comfort of routine, and no member of the Mod Squad ever got up to greet the other. Among merchants of death, equality rules. Polly actually kissed him and hugged him. It was unsettling. He was tired of being fussed over.

"I'm *fine,*" Nick said. "It's no big thing."

"You look great," Bobby Jay said.

"Yeah, you really do," Polly said. "You look great."

Nick stared at them. "What are you two, from Hallmark Cards? I look like shit."

Bobby Jay and Polly exchanged glances. Polly touched his forearm. "We're just glad to have you back."

"Don't patronize me."

"Sorry," Polly said, withdrawing her arm, "I didn't realize you were having a bad hair day."

"BR just told me the Captain wants me to go bribe the Tumbleweed Man, who's dying of throat cancer, so he'll stop badmouthing us. I have to accept every goddamn interview request—I'm on Larry King tomorrow night, he and the FBI want to use me as bait to draw out this Peter Lorre maniac—and some woman on the street just hissed at me that I deserved to get kidnapped. Yes, I'm having a bad hair day."

"It's a tough town," Bobby Jay said.

"Tell me about it. Check out my new bodyguards."

"Where?"

"Fooled you, didn't they? The one in the jeans and the woman with the handbag the size of a duffel? Former Secret Service. Do you know what she's got in there? Sawed-off shotgun. I *hope* they'll try it again. Do you have any idea what a ragged hole a fistful of double-ought buckshot makes?"

"Yeah," Bobby Jay said, "I do."

"They're supposed to blend. Unlike my former bodyguards with the suits and earphones. 'Attention everyone! We're bodyguards! Come attack our client.' Lot of good *they* were."

"I thought you kept trying to lose them," Polly said.

"Polly," said Nick condescendingly, in tones suggesting that security matters were beyond women, "*good* bodyguards don't get lost by the people they're supposed to be protecting." He sighed. "Jesus. Look at me. *Bodyguards.*"

"We're *all* going to need bodyguards soon," Polly said, "the way things are going. Did you *see* the coverage the fetal-alcohol people got themselves over the weekend?"

"Pathetic," Bobby Jay said.

"Don't you think the *Sun* sort of debased itself giving that kind of space to those people? I spoke to Dean Jardel over at S and B. They distribute two-thirds of the liquor in the D.C. area, and he says the *Washington Sun* is going to find itself without *any* liquor advertising for the next month."

"I wish we had that kind of leverage," Bobby Jay said, "but they don't take gun ads. Not that you *can* buy a gun in D.C."

"They made it sound like we encourage pregnant mothers to drink. It was so . . . pc I wanted to . . ."

"Frow up."

"I'm surprised *I* didn't get kidnapped on the way to work this morning."

Nick, taking all this in, brooding over the woman on the street, felt suddenly that his nicotine patch of courage was being co-opted. *127*

"Polly," he broke in, "I don't think people who work for the alcoholic beverage industry have to worry about being kidnapped, just yet."

Awkward silence. He'd made *alcoholic beverage* sound like *laxative* or *pet supplies*. Polly did a slow burn, blew a deep lungful of smoke out the side of her mouth in a cool, focused way, her eyes never leaving his, tapped her toe against the floor a few times. "Aren't we unholier than thou, today."

"Look," Nick said, "nothing personal, but tobacco generates a little more heat than alcohol."

"Oh?" Polly said. "This is news."

"Whoa," Nick said. "I'll put my numbers up against your numbers any day. My product puts away 475,000 people a year. That's 1,300 a day—"

"Waait a minute," Polly said. "*You're* the one who's always saying that 475,000 number is bull—"

"Okay, 435,000. Twelve hundred a day. So how many alcohol-related deaths a year? A hundred thousand, tops. Two hundred and seventy something a day. Well wow-wee. Two hundred and seventy. That's probably how many people die every day from slipping on bars of soap in the bathtub. So I don't see terrorists getting excited enough to kidnap anyone from the *alcohol* industry."

Bobby Jay said, "You two sound like McNamara, all this talk about body counts. Let's just chill out here."

Nick turned to him. "How many gun deaths a year in the U.S.?"

"Thirty thousand," Bobby Jay said, "but that's gross."

"Eighty a day," Nick snorted. "Less than passenger car mortalities."

"It nets out to even less," Bobby Jay said mildly. "Fifty-five percent of those are suicides, and another eight percent are justifiable homicides, so we're really only talking eleven thousand one hundred."

"Thirty a day," Nick said. "Hardly worth counting. No terrorist would bother with either of you."

"Would you like to see some of *my* hate mail," Polly said, flushing. Nick hadn't seen her look this *up* since she went on *Geraldo* with the parents of an entire school bus that had been wiped out by a drunk driver.

"Hate mail? *Hate* mail?" Nick laughed sarcastically. "*All* of my mail is hate mail. I don't even open my mail anymore. I just assume it's a letter bomb. My mail goes directly to the FBI lab. Technicians in lead suits steam-open it. Please, don't even try to one-up me on the subject of *mail*."

"Why don't we put away the gloves and order," Bobby Jay said, "I'm starved."

"*Fine,*" Nick said, grinding his teeth. *Expect a little sympathy . . . wait, she* was *being sympathetic until you told her she sounded like a get-well card.* There was that awful taste in his mouth again, like there was a cigarette butt under his tongue. The doctors had told him that his system was going to be flushing nicotine for the next three months. Food wasn't tasting very good these days, and spices made it taste like Drano.

Nick forced himself to say, "I wasn't *trying* to be unholier than thou."

"No big deal," Polly said tersely. The two of them concentrated on their menus so that they wouldn't have to look at each other.

It fell to Bobby Jay to make conversation in the form of a monologue. He bemoaned the upcoming anniversary of the assassination of President Finisterre, as these occasions always occasioned an orgy, as he put it, of calls for gun control on the op-ed pages of newspapers, never *mind* the fact that Finisterre had been blown away with a scope-mounted hunting rifle. "What are they going to do, take away our deer rifles?"

"Not until they pry them from our cold, dead fingers," Nick murmured, settling on pasta in the hopes that it wouldn't taste like stump dissolver. Bobby Jay said SAFETY was planning some proactive publicity in anticipation of the anniversary. They were also trying to get their friendlies in the Congress to get the White House to sign off on a Firearms Safety Awareness Week that would bracket the anniversary day. The White House was so far stonewalling them, but by their doing so, SAFETY was maneuvering them into a box: *We asked the White House, begged the White House, to get behind a national, week-long consciousness-raising initiative, and what happened? Nothing. . . .* Additionally, Stockton Drum, having been recently accused on *Face the Nation* of perpetrating "genocide" among black inner-city youth, had given orders that all senior SAFETY staff were to perform one hour a week of public service with black inner-city youth. This way, the next time some prissy-ass liberal accused him of enabling mass murder, he'd be able to cut him off at the balls. Drum's executive order was being met with mixed enthusiasm by most of the staff, though with genuine civic-mindedness by some. One staffer had proposed giving free handgun instruction in the inner city. If these kids were going to turn the city streets into free-fire zones, he reasoned, they might as well be taught how to be accurate so that they'd kill fewer innocent bystanders. Bobby Jay had nixed the proposal. "The sad thing," he said, fixing his special knife into his hook as the food arrived, "is that it's probably not such a bad idea."

The iced coffee had arrived. Polly hadn't said much over the food. Nick was feeling worse about how he'd acted and was working up to a rapprochement when Bobby Jay brought up a story in that day's *Washington Moon.*

"So," Polly said in a studiously casual way, "how's Feather?"

"Feather?"

"Heather."

"Fine," Nick said. "I guess. I don't know. She's trying to get a job on the *Sun.* She's interviewing with Atherton Blair."

"*That* asshole. He's probably the one who decided to put the fetal-alcohol convention above the fold. You know he doesn't *drink.*"

"A newspaperman who doesn't drink," Bobby Jay said. "Things have *changed.*"

"Not only that, he's in AA."

"He is?" Nick said.

"Our information is that he's in AA. He goes all the way out to Reston, so no one will know."

"No kidding," Nick said. "I should mention that to Heather."

Polly frowned. "What do you mean?"

"I don't know. Could come in handy. Maybe she should pitch him a story on how great AA is or something."

"And score points off alcohol-bashing? That's privileged information. Like *everything* that gets said around this table."

"Well, don't get your panty hose in a knot. I was just—"

"About to pass confidential information to your squeeze."

Bobby Jay put in, "I don't think any of us supposes, for a second, that anything that's said at this table goes any further than the sugar shaker."

"Right," Nick said.

"Right," Polly said.

Nick added companionably, "Nothing's, you know, happened, anyway. I've had other things on my mind these last few weeks, like wondering if I'm ever going to get the feeling back in my fingers. Or am I going to need a liver transplant."

"You better get to work if you're developing her as a mouthpiece," Polly said. She looked at her watch and said she had to go. Her wine people were in town from California to work the Ag Committee on phylloxera. Also to brainstorm with their ad agency on how to counter the disastrous misimpression that only French red wine kept you from getting a heart attack.

Nick and Bobby Jay watched her walk out, her bag slung over her shoulder, cellular antennae sticking out of it, heels going clickety-click on the floor. She was wearing a shorter skirt than usual, Nick noticed; sexy, with pleats.

Nick said to Bobby Jay, "Something going on with Polly? She seemed kind of bent out of shape."

Bobby Jay said, "She got a letter from Hector. He wants to try again. But he wants her to come live with him in Lagos."

"Oh, well, hell," Nick said, "no *wonder*."

Back in his office, Nick was squirreled away with a stack of paperwork when Gomez O'Neal came in and shut the door behind him.

"What's up?"

"I don't know," Gomez said gravely.

At a loss, Nick said, "Is this some Zen thing?"

"Watch your back, kid," Gomez said, and left.

14

Nick put in a call to the Captain. He was alarmed when his secretary told him that the Captain was in the hospital. "Nothing to worry about," she told him, "just in for repairs." Apparently some of the fetal pig valves that had been installed in other people had been giving out, and the Captain's doctors didn't want to take any chances. He did not sound well.

"Hello? No, goddamnit, I do *not* wish to move my bowels. Told you that four times already, it's none of your business. Hello? Nick, son! Bless my heart but it's good to hear your voice. How am I doing? I was doing fine until I was dragooned into this medieval house o' horrors. I'll tell you what's wrong with health care in this country. *Hospitals.*"

In the background Nick could hear the Captain's nurse, who sounded like a large, middle-aged black woman of supreme authority, demanding that he postpone his phone call until he had transacted more urgent business. Being a southerner, the Captain was helpless before her. It made no never mind to her that he was the Captain, titan of industry, the most important man in Winston-Salem. "I'll call you right back," he said, "after I have *dealt* with this female."

He called back ten minutes later. "It'll be a cold day in the infernal regions before *she* gives another order." In the background Nick heard, "I'm not going anywhere until you take that *pill.*"

"I *took* the damn pill. I watched you on the Larry King show last night. You did fine. Superb job. Too bad that fellow kidnapped you didn't call in."

"He probably figured the FBI had a tap on all incoming calls. Say, I'm calling about two things, Lady Bent and Lorne Lutch."

"Yes," the Captain said, "the gas guzzler and the nematode." The latter was a reference to the tobacco plant–eating worm. The first turned out to refer to the former British PM's liberal use of the Captain's Gulfstream. A man with a Gulfstream jet is always in demand.

"BR says you want me to read her the gospel?"

"That's right. You're young, good-looking, you been kidnapped. She'll listen to you. She won't listen to me, I'll tell you that."

"Uh-huh. He also told me you want me to bribe Lutch when I go out to California on that movie project. I think that's not a good idea."

"It was my idea."

"I see some downside potential."

"Every time I turn on the television, there he is croaking through that device to some bleeding heart talk show host about how he's only got two months left and he wants to spend every last minute of it pleading with the youth of this nation not to start smoking. For a man who's running out of breath, he does a *lot* of talking. Be a whole lot easier if he'd just died from smoking in bed like those others who were suing us, but we can't rely on *that* kind of luck every time."

Recently, three people who were suing the tobacco companies because they'd gotten cancer had managed to fall asleep with lit cigarettes and die.

"I don't think he's doing us any serious harm," Nick said. "He's just blowing off steam."

"Tell that to my senior VP for sales. Lutch was on *Donahue*—the thought of *those* two cozying up to each other gives me the rickets— three weeks ago and sales of Tumbleweed dropped off six percent. Six percent."

"It'll go back up after he goes."

"I wouldn't count on it. This is a very *high*-level defector. The gaspers are fixing to make a martyr out of him." The Captain lowered his voice to a whisper. "Gomez O'Neal's information is they're gonna start a foundation. The Lorne Lutch Foundation. They're going to build a ranch, for kids with . . ." He couldn't bring himself to say it.

"Cancer?"

"Gives me the willies just thinking about it."

"*Exactly* why we need an anti-smoking campaign aimed at kids."

"It's got so every time I turn on the television and see someone who used to do cigarette commercials, I think, What if *they* get it? Remember all those commercials Dick Van Dyke and Mary Tyler Moore did for Kent in the sixties? My God, what if *she* gets it? Can you *imagine*? America's sweetheart, on the *Donahue* show, wheezing. . . . I want you to go see him, son. He'll listen to you."

"Why," Nick said, "would he listen to me?"

"Because he knows that it was you talked us out of suing his saddle-sore butt when he first started making this fuss. And because of this kidnapping, you been blooded. You've suffered. He's a cowboy, he'll respect that. He's also a snob—I happen to know that personally—and now that you're a big media star, he won't be able to resist. Do it for me, son."

Nick sighed. "All right, but I honestly—"

"*Good.* Now obviously, we don't want to get into a bidding war with him, so we want our first offer to be impressive enough to get his attention. Where are my glasses? That woman stole them, I know it. Here they are. Now I'm looking at Gomez O'Neal's background report. . . . I see he had a little alcohol problem in his background, couple of bar fights, nothing too out of the ordinary, no wife beating. Stopped drinking . . . joined AA. No one drinks anymore, do they? It's all about health, these days. Health, health, health, jog, jog, jog. Life used to be so much more interesting. Went out to California myself last year on business, and you go to a cocktail party and all anyone's talking about is their cholesterol levels. The last thing I want to know about a man is the ratio of his bad cholesterol to his good cholesterol. Three children. From the looks of this report I don't think *they'll* be going too far in life. But there's five grandchildren in their teens. Five times twenty-five thousand dollars . . ." Nick heard him mumbling through some calculations ". . . times four makes five hundred thousand. Throw in a little more for his troubles. An even million dollars. We'll pay the IRS's share so everything'll be above-board, all nice and clean and legal. We could always write the check on the Coalition for Health. . . . No, I suppose we don't want any reporter getting his hands on a canceled check. Wouldn't they just go to town over *that?* Let's make it cash. Anyway, there's nothing so dramatic as a great big pile of cold, hard cash. When I was first starting out in the business, in sales, I'd fill a satchel full of five- and ten-dollar bills and drive around to country stores paying off the owners to give us rack space. Those were the days. Yes, let's make it cash, cash on the barrelhead."

Nick said, "Let me try out a headline on you: DYING TUMBLEWEED MAN REJECTS TOBACCO LOBBY HUSH MONEY. And that's *The Wall Street Journal* headline. The tabloid version would probably be something like MERCHANT OF DEATH TO TUMBLEWEED MAN: SHUT UP AND DIE!"

"It's not a bribe," the Captain said with feeling, "not at all. You're going out there on wings of *angels,* son. This is altruism at its finest."

"Now, honestly . . ."

"Absolutely. A gesture of profound humanitarianism. Here's a man going around calling us merchants of death and how do we respond?"

"By trying to sue him for breach of contract."

"That's water under the bridge. We're proposing to put his grand-children through college so that they won't have to pump gas and night-manage convenience stores like their parents. Plus we're throwing in a half million dollars just to say, 'No hard feelings.' Talk about turning the other cheek. I think Christ himself would say, 'That's mighty white of you, boys.' And he merely admonished us to love our enemies. He never said we had to make the sumbitches *rich.*"

"You're saying," Nick said, "that we're just . . . giving him the money?"

"Well, what have I been saying? Of course that's what I mean."

"He doesn't have to sign anything?"

"Not a thing."

"No gag agreement?"

"What's your problem, son. Do you not understand the mother tongue? No. Though, obviously, you might tell him that we would appreciate it if he kept our gesture private. A family matter. You might add that if he'd come to us in the first place, instead of to the press, we would have helped him out. Tobacco takes care of its own."

"Well," Nick said, feeling relieved, "I don't have any problem with that." The Captain, in his hospital bed, contemplating his own mortality, must have decided to make his peace with his enemies.

"The way I see it," the Captain chuckled, "is the sumbitch'll be so damn overcome with gratitude he'll have to shut up. Or if we get *truly* lucky, he'll have a heart attack at the sight of all that money."

Gazelle buzzed him on the intercom to tell him that agents from the FBI were here to see him.

Agent Allman, the friendly-looking one, shook Nick's hand. Agent Monmaney, looking like he'd just had a lunch of ground glass and nails, merely nodded.

"Did you get them?" Nick said.

"Who?" Agent Monmaney said.

"The kidnappers. Who else?"

Monmaney stared. What was it with him? Nick turned to Allman, who seemed to be giving Nick's office the once-over. Strange bedside manners, these two.

"Am I missing something here?" Nick said.

"The investigation is proceeding," Monmaney said.

"Well," Nick said, "is there something I can *help* you with?"

"Is there?" Monmaney said. Great, more tough-guy Zen.

Nick said, "Is there something you fellows want to talk about? Or did you just drop by to reassure me?"

Agent Allman was looking at the poster of the Lucky Strike–endorsing doctor. He chuckled. "Funny."

"Yes," Nick said. "My job would have been a lot easier back then."

"My dad smoked Luckies."

"Is that a fact?" Nick said.

"Uh-huh," Allman said, in a tone that made Nick suspect that his father had died a ghastly, protracted death from lung cancer. Swell, just what he needed on his side, an anti-smoking zealot.

"Is he," Nick groped, "was he . . . in law enforcement?"

"No, he owned a garage. He's retired, in Florida."

Nick felt great relief that Papa Allman was still among the living. Allman said, "The sun'll probably get him before the cigarettes."

"Hah," Nick said.

"Does anyone else use your office phone?" Agent Monmaney said.

"My phone? Uh, sure, possibly."

" 'Sure, possibly'?"

"Maybe. Why?"

"No reason."

Nick and Monmaney stared at each other. Allman said, "Have you ever used nicotine patches before, yourself?"

"Me?" Nick said. He was getting a very uncomfortable feeling from this line of questioning. "I used to enjoy smoking. I wish I still could."

"You certainly picked an extreme way to give up," Allman said, holding up Nick's World War I trench-knife paperweight. "This is mean."

"Excuse me?" Nick said. "You said, 'Picked'?"

"I said that?"

"Yes," Nick said firmly, "you did."

"Did I?" Allman said to Monmaney.

"I didn't hear," Monmaney said.

Nick sucked in his chest. "Why," he said, "do I get the feeling this is an interrogation?"

"I just saw an article in one of the scientific journals on skin cancer," Agent Allman said. "Pretty scary. You've really got to watch it these days."

"Yes," Nick said with asperity, "you certainly do."

"Mr. Naylor," said Agent Monmaney, "you're getting a lot of favorable publicity as a result of this incident."

"Well, it's not every day a lobbyist is abducted, tortured, and nearly killed," Nick said, "though a lot of people probably think it should happen more often."

"That wasn't my point."

"What was your point, exactly?"

"You're portraying yourself as a martyr. A hero."

"Agent Monmaney," Nick said, "do you have a problem with cigarettes?"

The faintest trace of a smile played on Monmaney's lupine features, not a nourishing smile. "Not since I quit."

"I'd say this," Nick said. "For the first time since I took this job, I'm getting *fair* publicity. Now at least they wait until the fourth paragraph in the story to compare me to Goebbels."

"Funny," Agent Allman said. Agent Monmaney did not share in the amusement.

The three held a staring bee. Nick was determined not to break the silence.

"You received a raise recently," Agent Monmaney said.

"Uh-huh," Nick said.

"A very considerable one. They doubled your salary."

"More or less," Nick said.

"I'd say," said Agent Allman, rising up off the sofa beneath the Luckies doctor, "that you deserve it. You seem to be doing a very competent job promoting cigarettes."

"Thank you," Nick said tartly.

"We'll be in touch," Agent Allman said.

15

Stress—which Nick was now distinctly feeling—tended to make him horny. He went out onto the balcony off his office and looked down at the fountain. It was a warm spring day outside and the office women were in their summer dresses. He found himself watching one, below, walking along as she ate her frozen yoghurt, a lovely, tall, busty blonde in a sheer sleeveless dress, stockings, and heels, taking long, slow licks of her cone. Even at this altitude he could make out her bra straps. Heather did the bra strap thing to very good effect. It was a trick among certain professional Washington women of bounteous endowment. They wouldn't go so far as to wear too-small sweaters or appear too decolleté—sex had to be flaunted in a more subversive way here—so instead they'd make sure a bit of strap showed for the photographer and pretend to be embarrassed when they saw it.

Looking down on the atrium, he began to dream. He dimmed the lights, got rid of all the people eating yoghurt and calzone. Around the fountain he assembled a full orchestra consisting of stunningly toothsome women wearing nothing but their instruments. He put the cellists out front. Yes. There's just something about nude women cellists. He had them play the cigarette song from act I in *Carmen,* where the young Sevillian men are serenaded by their sweethearts, the girls who work in the cigarette factory. The Academy had underwritten the opera at the Kennedy Center two years ago. Ever since, Nick had been humming it in the shower. *C'est fumée, c'est fumée!*

In the air, we follow with our eyes,
The smoke, the smoke,

that rises toward the sky,
sweet-smelling smoke.
How pleasantly it goes,
to your head, to your head,
so sweetly
and fills your soul with joy!
The sweet talk of lovers—
that is smoke.
Their transports and their vows—
all that is smoke.

The scene was set. There remained only the pièce de résistance: Heather, buxom, pink, and entirely au naturel, looking like one of Renoir's bathing beauties, sitting in the uppermost bowl of the fountain, with him, drinking champagne (Veuve Clicquot, demi-sec) from iced flutes.

He went back inside and called Heather.

"Hi," Heather said, sounding very throaty, "I can't come to the phone right now. Leave a message and I'll call you back as soon as I can. If you want to speak to an operator, press zero."

He left a message asking her if she wanted to have dinner that night at Il Peccatore, then went back outside to see if his *tableau* was still *vivant*. It wasn't. The orchestra had been replaced by worker bees eating calzones and frozen yoghurts.

He sat at his desk and turned to the work at hand with the enthusiasm of a man changing a flat tire on a sweltering day on the interstate. It was to ghostwrite an op-ed piece for congressman Jud Jawkins (D-Ky), challenging an NIH study showing that children of smoking mothers have 80 percent more asthma attacks than children of nonsmoking mothers. Nick sighed.

He wrote: "No one is more respectful of the work carried on at the National Institutes of Health than I, yet it is unfortunate that at a time when so many ghastly severe health problems face our nation—AIDS, skyrocketing cholesterol levels, and the recent outbreak of measles in my own home state, to name but a few examples—that the NIH has become so riven with political correctness that it is spending precious resources to bombard the American people with information that they already have."

It was one of his more conventional devices—the old Dejà Voodoo—but it would have to do. He was just cranking up some moral counteroutrage and pleas for common decency and fairness when there was a rap on his door and Jeannette said, "Am I interrupting?"

He looked up from his dissimulations to see Jeannette's head sticking out from behind the door. She looked much more relaxed than she usually did. She'd furloughed her ice-blond hair from its normal prison of a bun at the back and had it loosely ponytailed with a barrette. She was in her standard Don't Mess With Me dark blue suit, worn tightly so as to show off every minute of every sweaty hour at the health club; but she'd added an explosively colorful silk scarf from Hermès or Chanel that gave her the look of a rich woman on the prowl for fun. Nick had to admit that Jeannette was looking mighty fine this afternoon. Maybe one of her focus groups had told her to lighten up and lose the dominatrix look. After all, the whole idea of having a spokesbabe was to take the viewer's mind off cancer and heart disease and emphysema, not to beat back their own libidos with a chair and whip.

"Hi," she said in a friendly way. "Am I interrupting?"

"No," Nick said. "I was just making some op-ed mush."

She closed the door behind her. "God," she said, "I'd *kill* to have your touch with op-eds."

"Ah," Nick said, "easy as breathing."

"I can recite the one you did for Jordan when Deukmejian banned smoking on flights in California. 'I have a lot of respect for Governor Deukmejian. It's his respect for the Constitution that concerns me.' October eighty-seven, right?"

Nick blushed. "Lot of good it did."

She sat down, crossed her stockinged legs, which, Nick noticed, looked very sleek today. He looked up and saw that she'd seen him purloining a glance at her gams. He looked down at his op-ed and frowned as though he were trying to think of the right word.

"What's up?" he said in a businesslike way, though it was by now obvious to both of them what, precisely, was up.

"I've got this idea that I'm really excited about."

"Oh?" Nick said, still looking down at his op-ed piece.

"A magazine for smokers."

"Hm," Nick said, sitting back and looking at her, careful to keep his eyes above the waist. "Couple of the companies tried it. Controlled circulation, no newsstand."

"Precisely," Jeannette said, "where I think they went wrong. I want this on the newsstands. In their faces. Look at newsstands these days. Magazines for everyone, except smokers."

"What would you call it?"

"*Inhale!*" Jeannette said, "with the exclamation mark in the form of a cigarette, you know, with the ash. Dynamic, unapologetic, and *hot*."

"Hot?"

"Sexy," Jeannette said. *"Dripping."*

" '*Inhale!* '" said Nick. "Tell me more."

"We've got fifty-five million customers out there, huddling outside in doorways, feeling persecuted. Why wouldn't they want a magazine all their own? We're talking more readers than *TV Guide*. A magazine for the smoking lifestyle. Overweight women, minorities, blue-collar workers, depressives, alcoholics—"

"Rugged individualists," Nick said. "Independent spirits. Risk takers. Which is quintessentially American. I sometimes think that our customers are the most American people left."

"And dying out fast."

"Feature stories on the American West, fast, sexy muscle cars—"

"Bungee jumping."

"Yes."

"Listings of smoker-friendly restaurants. A real service magazine."

"But sexy."

"Hot. *Sports Illustrated*–type babes in swimsuits, only holding cigarettes. So much of the *sex* has gone out of smoking."

"But with substance."

"Absolutely. Interviews with prominent smokers."

"Are there any?"

"Castro."

"He gave up. Anyway, I'm not sure Caribbean Commies are sexy anymore. Nixon. Nixon smokes. Not many people know that."

"Is Nixon *sexy*?"

"Clinton. Cigars."

"He doesn't light them."

"We'll find someone."

Gazelle came over the intercom. She sounded amused. "Nick, the two gentlemen from *Modern Man* magazine—"

"*Young Modern Man*," corrected a Japanese voice in the background.

"Sorry. To see you."

Nick rolled his eyes. "BR's idea."

"Later," Jeannette said.

"Later when?" Nick said.

"Later-later? I'm crashing on sick building syndrome, but I'd really want to get with you on this."

"You want to grab a drink later-later? Or a bite later-later-later?"

"Perfect. BR wants me to do a drop-by at the Healthy Heart 2000 thing at the Omni-Shoreham. You know, show the flag."

"Uch. Bring your flak jacket."

"Believe me, I'm not sticking around. Eight?"

"Great. You like soft-shell crabs?"

"I *love* soft-shell crabs."

Heather called in the middle of his session with the reporter and photographer from *Young Modern Man,* who, to judge from the questions—"Who do you consider are the true smoking heroes in America today?"—were on the side of the angels. But then the Japanese were amazingly tolerant where it came to smoking: they allowed cigarette advertising in *children's* TV programming. Maybe he should ask for a transfer to Tokyo. . . .

"I can't do dinner tonight," said Heather, sounding busy, sounds of the newsroom about her. Thank God. Nick realized that he had asked two women to dinner.

"No sweat. By the way, we're going to roll out the new anti-underage smoking campaign next week, and I wondered if the *Moon* wanted an exclusive preview."

"Nick, I told you I don't do propaganda."

"Look, we're committing economic suicide. Tell me that's not news?"

"Maybe to Oprah."

"What's the matter, are you worried that jerk at the *Sun* will think you're soft on tobacco?"

"Hardly."

"All right," Nick said, "but don't blame me if something interesting happens at the press conference."

"Like what? An announcement that smoking cures cancer?"

"You laugh," Nick said, "but we've just seen a study showing that smoking retards the onset of Parkinson's."

"In what? *Tobacco Farmer's Almanac?*"

"Half my job," Nick said to *Young Modern Man* after hanging up, "is maintaining good communications with the media. Information doesn't do any good if you don't get it out there. Right?"

The maître d' at Il Peccatore led Nick to the same corner booth where he'd had the first lunch with Heather. It made him hope Heather didn't show up; though what the hell, to her it would just look like he was having dinner with a co-worker.

His bodyguards sat at a nearby table with their Velcro bags, ready to turn Il Peccatore into an abattoir if Peter Lorre and his gang of dispatchers made another move. They were two taciturn women, steely-eyed and *very* butch, admittedly, but *women* bodyguards? He said something about it to Carlton, who just laughed and said, "Listen to me, Nicky, Godzilla wouldn't want to fuck with these babes, believe me. Anyone so much as brushes up against you is to become a major organ donor. If there's anything left whole enough to donate."

Jeannette arrived ten minutes after eight, full of apologies, and carrying tchotchkes that she presented to Nick: a Healthy Heart 2000 tote bag.

"Double Dewar's, up," she told the waiter. She lit a Tumbleweed Light and exhaled. "Christ, I didn't think I'd make it out of there alive. Wall-to-wall cardiologists." She shuddered.

"I won't do the cocktail parties anymore," Nick said. "I'll sit on the panels, I'll eat lunch with them, but I will not be in a room with them while they're sucking up chardonnay and vodka. It's just *too* volatile."

"Farkley Krell was there," Jeannette said. Krell was Senator Ortolan K. Finisterre's gray eminence, his chief aide, speechwriter, press secretary.

"Did he throw his drink in your face, or merely ignore you?"

"I was very polite. I went over, stuck out my hand, which he did not shake, and told him how much we were looking forward to working with him on secondhand smoke."

"That *was* brave."

"What else am I going to say? BR said show the flag, so. . . . He looked at me like I was wearing mustard-gas perfume and said, 'I'm sure we'll be working together on a *lot* of issues, soon.' "

"Hm. What did *that* mean?"

"I don't know, but I thought I better call BR about it. That's why I'm late. He got Gomez in on it. And guess what? Finisterre's got this Guatemalan housekeeper named Rosaria. She's been with the family since when Romulus was president. Since before, since the Devonian era, whenever. Anyway, she smokes. And guess what?"

"Don't tell me."

"Uh-huh. They give her six months, tops."

Nick sighed. "You know, there's never any good news. At least Polly and Bobby Jay get some good news sometimes. *Sixty Minutes* does a show saying red wine keeps you from having a heart attack, or someone uses a gun to do some good, like kill a serial murderer." He shook his head. "How does Gomez know this about the cleaning lady?"

"Gomez? Are you kidding. Gomez knows everything. I think he still works for the CIA. But I've got a bad feeling about this. Finisterre's up for re-election next year, his numbers suck, he's looking for an easy win. . . ."

Nick stirred his vodka with his forefinger.

"Well," Jeannette said, leaning into him, "let's talk about something else."

The soft-shells arrived. They were tiny, delicate, crispy, dusted with just a hint of ginger, and topped with a lobster roe sauce. Refusing the wine list, Nick asked the waiter if they happened to have a particular thirty-eight-dollar bottle of Sancerre, which he knew they definitely did have because he'd checked before Jeannette arrived. The maître d', playing his role, cooed over Nick's arcane selection. It turned out to be delicate yet assertive, dry yet full-bodied, tangy yet smooth, fruity yet not fruity. It was everything a thirty-eight-dollar bottle of wine should be, namely, good.

"You certainly know your wines," Jeannette said, leaning in even closer.

"Why don't we have another bottle."

"Absolutely. No one drinks anymore. No one drinks, no one smokes. . . ."

In the car, Nick tried to concentrate on staying in his lane and on praying that there were no breathalyzing cops with roadblocks tonight. His BAC had to be in triple digits.

"Let's have a nightcap," Jeannette said.

"We could go to the Jockey Club?"

"Too crowded," Jeannette said. "What about your place? Isn't it just off DuPont Circle?"

"Yeah."

She touched his arm as he shifted gears. "Then step on it," she said silkily.

"Ohh," she said.

"Ahh," he said.

"Uhh," she said.

"Ooo," he said.

"I've wanted to do this ever since I first saw you," she said.

"Mrrr," he said. "Urr."

"Do you want me to tie you up?"

"Hm? Uh-uh."

"Do you have any rope?"

"Uh-uh."

"Clothesline?"

"Uh-uh."

"Bungee cord?"

"Uh-uh."

"Garbage-bag ties?"

Nick sat up. "No. Don't we want *some* light in here?" Jeannette had insisted on pitch-blackness. Nick heard the sound of stretching rubber.

"What are you doing?" he asked.

"Putting on latex gloves."

"Gloves?" he said. "Why are you putting on gloves?"

"I love gloves. I think they're soo sexy."

146

"Uh . . ." She chewed his earlobe. "Here," she said, handing him a box in the dark.

"What's this?"

"Condoms," she moaned. "Extra large."

"Oh."

He started to open the flaps on the box. Were they the glow-in-the-dark kind? Was that why she wanted the lights out?

"You're not offended? It's just, I'm *so* fecund."

"No," Nick said, "of course not." He ripped open the box.

"Here," she said, taking it from him, "let me."

"You're not going to tie me up with them?"

"Silly," she said.

"Ohh," he said.

"Ahh," she said.

16

BR called him at seven-thirty in the morning while he was humming *C'est fumée, c'est fumée!* in the shower—Jeannette had slipped away sometime in the predawn—to say that he'd just had a call from the Captain. Lady Bent was addressing the Trilateral Commission in New York and a rare fifteen-minute window had opened up in her schedule. He wanted Nick to go up to New York and talk turkey to her.

"Why me?" Nick said.

"The Captain thinks the sun rises and sets on your ass."

"But what am I supposed to tell her? 'Mention cigarettes next time someone asks you about the Middle East'?"

"The Captain thinks she'll go for you because you're young, good-looking—"

"Oh, come on, BR."

"And because you, like her, have been the victim of terrorism."

"Look, I don't even speak British."

"Okay, then call the Captain and tell him you refuse to meet with the former prime minister."

Nick sighed. Two, alas, could play the old *You tell the Captain* game.

"All right. But I've got the puffers coming in at nine."

"Fuck the puffers. Let Jeannette speak to them."

"They're expecting me. I can't let them down."

"They give me the creeps, those people. What a bunch of losers."

"They're dedicated. Look, I can do both the puffers *and* Cement Knickers."

"As long as you're on that ten o'clock shuttle. By the way, *top* security on this. If that Holloway broad or any other reporter finds out that Nick Naylor is giving motivational training to Penelope Bent, it'll be raining shit for forty days and nights, so not a word to anyone, even your staff."

Nick got back into the shower and lathered. He felt curiously neutral about the prospect of meeting the most famous woman in the world—British princesses and Liz Taylor aside—because he knew exactly how it was going to turn out. She'd cut him into tiny, bite-size morsels, eat him, and afterward floss her teeth with his guts.

He relathered. Making the ten o'clock shuttle would be tight . . . but he couldn't let down the puffers. It was a big deal, to them.

These were the smokers' rights groups that had spontaneously popped up around the country as the anti-smoking movement had gathered momentum. They championed the rights of the oppressed smoker who couldn't find a smoking section in a restaurant, or who had to leave his desk and go stand in the snow to have a cigarette. They targeted local politicians who favored anti-smoking ordinances, attacked the surgeon general much more viciously than the Academy itself could, organized "smoke-ins"—pathetic as they were, Nick had to admit—and "seminars"—also pathetic—sent out form letters pre-addressed to anti-smoking congressmen and senators in Washington, gave out "Smoker Friendly" awards, mostly to restaurants that didn't put their smoking sections in the back next to the Dumpster, and distributed morale-boosting T-shirts and caps with pro-smoking emblems modeled on the old Black Panther salute: upraised fists holding cigarettes. Ostensibly, these were grassroots, heartbeat-of-America (or heart-attack-of-America) citizens groups that showed just how committed and politically active the fifty-five million smokers were. Look at all the money they were able to raise to support all these activities.

In actual fact, there wasn't really anything spontaneous about the rise of these groups. They were front groups: the Captain's brainchild, modeled on the CIA-funded student organizations of the 1950s. They were almost entirely funded by the Academy, with the money being laundered—legally—by giving it to various middlemen who, posing as anonymous donors, passed it along to the groups as contributions. The whole operation cost next to nothing, relatively, and this way tobacco's friends in the House and Senate could stand up and point to them as evidence of a groundswell.

Also, every now and then, if it was a very slow news day, the local newspaper might send a reporter out to interview the local head of the Coalition For Smoking Indoors or Smokers United For Freedom, or the more militant Hispanic group, Fumamos!

Once a year all the groups came en masse to Washington to hold a smoke-in on the Mall and roam the halls of the Capitol building in search of health-conscious congressmen to harass.

Though the Academy naturally preferred to keep a low profile in its contacts with the front groups, Nick felt it was important to have them in for a pep talk. So what if they were stooges. *They* didn't know that. BR was right, in his snobbish way: they were all, as a rule, a bubble off plumb. Nick at least was paid to be passionate about smoking. These people did it for free. In a funny kind of way, the puffers were just like the gaspers: humorless, obsessive, pissed off.

And yet Nick felt that the least the Academy could do was spend half an hour with them. He wasn't about to shortchange them for some retainer-grabbing former British PM. This morning Nick was at peace with the world, despite the fact that he'd gotten almost no sleep the night before. Getting laid has that effect. And he had gotten laid. She'd put him through two boxes of her condoms. Jeannette definitely knew her way around the sack. She was thoughtful, too; he didn't want empty condom boxes strewn around for Heather to see, and when he went to throw them out, he saw that she'd taken them with her. Tidy; probably went along with the compulsion to want to tie people up.

As he walked in, Gazelle announced that Agents Monmaney and Allman were waiting for him in his office.

"Good morning," Nick said grimly. "Have you found them yet?"

Agent Allman returned his greeting. Agent Monmaney did not.

"What can I do for you?" Nick said, dispensing with further pleasantries. "I've got a very full morning."

Monmaney took out a notepad. "Six years ago, when you were

working for WRTK, you went on the air live and said that President Broadbent had died."

"Uh-huh," Nick said.

"How did that come about?"

"An honest mistake."

This elicited one of Monmaney's slow-fuse stares.

"Does this have any bearing on finding my kidnappers?"

"No," Agent Allman said. "Well, you're busy. We can talk more later." They left. Nick wondered: could you request a change of FBI agents?

They were all waiting for him in the small auditorium. Nick was taken aback at the atmosphere in there, which was so full of smoke he could hardly make out the back row. These people did *love* to smoke.

They gave him a standing ovation. It was gratifying. *My people,* he thought. The head of United Smokers of America, Ludlow Cluett, gave him a rousing introduction, making it sound like he'd fought off his kidnappers with bare fists, and said how much the Academy meant to them. Little did he know.

Nick took the podium and started in on the speech he'd composed in the shower, in which he likened them to a long line of American freedom fighters stretching all the way back to Ethan Allen's Green Mountain Boys. It required some rejiggering of American history, but it could be done.

He got as far as World War I and Pershing's urgent telegram to Washington saying the doughboys needed more cigarettes—leaving out the part about how that had produced the first cases of lung cancer in America—when all the smoke in the room started to get to him. His head spun and throbbed and he started to cough. Really cough, the kind where you have to hold a handkerchief in front of your mouth or people around you get sprayed.

"Excuse . . ." he gasped, "flu . . . *harrrrg* . . ."

He managed to pull himself together and was in the midst of a little Lucy Page Gaston–bashing when he was struck by a hurricane-force coughing spasm that left him with stars in his eyes and his heart approaching paroxysmal atrial tachycardia. *Tobacco Spokesman Suffers Fatal Heart Attack While Addressing Pro-Smoking Groups.* People would laugh as they read his obituary. He had to get out of there.

"In conclusion," he wheezed, "let me leave you with the thought that . . ."

They were looking at him adoringly, hanging on his words. *My people. . . .*

". . . that it's people . . . like you . . . who are . . . lighting the . . . *harg harg* . . . fires of freedom around this . . . *harg harg harg* . . . great nation of . . . *wheeze* . . . ours."

He reelingly stuck around to sign a few autographs, mostly on cigarette packs, and fled for the shuttle, where he opened his *New York Times* to the front page and read: "To save money, airlines in the United States are circulating less fresh air into the cabins of many airplanes." And they were mad at the cigarette companies?

He ducked into the men's room at National Airport while waiting for the shuttle. It was the one place his women bodyguards couldn't follow him into. He was standing in front of the urinal minding his business when he heard a voice behind him say, "Hello, Neek!" *Peter Lorre!*

Nick whirled around, still holding his spigot, which was at this point in full flow, only to find himself spraying the pants leg of an innocent and very aggrieved businessman.

"Hey! *Damnit!*"

"Sorry. Sorry," Nick stammered. "I . . ."

The businessman furiously cleaned himself. Nick looked around. There was no one else in the bathroom. Nick spent most of the flight up staring at the back of the seat in front of him. He called Dr. Williams on the Airfone and described the episode. In his sympathetic way, Dr. Williams reiterated that Nick had undergone great trauma, and offered the number of a psychiatrist. Nick said he'd think about it, hung up, and went back to staring blankly at the back of the seat.

Lady Bent was installed on a high floor of the Hotel Pierre. To get to her floor a special key had to be inserted into the control panel by an assistant manager, and as you rode up you had the feeling that sensors were examining your body; every part of it.

The door *dinged* open to reveal three athletic men with bulging armpits; Nick recognized them immediately as Security, and they fixed him with the usual evaulating stares. Though out of power, Lady Bent was still under Special Branch protection on account of what she'd done to the IRA after they blew up her bulldogs. They'd vowed to get her, someday.

Her bodyguards did not like the fact that Nick had arrived with some of his own armed guards—thank God they hadn't brought their sawed-off shotguns. A Mexican standoff developed, because Nick's Valkyries were under strict orders not to let him out of their sight, and Lady Bent's people weren't about to let them get near Lady Bent. A factotum arrived and made diplomacy between the two armed camps and asked Nick to follow him.

They went into a vast and endless suite. The factotum knocked softly on a door, which opened to reveal not Lady Bent but her private secretary, a man of viceregal air, tall, thin, exquisitely tailored. He had strange, transparent skin—you could almost see his skull underneath—and a nose so aquiline that Nick was tempted to offer it a fish to eat.

"Ah, yes, Mr. *Naylor*," he said, unsmilingly offering a hand. "I'm afraid we're running a bit over this morning so if you wouldn't mind having a seat I thought we could use the time to talk about what it is, exactly, you'd like to discuss with Lady Bent."

"Sorry?" Nick said dumbfoundedly.

The viceroy gave a brief show of pain, suggesting that he had not achieved a double first at Cambridge in order to waste his time repeating his beautifully crafted questions for the benefit of mentally defective post-colonials. He repeated himself word for word, slowly.

Clearing his throat, Nick asked, "I meant, what were you under the impression I was here to discuss with Lady Bent?"

"We were *told,* simply, by Mr. Boykin's people, that you desired to speak with the former prime minister in connection with her arrangements with Agglomerated Tobacco. The precise nature of the discussion was never in fact specified, despite our, I must say, repeated requests for clarification on the matter. So here, as it were, we are; though I certainly hope, not at odds."

Enough words there to choke a giraffe, but it was gradually dawning on Nick that the Captain, titan of industry and leader of men that he was, was completely *cowed* by this woman, despite the fact that he was paying her a small fortune and flying her around in his Gulfstream at $15,000 an hour. He couldn't quite bring himself to come right out and tell her: *"Damnit, start saying nice things about my cigarettes!"*

And from the looks of it, the viceroy wasn't even going to give him any face time with old Cement Knickers unless he was first satisfied that the topic was worthy of her precious time.

"Uh," Nick said, trying desperately to think of something to say. The viceroy stared. Nick whispered, "Is this room clean?"

"I *beg* your pardon?"

"Has it been, you know, swept?"

"Swept? What do you mean? For *bugs*?"

Nick nodded.

"I . . . should think not, in all likelihood. But why on *earth* would you be concerned about that?"

Nick took out his notepad and wrote, "Is there a bathroom where we can talk?"

"A *bathroom*?" the viceroy said. "What *are* you talking about?"

Nick wrote: "Concerns L.B.'s personal safety."

The viceroy looked up, confused, and said impatiently, "Very well, then." Nick followed him into the bathroom and after making a show of examining it for listening devices, opened up all the faucets so that it sounded like Niagara Falls. He whispered, "As you may already know, I was the target of an attempt by a radical anti-smoking movement."

"Oh. Yes, I thought you looked a bit familiar. But what on earth has all this to do with Lady Bent?"

"We don't know how far this group might prosecute their agenda. If you see what I mean."

"But this has nothing to do with her. Her connection with your business is extremely remote. A few appearances at board meetings, the occasional dinner, that sort of thing."

"She *is* accepting money from the industry."

"Well, yes, but . . ."

"And traveling in Ag Tobacco's plane."

"Yes, but she's hardly . . ."

"All the same, we're very concerned for her."

"I think you're overreacting, frankly. I can't see how this affects the prime minister."

"If you're willing to take that risk on her behalf, fine. You're probably right. They probably wouldn't go after her. I'll just go back and make my report, in writing, that you didn't think it was a problem."

"Perhaps you should speak with her. But only *very* briefly, please. We are very pressed this afternoon."

He opened the bathroom door and there was Lady Bent, standing in the middle of the room. She was a handsome old girl with a great matronly bosom, mongoose eyes, and a helmet of hair that looked as if it could deflect incoming nuclear missiles.

"Ah," she said, "I've been looking all over for you. What on *earth* were you both doing in *there*?"

The viceroy blushed.

Lady Bent offered Nick a chair and said, "What may I do for you?" making it clear that she did not want to engage in small talk about the Pierre, New York, or her private secretary's penchant for luring younger men into toilets. Before Nick could answer, she looked at him curiously and said, "You're the cigarette man who was attacked, aren't you?"

"Yes ma'am," Nick said.

She instantly warmed. "You needn't call me ma'am. I'm not the queen. It must have been quite ghastly."

"Well, it wasn't *fun*," Nick said. "But nothing like what you've been through."

"We have something in common, then. We know that terrorism must never, ever, be countenanced."

"You bet," Nick said. "However, Lady Bent, our people are very concerned that this group—which is still very much at large—might target you, and we would obviously feel awful if anything happened. So I've come to ask that in all your public and even private statements, you absolutely *refrain* from mentioning tobacco. Or, God forbid, from saying anything positive about it."

She drew herself up like an aroused lioness and fixed him with a withering look. Nick thought, it sure must have been fun to be in her cabinet and face that look across the table.

"Mister Naylor," she said, like an arctic wind, "I have never been one to shrink from principle out of fear for my own personal safety."

"Of course not," Nick said. "And I certainly didn't meant to imply that you were. It's just that we feel—"

155

"If we let terrorists dictate what we do not say, then we are as good as letting them dictate what we do say. And when we do that, we are finished as a civilized people."

"Nicely put," Nick said. "Still, I must insist that you not mention tobacco. You don't want to get these people mad. I don't know about the IRA, I know they're bad news bears and all—and that was a terrible thing they did to your dogs—but things can get pretty nasty in America."

The color rose in Lady Bent. She stood, signaling that their interview was at an end, and proffered her hand. She said tersely and without smiling, "Good to see you," and with the viceroy following, walked out of the room, whose doors opened as if by magic.

Two days later, back in Washington, Nick was getting ready for his trip out to California when BR called him in.

"You see this?" he said, tossing him *The Wall Street Journal.*

Nick hadn't. He read:

After the dinner at the Pierre, Lady Bent spoke for an hour and twenty-five minutes, lengthy even by her standards. The theme of her speech was free enterprise in the post–Cold War era. It surprised no one at the dinner, consisting largely of business and international commerce officials, to hear the former British Prime Minister issue a ringing defense of open trade and a stinging attack on protectionism; she also included an unusually passionate endorsement of the right of American and British cigarette companies to compete in Asian markets.

Lady Bent serves on the board of Agglomerated Tobacco, which has been especially aggressive in trying to break down Pacific Rim trade barriers to U.S. tobacco products. In an informal exchange with a reporter after the dinner, Lady Bent said that her remarks on tobacco were unrelated to her connection with Agglomerated. "My views on the tobacco business are the same as my views on the ice cream business," she said, "and they have been consistent throughout my career." She went on to rebuke the anti-smoking movement for being "anti-business."

"I don't know what you told her," BR said, "but it sure worked. I've been instructed to give you another raise. To two-five-oh."

Nick ran into Jeannette in the hallway. She was all smiles.

"We still never talked about *Inhale!*" she said.

"I have to go to California tomorrow."

"Then we better have another nightcap tonight," she purred. She wanted to come over to Nick's place again. And everything was the same, the lights out, the condom boxes—Jeannette was definitely into latex—the oohs, and the aahs. The next morning, sore, Nick caught the flight out of Dulles to L.A. for his big meeting with the big guy.

17

He flew First Class, which BR had okayed since he was carrying an attaché case containing a half million dollars in fifty- and hundred-dollar bills. Lorne Lutch's hush money. It was a strange sensation, carrying all that money. It made him feel like a drug dealer or a Watergate bag man. Going through the X-ray machine at Dulles, the eyes of the guy monitoring the screen went buggy when he saw all that cash. No law against carrying around money, but there was a minor scene when his three women bodyguards declared their 9-millimeters. But once he was seated up in First and hovered over by stewards dispensing hot towels and Bloody Marys, he began to relax. Nick liked airplanes, even if the airlines were circulating less fresh air in the cabins to make more money. In a way, he mused, he and they were in the same business.

First Class was full. There was a lot of traffic back and forth between D.C. and L.A. these days. He recognized Barbra Streisand's issues person, whom he'd read had flown in to brief the National Security Council on Barbra's position on the developing Syrian situation. Richard Dreyfuss's issues person was also on board, having given a presentation to the cabinet on Richard's feelings about health reform.

It wasn't until two hours into the flight that Nick realized that the woman sitting next to him, underneath Jackie O–sized dark glasses, was Tarleena Tamm, the television producer friend of the First Family. Nick didn't introduce himself, knowing how celebrities, especially controversial ones, value their privacy in the air. But then he became aware that she was sneaking furtive glances at him. When their eyes connected for the third, embarrassing time, he smiled at her. She said, "Aren't you the tobacco person who was kidnapped?"

"Yes," Nick said, flattered at being approached by a celebrity. He was about to reciprocate when she set her jaw and said, "I know a lot of people who died of lung cancer. *Good* people."

Nick said to her, "No *bad* people?"

She gave him a fierce look, craned about to see if there was an empty seat, and finding none, went back to angrily marking up the script on her large lap with a big, angry red pen. Some screenwriter would pay for Nick's insolence.

Nick loved L.A. Arriving there always made it feel like Friday, even in the middle of a week facing a full workload. He felt exhilarated walking off the plane and imagined himself at the wheel of the sporty red Mustang he'd had Gazelle rent for him, driving along Mulholland Drive at night and looking down on all the lights of the city, spreading out as far as the eye could see. Too bad Heather or Jeannette wasn't here. Maybe he could entice Heather to fly out. Or Jeannette.

Shattering this pleasant reverie was the sight of a Middle Eastern–looking chauffeur with a hundred-dollar haircut waiting for him at the gate holding up one of those signs: MR. NAYLOR. When he innocently reached for Nick's attaché case, Nick's bodyguards nearly wrenched his arm out of its socket. The chauffeur apologetically introduced himself as Mahmoud and said that he'd been sent by Mr. Jack Bein, of Associated Creative Talent, and handed Nick an envelope with a note inside from Bein asking Nick to call him immediately.

Nick was sorrier still for his canceled Mustang when he saw Mahmoud's vehicle, a white stretch limousine the length of a lap pool. People standing on the curb nearby waiting for the shuttle bus saw Nick with his entourage and Moby Dick limousine and demanded his autograph, which made the bodyguards nervous. Nick signed one and the person who'd asked for it examined it, frowned, and said, "It's not him." The small crowd dispersed.

It was cool and cavernous inside and lit with scores of tiny Christmas tree lights. A huge TV screen in front displayed computerized fireworks that formed the words "Welcome to Los Angeles, Mr.

Naylor." A microwave oven beeped open with a bowl of hot towels; a wet bar opened with four kinds of freshly squeezed juice, as well as liquor. On the seats were fresh copies of the *L.A. Times, Variety,* and *Asahi Shinbum.* So where, Nick wondered, was the terry cloth bathrobe?

Suddenly the fireworks display vanished from the screen and was replaced with a huge face: deeply tanned, teeth so white they hurt to look at, eyes masked by tinted aviator glasses. Nick was trying to figure why the TV had gone on and what game show host this was when the face said: *"Nick!"*

Nick started.

"Jack Bein. Is everything okay?"

It was asked with urgency, with fear, as if he expected Nick to tell him, *No, everything is* not *okay, Jack. Things are very* un-*okay. And you, your family, and your dog are going to suffer for it.*

"Yes," Nick said, recovering his composure. "Fine. Thank you."

"I can't believe I'm not there to greet you personally." Nick was left to interpret this as he chose. "Jeff is really looking forward to meeting you. I'll pick you up at the hotel first thing. Here's my home number, call me anytime, in the middle of the night, whenever. Whatever you need. I mean that, okay?"

"Okay," Nick said.

A half hour later they pulled up in front of a hotel. It was not the Peninsula, where Gazelle had made reservations, but the Encomium, very palmy, open, and grand, with an enormous Yitzak McClellan fountain *bleu* outside. An assistant manager was waiting for him at the curb.

"*Yes,* Mr. Naylor, we've been expecting you. The manager asked me to relay his sincere regrets that he couldn't be here to greet you personally. Are these," he said, regarding the three brutish women surrounding Nick, "ladies in your party?" Nick said that they were.

"Will you all be staying together?"

"No, no," Nick said.

"If you'd follow me, please."

Nick's bags were whisked away. Check-in formalities were dispensed with. The assistant manager handed him a magnetic card to operate his own private elevator, and led him up in the outside glass elevator to a huge penthouse suite with sunken marble bathtub, fireplace, balcony, waterfall, and immense bed already turned down. There were Hockneys on the wall; originals. Nick's very own butler, an immaculate young Asian fellow, was standing there in white tie holding a silver tray with a vodka negroni on the rocks in a Baccarat tumbler. Nick's drink. Now *this* was good advance.

"We took the liberty of calling your office this morning as soon as we knew you were coming," explained the assistant manager.

"May I pour your bath?" the butler said.

The phone rang.

"May I get that for you? Mr. Naylor's suite. Yes, please hold. It's for you, sir. Mr. Jack Bein of ACT."

"Nick, Jack. Is everything all *right*?"

"Yes, Jack," Nick said. "Everything is fine."

"You're *sure*?"

"I think so."

"Just sign for everything. Don't worry about it."

All this was—free? What a great town.

"I want you to call me if you're not happy," Jack said, "for whatever reason. If you wake up in the middle of the night and you just want to talk. I'm here. I know what it is to be alone in a strange town. Take this number down, it rings on my bedside table. Only three people in the world have this number, Michael Eisner, Michael Ovitz, Jeff, of course, and now you. And my mother makes five. Do you have a mother? They're great, aren't they? I'll see you for breakfast. Is Haiphong there?"

"Who?"

"The butler. They did give you a butler, didn't they? Jesus Christ on Rollerblades, what's going on there?"

"Is your name Haiphong?" Nick asked the butler. "Yes, Jack, he's here."

"Put him on."

"He wants to speak with you," Nick said, handing over the phone. Haiphong said "yes sir" crisply many times and hung up.

"May I send up the masseuse, sir? She's very good. Highly trained."

"Well, I . . ."

"I'll send her right up."

"Haiphong," Nick said, "can I ask you something?"

"Yes, sir."

"Is Mr. Bein *connected* somehow with this hotel?"

"All ACT guests and out-of-town clients stay at the Encomium, sir."

"Ah," Nick said.

"I'll send Bernie right up."

Nick sat back in a chaise longue and sipped his vodka negroni and looked out the window at the sun setting over Santa Monica and the ocean. The Campari and vodka was just starting to make him comfortably numb when Haiphong knocked to announce that Bernie had arrived. She was in her mid-twenties, pretty, muscular, and blond, with a big California smile—"*Hi* there!—in a white V-necked leotard.

The few times he'd indulged in massage—never in a "massage" parlor—Nick had always felt a little awkward, but Bernie put him at ease with her friendly, open manner and soon he was starkers on the slanted table, with a towel over his privies. She gave him a massage menu—Swedish, Shiatsu, hot oil, Tibetan, etc.—but strongly recommended something called NMT, or Neuro-Muscular Therapy, which, she said, had been invented by a much-wounded Vietnam veteran who, fed up with Western medicine, had studied Oriental healing techniques. It wasn't very relaxing; in fact it caused Nick significant, groaning, teeth-clenching pain as she knuckled into his vertebrae, kneaded his sternocleidomastoids and traps, crunched his lumbar region with her elbows, and then pinched his skin till it burned—in order, she explained, to bring the blood up to the surface. This last torture she called "bindegewebs," a technique that had been invented by the Germans; *naturlich*.

She put on a tape called *Pelagic Adagios*. New Age muzak consisting of squealing humpback whales and synthesized musical gibberish. Actually, it was pleasant enough, since it took his mind off the pain. After pressing her thumb tips along the rims of his eye sockets, producing an aura of light—aggrieved signals from the optic nerve, no doubt—she maneuvered his head off the edge of the table and put his face down into a "face cradle." With the table slanted up at his legs, the blood was soon puddling in his sinuses, making him feel as if he had a severe head cold. She stood, bending over his head as she attacked his lower back, her breasts grazing the top of his head. Back and forth, back and forth. After a few minutes of this he had to start counting backward from one hundred in intervals of seven, a delaying tactic that he'd learned many years ago. He lay there, facedown, snuffling through his clotted nasal passages like a truffle pig, listening to humpbacks squealing and gamboling in the deep.

"Do you like the music, Nick?"

"Urhh."

"I love whales. They're the most majestic of the creatures, don't you think?"

"Rhhh."

"I can't *believe* that the Japanese are going to start hunting them again."

"Wrrhl."

"You kind of have to be sort of careful saying that here."

"Nrrll mhh?"

"Have you ever swum with dolphins, Nick?"

"Nrnh." Where was *this* going?

"My boyfriend and I did, a couple of weekends ago." Aha. Boyfriend. Code for *Don't get any ideas. This is strictly professional.*

"There's a place north of San Diego where you can swim with dolphins for ten dollars. Mark and I were out riding on his motorcycle. He has a Harley-Davidson. A big one?" She had the habit of turning everything into a question, even the most basic declarative sentences, just in case you weren't able to follow *along?* "He's in the navy, stationed there. He's a SEAL? He can't talk about what he does. Anyway, he didn't want to swim with the dolphins, but I really wanted to, so we did. Their skin is really incredible and soft, and when they breathe, it's like they're sighing? They go, *Poosh.* That's what they sound like. It was so sensual, you know? Riding on them, holding on to the fin? It was almost . . ." She sighed. "Mark didn't like them. He kept punching them whenever they came up to him. The man who owned the place got angry and told him to get out, then Mark said he was going to throw him in with the dolphins."

More code: *My boyfriend is a short-tempered, highly trained professional killer. What was that about a hand job?*

"But I stayed in," she continued, "I could have stayed in there *forever,* it was so wonderful? The other night I even dreamed about it. I was riding dolphins in the moonlight, leaping up and down over

163

waves. No swimsuit on or anything, and the amazing feel of his skin on mine. And him sighing? *Push* . . . I woke up all excited? And there's Mark next to me, snoring. Mark *really* snores? And when I tell him about it, he gets angry? I bought him this thing for his birthday, it's like a microphone that you clip on to your jammy tops and it goes to this thing like a wristwatch, only you strap it to your arm, and every time you snore it like zaps you with a little electricity? And he got so *angry?* It ruined the evening. Everyone went home early. Mark can get so angry at times? You'd think a Navy SEAL would get all his anger out at work?"

"Yurnh."

She was working on his neck muscles with her thumbs and forefingers. "Your bands are hypercontracted, Nick. You're kind of tense."

"Urnh." Her breasts were pressing against his head again. 100 . . . 93 . . . 86 . . .

"Would you like me to relax you totally, Nick?"

"Hurnh?" Was this an honest-to-goodness question?

"Mr. Bein said to take *real* good care of you."

He saw a large Navy SEAL—a large, angry Navy SEAL—dripping wet, face blackened, framed in the doorway, a gigantic Ginsu knife in his hands. . . . 79 . . . 72 . . . 65 . . .

"Would you mind if I took this off? I feel real *warm* all of a sudden?"

. . . 65 . . .

"Ohh, that's much better. Is that better for you, Nick?"

"Nick," Jack Bein said with blasting intensity in the lobby early the next morning. The face that Nick had seen on the big-screen limo TV yesterday turned out to be connected to a short but muscular body in a linen suit with a bit of expensive turquoise silk protruding from the breast pocket. A watch worth a year's factory wages was gleamingly clasped outside the shirt cuff of his right hand. "Saves time," Jack said. "You don't have to pull it out from under the cuff. I figure over the course of my life I'll save two hundred man-hours."

Jack looked to the women bodyguards and made a question mark with his face, so it became Nick's turn to explain his odd accessorizing. Jack was very impressed.

"We had to do that for Jeff two years ago. Maybe you remember."

Nick didn't. "One of his former martial arts instructors went a little nuts. He had some idea that Jeff was going to make him into the next Steven Seagal. Personally, I think Jeff could've cleaned his clock, but when you're talking about a two-hundred-fifty-pound Korean with more black belts than Liz Taylor, you don't want to take chances, do you? Did you sleep okay? Did you get your massage? Was it Bernie who did you?"

Nick mumbled embarrassedly that yes, Bernie.

"Nice kid. And don't worry about the Navy boyfriend. He's big, but harmless. He was one of the ones they sent into Baghdad during Desert Storm to try to kill Saddam Hussein. They missed him by like five minutes. Know why? He was at his girlfriend's getting laid. Bombs coming down like rain and he's getting his rocks off. What a schmuck. No wonder he lost the war. No one's supposed to know that, by the way. *I'm* not even supposed to know that, but we're putting her through college. What's the matter, something wrong with your breakfast? You're jet-lagged. It's ten in D.C. Try some vitamin B, Jeff swears by it. Do you want an injection? How is it, living in D.C.? Is it all right? The new guy, is he going to make it?" Nick gathered he meant the President of the United States. "Frankly, Jeff is a little disappointed in him. Jeff went all *out* for him. Introduced him to all the right people. Jeff is the one who introduced him to Barbra. Other people have taken credit for it, but it was Jeff who made it happen. I shouldn't be telling you that, but I like you, so I'm telling you."

They drove in Jack's car, a red Dodge Viper, a muscle car on steroids. Jack explained that he was trying to do what he could for the U.S. economy. "Jeff *strongly* believes in America. That's why he's so excited by this project. It's a chance to help a truly American industry. What could be more American than tobacco, right?"

"Absolutely," Nick said, relieved finally to be talking about tobacco.

"So what do you think of the new building?"

It loomed, frantically, like a Mormon temple, occupying an entire city block, a crystal palace of curving mirrors.

"We had some problems after it was first built. The mirrors were reflecting the sun down onto the street in such a way that it was cooking the pedestrians. A couple actually had to be taken to Cedars-

Sinai and treated for hyperpyrexia. Not that you get many pedestrians in L.A. But don't want to cook the ones you have. We had to redo a section of the outside, and let me tell you, it was not cheap."

"It's very nice," Nick said, sensing that a compliment was awaited.

"Tell Jeff how much you like it. He put a lot of himself into this building. And you know something? It *shows*."

Nick looked up and saw the Viper reflected on the shimmery wall of ACT's headquarters. "Not bad for someone who started out in the mailroom," he said.

"I'll tell you something. We now have foreign *governments* coming to us."

"Really? Which ones?"

"I really shouldn't be talking about this, Nick. Point is, you're right—Jeff is a very long way from the mailroom."

They drove past the main entrance, which was flanked by significant Nanomako Yaha sculptures.

"Very nice," Nick said.

"Those? Those were an office-warming present from Deke Cantrell."

"That was generous."

Jack laughed. "Generous? Please. Deke Cantrell made enough from *Spud* to buy Nanomako Yaha's frozen corpse. Don't get me wrong. Deke is a tremendously talented human being and an extremely decent human being, despite what you hear, but the fact of the matter is, before Jeff took him on, he was a face. Now he's a name. He gets ten to twelve per film."

"Still, nice presents."

"It's not the thought that counts. It's the money." Jack laughed. "We're not going in the main entrance. We call it the Potemkin entrance. Very few people use it. Want to know why? The other agencies rent rooms in that building across, there. They keep people with binoculars and telescopes to see who's coming and going. Sometimes, just to fuck with their heads, we hire doubles of famous actors to walk in. Drives C.A.A., William Morris, and I.C.M. *crazy*. They think their clients are defecting. I *really* should not be talking about that. Anyway, now that we're advising foreign governments, we'll probably get real spies watching across the street. Do you know any spies in Washington?"

"We have some former spooks on staff," Nick said. "I shouldn't be telling you that."

"We've got this CIA movie deal project in the works, it's going to be *very* big. The idea is the CIA thinks Franklin Roosevelt is too cozy with Stalin, so they kill him so Truman will get in and nuke the Japanese. Fabulous film."

"Sounds great. But I don't think the CIA existed back in 1945."

"It didn't?"

"I think it started in '47."

"It's a little late change the whole premise. Principal photography starts in two weeks. We'll have to fudge. What the hell, according to these surveys, high school students think Churchill was Truman's vice president. As a matter of fact, we were thinking of you in connection with the project."

"How's that?"

"Roosevelt smoked, right?"

"Yes he did," Nick said. "But I think we're looking for someone more contemporary."

"You're probably right. How many girls want to fuck a dead guy with polio?"

"Uh, right."

They parked in the underground garage and took an elevator. So far, Nick had only ridden in private elevators since arriving in L.A. "By the way," Jack said, "don't be nervous when you meet Jeff. You'd be surprised at the names of some of the people who've frozen up when they met him for the first time." He lowered his voice, which made Nick wonder if the elevator was bugged. "Tom Sampson, Cookie Perets . . . Rocco Saint Angelo?"

"Rocco Saint Angelo? Really?"

"Comatose. I thought I was going to have to start cracking ammonia pellets under his nose. But you'll be fine. Jeff is basically a very human person underneath."

The elevator doors opened to reveal a fish pond. Nick followed Jack across stepping-stones. Large white and red carp lazed beneath the surface. "That one over there," Jack whispered, "seven thousand dollars."

"Seven thousand? For a fish?"

"Go figure. No wonder sushi over there costs a hundred bucks *167* apiece. Do you like sushi? I worry about worms. They can go into your brain. Every time I eat sushi now, which you kind of have to do—right?—I think I'm going to end up like John Hurt in *Alien,* with the thing coming out of my chest. Anyway, the fish was a gift from Fiona Fontaine. Another face Jeff made into a name. That one over there, with the black speckles? *Twelve* thousand. From Kyle Kedman. Jeff got him the lead in *Mung,* and Columbia was set, and I mean *set,* on Tom Cruise for that part."

"Do you keep sharks in here?"

"Nah," Jack laughed. "We're very nice here."

They were met at the end of the stepping-stones by an extremely attractive, fiftyish woman who introduced herself with a handshake and "I work with Jeff." She whispered into Jack's ear. Jack took Nick by the arm and led him back to the water's edge. "His Serenity just placed a call to Jeff."

"His Serenity?"

"The Sultan of Glutan," Jack whispered. "New client."

"Aha," Nick said. "Richest man in the world."

"Not anymore." Jack grinned. "Just joking." He led Nick over to what appeared to be a waiting area, by the pond. Nick looked at the man sitting there reading *Golf Digest*. No. Was it . . . wow, it was.

"Sean!" Jack said. "So where's the kilt?" Jack introduced Nick, and for the first time in his life, Nick felt the tongue-tying terror of encountering a true movie star hero. He'd grown up on the man's movies. He could recite some of them by heart, practically. He'd dreamed of *being* him. And now here he was, at the other end of a handshake. He couldn't have been more pleasant and courtly, even seemed interested in Nick. For his part, Nick could manage only a rictus of a smile and nod vigorously to every remark. He and Jack talked a bit about the golf tournament he'd just played in, and then obliquely about the project he was obviously here to discuss with Jeff. After about twenty minutes the attractive woman reappeared to say that Jeff was off the phone and would see them.

"You mean," Nick whispered to Jack as they followed her, "that we're ahead of *him*?"

"You should have seen the waiting room yesterday," Jack said. "Goldie, Jack, *and* Mel."

Two doors of polished Burma teak carved with ideograms opened to reveal a vast, cathedral-like space, with a mind-boggling view of the city and the Pacific Ocean beyond. Jack whispered, "On a clear day, you can see Tokyo." At the center of it was a glass-top desk with nothing on it—now *that* was power: a totally clean desk—and behind it a man in his mid-forties, short, tanned, thinning hair, extremely fit, chest muscles bulging under a blue shirt that looked one size too small. He had a bland face, sparkly, gapped teeth, and pale laser eyes.

He smiled broadly and rose from his crystal throne and came out from around the desk to shake Nick's hand. "Jeff Megall," he said, surprising Nick again; most of the exalted pooh-bahs Nick had experienced tended to dispense with self-identification. *We all know who I am.* . . .

"How was your flight?" he asked.

"Fine, thank you."

"Jack, would you see that Mr. Naylor travels back to Washington on our plane? What about your hotel?"

"He's at the Encomium," Jack interjected.

"Good hotel," Jeff said. "Let us know what we can do." He gestured to a sofa. "May I offer you anything? Coffee? Tea? Mineral water?"

"If it's not too much trouble."

"How do you take it?"

"Black."

"Black mineral water?" He laughed. "Could we have some black coffee for Mr. Naylor?" He said it into the thin air; there was no one else in the room, and within seconds a woman, a very beautiful woman with long hair, long legs, and a short skirt, appeared with a steaming cup of perfect black coffee.

Jeff said, "Would you like an ashtray?"

"Oh, no," Nick said, "that's okay. I'm . . ."

"Please, it doesn't bother me in the least. In fact, I enjoy watching people smoke. It's so rare these days."

"Well," Nick said, "that's what I'm here to talk about."

"By the way, I thought you handled the kidnapping extremely well. It must have been an awful experience. But your statements to the media indicated a fineness of spirit. I congratulate you for that."

"Well . . ."

"I've been thinking about the tobacco industry as a result of your   *169* interest in working with us, and I've come to the conclusion that if things continue as they have been, the American tobacco farmer will vanish, and with him, a way of life."

"Yes," Nick said, "we're very concerned about that ourselves."

"So," Jeff said, "let's see what we can do to help these people."

Nick was *very* impressed. Jeff already had his reason: he wasn't in this for the money—he was in it to save the farmers. Nick had to ask it—out of collegial admiration, he just had to hear the answer: "You don't have any problems with the health question?"

Jeff responded without hesitation: "I don't have the answers on that. I'm not a doctor. I'm just a facilitator. All I do is bring creative people together. What information there is, is out there. People will decide for themselves. I can't make that decision for them. It's not my role. It would be morally presumptuous."

"Yes, right," Nick said. He was dazzled. The man was a *titan* of ambiguity. He could learn from this man.

"So," Jeff said, "why don't we talk. You're looking for some aggressive product placement."

"Jeff is too modest to mention this," Jack stepped in, "but he was the driving force behind product placement."

"Jack, Mr. Naylor did not fly all the way out here from Washington to listen to you recite my résumé."

"Excuse me, Jeff, but I think it's relevant for Nick to know that you pioneered the entire field of product placement. Nick, do you remember how in movies whenever someone drank a beer or soda, or whatever, either the label was generic or it was covered? Then gradually you started to see the labels? And now you can see them so close up you can read the ingredients? Jeff did that. I'm finished."

"That's why we came to ACT," Nick said. "We knew that Mr. Megall was the best."

"Forgive me. I wasn't sure you knew."

"Can we continue, Jack?" Jeff said in a tone of mild impatience. "Or do you want to tell Nick what position I played for the Bruins?"

"Continue, please."

"In point of fact," Jeff said, "we *were* the first to recognize the importance of product placement. What isn't so widely known is, and I know this surprises some people, but at the time, we did not do it to raise more investment."

"You didn't?" Nick said.

"Absolutely not. We wanted to involve the audience more fully in the character. People see their heroes up there on the screen. They want to know everything about them. Take James Bond. He drinks, what is it, a 'medium vodka dry martini shaken not stirred'? Don't you think people want to know what *kind* of vodka James Bond drinks? I can tell you this," said Jeff, "they *will* find out what kind of vodka James Bond drinks in the next James Bond movie."

"Aha," Nick said.

"Now, as it happens, the makers of that particular vodka—whatever it ends up being—are more than happy to participate financially in the creative process. But the money was all along a byproduct of a creative decision." He grinned. "It's nice when that happens."

Dazzling. Absolutely dazzling. The man made it sound as though product placement was crucial to character development. *Call me Ishmael, and hand me a Coca-Cola.*

"We were thinking maybe Mel Gibson," Nick said, blurting it out, unable to contain himself any longer.

"That might be difficult," Jeff said. "He just quit. You know, he's got six kids. Not that he couldn't live forever and smoke, but, listen, I know where you're coming from. Mel was a beautiful smoker. The best contemporary smoking I've seen was in *Lethal* One. He took that smoke in so far you weren't sure it was ever going to come out. And when it did, it was like the breath of a dragon."

"It made me want to start smoking again," Jack said. "I almost did, in fact."

"Remember, however," Jeff said, "that Mel was playing a cop on the edge, someone with some pretty severe psychological problems. What else does he stick in his mouth during that movie? The barrel of his gun. You see, today, when you see people smoking in films, it's generally a sign that there's something wrong with their lives. It's not Humphrey Bogart in *Casablanca* anymore." Nick shuddered as the image of Peter Lorre flickered past. Jeff continued, "It's Bobby de Niro playing a chain-smoking, tattooed psycho in *Cape Fear*, Andy Garcia smoking through a hole in his throat in *Dead Again*, Thelma and Louise lighting up and getting loaded then going out to the parking lot to blow the balls off a rapist. It can get *very* weird with cigarettes these days. Pat Hingle branding Anjelica with a cigarette in *The*

Grifters. Laura Dern and Nick Cage chain-smoking through *Wild at Heart,* talking about how their parents all died of lung cancer and cirrhosis. Nick Nolte in *Prince of Tides.* Definitely a man with problems. Or Harrison Ford in *Regarding Henry.* He goes into a convenience store to buy a pack of cigarettes and ends up on the floor with his brains splattered all over the place. He didn't even have time to read the surgeon general's warning. What message is being transmitted in these films, do you suppose? That smoking is cool? I think not."

"Exactly," Nick said. "We need a winner. A smoking role model."

"Yes. Set in the 1950s, before all the health stuff got out of hand."

"We'd *like* it to be contemporary," Nick said. "We want people to feel good about smoking now. *Everyone* felt good about smoking in the fifties, at least until they read *Reader's Digest.*"

Jeff rested his chin on steepled fingers. "We'd have to move quickly. Principal photography starts in two weeks. How do you feel about Franklin Delano Roosevelt? Talk about a role model. And a *very* elegant smoker. That holder, almost feminine . . ."

"*Beautiful* smoker," Jack said.

"We could fix the script. As a matter of fact . . ."

"What are you thinking?" Jack asked.

"That the cigarettes could be central. The CIA puts the poison in the cigarettes. The cigarettes become the McGuffin."

"*Brilliant,*" Jack said.

Nick said, "So FDR dies . . . from smoking?"

"Yeah, but not from cancer."

"I think I'd have a hard time selling that to my people."

"Yeah," Jeff smiled, "I can see where that might be a problem. Contemporary is good, but the mind-set is already hardened against it. The L.A. City Council just voted to ban smoking in restaurants here."

"I know," Nick said lugubriously. "Seven thousand restaurants."

"So much for the Constitution. It's late in the game for mainstream. . . . Wait a minute, wait a minute. . . ."

"What? What?" Jack said.

"That's it."

"*What?*" said Jack.

"The future."

"Brilliant," Jack said.

Jeff turned back to Nick. "I shouldn't really be telling you this, but UFA has a womjep sci-fi picture in development that's going to be very, *very* big."

" 'Womjep'?"

"Woman in jeopardy. *Alien* meets *Dune* meets *Star Wars* and Darth Vader is gay. A *screamer*. I've seen the script. It's a very funny part, an Oscar part. The hero is a disgraced space baron with an alien kid sidekick who can turn into anything. The girl is the emperor's daughter who's run away and gotten into some seriously bad company. It's called *Message from Sector Six*. The effects are going to be amazing. Half an *hour* of morphing. You know what morphing is? What they did in *Terminator 2*."

"They're calling it *Morph and Mindy*," Jack said.

"A million dollars per minute. They've already reserved advertising space on the fuselage of a space shuttle launch. They've budgeted a hundred and twenty million dollars. It will be the most expensive film ever made. And they're making it in *Mexico*."

"I heard they're already up to one-forty."

"It better be good. UFA is going to be wide open to product placement."

"Cigarettes?" Nick said. "In outer space?"

"It's the twenty-sixth century," Jeff said. "They're not bad for you anymore. In fact . . . in fact . . ."

"What?" Jack said.

"They're *good* for you. The *Sleeper* idea. That reminds me, I need to call Woody, though I don't know what I'm going to tell him. Jack, call Bill Hyman, Jerry Gornick, Voltan Zeig, set up a meeting for this afternoon."

"Done."

"I've gone blank. Ginseng depletion. Who's directing?"

"Chick Dextor."

"Going to be a loong shoot."

"Tell me about it."

"Nick," Jeff said, "this could be very exciting for all of us."

"I . . . but don't you explode if you light up in a spaceship? All that oxygen?"

"It's the twenty-sixth century. They've thought that through. That can be fixed with one line of script."

"It sounds like . . . I don't know . . ."

"Nick. The leads in this movie are Mace McQuade and Fiona Fontaine."

"No kidding."

"No kidding. Can you see them, sharing a postsex cigarette in their spaceship, in a round bed with satin sheets and a clear bubble top. The galaxies go whizzing by, the smoke curls weightlessly upward. That doesn't prime your pump? You don't think that would sell a few cartons?"

"Yeah," Nick said. "I guess it would."

"I'll tell you something else. It's not my role to get involved in this part of it, unless I'm asked, but if I were you I would *right away* get started on launching a whole new brand of cigarettes and launch it simultaneously with the movie. Sector Sixes. No one has ever done that with cigarettes."

Jeff stood. The meeting was over. He shook Nick's hand. "You've done something to me that I try very hard to resist. You've gotten me emotionally involved."

Outside, Sean was working on a crossword puzzle. In the elevator, Jack said, "You should be pleased with yourself. Jeff *really* liked you."

18

Lorne Lutch lived on an avocado farm sixty miles east of L.A. Feeling the need to have his own hands on the wheel, Nick dispensed with Mahmoud and his Great White Whale and drove himself in a rented red Mustang, with his bodyguards following in their own rented tan sedan with the half million dollars of cash. Maybe Lutch would appreciate the symbolism of Nick's showing up in a Mustang. Or maybe he'd come out with a double-barreled shotgun and blow Nick out of his bucket seat. It could go either way.

He'd read Gomez O'Neal's amazingly thorough briefing book on the man's personal and financial history, detailed enough to make the wiretappers at the National Security Agency blush—where *did* Gomez get all this stuff?—already he knew to the penny how much Lorne Lutch was carrying on his Visa and MasterCard and how much albumin he had in his last urine test. Gomez's boys had their fingers in every urine test that affected tobacco, avid for traces of dope.

This was a very strange mission, one he would only have taken on for the Captain. The night before, he'd placed a call to Polly, the only person, aside from Bobby Jay, to whom he could turn for pointers on bribing dying product spokesmen. Polly had whistled when he told her what he was up to.

"Hm," she said, "if I were you I'd put a get well card in it, leave the bag by the front door, ring the bell, and run like hell." Actually, not a bad idea.

While he was on the phone with Polly, Jeannette called, all sex and heavy breathing, wanting to know if she should be jealous of Fiona

Fontaine yet. And while she was on, Heather called, lighting up the third button on the phone console and making Nick feel like an air traffic sex controller.

Heather wasn't calling to whisper sweet num-nums into his ear long-distance. She was all business, except to complain about the Washington heat and the cab drivers. Most cab drivers in Washington are recent arrivals from countries where driving is the national blood sport; confronted in the rear-view mirror with an attractive female passenger with a nice figure in a thin summer dress, they tend completely to ignore the road ahead while suavely propositioning their passengers with the likes of *You like Haiti food?* Today, Heather had had enough of being hit on by sweaty Tonton Macoutes. What she wanted from Nick was what he knew about the bill Ortolan K. Finisterre was reportedly gearing up to introduce. They were being very close-mouthed about it on the Hill, and that was *very* unusual. She said that the *Sun* had called her back for more interviews, so now was definitely the time for her reporting to shine. Nick said he was a little out of the loop out here in Hollywood, but would see what he could find out from Leg Affairs.

"By the way," Heather said, "what *are* you doing out there?"

"Not much," he said, "just pumping up our West Coast office. Morale-boosting visit with the troops."

"Uh-huh." Silence. She was too good a reporter to swallow that. The Senate gearing up to something big, and you're in L.A., for no good reason? "What are you really doing?"

"Off the record?"

"Okay." She sounded a little offended.

"I'm out here to bribe the Tumbleweed Man, who is dying of lung cancer, to stop attacking us in the media."

Heather laughed. "You know, I wouldn't put it past you."

It left Nick a little unsettled that she hadn't believed him. Polly was annoyed at having been put on hold for five minutes.

"I was talking to a reporter," Nick said, invoking a reliable Mod Squad dispensation.

"Heather Holloway?" said Polly.

"No," said Nick, "Just . . . a reporter."

" 'A reporter'?"

"I'm not sure I even remember her name."

Why, he wondered, after getting off, was he lying about Heather to Polly?

The Lutch avocado spread was a modest one called Fault-Line Farm, a name that made sense when Nick saw a gaping crevasse across the scrubby field in front of the house, rimmed by a tangle of dead avocado trees.

He took the attaché case from his bodyguards and ordered them to stay in their car. They argued about letting him disappear behind enemy lines without protection. Mame, the detail commander, made a persuasive case that Lutch had very little to lose by shooting Nick. Nick considered bringing her along for a moment, but then contemplated the headline, TUMBLEWEED MAN SLAIN IN SHOOT-OUT WITH TOBACCO SPOKESMAN'S SECURITY GUARD and decided it would be good to avoid that, so he put his foot down and started up the steps alone. A large Rhodesian Ridgeback lazed in the heat on the porch, barely looking up at Nick as he approached. There were a number of steel bottles on the porch labeled OXYGEN.

Nick took a deep breath and banged on the screen door. Today, he said to himself, you will earn your salary.

He felt a poke in his back, and heard a croaky voice say, "Don't move or I'll blow a hole the size of a grapefruit in you. Now raise your hands and keep 'em where I can see 'em."

Nick did as instructed.

"Now turn around. *Slow.*"

Nick slowly rotated and found himself facing Lorne Lutch himself. He was still recognizable as the Tumbleweed Man, even fifty pounds lighter and with yellow skin. He was in a bathrobe and slippers and wouldn't have looked at all threatening without the shotgun that was aimed at Nick's stomach.

He peered at Nick. "You're Nick Naylor, aren't you?"

"Yes sir. I was just . . ." Passing through, carrying half a million dollars in cash. "Do you, could I, do you have a minute? If it's inconvenient, I could, uh, come back."

Lutch said suspiciously, "What do you want here?"

"Just . . . to talk."

"All right," he said, lowering the shotgun. He pushed open the screen door with the muzzle. They sat. "Didn't mean to startle you," he said. "But someone's been following me."

Gomez?

He croaked, "Roberta, company." It made him cough. And cough, and cough.

Mrs. Lutch entered, took one look at Nick, and went cold as a bucket of liquid nitrogen. Lutch continued to cough, leaving Nick to stand there waiting for it to subside so that he could be introduced. It was awkward, frankly. When Lorne's coughing showed no sign of subsiding, Nick mouthed a "Hello."

"What do *you* want?" she glowered with such intensity that Nick almost regretted leaving his Praetorians outside in the car. He hadn't counted on being shot by the *wife*.

"Now now, Roberta," Lutch wheezed, wiping his mouth, "let's not be rude to our guest. I don't suppose he's come all the way out here for no good reason. Remember he's the one talked the company out of suing me for breach of contract."

"I'd as soon feed him to the hogs as have him in my house." Fixing Nick with one last copper-jacketed shot of eyeball, she turned her back and started to leave. On her way out, she stopped and said, "You want some more morphine, hon?"

"No thanks," Lorne said, "I'm doing just fine. But maybe our guest would like something."

"Some morphine would be fine, thank you," Nick said. Mrs. Lutch disappeared, probably to mix Drano in with Nick's morphine.

"I'll tell you," Lorne said, settling back into a big, torn armchair, "about the only *nice* thing about dying of cancer is the dope. The *dreams* I've been having . . . and in technicolor."

"Must be amazing," Nick said.

"Do you know what the word 'heroin' comes from? It's German. It was the Krauts who first come up with it, back in the nineteenth century; nicest thing Germany's ever done for the world, let me tell you. *Heroisches.* That's what it made people feel like. Heroic. Do you know, when I first started in on the chemotherapy, people for miles around here started bringing me marijuana brownies. Keeps the nausea down. You can get it in pill form, but they make you jump through flaming hoops for it and then they put it in sesame seed oil so you won't get high. Don't you love that? God forbid people dying in pain should have a little pleasure on the way out. Anyhow, I got about ten pounds of pot brownies in the freezer."

Nick thought: wouldn't Gomez love to know that. TUMBLEWEED MAN ARRESTED ON DRUG CHARGES.

"Reckon I must have enough to get me sent away for the rest of my life," Lutch said. "You want one?"

"No, thanks," Nick said. "Just the morphine. I better not mix."

Lutch laughed, which made him cough again. This one went on longer than the last. Mrs. Lutch came running out with a nebulizer.

"*Excuse* me," Lutch said, recovering finally. "Do you smoke?"

"No," Nick said. "Since the kidnapping, I haven't been able to."

"I read about that. Saw you on—weren't you on the Larry King show? Roberta said you were on same night as me. Funny we didn't run into each other in the studio."

"Yeah," Nick said.

"That must've been something. My doctor said you were one lucky son of a bitch." Lutch chuckled. "Said a few other things, too, I won't share with you. You know, doctors used to *promote* cigarettes."

"That's right," Nick said, "twenty thousand six hundred seventy-nine physicians say, 'Luckies are less irritating.' "

"I wonder how *they're* doing?" Lutch said caustically. "Strange business. In the early fifties, they had the first cancer scare, so they started making filter cigarettes. Then they got worried that men would think filter-tips were for pussies. That's where I came in."

"You were great," Nick said. "I used to want to be you. I mean, when I was growing up. We all wanted to grow up and be cowboys."

"Don't I know it. You know a song by George Jones, 'Hell Stays Open All Night Long'? I listen to it over and over."

"You're being kind of tough on yourself, aren't you?"

"Last year, after I got diagnosed, I flew East to attend the annual stockholders' meeting of Total Tobacco. And I stood up and told them that they at least ought to limit their advertising. And do you know what the president said to me?"

Nick did know, but he shook his head.

"He said, 'We're certainly sorry to hear about your medical problem. Without knowing your medical history, I don't think I can comment further.' Then they tried to pretend I never worked for them. I couldn't believe it. Even when I showed reporters my pay stubs, the company went on saying it wasn't me in those photographs. Then when I kept on making a fuss, they told me they were going to sue me—for breach of contract! I guess you were the one to put a halt to that."

"Yeah," Nick said. "I told them it was a pretty dumb idea. Well, they can be assholes, there's no doubt about that."

"Tell you something else. I never even *smoked* Tumbleweeds. I smoked Kools."

Nick laughed.

"You look like a nice enough fellah. What are you doing working for these assholes?"

Somehow the usual business about needing to pay the mortgage didn't seem appropriate here. Nick looked about at the things on Lorne's wall—rodeo trophies, stuffed trout, family photographs mounted on brightly lacquered wood—and said, "I'm good at it. I'm better at doing this than I ever was at doing anything else."

"Well hell, son, I was good at shooting Koreans, but I didn't make it a *career*."

Nick laughed. Lutch looked at him for what felt like a long time, and said, "I suppose we all got to pay the mortgage somehow."

Nick could have kissed him.

"I was good at playing my role. People used to recognize me and ask me for my autograph. I don't know how much that's going to count for at the Pearly Gates, but I was just a dumb cowboy who wanted to be in pictures, whereas *you*," he smiled slyly, "look like about twenty thousand dollars' worth of college education." The smile was gone. "So why'd you come all the way out here for?"

"Good question," Nick said, staring balefully at the attaché case.

"You here to talk me into shutting up? Is that what's in that case of yours?"

"Yes, basically," Nick said. "No, not basically. That's exactly it."

Lutch gave him a steely stare. "Look here," he said, "my dignity ain't for sale."

"No," Nick said, "it's more complicated than that."

"How do you mean?"

"This is supposed to be an outright gift, no strings attached. The taxes have all been paid. You get to keep it no matter what you do. You're free to go bad-mouthing us. The idea is that you'll feel so guilty about trashing us that you might just say no the next time a producer for Oprah calls."

Lutch stared at Nick. "Were you supposed to tell me all this?"

"No. Just apologize, give you the money, and leave."

"Then why are you telling me this?"

"I don't really know," Nick said. "Not for reasons you might think. I don't believe in the Pearly Gates, or an open-twenty-four-hours hell. I like the guy I work for, the one who cooked up this idea, even though I told him we ought to just leave you alone. He's just freaked out, like the rest of them. And, I'll probably go on doing what I do. So I don't know why I'm doing it. Beats me."

"You're a strange fellah, Nick."

"I know people who'd agree with that. No," Nick said, "I should be honest, for once. I know why I told you."

"Why?"

"Because this way, you'll take the money."

"Why would I do that?"

"Because you're mad. The first thing you'll do is call the *L.A. Times*, KBLA and tell them to get out here right away."

"You're damn right about that."

"By the way, don't forget CNN. And *insist* on Bonnie Dalton, their top L.A. person. Do you remember her from the cracks in Hoover Dam story last year? She's got the perfect touch for something like this. She does very good controlled outrage without going overboard. Also, she's good-looking. Bonnie Dalton. Tell them no Bonnie, no story, they can watch it on KBLA."

"Okay," Lutch said. "Bonnie Dalton."

"Now if I were you, I'd open up the case and dump all the cash out onto the floor."

"Why?"

"It'll look much more effective. Here, look." Nick dumped the money out. "And shake it like this to get the last bundle out. Also, it would be great if you could cough while you're doing it. The whole time you're dumping, you should be denouncing, sort of build up to the last piece of silver. You might even call it that. You know, as in the thirty pieces of silver, from the Bible, the Judas payoff. Then you tell them what you're going to do with it."

"What *am* I going to do with it?"

"You're going to give it to the cancer ranch. Of course."

"Well, I do have a family. . . ."

"Whoa, Lorne. You can't *keep* the money."

"Why the hell not?"

"How's that going to look? Denouncing us and then keeping it? It's blood money. Look at it." They both stared at the bundles of hundred-dollar bills on the floor. Lot of money.

"I'm going to have to talk this over with Roberta," Lutch said, shifting uneasily in his seat.

Nick drove back to L.A. fast. He got pulled over for going ninety-two miles an hour. The cop wrote him up for the full amount. Nick didn't argue.

The next morning Gomez O'Neal called Nick at the Encomium. "We just heard that Lorne Lutch canceled out of a local TV talk show for next week. Nice going."

The Captain called five minutes later. "Gomez O'Neal tells me it worked. I knew it would. Good *work,* son."

BR called. "I gather things are going well out there."

Nick hung up and called Lutch. "Lorne," he said, annoyed, "what's going on?"

"Roberta and I are still thinking about it," he said.

"Look, it's not going to do any good to denounce us a week or a month from now. Outrage is like fish, it's got to be fresh. Do it today. It really should have been yesterday."

"Suppose," Lutch said, "I denounced you for giving me a hundred thousand dollars? Would that be all right with your people?"

19

Jack Bein called to say Jeff had news and wanted a meeting at seven the next morning. "That's not too early for you, is it?" Nick told him that in Washington, too, business started early.

"I spoke with everyone involved in *Sector Six,*" Jeff said, sipping on a cup of ginseng tea. "I told them what we wanted, and," he smiled cynically to let Nick know that their response had come as no surprise, "they told me what *they* want, which is a lot of money. An amount of money that," he chuckled smoothly, "surprised even me. And I like to think that I do not surprise easily."

"How big an amount of money?" Nick asked.

"This is a movie about outer space. The sum of money is appropriately astronomical, you might say."

"Well," Nick said, "my industry does forty-eight billion a year, so I'm probably not going to faint. So what are we talking about?"

"For Mace to smoke, ten. For Fiona and Mace to smoke, twenty-five. I said to them, wait a minute, so where's this extra five coming from? Usually when you buy two of something, there's a discount. They said it was for the synergy. These are not dumb people. They got it right away: Mace and Fiona lighting up after some cosmic fucking in the bubble suite is going to sell a *lot* of cigarettes."

Twenty . . . five? "We only want to rent their lungs for two hours," Nick said. "We're not asking them to get cancer."

"That's funny," Jack Bein said.

"I wouldn't take these numbers as being set in concrete," Jeff said. "The point is, they want to play. This is a very expensive film, even with the additional financing. I shouldn't be telling you this, but the Sultan of Glutan is looking to expand his presence in this country, and is getting into the film business."

"Getting *into* it is right," Jack said.

"The reason I mention this, in the strictest confidence," Jeff went on, "is that I wanted to ascertain if you'd have any problem being financially co-involved with the sultan."

So that's why he's telling me all this, thought Nick. Jeff Megall did not make small talk, or lightly breach confidences. The sultan had been in the news lately. They had discovered more oil on one of the more remote islands in his archipelago. It was inhabited by several thousand primitive tribesmen who quaintly thought the oil drillers were raping their earth-mother by sinking their shafts into her, and so, logically, hacked them to pieces. The sultan, being the richest man on earth and therefore impatient with inconvenience, responded by ordering his air force to bomb the island until nothing remained alive on it but the especially hardy species of lizard, *Komodo terribilis*. The U.N. had denounced the action, and world opinion was strongly against him; so much so, in fact, that a half-dozen international celebrities had cancelled out of his annual yacht party in Costa Splendida that year.

"Let me add," Jeff said, "that the sultan's participation in the financing will be completely anonymous. We're doing it through one of his off-*off*-shore corporations." He spread his hands, palms up, in the international gesture of helplessness. "As for the controversy, that's not for me to say. I try very hard not to get involved in politics."

"Speaking of which," Jack said, "have you decided whether you're going to his birthday, yet?"

This would be the President's birthday, thought Nick. Heather had mentioned it. A big affair, on the South Lawn of the White House. It was being done as a benefit, of course, for homeless children. These days you couldn't just throw a party for yourself.

"I don't know," Jeff said with an air of exhaustion. "I don't know yet. I just don't."

"It's tomorrow, Jeff."

"Yes it is. Maybe I'll be there. I don't know. The whole thing to me is very . . . sad."

184   Once again Nick was dazzled. The death of thousands of Glutanese

had been displaced by a discussion of whether Jeff was going to attend a party for a President who had disappointed him by not staying as a guest at his house, all because the press was making a thing out of how he was star-struck by Hollywood. Yet clearly Jeff was a man of sensitivity: he had extended to Nick the professional courtesy of asking one mass murderer if he had any objection to co-sponsoring a movie with another mass murderer. In a crazy, mixed-up world, Nick reflected, it amounted to manners.

"So," Jeff said, "would that be a problem for you?"

BLOODY SULTAN AND TOBACCO COMPANIES TEAM UP IN MOVIE DEAL. Nick sighed. "I'd better run it by my people."

"Of course," Jeff said, sounding disappointed.

Nick sensed that he was not used to being told, *I'll get back to you.*

"And those numbers," Jeff said, setting down his cup of ginseng. "You'll want to run those by your people too," in a tone of mild, but unmistakable disparagement.

It was time, Nick reckoned, for some counter-peckerflexing. A forty-eight-billion-dollar industry had no apologies to make for the size of *its* penis.

"Of course," Nick smiled, "those numbers are *completely* out of line. Especially in light of the fact that we're being asked to participate in the venture with someone who's being called the Hitler of the South Pacific. Not that we get involved in politics, either."

Jeff stared. Jack finally broke the silence. "There's a lot that didn't come out in the press. He *did* offer to relocate them, first. And what did they do? Stuck a spear through his emissary. My understanding is that if you're a sultan, you just can't let that kind of behavior happen, cause pretty soon *everybody's* going to be in your face. It's not like being governor of, I don't know, Kansas."

"I think we're getting a little off the track here," Jeff said. "I personally can say that in my dealings with the sultan, he's been a very reasonable and sensitive individual. As for those numbers, we can get them down. We're all looking for comfort. At the same time, Nick, we have to be realistic. We're talking about two of the hottest stars in the business, supernovas. And some technical considerations. Like why they don't blow themselves up when they light up in a spaceship. We're still going to be talking serious money."

"Uh-huh," Nick said. "Of course we'll want everything all spelled out, contractually. Script approval. Brand of cigarettes, number of cigarettes smoked, spoken references to the cigarettes, specifically to how enjoyable they are to smoke. And so forth. In fact, for this kind of money, I'm certain that we'll want it specified how many puffs they take off each cigarette. Can Mace McQuade blow smoke rings?"

"I don't know," Jeff said. "I don't have that information."

"For this kind of money, we'd want smoke rings."

Jack said, "He learned how to scuba dive for *Kraken*. I don't see a problem learning to do smoke rings."

"Good," Nick said. "Because for the kind of money we seem to be talking about, my people would expect some very serious smoking in Sector Six."

"Let's see what we can work out," Jeff said. "We'll be in touch."

This time, Jack Bein remained behind with Jeff. Stepping across the fish pond, Nick felt like one of the people in the James Bond movies who, having displeased Number One, are dropped through the trapdoor into the shark pool; but he made it to the elevators without being nibbled to death by expensive carp.

Back at the Encomium, there were urgent messages from the Captain, BR, Heather, Polly, Jeannette, and Jack Bein. He wasn't sure whose to return first, but with phone messages, as with life, it's always prudent to give priority to the person paying your salary.

The Captain was out of the hospital, but sounded as though he should be back in it. He was not in a good way.

"I assume you heard this . . . *grotesque* news," he said. Nick said he'd been in a meeting all morning with Jeff Megall. The Captain didn't even ask how that was going.

"Finisterre?"

"Means end of the earth, in French," the Captain said, pausing to swallow something. Nitroglycerin? "That's appropriate. Gomez O'Neal reported in last night. One of his Senate people finally dug it out. Wasn't easy, or cheap. The son of a bitch is going to introduce a bill by the end of the week mandating that cigarette packages carry a skull and crossbones."

"Ouch," Nick said. Of course—the Hispanic housekeeper. A warning that even non-English speakers could understand. Should have been able to see it coming a mile away. Was he losing his touch?

"We're going to look like *rat* poison," the Captain said. "You better get back on the first flight home."

He called BR. He wasn't taking the news as emotionally as the Captain, but he was on edge. There was a definite smell of paranoia in the air. The first thing he asked was if Nick was on cellular. Even after Nick assured him that he was on a ground line, BR refused to reveal how, precisely, Gomez had come by this gruesome intelligence, but he did say that it was solid. Furthermore, he told Nick, Finisterre had gotten Representative Lamont C. King of Texas—one of the more conservative boll weevils in the Congress—to co-sponsor the bill in the House. An odd couple. King loathed Finisterre; but Finisterre sat on the Military Base Closings Commission.

"We did a quick and dirty whip count," BR said, "showing the bill *will* pass. Don Stookey is predicting a twenty-five percent drop in all tobacco stocks within a week."

"Ouch," Nick said.

"It's going to get pretty hairy," BR said. "You better get back on the next flight."

Nick called Heather. He hoped she hadn't called about this. She hadn't.

"Two FBI agents were here to see me," she said in a strange tone of voice. "They were asking questions."

"That's what FBI agents do," Nick said. "It's their job. They're trying to find the people who tried to kill me."

"They wanted to know how well I knew you."

"Oh?"

"They stopped just short of asking if we'd slept together. *Exactly how well do you* know *Mr. Naylor?* There were two of them. A good cop and a bad cop. The bad cop did most of the talking. Monmaney. Handsome, if your taste runs to wolves. He wanted to know quote what sort of person unquote you are."

"Well," Nick said, "I suppose there's nothing too unusual in that."

"He asked if you were especially ambitious."

"Ambitious?"

"Uh-huh. They also wanted to know if I thought you were still quote psychologically grappling unquote with having told the world that the President was dead. Hello?"

"What did you tell them?"

"Obviously, I refused to tell them anything."

"You refused? Why?"

"Because, I'm a reporter. Reporters don't divulge things to FBI agents."

"*Divulge?* What's to *divulge?* They were just asking routine questions."

"You call those routine?"

"But now they're going to think you're protecting me."

"I'm not protecting you. I'm protecting a principle."

"But why couldn't you just tell them the truth? *That's* a principle, isn't it?"

"Listen to Mr. There's No Link Between Smoking and Disease. Honestly. Hello?"

"I'm here," Nick sighed, massaging the bridge of his nose with his thumb and forefinger.

"Why are you getting so worked up? You sound . . ."

"What?"

"Guilty."

"Guilty? Guilty of what? Covering myself with nicotine patches? I almost died!"

"Calm down. They're just fishing. They don't have anything." Pause. "Do they?"

"Heather," Nick said, "*what* are you *talking* about?"

"Hey, *I* don't know why the FBI is asking questions like these."

"Well you might be a little more skeptical. Jesus, most reporters I know are so skeptical they don't believe in anything. Except Mother Teresa, and some I know think *she's* on the take."

"Hold *on.* How did Mother Teresa enter into a conversation about the outraged principles of a tobacco lobbyist?"

"Thank you," Nick said sullenly. "You're really being tremendously supportive today."

"I'm *going* to help. By writing about this."

Nick said, "You're what?"

"We'll put the FBI on the defensive. Let them explain why they're harassing kidnap victims. Politically Correct persecution. Escalation in the continuing vilification of tobacco. Tobacco as the new evil empire. I'm surprised you hadn't thought of that. It's a great story."

"You want to *write* about this?"

"I *have* to write about this."

"And tell everyone that I'm, I'm, I'm under suspicion by the FBI? Uh-uh. No thank you. I think not. Hello? Heather? Heather, this conversation is off the record. Heather?"

"Stop being so paranoid. This will be very positive for your side. Now, have they approached you directly yet? Hello?"

He called Polly. She sounded alarmed.

"Nick," she said, "thank God. I've been trying to reach you. Uh, you're not on cellular are you? Good, because the FBI came to see me yesterday. They . . ."

. . . had asked her the same questions as Heather. Now Nick *was* paranoid. He knew the FBI was good, but how did they know about Heather, and Polly? How did they know all this *personal* stuff?

"Don't worry," Polly said. "I didn't tell them anything."

"What do you mean?"

"Is there anything I can do? Marty Berlin says the lawyer to have is Geoff Aronow. He's at Arnold and Porter. Expensive, but really good."

"Polly . . ." But Nick was too morally exhausted to proclaim his innocence twice in an hour. Then it occurred to him that if the FBI was listening in on this conversation—and God knows they were able to listen in on ground lines, too—he'd better at least go through the motions of being outraged. Yet Polly, dear Polly, only made it worse by continuing to say that she didn't *care,* it didn't *matter,* she was behind him 110 percent. If there was a phrase to titillate the tappers, surely it was that, from a woman: *I'm behind you 110 percent.*

Jeannette hadn't been questioned by the FBI, thank God. She'd called because she'd wanted to "do a quick mind-meld" with him on the Finisterre bombshell. She was wondering if it wouldn't make sense to leak it themselves ahead of Finisterre's announcement, so that they could give it their own spin: *Pitiful, isn't it, that Senator Finisterre, in order to get people's minds off the fact that he's getting divorced yet again, is grandstanding with this hysterical nonsense, and in the process, insulting the intelligence of the American people by treating them like illiterate rats?* Not bad, Nick thought. Smart, Jeannette. He complimented her. She purred, "I have a good mentor."

"By the way," he said, sounding suavely casual—no sense in BR freaking out at a time like this over one of his employees being under suspicion—"the FBI is apparently poking around asking dumb personal questions."

"What jerks," she said.

"Yeah, but do me a favor. If they come to you, tell them everything."

"Everything?" she laughed.

"Well," Nick said, "by way of the facts. I don't have anything to hide from them."

"Get an early flight back," she sizzled. "I *want* you."

Nick was zipping up his garment bag when Jack Bein called, aggrieved that nearly an hour had gone by without Nick's having returned his call. In a city where everything took forever, forty-five minutes was an eternity.

"Jeff thought the meeting went *really* well, and," Jack said, with the air of announcing the winner of a lottery, "he wants you to come to dinner tonight at his home. Normally, Jeff doesn't invite new clients to eat with him at home. He's a very private person. It's a sign of how much he respects you. It'll be just you, Fiona, and Mace. Plus Jerry Gornick and Voltan Zeig, the producers. He's serving something very special. I can never get the name of it straight, I'm not very good at Japanese—I better get better, right?—but it's transparent sushi. They bring it all the way up from the bottom of the Mariana Trench. From like thousands of feet down, where the really strange creatures are. Jurassic squid. You know, those things with eyeballs on the end of their antennae? Frankly I'm not so crazy for it. Personally, I like fish you can't see through, but it's incredibly rare, and you cannot get this stuff in even the best restaurants. Jeff has a connection through Sumitashi International, which you didn't hear from me about. Usually, Jeff only serves it if like Ovitz or Eisner are coming, so it's a terrific tribute to his feelings for you."

Nick explained that, honored as he was, he'd just been called back to Washington on urgent business. There was a long pause. Jack sounded mortally wounded. "Nick, I don't know how to put this, but what could be more important than *this*?"

The bellman was knocking on the door. His flight left in—Jesus—fifty-five minutes. "Trust me, Jack, it's big. I'll call you later, from my coast."

20

The conversation over the table by the fake fireplace at Bert's was strictly sotto voce today. Nick, Polly, and Bobby Jay hunched inward, like revolutionaries discussing bombs in a Paris café.

Bobby Jay was livid over this news about Finisterre. When he was governor of Vermont, Finisterre had pushed through a very tough anti-handgun bill—as far as SAFETY was concerned—requiring a forty-eight-hour waiting period *and* limiting purchases to one per week. Now that he'd bought himself a Senate seat with family money, he could inflict his Neo-Puritanism on the national scene.

"There's nothing wrong," Bobby Jay said, crunching into a large Italian pepper, squirting a bit of fiery green juice onto Polly's dress, "with that little buck-toothed son of a bitch that a hundred grains of soft lead couldn't set right."

Much as it did Nick's heart good to get such sympathy, Bobby Jay's reaction seemed a tad extreme, especially for a born-again Christian.

"Do you have any ideas for me," Nick said, "short of assassinating him?" Nick pulled the carnation out of the vase and examined it closely.

"What are you doing?" Polly said.

"Checking for bugs. As long as we're discussing shooting U.S. senators."

Bobby Jay took the flower and spoke into it. "I have the highest regard for Senator Or-to-lan K. Finisterre."

"He's just in a bad mood," Polly said, "because another mail carrier went berserk this week and turned a post office into a slaughterhouse.

By the way, I meant to ask you—how was he able to legally purchase a *grenade* launcher?"

"Do I get on your case every time some drunk teenager runs over a Nobel laureate?" Bobby Jay said. "And by the way, pepper juice doesn't come out."

Nick said, "I believe we were talking about my problem."

"I assume you're backing Finisterre's opponent," Polly said.

"Oh yeah. He's going to be *rolling* in soft money. And hard money. But that doesn't do us a whole lot of good. The election is in November, and this is now."

"Well," Polly said, "do you have anything on him?"

"He's a fornicator," Bobby Jay said. "Married and divorced three times, and Lord only knows how many pop tarts in between."

"Shocking as that may be to the American people, I was thinking something more, I don't know, lurid. Kink, whips 'n' things? God," she said, exhaling a long, philosophical stream of smoke, "listen to us. I was going to be secretary of state."

"What's the matter?" Bobby Jay said. "Can't stand the heat? Life is a dirty, rotten job and someone's got to do it."

"Go shoot a whale." She said to Nick, "Isn't your guy—Garcia?—on the case?"

"Gomez. Yeah. They're probably going over his credit card slips right about now."

"Don't forget his video rental records. Remember what those swine did to poor Judge Thomas."

"I'm confident," Nick said, "that Gomez O'Neal isn't one to overlook those."

"Won't do any good. They all use cutouts now. Probably has someone on his staff renting his dirty movies. Pharisee."

"He was a bit of a playboy when he was younger. And thinner. He did used to get drunk a lot. Got stopped for DUI once."

"Oh, *please*," Polly said, "stay off that if you can. Anyway, it's ancient history. He was the one who lowered Vermont's legal BAC to .08, hypocritical bastard. Typical. Just because he used to get loaded and drive, now anyone who takes two sips of chardonnay loses their license for six months. And what are you supposed to do, in Vermont? Call a cab?"

"You realize you're next, don't you?" Nick said. "If he gets away with putting skulls and bones on cigarettes, how long do you think it's going to be before he's going to want to slap them on scotch, beer, and wine?"

"There's no *room* for any more warning labels," Polly said bitterly. "I'm surprised we don't have to say that you shouldn't swallow the bottle."

"We're all finished," Nick said morosely.

"Despair is a mortal sin," Bobby Jay said.

"My entire product line is about to be moved from the cash register over to the "Household Poisons" shelf and the FBI thinks I covered myself with nicotine patches. I think frankly that I'm entitled to a little despair."

Polly put her hand on top of his. "Let's take it step by step."

"She's right," Bobby Jay said. "There's only one way to eat an elephant. One spoonful at a time."

"What is that supposed to be, redneck haiku? Can we please get *real*?"

Bobby Jay leaned in close. "We have friends inside the J. Edgar Hoover building. Lemme see what I can find out."

"About an ongoing investigation? Good luck."

"You might be surprised. A whole lotta bonding goes on at a firing range. Never know what you might pick up with the empties."

"Well," Nick sighed, "tell them to go arrest some more Islamic Fundamentalists."

"All right, we're making progress," Polly said. "Bobby Jay's taking care of your FBI problem. So now you only have to figure out what to do with Finisterre. He's got to have a weak spot. Everyone does."

"What am I going to do? Attack him on *MacNeil-Lehrer* for renting *Wet Coeds*?"

"Heyy," Polly said, taking him by the shoulder, "where's the old Neo-Puritan dragon slayer? Where's the guy I used to know who could stand up in a crowded theater and shout, 'There's no link between smoking and disease'?"

Nick looked at her, and was seized with the old swelling for Polly. But this was no time to think about that, as he was semi-involved with Heather and certainly involved with Jeannette. Pity. He and Polly would be . . . well, anyway, she was right. You want an easy job? Go flack for the Red Cross.

The waitress arrived to tell them about the dessert specials. She was new; Bert hadn't briefed her that table six was never, ever, to be told about the day's specials.

"We have apple *pie*," she said, "and it's served à la mode, with ice cream, or with Vermont cheddar cheese, which is *real* good."

"So," Polly said, once the waitress had been shooed away, "so what's the deal with Fiona Fontaine's hair? Nick? Nick?"

It felt like he was in an isolation chamber, being observed by scientists on closed-circuit TV. He didn't even get to watch his interrogator and the other guest on a monitor. All he'd get was audio—and that lens, staring at him unwinkingly like a great, glassy, fish-eyed, man-eating cyclops.

Koppel preferred it this way—himself alone in the studio, his interviewees off in others. TV news's equivalent of the one-way mirror in police stations. It gave him the advantage of not having to cope with his subjects' corporeality. This way he would not be distracted by their nervous body language and take pity on them. Only special guests got to sit next to him, such as the disgraced former presidential candidate who, months later, selected *Nightline* to try to explain why—on earth—he had blown his kingdom for a blow job.

"Thirty seconds," Nick heard in his earpiece. He was nervous. He'd been on *Nightline* before but the stakes had never been this high. He could *feel* himself being watched, could sense on the other side of the lens the Captain, BR, Polly, Jeannette—watching in the greenroom, a few doors away—Heather, Lorne Lutch, Joey, his proud mother—my son, the tobacco spokesman—Jack Bein and maybe even Jeff Megall, who would be hoping that Nick would fail miserably, for the *lèse majesté* of having declined his meal of transparent raw fish.

Be cool, he told himself. In a hot medium, coolness is all, limpidity is better, and not picking your nose is key. He did his breathing exercise, a ten-second breath let out in twelve. He closed his eyes and tried to empty his mind. Somewhere he had read that it takes Japanese monks twenty years of silence, green tea, and brown rice to empty theirs. Tonight, however, he wasn't looking for enlightenment, just a reduced pulse rate.

Suddenly through the earpiece he heard—violent coughing. Was it the engineer?

Oh no, for up came the familiar voice-over: "Cigarettes . . . some estimates are that as many as half a million Americans will die this year from smoking."

Swell, Nick thought, we're off to a fine start: an image of a terminal cancer patient spitting up burst alveoli.

"Yet despite," Koppel continued, "the Federal Cigarette Labeling and Advertising Act of 1965 requiring stiff warning labels on cigarettes, people continue to smoke. Now, a U.S. senator . . ."

Nick did another breathing exercise.

"Good evening. From Washington, I'm Ted Koppel and this . . . is *Nightline.*"

That trademark pause reminded Nick of the beat that Edward R. Murrow used to insert in his famous wartime radio dispatches from London during the blitz. "This . . . is London." Dear old chain-smoking old Edward R. Murrow. Dear old, dead old Edward R. Murrow.

". . . later, we'll be joined by Vermont Senator Ortolan K. Finis-terre, author of the Senate bill, and by Nick Naylor, chief spokesman for the tobacco lobby. But first, this report from correspondent Chris Wallace. . . ."

Wallace's wretchedly thorough report brought up the *Lancet* study predicting 250 million deaths worldwide from smoking by the end of the century—one in every five people in the industrialized nations. Bitch of a study, that one. Nick made a mental note to try, anyway, to cast aspersions on the world's most respected medical journal.

"Let me start with you, Senator. Cigarettes already carry explicit warnings. Why do you need this additional label?"

"Well, Ted, as you pointed out in your excellent introduction . . ."

Brown-nose. But—a miscalculation! Koppel was too proud to be blatantly sucked up to, especially by a politician.

"But surely the warning is *already* dramatic," he riposted. Nick cheered him on. "It states the risks. 'Lung cancer,' 'emphysema,' 'heart disease,' 'fetal asphyxiation.' Why do we need a skull and bones?"

"Unfortunately, Ted, many people in America can't read, or can't read English, so this measure is very specifically intended for their benefit. I think we have a responsibility to those people."

"All right. Mr. Naylor, and I should point out that however people feel about smoking, you've certainly been a front-line warrior for your industry, by virtue of having been recently kidnapped and nearly killed by an apparently radical anti-smoking group—"

"Apparent to *me*," Nick said.

"Perhaps I should start by asking you if you believe that cigarettes are harmful."

A softball.

"Well, Ted, I take what I'd call the scientific position, namely that a lot more research is needed before we come to any responsible conclusion on the matter."

Good, excellent. In a single sentence he had allied himself with Responsible Science.

"Even though there have been to date more than sixty *thousand* studies showing a link between smoking and cancer alone?"

Nick gave a world-weary nod of the head to indicate that he was not surprised that this raggedy-ass canard had been dragged out. "I think I recognize that figure you just cited, Ted. If I'm not mistaken, it comes from former Surgeon General Koop's book, the one he got a rather substantial advance for."

"I'm not sure what you're suggesting."

"Just that Mr. Koop, like many other political figures, is not without his own agenda."

A bit tortured, perhaps, but he'd at least kicked a little putative dirt onto the shoes of a venerable doctor, a pediatric surgeon, at that. A man who saved the lives of . . . little children. *Don't think about that!* Thank God Koop looked like Captain Ahab with that scary beard of his.

He could sense Ortolan K. Finisterre frantically waving his arms in the air at Teacher. "Ted, may I comment on that?"

Koppel, however, was not about to yield his conch shell to a brown-noser who owed his political career to some nut who'd blown up his president-uncle thirty years ago at Disney World.

"I'm not sure if I understand, Mr. Naylor. You're saying that after tens of thousands of studies and, frankly, an overwhelming amount of scientific evidence that cigarettes are harmful, that it's *still* an open question as to whether or not they're harmful?"

"Ted, twenty years ago the scientists were telling us that we were all going to die of artificial sweeteners. Now they're telling us—we goofed, never mind. The more cyclamates, the better. So I think any scientist worth his or her salt—or in this case, sugar—would tell you that the first principle of science is—doubt."

Koppel sounded amused, in a disgusted sort of way. "All right, let's for the sake of argument suppose that it is still an open question. But would you agree that until such a time as there *is* conclusive evidence that smoking is harmful, that we ought to err on the side of prudence and protect society against the possibility—to use as *neutral* a term as I can—that it *might be* harmful, and therefore put Senator Finisterre's labels on cigarettes?"

Subtle bastard.

"Well," Nick laughed softly, tolerantly, *"sure,* but we're going to have to print up an awful lot of warning labels to cover *all* the things in life that might not be a hundred percent safe." But enough palaver. It was time to pull the pin on the hand grenade that the waitress had given him. "But the *irony* in all this, Ted, is that the real, *demonstrated* number-one killer in America is cholesterol. I don't know *any* scientists who would disagree with that. And here comes Senator Finisterre, whose fine and beautiful state is, I regret to have to say, *clogging* the nation's arteries with Vermont cheddar cheese, with this proposal to plaster us with rat-poison labels."

"That's absolutely absurd. Ted, may I—"

"If I might be allowed to finish?" Nick said, snatching back the mike. "I was merely going to say that I'm sure that the tobacco industry would consent to having these labels put on *our* product, if he will acknowledge the *tragic* role that *his* product is playing, by putting the same warning labels on these deadly chunks of solid, low-density lipoprotein that go by the name of Vermont cheddar cheese."

"Ted!—"

21

He picked up Jeannette in the greenroom after the show. There were other people milling around, mostly trying to get her phone number. She was looking very sleek tonight. With Nick she was the soul of cool professionalism, confining herself to complimenting him on having made "some very important points." Then when they were alone in the elevator, she grabbed him by the neck and put a kiss on him like a NASA air lock.

"You were incredible. I'm going to make you *moan*."

Jeannette sure knew how to make a guy feel like he'd done an honest day's work. She kept attacking him in the car on the way back to Nick's place. Disinformation was certainly an aphrodisiac to Jeannette. They tumbled through the door and onto the bed. As usual, the lights stayed out and Jeannette did her kinky latex number with the gloves and condoms.

Just as things were getting truly sweaty, the phone rang. Polly's voice came over the answering-machine speaker. It was distracting, making love to one woman while listening to another.

"Killer *cheese*?" Polly laughed. "Well done. Finisterre looked like he was having an outbreak of shingles. Bobby Jay said to tell you that you did the Mod Squad proud tonight. Congratulations. Give me a call when you get back. I have to do a panel tomorrow, so I'm cramming about the effects of alcohol on neural function. Did you know that alcohol actually *strengthens* the flow of ions through the GABA$_A$ ion channel and produces a calming effect, much like Valium? In *moderate* doses of course, but I can fudge that. If it's one thing the

Moderation Council hates, it's moderation. Anyway, kiddo, you were really great. You made my ion channels hum. Bye."

"Who was that?" Jeannette said.

"Don't stop. *Oh.*"

"She sounded kind of friendly."

"Polly Bailey. Just a friend."

"What's the Mod Squad?"

"Merchants of Death. We do lunch. Oh, *yes, definitely. Ohhh.*"

The phone rang again. "Hi Nick, it's Heather. *Cheese?* I gotta hand it to you. You could make the Serbs sound like humanitarians. Give me a call, okay? We need to talk about this piece. Can you do dinner tomorrow night?"

"Was that Heather Holloway?"

"Ohhhhhhhhh. Yeah."

"Aha. I *knew* you were her Deep Throat. Naughty boy. You should be spanked. *Do you want me to spank you?*"

"No."

"So, are you fucking her?"

"Who?"

"Heather Holloway."

"Can we talk about this later? Ow! Hey!"

The next call was from the Captain. "Nick, son. You were magnificent! That buck-tooth, pimply-assed son of a bitch looked like he was going to shit his britches. In fact I think I heard him do just that. Well *done,* sir. You're the only good thing's happened to tobacco in the last ten years. And don't you think I don't plan to show my appreciation."

"Was that—the Captain?"

"Oh, oh, oh, oh . . ."

"Niick."

"*What?* Yes."

"He certainly sounded happy."

"Mrrmph. Baby, baby—"

"What did he mean by showing his appreciation?"

"Rmmmm. Oo, oo, oo. Yesyesyesyessssss."

She was gone, as usual, by the time he woke up, and once again had cleaned up, sparing him having to dispense with nookie detritus. Very orderly woman, Jeannette. Probably went with the S&M fetish. What a littered scene it would have been this morning, boxes, wrappers, little limp love zeppelins lying all over the floor. Five times! Reassuring, in your forties, to know that the old cobra could still stand up and hiss five times in one night.

The phone rang. It was Gazelle, panicking because it was 9:15—he hadn't gotten to sleep until after four—and his phone was already in meltdown from outraged calls, mostly from Vermont, including from the governor's office. "You better tell those dykes they got protecting you to look sharp," she said, " 'cause these people sound like they're going to drive down here in their cheese trucks and park them on top of your *ass*."

When he got to the office, it was high-fives in the hallway and hurrahs for the conquering hero. Tobacco might be going down in flames, but its paladin was wielding a sharp lance.

BR was a tad subdued. A tad cool, even. "I just got off the phone with the Governor of Vermont," he said. "I would not describe him as a happy camper."

"That'll teach him to ban smoking in his prisons." Nick shrugged, pouring himself some coffee. After intense internal debate, the Academy of Tobacco Studies had decided *not* to go to court on behalf of the smoking rights of the Green Mountain State's murderers, rapists, and thieves.

"Legal Affairs says that we're going to be sued by every cheddar cheese manufacturer in the state," BR said. " 'Tragic role of cheese'?"

"Let them sue." Nick said. "Let cheese take the witness stand for a change. For the first time since I can recall, we're on the attack instead of circling the wagons."

"We are that. I only wish we were attacking on better ground than cheese."

"Such as? Health?"

BR frowned.

"I thought you wanted a challenge. We're going to need to get our research ducks lined up. You better get Issues Intelligence cranking. You know what we're looking for."

"Cheese fatalities?"

"Atherosclerosis rates in Vermont. No reason we can't correlate Vermont cheddar production with heart disease, nationally. Any cholesterol injuries will do. Hell, we can probably attribute every heart attack in the country to Vermont cheddar cheese. Get Erhardt on the case. Erhardt could make oat bran sound lethal."

"I wouldn't plan on doing any leaf-peeping in Vermont this fall unless you put on a fake beard and register under an assumed name."

"Yeah, well, there's always New Hampshire," Nick said, turning to go.

"Nick," BR said uncomfortably, "something's come up that I need to talk with you about. Those two FBI agents, Monmaney and Allman, came in to see me yesterday late afternoon and, well, why don't we say that you and I never had this conversation."

"What's the problem?"

"They want to see your phone records."

"Uh-huh," Nick said. "And why would they want to do that?"

"I don't know. But it was pretty clear that if I didn't volunteer your phone records, they'll come back with a subpoena. I don't think either of us wants that. But I wanted to talk with you first." He gave Nick a pained look. "What do *you* want me to do?"

"I'm not sure I'm tracking here, BR. Am I under suspicion of something?"

"I asked them just that."

"And?"

"They gave me some bullshit boilerplate nonanswer out of the G-man's training manual. Made me madder than a hornet and I gave it to them, believe me. But obviously, yeah, they seem to be . . . curious about you at this point."

"What do they think happened? I kidnapped and almost killed myself with, with, with *nicotine* patches?"

"I suppose for the same reason that it occurred to me. All the great press we got afterward. At the time, you'll recall I told you I wished *I'd* thought of kidnapping you. The same motive seems to have occurred to them."

"Let them *have* my phone records. I don't have anything to hide. They can have my dry cleaning bill, too."

"Nick," BR said in a parental tone, "I think it's time you had some representation. Just . . . in the event."

"In the event of what? I didn't do it. It's the one thing in my life about which I can say, with actual conviction—I am innocent."

"Nick, you don't have to convince me. I'm on your side. But let's at least do this thing right."

"Great. TOBACCO SPOKESMAN HIRES LAWYER."

BR winced. "I see your point. But if this goes any further, I'm calling Steve Carlinsky."

"Steve Carlinsky? Who defended whatsisname, the Dip 'n' Glow guy, Scarparillo?"

"He's the best. And he got him off, which, considering he was facing fifteen to twenty-five for selling repackaged radioactive waste as furniture stripper, was something of a legal triumph. Tom Salley told me it was the most brilliant defense he's ever seen, and he worked for Edward Bennett Williams. Where are you going?"

"To blow up the Holland Tunnel."

"What?"

"If I'm going to be arrested by the FBI," Nick said with asperity, "I might as well have some fun."

Nick was sitting in his office staring at the poster of the Lucky Strike doctor, stewing, when Jack Bein called. "*Nick!* You were tremendous."

"You saw it?" Nick said, surprised. Jack didn't strike him as a *Nightline*-watching type.

"Not personally. But you were fabulous. And I voted for the guy's uncle, so you know where *I'm* coming from. You know, I can't eat cheese. Gives me a headache. Listen, I was just with Jeff, and by the way, there's no hurt feelings about the dinner, so put it out of your mind."

"A great relief," Nick said.

"Now we've got some incredible news. Jerry and Voltan—the producers—have agreed to come down on their percentage of Mace and Fiona's product placement compensation, so that means Mace and Fiona will have to come down."

"Well there's certainly a lot of room for improvement, Jack. I gave my people those numbers and they went into cardiac arrest."

"Nick, Jeff wants this to happen, so it's going to happen. Don't worry about the numbers. We'll make the numbers fit. Now, Jeff met with Mace and Fiona's reps and here's the situation vis à vis them. . . ."

* * *

Nick stared into Bert's fireplace and watched the rotating purple and yellow light pretending to be flames. Bobby Jay had not found out anything from his FBI contacts. And Polly thought he ought to hire Steve Carlinsky right away, which annoyed Nick so much he changed the subject.

"Mace McQuade and Fiona Fontaine have quote qualms unquote about quote glorifying smoking unquote."

Bobby Jay shook his head as he stirred his coffee with his steel hook, a custom Polly found uncouth. *"Qualms,"* he snorted, "from people who make their livelihood glorifying sex and violence."

"What about your Durk Fraser ad campaign?" Polly said. "He made *his* millions playing a savage policeman, and now he's your poster boy. 'I'm on SAFETY.' "

"Durk Fraser is a highly moral human being," Bobby Jay said, "who always stood up for what was right and fine."

"Right, while torturing confessions out of minorities."

"That was one movie, and the fact is that most crime is committed by minorities, a point that some bleeding heart liberals find difficult to admit."

"Just because I find Durk Fraser repellent—*and* a bad actor—doesn't make me a liberal."

"Durk Fraser," Bobby Jay said, "is five times the actor Mace McQuade is, and he never had to wiggle his bare butt on the screen. If I were Nick, I'd tell that boy and his agent to go straight to hell and don't even stop to clean the bugs off the windshield. And as for that Rahab . . ."

"Who?"

"The painted whore of Babylon." Two espressos and Bobby Jay became a flame-snorting Old Testament moralist. "I am familiar with the complete *oovvre* of Fiona Fontaine, and while I do not deny that the Lord endowed her with natural beauty—which she defiled by having her tits pumped full of plastic—I do not frankly see what all the fuss is about. Not wearing underpants does not make you an actress."

"So," Polly said, "does this mean no smoking in *Sector Six*?"

"Oh no," Nick said, "two million dollars—each—goes a long way toward qualm abatement. I have to hand it to Jeff Megall; for a guy who eats transparent sushi, he's very smart. He came up with a brilliant solution: shooting duplicate scenes, in which Mace and Fiona smoke, but only for foreign distribution. This way no one here at home will see them smoking. Just billions of Asians, who want to be just like Mace and Fiona. Jeff calls it 'product-smart placement.' Like the bombs."

"That *is* smart. So Mace and Fiona don't mind quote glorifying smoking unquote as long as it's for the benefit of . . ."

"Gooks," Bobby Jay said.

"I hate that word," Polly said.

Bobby Jay held up his hook. "I left twenty pints of blood and half an arm over there," he said, "so I suppose I can call them anything I *please*."

"He's got a point," Nick said. "Megall came up with even another idea: shooting the scenes with blank cigarette packs, then they can digitalize in different brand names, according to country."

"Wow," Polly marveled.

"So in the movie print that goes to Japan, they're smoking a Japanese brand, in the one that goes to Indonesia, Indonesian, and in the Hungarian print, a Hungarian brand like *Throatscraper*. An actual name. In Eastern Europe they *want* more tar and nicotine."

"Smart."

"Actually," Nick said, "I don't know why we didn't think of it. It's already being done abroad, using transponders to superimpose logos on satellite TV transmissions. So the Madonna concert in Spain becomes the Salem Madonna concert in Hong Kong. You can do things over there you just can't here. Laura Branigan, Tiffany, Stevie Wonder, Roberta Flack, Huey Lewis, Luciano Pavarotti, Tom Berenger, Roger Moore, James Coburn, Jimmy Connors, and John McEnroe have all endorsed cigarettes overseas, either directly or indirectly. And they don't get any grief about it here, because nobody sees it."

"But what about here? The whole idea was to promote the product here, wasn't it?"

"Jeff says no problem. It's only the big actors who pull down eight, ten million a picture who can afford the luxury of quote qualms unquote. He says we'll be in three Christmas movies. By *this* Christmas."

"How would I go about getting in touch with Jeff Megall?" Polly said.

* * *

Under the circumstances, Nick thought it made sense to meet Heather not at Il Peccatore but at a more out-of-the-way place, so he picked the River Café in Foggy Bottom. He got there first. It had been a trying day, listening to threats by the governor of Vermont, among others. He ordered a vodka negroni on the rocks, but reminded himself, as it massaged its way up his brain stem, of the need for mental clarity. On tonight's agenda was not how to get Heather into the sack, but how to keep Heather from getting him sacked. At this point, she seemed hotter to impress her prospective employers at the *Sun* than she was for him.

She arrived, right on time, all smiles, and in a dress that surely had been put on after work, for his benefit. It would have created havoc in any newsroom.

"Hi!" she said. "Am I late? I came right from work."

They started with a little small talk, then moved on to major media gossip—who was going to replace Morton Kondracke on *The McLaughlin Group*. Boy, Nick thought, the things we care about in Washington. . . .

Finally, after they'd both refused dessert and settled in with their decaf cappuccinos, Heather ventured: "You know, the more I think about the FBI investigating you, the more burned I get."

"Appalling, isn't it?"

"That's why I think it's so important to get it out there. Your tax dollars at work. I think they'll back off the moment this sees print."

"*Is* this seeing print?"

"Yes," she said nervously, "I was able to confirm independently that they're looking into you. So I wouldn't be violating any confidence."

Nick suppressed the urge to congratulate her on having sunk to his own chthonic ethical level. He merely nodded. "Fair enough."

Heather seemed surprised by his compliance. "You're not pissed?"

"No. Actually, I think you're right. I think they probably would back off. Write as you will. Though I'd certainly appreciate it if you didn't quote me."

"No, of course. You're sure?"

"Sure. In fact," he leaned forward in his best revolutionary hunch and whispered, "completely, utterly, and totally off the record, that would be kind of . . . for the best."

"Oh?"

The hook was in.

"Let's get out of here," Nick said.

They walked down I Street toward the Watergate. An appropriate direction, given what he was up to. Heather said, "What did you mean, 'for the best'?"

"Well," Nick laughed, "would you want the FBI going through *your* drawers?"

"Nick, are you trying to tell me something?"

Nick grinned. "Only that people will do amazing things if the stakes are high enough."

"You did kidnap yourself?"

"I didn't say that."

He dropped Heather off at her front door with a chaste kiss, confident that there would be no story. She would now have her eyes set on a much bigger story, and there wasn't one. She'd end up stuck in gridlock.

22

Ordinarily, Nick enjoyed appearing before Senate subcommittees. It made you feel that for a brief, shiny moment, you'd taken part in the great serial drama of American history. The bright TV lights, the pitcher and glass of water, the green felt tabletop, the hum and thrum of the spectators, the senators trying to look like Roman busts, the crab-scuttling of their aides as they pretended to avoid the TV cameras, and now, Nick noted, this new twist on stenography—stenographers speaking into cones held over their mouths.

Today, however, Nick was not enjoying his small role in the great serial drama of American history. Today was more of an exercise in waiting, a combination of jury selection and Disney World. It was now a few minutes to four, and Nick had been waiting to testify since ten A.M. Finisterre's petty revenge. At first he wasn't even going to allow Nick to appear before his subcommittee, but he relented when Senator Jordan privately threatened to cut off his highway improvement funds. (After the Captain privately threatened to cut off his free jet.)

So far, Nick had listened to tobacco—and himself in particular—be denounced by adversaries familiar and new: Mothers Against Smoking, Teenagers Against the Exploitation of Youth (*what* a bunch of dweebs), the head of the National Institute on Drug Abuse (Finisterre, subtle fellow that he was, wanted to jackhammer home the point that tobacco was just another drug, like crack), and the Coalition for Ethical and Responsible Advertising (a rather small group).

At four, after a weepy Hispanic woman finished a lurid description of how her husband, Ramon, had been killed by the evil weed—"He no can read so he no know is so bad for him"—Finisterre tried to adjourn the proceedings for the day. At which point Senator Plum Rudebaker of North Carolina, tobacco's man on the subcommittee, growled into his mike that this "lynchin' " had gone on long enough and demanded that Nick be heard, today.

Nick graciously thanked Chairman Finisterre for the opportunity to present his views before such a distinguished committee. How proud the founders would have been of the senators before him: over two thousand bounced checks between them, a seducer of underage Senate pages, three DUIs, one income-tax evader, a wife beater whose only defense was that she'd beat *him* up first, and a case of plagiarism, from, of all sources, a campaign speech of Benito Mussolini. (The senator later blamed the episode on an "overzealous staffer.")

As soon as Nick launched into his prepared statement, which consisted of an eloquent plea not to turn the American tobacco farmer into the Dust Bowl Okies of the nineties—complete with tear-duct-pumping quotes from *The Grapes of Wrath*—two of the senators ostentatiously stood up and left, without even going through the usual pretense of telling the chairman that the safety of the Republic depended on their immediate presence elsewhere. Nick paused in his recitation long enough to reflect that it's a sorry state when seducers of teenagers and Mussolini-quoters feel morally superior to you. He would shore up his prepared statement by proudly pointing to the Academy's vigorous anti-underage-smoking campaign. That done, Rudebaker tossed out the softball, right on cue.

"Ah'd lak to thank Mistuh Nayla fuh his courage in attendin' today's hea'ngs," he intoned in his Tarheel baritone. "And ah'm not just speaking to his mor'l courage, but his *physical* courage." Nick modestly lowered his eyes, an appropriate gesture, considering that he'd ghostwritten these very words of the senator's. "For it's mah understandin'," Rudebaker continued, "that he has been *threatened* by a number of mah distinguished colleague from Vuhmont's con-stit-uents."

"Just what," Finisterre barked, "does the gentleman from the to-bacco-producing state imply by that remark?"

"Ahh'm not *implyin'* anythin'." Again on cue, Plum held up a fistful of papers, spilling them all over. Photographers, by now near coma from boredom, fired away, filling the room with the cricket-sound of motorized drives. "An' neither do these death threats, *all* o' which are postmarked from the great state of Vuh-mont."

Murmur murmur, gavel gavel.

"I certainly hope that my distinguished colleague . . ." Amazing, senatorial courtesy. ". . . isn't suggesting that these *alleged* letters were somehow the result of some coordinated effort—"

"Ah'm not *sayin'* or *suggestin'* or otherwise *hintin'* at *anythin'* of the *sort*. Ah'm merely sayin' that it's a saad day when a man whose only crayhm is representin' the interests of a *legal* product becomes a hunted man. In that regahd, ah'd like to point out to the distinguished chairman that Mistuh Nayla has already suffuhd kidnappin' and torcher fuh doin' his job. An' now he's got to live with thiyuss. Myself, ah don't know who put these cheesemongerin' assassins on his case, but ah *am* proposin' that their elected representatives show a little leadership and call off these dogs of wah, before someone gets *hut*."

"Gets *what*?" said a reporter sitting behind Nick.

"Plum certainly rose to the occasion," BR said the next day as he and Nick scanned the media coverage. FINISTERRE DISAVOWS THREATS AGAINST TOBACCO SPOKESMAN.

"Don't think it's not going to cost," the Captain said over the speakerphone. It was dark in BR's office. The new "tempest-hardened" curtains that Carlton had had installed were drawn. They were supposed to foil electronic eavesdropping. Between the FBI investigation of Nick and the tobacco lobby's frontal assault on a U.S. senator, the paranoia level was rising like the Mississippi during a wet spring. "But," the Captain continued, audibly short of breath, "we got the sumbitch on the defensive. Brilliant idea, son, brilliant."

Nick, exhausted from another night of making whoopee in the wee hours with Jeannette, yawned. "We're not going to win this one, Captain. Leg Affairs says it's going to pass committee by twelve to five. And when it hits the floor, watch out. We might as well face it. We're going down."

"Don't talk defeatism to a southerner," the Captain said.

"I'm just trying to be realistic."

"What about your Kraut doctor's report?"

Erhardt's Institute for Lifestyle Health had cranked out a document entitled *The Silent Killer,* estimating that over two million Americans a year were dying from Vermont cheddar–clogged arteries. (Based, to be sure, on the assumption that anyone who ever ate so much as a mouthful of Vermont cheddar cheese had ultimately died from it.) Nick was recommending against releasing it. Indeed, was recommending that all copies of *The Silent Killer* be immediately shredded.

"Gomez?" the Captain said in a lowered voice.

"We're pretty sure he made a pass at an au pair a couple of years ago," BR said.

"A what?"

"A foreign nanny. Icelandic girl, twenty-one, named Harpa Johannsdottir. She's back in Iceland. I have a man over there now looking for her. It may take some time. The Icelandic phone book is listed by first name and—"

"Can I interject?" Nick said. "Much as I regret to say it, I think we need to start planning, and now, for a post–skull and bones labeling environment."

"That's Appomattox talk." The speakerphone filled the room with the Captain's coughing. He didn't sound well at all. There was talk of installing a new fetal-pig heart valve.

Nick felt badly for the old boy and wished he had more positive thoughts for him. "Maybe," he said, "there's some way we could make it *our* skull and bones."

"What does *that* mean?" the Captain said.

"I don't know yet. Let me get with our creative people and try to work something up. In the meantime, maybe Gomez's man in Reykjavík will come up with an Icelandic love child with buck teeth."

Gazelle was waiting for him outside BR's office, looking worried. "It's them," she whispered.

"Them who?"

"FBI."

"Well don't look so guilty," Nick said, annoyed.

They were in his office. Monmaney, to Nick's considerable annoyance, was looking over the top of his desk. Allman—the more humane of the two—was looking with bemusement at the Lucky Strike doctor.

211

Nick closed the door behind him and said, "So, you've found them."

"Who?" Allman said pleasantly.

"My kidnappers."

"Oh," Allman said.

"Are you planning to travel, Mr. Naylor?" Monmaney asked.

"What?"

"Travel."

"No."

Agent Monmaney read aloud off the memo paperclipped to Nick's plane tickets. "Dulles-LAX. Mahmoud will meet you at the gate."

"Oh, that. Business. I thought you meant pleasure." Agent Monmaney gave Nick his timber wolf stare.

"Why are you asking me this?" Nick said.

"Don't worry," Allman said. "He's just that way. Could we see your apartment?"

"My apartment?"

"Yes."

"Well . . . are you looking for something?"

"In cases where there's loss of memory due to trauma, it makes sense to take everything into account."

"You understand," Agent Monmaney said, "that this is a request. You're not required to comply with it."

"I'm not?"

"No. You're only required to comply with a search warrant."

"Right," Allman said. "But we don't have a warrant."

Nick thought: was there anything in his apartment he needed to worry about? Anything indelicate? No . . . Jeannette was so meticulous about picking up the limp love zeppelins. . . . Oh Christ. *The hash brownies in the freezer.* Whatshername, Paula, the stewardess, had brought some over one night two years ago. His cleaning lady had eaten one by mistake and cleaned the toilet with the vacuum cleaner. He meant to throw them away. *Why* hadn't he thrown them away? Fool! Idiot! Sent to prison for stale hash brownies!

Agents Monmaney and Allman were looking at him.

"Uh, yeah, sure. When would you like to stop by?"

"What about right now?"

"Now?" Nick said looking at his schedule. "Now . . . today . . . kind of . . . How about tomorrow?"

That look again. Monmaney said, "You're going to Los Angeles tomorrow."

"Right." He took out his keys and handed them over. "Help yourself."

Monmaney shook his head. "It would be preferable if you were present."

"I'm trying to help, but it's kind of hard to run a staff meeting and give two interviews and prepare for a panel on secondhand smoke but . . . fine." He buzzed Jeannette and asked her to cover for him.

He drove in the back of their sedan, imagining his next ride in it, handcuffed, on the way to being booked for possession of drugs. He foresaw it all: *You say her name was Paula? What airline did she work for?* Allman, the cheery swine, was intent on making small talk. It was difficult to rehearse your explanation for possession of narcotics while making small talk with a fed.

Wait a minute, that's not my refrigerator!

"I don't see why you're so worried," Polly said.

Nick had convened an emergency meeting of the Mod Squad. Bobby Jay had been a bit put out since this was his bowling-prayer-and-pizza night with the born-agains, but recognizing the note of panic in Nick's voice, he was here. At night, the flames from the fake fireplace looked slightly more realistic.

Nick was sucking down his third vodka negroni.

"You're kind of guzzling that," Polly said.

"You still haven't explained what the problem is," Bobby Jay said. "Since they didn't find your *drugs.*"

"*Shh,*" Nick said. "Jesus."

"Let's leave Jesus out of this."

"He had his hand right *on* it," Nick said, reliving the horror afresh: Agent Monmaney opening the freezer, feeling around amidst the frozen bagels and the cookie-dough ice cream and piña colada concentrate. "I was going to try to grab it out of his hand and try to eat it when the other one, Allman, comes into the kitchen with this look on his face like he's saying, *I found it.*"

"Found *what*? What could he have found?"

"I don't know. It was this silent thing between G-men. Whatever it was, Monmaney caught it. He stopped feeling around in my freezer. They said goodbye and left."

"But what could they have found?"

"Nothing."

"You're sure you didn't have any more *drugs* stashed away somewhere?"

"Will you please shut up, Bobby. And what happened to all that male bonding at the firing range? Instead I call you up and you're out bowling for Jesus."

"I'm *working* on it."

"Well work harder, would you, please? If this is the best you can do, no wonder the handgun control lobby is getting the upper hand."

23

The next night, Nick was riding in Mahmoud's great white whale, on the way from the airport to the Encomium, when he looked out the window at the Los Angeles skyline and saw the billboard, bold as one of his lies. It showed a huge skull with crossbones. The copy beneath read: DON'T SMOKE DEATH CIGARETTES.

Nick knew all about Death cigarettes. Everyone at the Academy kept a pack, with its distinctive skull and bones logo, despite the fact that the industry's official attitude toward Deaths was not exactly collegial. It was the perfect cigarette for the cynical age. It said—shouted—*Our product will kill you!* What product advertised itself more honestly than that? The surgeon general's warning on the side was positively ludicrous. And they were *flying* off the shelves, though their appeal tended to concentrate on young urbans for whom coughing up blood was still a sign of manhood.

It was late in Minneapolis, but for a thirty-million-dollar-a-year account, your creative ad director should take your call even if it is late in Minneapolis. Nick explained his idea to a groggy Sven, who said he'd get his Skunk Works right on it and would fly to Washington on Friday.

Early the next morning, Nick found himself sitting next to Kevin Costner outside Jeff Megall's office. He barely had time to tell him how much he liked *Dances With Wolves* before he was ushered in by the efficient older lady.

They were all sitting around the malachite conference table.

"*Nick,*" Jeff said warmly. Jack Bein made a sign to Nick that he should be impressed by the warmth of Jeff's greeting. "Nick, this is Jerry Gornick and Voltan Zeig, whom you know of. And this is Harve Gruson. Harve has been involved with the final polishes on *Sector Six*. Since the arrangements worked out by everyone's legal people are so specific as to the content of the extra scenes, it makes sense for all of us to get together. Harve, bring us up to speed."

"Okay," said Harve, a mostly bald, overweight, and exhausted-looking man in his early thirties. "We've got ten scenes where there's ambient smoking. They're doing whatever they're doing—navigating, eating, getting dressed, whatever—only they're also smoking. Then we've added scenes. So far, we've got two postcoital scenes, at almost a minute per."

"Is that where he does the thing with the smoke rings?" Jeff asked.

"No. *She* does the thing with the smoke rings. She teaches him how to blow smoke rings. It's hot. My computer screen went into meltdown."

"May I?" Nick held out his hand for the script.

POV over Slade's shoulder.

SLADE
Bull's-eye. Where did you learn to do that?

ZEENA
My programmer was into horseshoes.

"You mean," Nick said, "that she's blowing smoke rings at his . . ."

"Told you. *Hot*."

"Too bad we can't put it in the U.S. version," said Jeff. "That's a great scene."

"We need the PG-13," Voltan shrugged.

"Fiona plays a robot?" Nick said.

"Not a robot. A Format Seven Gynorg. The brain of Einstein and the body of Jamie Lee Curtis."

"Dream date," Jerry said.

"Not *my* dream date." Voltan laughed crudely.

Jeff said to Harve, "What else do you have for us?"

"We've changed the scene where Mace escapes from the prison on Alar. In the U.S. version, he puts out the guard's eye with the icicle.

In this version, he'll put it out with a cigarette. Alarians only have one eye, so it's no more sightseeing for *him*."

"I don't think putting out eyeballs with our product . . . I'm pretty sure that's not what we're looking for."

Harve turned to the producers. "I was told cigarettes had to be integral. How much more integral can you get? Mace gains his freedom with a cigarette. It's a very powerful message."

"I think," Jeff said, "that Nick is uncomfortable with it."

"Okay," Voltan said, "lose the eye."

Harve shrugged.

"By the way," Nick asked, "how are we explaining why the oxygen inside their spaceship doesn't blow up every time they light up?"

"It's the twenty-fifth century," Voltan said. "By then they'll have it figured out."

"We could drop in a line that they mix Freon in with the air supply," Harve said.

"That's good," said Jack. "Would that make them talk funny?"

"Like fags," Voltan said.

"Nah," Jerry said. "That's helium."

The Captain reached Nick in the great white whale on his way to the airport. He didn't sound very good, and there was a lot of static on the line. "I'm in my bass boat," he coughed, "up at the lake in Roaring Gap for a few days. Thought I'd get some fresh air and prove to those idiot doctors down there there's nothing wrong with me that some *competent* medical advice couldn't solve. I'm beginning to suspect they all got their medical degrees in Grenada. They're saying they want to open me up and stick another pig heart in me. Only good thing about it is you don't have to wait to find a donor. They just go out back with an axe. Oop, hooked one. Call you back."

The phone rang a few minutes later, just as Mahmoud was turning off at Century Boulevard toward LAX. "Sumbitch wrapped me around a log. Felt like a six-pounder, too. Now son, uh, BR tells me the FBI is poking around, asking questions. Can you shed a little light on it for me?"

The Captain's tone took Nick by surprise. He told him everything, except about the hash brownies.

"Huh," the Captain said. "Well, they're probably on a fishing expedition, just like me. But I don't like it. With this Finisterre thing, the last thing we need right now is something like this." There was a pause. "There isn't anything going on I oughta know about, is there?"

"What do you mean?" Nick said.

"Nothing. BR's a little squirrelly."

"What," Nick said, "did BR tell you, exactly?"

"He seems to think we ought to hire you a lawyer. Jewish name. One who got that fellah off was making his clients glow in the dark. Carlinsky."

"I'm not quite clear why you should be hiring me a criminal lawyer."

"Now don't get yourself all in a sweat. Stress is a killer. You fish?"

"A little."

"If you want to take a vacation right now, you go ahead."

"A vacation? With everything that's going on?"

"You know what Winston Churchill said. He said there's never a convenient time for taking a vacation, so go ahead and take it."

Nick sat in First Class grinding the enamel off his teeth and feeling the bands in his neck muscles hypercontracting. He called Jeannette. There was something in her voice, too. She sounded like the old Jeannette, the one who'd shown no interest at all in staying up all night to make him moan.

"My flight gets into Dulles at six," Nick said. "Can you meet it? I need to talk to you."

"I'm really busy," she said. "What do you need to talk to me about?"

"BR talked to the Captain about the situation, you know, about the two people who came to see me—"

"The FBI?"

Terrific. Half the ham radio operators in America were listening in. "All I know is BR called the Captain about my situation and the Captain just called me to suggest I take a vacation."

"I wish the Captain would call *me* and tell me to go on a vacation."

"That's not really the point. Do you have *any* idea what it is BR told him?"

"No."

"Do you want to get together later?"

"No." The next sound Nick heard was a recorded voice telling him that if he wanted to make another expensive call from thirty-five thousand feet up, all he had to do was press 2.

He called BR. He was put on hold for eight minutes.

"Yes, Nick?" Again the tone of voice. Had everyone at the Academy been breathing Freon?

"I was wondering what you told the Captain that made him suggest I hire a lawyer and go fishing."

BR cleared his throat. "I thought I owed it to him to bring him up to speed vis à vis this FBI thing."

"I see. Did you tell him anything else?"

"Only what I know."

"Well, what do you know?"

"That the FBI has been taking a very active interest in you. I've gone ahead and retained Steve Carlinsky for you—"

"Oh."

"Look, Nick, the FBI was in here today, again. People are talking. I think at this point we all need some counsel."

"What did the FBI want this time?"

"Nick, I don't think I'm in a position to discuss that with you."

"What?"

"It's for your protection. But, clearly, I have a responsibility to think about the Academy's position."

Nick buzzed for the flight attendant. "Do you know to make a vodka negroni?"

"I sure don't!" she said brightly.

"What I *don't* understand," Steve Carlinsky said the next morning in his office, the walls of which were taken up with many photographs of famous people posing with him, "is why you waited until now to call me."

Carlinsky was tall and gaunt with close-set eyes that had a look of permanent astonishment. Everything about him was gray, except for a splash of floppy silk bow tie that, in his universe, amounted to almost raffishness. His only passion, aside from billable hours, was said to be wine, which he didn't drink but only collected.

"People make the same mistake with lawyers," he continued, "that they do with doctors. They wait too long. And by then the tumor has . . ."

"I didn't call you," Nick said. "And how did *tumors* get into this?"

"I apologize. That was insensitive. In your business, I'm sure you hear more than you want to about tumors. Now, tell me everything. The more I know, the more I can help you."

It was a bit like therapy, only at $450 an hour, more expensive. Carlinsky was a perfect Freudian analyst. He said nothing. When Nick had finished, Carlinsky said, "Though I *never* would have allowed you to let FBI agents onto your premises without a search warrant, in a way I'm glad you did, because we can use that against them when the time comes."

"When what time comes?" Nick said.

"For a rainy day. Would you like to smoke? I have no objection. Though I never smoked myself, candidly, I think the anti-smoking lobby has accumulated *far* too much power."

"I haven't been able to smoke since the incident," Nick said.

"We can use that, too. In your line, that's a disability. Now I want you to go back to work, forget about all this, and if the FBI shows up again, would you do me a personal favor and *call me*? In the meantime, let me make a few calls and see what I can find out."

That wasn't so bad, Nick reflected as he walked the three blocks from Carlinsky's office to the Academy. A perfectly decent fellow, and sensitive.

When he arrived back at ATS, Gazelle came rushing up to him with a phone slip. It said, "Heather Holloway, *Moon*, URGENT!!!"

"Heather? Nick."

"Nick, can you hold? Okay, I understand you've hired Steve Carlinsky? Hello?"

"I'm here."

"I need a comment. Nick."

"Still here."

"That's not a comment."

Think, man. "What gives you that idea?" *Oh, brilliant.*

"You just spent an hour with him at his office."

Self-promoting swine. "Yes," Nick said, reeling, "in fact I did, but

220   we were discussing a private ATS matter and I'm hardly at liberty to

discuss that." He heard the sound of fingers—fingers that should have been doing other things—taking it all down.

"You mean," she said, "pertaining to the FBI's investigation of you?"

"You're referring to their so far inconclusive investigation into my torture-kidnapping?"

Clickety clack.

"You deny, then, that Steve Carlinsky has been retained to act on your behalf in connection with the FBI investigation of your recent disappearance and reappearance on the Mall, covered with nicotine patches?"

"That's an artfully crafted question, I must say."

"Come on, Nick, it's me."

"I assume Ortolan Finisterre is behind this?"

"What?"

"Frankly," Nick said, in a world-weary voice, "I didn't think he'd stoop quite this low."

"What on earth are you talking about?"

"Using the FBI to pursue his private vilification agenda, in order to get everyone's mind off the real problem, which is his cheese. I find it very sad. A sad day for Vermont, a sad day for the U.S. Senate, and a sad day for the truth."

Nick was staring at the Lucky Strike doctor, trying to wonder how that canard was going to play when Sven arrived with the designs for the new warning label. He was grateful for the distraction.

"This was a challenge," Sven said, unzipping a snappy black and burgundy suede portfolio. "But we like a challenge. You all right? You look a little pale."

"Fine. What do you have for me?"

"Let's start with our base line." Sven pulled out a large photo of a package of Death cigarettes. "As you say, a brilliant concept. And prescient. I doubt the makers of Death cigarettes are sweating out this Finisterre bill. Okay. We tried a couple of different approaches, taking into account the size requirements specified in the bill, positioning on the packs, etc., etc. To keep each one straight, we gave them nicknames. This first one we call 'Jolly Green Roger.' " Sven revealed a pack of Marlboros with lime-green skull and bones on the side. "Our PCT people tell us—"

"Who?"

"Psychological Color Theory. They swing a big dick these days. Anyway, we know that green registers as soothing—lawns, money, mint, pool tables—"

"Surgical garb, pus. . . ."

"The specifications in Finisterre's bill don't say what color the skulls have to be, so we'd be okay, legally speaking. We did a quick and dirty focus group on all of these, and the Jolly Green Roger did pretty okay. Only forty percent said, 'I would not under any circumstances smoke if this was on the pack.' "

Nick sighed. "Forty percent?"

"That leaves sixty percent. What do you think?"

"I think it looks like a green skull and bones."

"This next one," Sven said, "is 'Have a Nice Death.' Basically, we took the Have a Nice Day face, made the eyes bigger, added teeth, contoured the jaw, and made the bones look like crossed arms across his chest."

"Jesus. It's awful. It's *frightening*."

"That's what the focus group told us, too. Very high negatives. But now, check out . . . *this*."

Nick wasn't sure what it was, other than a smiling skull. And yet the longer he looked at it, the more gentle it seemed. Almost . . . friendly.

"Who," Sven said, "is the nicest person in the world?"

"I don't know *any* nice people," Nick said.

"Then say hello to your new friend, 'Mr. Death's Neighborhood.' "

Nick stared at the skull. *It's a beautiful day in the neighborhood, a beautiful day for a neighbor, will you be mine?* "That's *his* skull?"

"In the flesh. Actually, without the flesh. The computer gives you a perfect image of what his skull looks like underneath. It's basically just a reverse of a program they developed for forensic anthropologists who're trying to figure out who the bones that just turned up in someone's basement belonged to."

"Wow."

"The program's called KCIROY. Yorick, you know, the skull in *Hamlet,* spelled backward."

"Oh, right."

"All that's missing here is the cardigan sweater. We didn't have room for that. The focus groups loved it. The nonsmokers actually wanted to buy this pack. I took it home and tried it out on my kids. And *they* loved it."

"Really," Nick said. "I must share it with my twelve-year-old."

24

TOBACCO SPOKESMAN RETAINS CRIMINAL LAWYER
AS FBI SHIFTS INVESTIGATION FOCUS ONTO HIM

Naylor Accuses Senator Finisterre of Initiating Federal Probe

BY HEATHER HOLLOWAY
MOON CORRESPONDENT

"I think," Polly said in the hushed tones that were now standard at Mod Squad lunches, "that your Heather Holloway strategy has not been a total success."

"I thought," Nick said, stirring his second vodka negroni with his finger, "that if I made her think I did kidnap myself, that she'd hold off rushing into print with a story about how the FBI was investigating me. And eventually trip herself up trying to prove that I kidnapped myself, which she can't, because I didn't. If you . . . see."

"Young Washingtonians in love," Bobby Jay snorted. "What a wonderful thing it is."

"For a Jesus freak," Polly said, "you're very cynical, Bobby Jay."

"It should have worked," Nick said. "Because I did *not* kidnap myself."

"Shh," Polly said, taking his arm.

"Why," Nick said, "do I get the feeling that I'm preaching to the *un*converted?"

"We believe you," Polly said, though it sounded sort of forced.

"Then that prick Carlinsky leaks it to her that he's representing me, and—*this.*" Nick whacked the newspaper.

"How can you be sure it was Carlinsky?"

"Because he told me he didn't. Would you believe a lawyer who managed to get acquitted a man who sold radioactive waste as furniture-polish remover, the head of the Teamsters union, and that German they caught trying to resell that submarine to the Iraqis?"

"See your point."

"I did some checking on him. He doesn't drink, he doesn't smoke, he doesn't do the woolly deed with females *or* males. All he cares about is publicity. Do you know that he charged Mr. Dip 'n' Glow for every time he was quoted in the press?"

"Really?"

"When he went on *Nightline,* his client got a bill for half an hour, which in his case is $225. Plus for the limo to take him to the TV studio. And he wasn't even discussing the Dip 'n' Glow case. It was a show about whether there are too many lawyers."

"Well," Polly said, "he'll do well for himself with your case. I have a feeling there are going to be a lot of mentions of you in the press."

"At least he's good," Bobby Jay said. "He'll probably get you off."

"I haven't been charged with anything, Bobby."

"I mean, if."

"We *believe* you," Polly said, giving him a squeeze.

"Would you please not talk to me in that *soothing* tone of voice. I'm not a mental patient." Nick looked glumly at the *Moon* headline. Front page, but below the fold.

"She did print my quote about how Finisterre put the FBI up to it," Nick said.

Polly read: " 'Leslie Dach, an aide to Senator Finisterre, dismissed Mr. Naylor's allegation as being 'lower than the scum on an eel's underbelly,' adding that it was 'the kind of odious insinuation that has come to typify the tobacco lobby as it becomes more and more desperate to maintain its stranglehold on the American public's lungs and wallets.' I'd say she gave the Finisterre camp equal time to answer your charge."

"Told you that woman was nothing but trouble," Bobby Jay said.

"Thank you, Bobby Jay," Nick said. "That's very helpful just now.   *225*

Something to tide me over until you give me your wonderful intel from the FBI firing range."

"I don't think bibulating yourself into stupefaction is going to help."

"Boys, boys," Polly said.

"If I can't smoke, I'm going to drink," Nick said. "It's the only way I know to avoid *karoshi*."

"What's that?"

"Japanese for 'sudden death.' It happens to their executives a lot. They work twenty-three-hour days, then one day they're walking along the Ginza, going back to their offices at ten o'clock after a business dinner, they just fall down on the sidewalk and die. One minute they're middle managers, the next, they're on their backs on the pavement like June bugs."

Nick's cellular rang. It was Gazelle and she was whispering. "Nick, it's those FBI people. They're headed your way."

"What do you mean?"

"Nick, I *had* to tell them where you were."

"Why? Did they beat you with rubber truncheons? Oh hell. All right, call Carlinsky. No, never mind, *I'll* call him."

"What about your panel this afternoon?"

"What panel?"

"The Healthy Heart 2000 panel."

"Call Jeannette. No, call Tyler. And tell him to expect a lot of questions about last week's *JAMA* story about clots. *Clots.* Erhardt's got some stuff on it. It's on my desk somewhere."

Nick hung up, drank the last of his vodka negroni in a swallow. "So, would you like to meet some FBI agents?"

Agents Monmaney and Allman arrived a few minutes later, suggesting that they had hurried, which was not particularly reassuring. Nick saw that they were followed by a uniformed D.C. policeman, which was even less so. Nick's three bodyguards, immediately assessing the situation, made no move to interfere with these more legitimate carriers of guns.

"Mr. Naylor," Monmaney said with his usual charm, "would you please stand up and move toward the fireplace."

"Why," Nick said, "would I want to do that?"

"Yeah. Hold on a minute," Polly said.

"Ma'am!" the D.C. cop said warningly. What a macho guy, talking tough like that to a size six.

But—what was this? Monmaney unmistakably placing his hand on his gun? "All right, Mr. Naylor, please stand up, keep your hands where I can see them, turn around and move toward the fireplace."

And so Nick found himself spread-eagled over the fireplace, staring down into the fake flames, as Agent Monmaney frisked him. And then handcuffed him. Dimly, he heard the words 'arrest' and the familiar lines about how he had the right to remain silent, et cetera.

"I'd like to see some ID," Bobby Jay said in a steely tone.

"Sir!" the D.C. cop shouted.

"Well you got *that* right, bub."

"Stand up, sir." Then Bobby Jay was being spread-eagled, or in his case, spread-hooked, and frisked by the cop.

"What's this?" The cop found something interesting in the vicinity of Bobby Jay's ankle. A bulge. Now there was a commotion and the D.C. cop had *his* gun out and was pointing it at Bobby Jay in what Nick thought was a slightly melodramatic way.

"Hunh," Bobby Jay said. "That's—you know, I didn't realize that I was wearing that. See, I live in Virginia and I wasn't actually planning to come in to the District today, and—"

"You're under arrest for possession of a concealed loaded firearm."

"Aw now, come on, there's no need for that. I'm a senior vice president of SAFETY."

"You have the right to remain silent. . . ."

The D.C. cop was stymied as to how to handcuff Bobby Jay's hook.

As Nick and Bobby Jay were being led away, Polly, who looked like she was going into shock, said to them, "I'll . . . get the . . . check."

FBI Arrests Tobacco Smokesman;
Charges Him in Kidnapping Scheme

Nicotine Patch Boxes With Naylor's
Fingerprints Are Found at Va. Cabin

Gun Lobbyist Is Arrested With Him
For Carrying an Illegal Handgun

BY HEATHER HOLLOWAY
MOON CORRESPONDENT

"What I *don't* understand," Steve Carlinsky was saying, "is why you didn't tell me about these boxes before."

Things were looking a little calmer through Nick's eyes, owing to the 10 mgs of Valium Polly had given him. He would have preferred a couple of stiff vodka negronis, or for that matter a hash brownie, but he refrained from asking for either since it was ten o'clock in the morning. It had not been a pleasant eighteen hours. His fingers still smelled of the stuff they'd given him to wipe off the fingerprint ink, and the rest of him felt stale and clammy, despite the clean shirt, underwear, and socks that Polly—dear Polly—had provided. All night she had shuttled back and forth between the FBI building, where Nick had spent the night being gone over by agents Monmaney and Allman, and the D.C. city jail, where Bobby Jay had spent his night, making all sorts of new friends, many of whom shared his views on gun control. Nick's one consolation was that the quality of person you meet in a federal lockup was, perhaps, slightly superior to the ones you met in the municipal jail. At his arraignment, Polly told him that Bobby Jay had inserted his hook deeply into a delicate part of a fellow prisoner who had expressed the desire to share intimacies with him in the toilets. There was now the possibility that a charge of assault with a deadly weapon would be added to the firearms charge, though his lawyer was optimistic on that count. As for Nick, Carlinsky had persuaded the judge that, grievous though the charge was—conspiracy to commit criminal fraud; criminal fraud; giving false evidence to federal officers; along with a few lesser charges that Carlinsky said were just plain "piling on"—Nick was unlikely to flee to the Canadian border in his BMW, and so he'd gotten him released on bail of $100,000, which the Captain, from his hospital bed, had ordered BR to post. So here he was in the offices of the man upon whom he was now dependent to keep him from being sent away for ten to fifteen years, doing his best to cope.

"Tell you *what* about the boxes?"

Carlinsky's already close-set eyes narrowed so much that Nick thought they were going to combine into one big eye, like the ones on the prison guards on the planet Alar.

"Nick, how can I help you if you won't help me?"

"Steve, I don't *know* how my fingerprints got on the boxes."

Carlinsky pensively made a steeple with his hands. "Let's review."

"Again?"

"They have ten boxes of NicArrest nicotine patches with your fingerprints all over them at a rental cabin in Virginia that was rented sight unseen over the phone. They have a record of calls made to that cabin from your office phone, the second call on the morning of the abduction, and a piece of paper found in your apartment with the phone number of the cabin. Okay, now any paralegal in my office could get that last piece of evidence thrown out on illegal search, and anyone could have placed the call to the cabin from your office— *provided* we can establish that you weren't in the office at the time it was placed. But the boxes. The boxes are a problem. As evidence goes, fingerprints are very, very tough. I'd rather go up against a DNA match than fingerprints. Do you know why?" Carlinsky was the kind who waited until you said, *Why?*

"Why?" Nick said.

"Because your average District of Columbia jury does not *understand* DNA. And being lectured about it makes them feel like they're back in high school, flunking biology. You have to present it to them so *sloowly* and *caarefully* that it makes them feel like idiots. They resent you for it, and little good comes of making a jury feel inadequate. But fingerprints—fingerprints are easy to grasp. Much easier than DNA, or such precious bodily fluids as blood or urine or sperm."

"Are you saying your job would be easier if they found boxes of nicotine patches with my blood or sp . . . ?"

"Nick, are you all right? Wait, we have work to do. Where are you going?"

"To kill someone," Nick said, heading out the door.

Nick stormed out of the Hill Building overlooking Farragut Square and made his way down I Street toward the Academy offices in what passersby could not have mistaken for anything other than what is usually called a towering rage. The only question he was still trying to resolve in his mind was—what instrument to use on Jeannette. His first impulse was to drag her, by that tight little bun of hair, to his balcony and toss her ten stories down into the fountain. He mused on other, less spectacular but equally efficient ways to devise her demise. But it is a scientific fact—and not one of Erhardt's—that in moments of stress we lose twenty-five percent of our powers of reason, and so as the first flush of rage subsided, fantasies of listening to Jeannette's death gurgle as his hands throttled her lovely neck were displaced by images of him being carted out of the Academy by the men in white and being taken across the river to Saint Elizabeth's, where his new padded-cellmate John Hinckley could critique for him, over and over and over, Jodie Foster's performance in *The Silence of the Lambs*.

25

There were no hurrahs this time for the returning conqueror as Nick made his way through the Academy. It was downright awkward. People kept saying, "Oh—Nick . . ." and kept right on going. Only Gomez O'Neal, whom he met by the coffee machine, greeted him with sympathy.

"You okay, Nick?"

"Fine, fine," grinding away on his back molars.

Gomez put his hand on his shoulder. "You hang in there."

Coffee in hand, Nick made his way past a gauntlet of averted glances toward BR's office.

"Oh—Nick . . ." BR's secretary said. "He's busy. He's in with Jeannette."

Nick thought there might be one superfluous word in that sentence. He barged right in, rather hoping he'd catch them *in flog-rante,* whacking each other with riding crops, but they were only going over papers.

"Morning," Nick said.

BR and Jeannette stared in surprise. "Are you all right?" BR asked.

"Fine, fine. There's something about staying up all night protesting your innocence to FBI agents that I find invigorating."

"Would you excuse us?" BR said to Jeannette.

"No, *please,*" Nick said. "I certainly don't have anything to hide from *Jeannette.*"

BR leaned back in his big black leather chair. "How do you think we ought to proceed?"

"In terms of what?"

"In terms of your situation."

"Oh *that*. Well, as you say, Steve Carlinsky's the best there is. I'm sure he'll figure out something. That's why you're paying him $450 an hour."

"I meant more in terms of the immediate situation. I don't need to tell you what kind of press we're getting. I have a responsibility to think of the organization. Jeannette thought a leave of absence might make sense."

"I have no objections if Jeannette wants to take a leave of absence."

"Uh, I think we're talking about *you* taking a leave of absence."

"Much too much to do. Finisterre, Mr. Jolly Roger's Neighborhood, Project Hollywood. Gotta keep up the Big Mo." Nick smiled. "Neo-Puritans never sleep."

"I'm not sure that's advisable, at this point. You've sort of become . . ."

"A liability?"

"An issue, certainly." BR held up the morning papers. "Your Ms. Holloway seems to be in hot pursuit of her first Pulitzer. She does have good sources."

"Not as good as the FBI's. Now *they* have sources."

"We're getting a hell of a lot of calls about this. Very, very angry calls."

"Yes, I can imagine what they must think."

"Jeannette's office has fielded one hundred seventy-eight calls this morning."

"Jeannette's office?"

"We obviously can't refer calls about you to your office."

"No, no. Naturally. Well, Jeannette can certainly handle it. In fact, I appreciate Jeannette's abilities more and more each day. But I'm not sure that a leave of absence is a good idea."

"And why is that?"

"Because," Nick grinned, "it would send the signal that you all think I'm guilty. Which of course is not the case. Right?"

BR and Jeannette stared.

"I mean, the notion that I would cover myself with nicotine patches to the point of giving myself several heart attacks, and throw up a hundred times, and then leave the empty boxes all over the cabin for the FBI to find, once they were tipped off. *And* call the cabin from my office phone on the morning I abduct myself. *And* leave the number of the cabin right out in the open in my apartment. I mean, who would believe that a smart guy like me would be so FUCKING *STU-PID*?!''

Jeannette started.

"Sorry," Nick said. "Don't know what got into me. Anyway, I know my colleagues, my trench mates, my brothers- and sisters-in-arms, could never believe that I'd be capable of such ineptitude. So," he said brightly, "let's fight this all the way to the Supreme Court."

BR said, "Do we have a defense strategy?"

"You bet. We're going to find the people who made me into the asshole."

"Do you have any idea who those might be?"

"Well," Nick said pensively, "they would have to be people who really despise me. But in my case that comes to about four-fifths of the U.S. population. Two hundred million. Sort of a big suspect pool, isn't it? You know, they'll probably be thrilled to see me get sent off to play love slave to the Aryan Brotherhood for ten to fifteen."

"I'm not sure it's going to come to *that*," BR said. "We ought to be able to get you into some minimum-security place."

"Oh," Nick said, "I wouldn't count on it. Carlinsky says he's never seen prosecutors so pissed off. Evil yuppie scum devises cheap stunt to promote himself and cancer. He says they're out for blood." Nick grinned. "Mine."

"Well," BR said, leaning forward in a way suggesting that he was tired of badinage about Nick having to spend his next decade behind bars being gang-banged by people with swastika tattoos. "Carlinsky is the best, and we are behind you. But I think under the circumstances a leave of absence does make sense."

"Why don't we just run that by the Captain."

"I wouldn't trouble the Captain with this right now. This has all come as a terrible shock to him. He's not doing very well."

"He's *not*?" Nick said.

"No," BR said, with the faintest trace of a smile. "I'm afraid he isn't."

* * *

As soon as the door to BR's office closed behind him, Nick dashed to his office, only to find yellow CRIME SCENE tape on his door and several FBI technicians in jumpsuits with FBI CRIME SEARCH TEAM in big, intimidating letters on the back. They were wearing latex gloves, and from the looks of it, ransacking every square inch of his office in the process, making it look like Nick's old room at college. God knows what they thought they were going to find in there, Nick thought— presumably a file in his computer labeled "SELF-KIDNAP PLAN. Things to bring to the cabin: 10 boxes NicArrest patches, rope, handcuffs . . ."

"Is this necessary?" he said to one of the FBI technicians, who pointedly ignored him.

He took Gazelle aside. "Get me on the next flight to Winston-Salem."

"They said you weren't supposed to leave the metro area. Conditions of your bail."

"*Gazelle.*"

"Is this going to make me an accessory?"

"All right, all right. Just look up the flights. Can your conscience handle that? I'll get the ticket myself."

He took the elevator down to I Street. A cab was parked, the driver, a Middle Eastern man with a close-cropped black beard, eating a knish from a sidewalk vendor. Nick waved him over and got in the back.

"National Airport. And hurry." It was unnecessary to say that to any foreign-born D.C. cab driver, since they only drive at two speeds, dangerously fast and really dangerously fast. Off they sped.

Nick looked out the rear window and saw a tan sedan with two athletic-looking types with sunglasses. Feds. The headline flashed before him.

NAYLOR IS BACK IN CUSTODY
AFTER VIOLATING BAIL TERMS

According to the license posted on the dash, the driver's name was Akmal Ibrahim.

"Mr. Ibrahim," Nick said, "are you in some sort of trouble with the FBI?"

"Why you say this?"

"Because you're being followed. That tan sedan. Those are FBI agents. I saw them watching you when you were parked."

Akmal looked nervously in the rear-view. "I have no problems with FBI."

"They seem to have some problem with you."

"Ever since World Trade Center bombing, FBI thinks all Muslim people are bad. Is not true. I have family in Reston."

"I know," Nick said. "It's awful the way they persecute people for their religious beliefs. I wonder what they want with you."

"I have nothing to worry."

"Why don't you take a sudden turn without a signal. See if they follow."

Akmal made a sharp turn onto Virginia Avenue at the last minute. The sedan swerved to follow, nearly colliding with a State Department staff car.

Akmal said worriedly, "They follow!"

"Yeah. You know, I saw them put something in your trunk while you were eating."

"What?!"

"It might have just been a listening device, but it might have been something else, like explosives. So they can arrest you for a bomber. I'm a reporter at the *Sun*. We've heard they're planning a big roundup of Muslims. They need hostages to trade with Saddam Hussein in case we go to war with him."

"But I have green card!"

"Well, good luck."

"FBI is arresting many wrong people. In New York they arrest people for the bombing, they are *not* the ones who do the bombing. The bombing is done by Israeli secret police, to make bad feelings about Muslim people in America."

"I know. It's awful. I'm writing a big article about it. But once they stop you and find whatever it is they put in your trunk, that's it, Akmal. That's how they got Sheik Omar, you know. And he's not getting out of prison until the twenty-second century."

"Sheik Omar is very holy man."

"Maybe they'll put you in the same prison. You and he could become friends."

Nick wondered, as he was forced back into his seat by the g-forces as Akmal hit the accelerator, if he had done a wise thing. There was a lot of honking and screeching of tires. When he opened his eyes and looked back, the tan sedan was fifty yards behind. Even highly trained government drivers are no match for the ordinary Middle Easterner.

By the time they'd reached the Arlington end of Memorial Bridge, Akmal had gained more yardage. Then, without any warning, he did a breathtakingly precise bootleg turn into the oncoming traffic, setting off an angry chorus of horns and anti-locking brakes. Nick was slammed into the side of the car.

"We lose them!" Akmal shouted triumphantly.

Nick peered cautiously through the rear window and saw the FBI sedan trying to catch up by speeding around the rotary in front of the cemetery. But by now Akmal had a couple of hundred yards on them. After another stunningly illegal turn, south onto Rock Creek, onto Independence, he did another 180-degree bootleg. Then it was back onto Rock Creek, right on Virginia, left onto Route 66, off at the Iwo Jima Memorial, left onto Route 50, and onto the George Washington Parkway south. Nick tipped Akmal fifty bucks and agreed with him that God was indeed great, then caught the flight to Charlotte, where he connected into Winston-Salem, arriving at the Bowman-Gray Medical Center after the Cardiac Care Unit visiting hours, making it necessary to adopt a rather broad southern accent as he told the head nurse that he was Doak Boykin III, uhgently come to see his deah old grandpappy.

"You're his grandson?" she inquired, a little suspiciously.

"Yay-ess," Nick said, sounding like Butterfly McQueen.

She peered at him. "You look familiar."

Doubtless, Nick's face had been prominently splashed across the front page of the *Tar-Intelligencer*.

"They say ah look *jus* like him. May I please see him? Ah been so *wurried*."

"Well," she said, "all right. But only ten minutes. He's very tired."

"Is he gone to be all rayht?"

"Oh, he just likes to make us all worried. He'll be all right. If he *behaves*."

The Cardiac Care Unit was top of the line, paid for with tobacco money, just another example of how tobacco and progress go hand in hand. The Captain was hooked up to a number of machines. In the semidarkness, their screens cast a cool glow of light onto the Captain's face, which seemed to Nick very pale and drawn. He stood next to the bed.

"Captain?"

The old man's eyes opened, blinked a few times. "I *told* you," he said, "that I will not have any more pig parts put in me. I want *human* parts, damnit."

"Captain. It's me, Nick."

The Captain looked up.

"Why *son*. Sit down, have some oxygen."

"I came to explain to you. About the arrest."

"Yes," the Captain said, coughing. "It could use some explaining. BR called me in the middle of the night to say you were in custody."

"Thank you for the bail money."

"I don't suppose it'll bankrupt us. That Jewish lawyer fellow we hired you probably will, though. Four hundred and fifty dollars an hour . . ."

"This is going to sound a little strange," Nick said, "but here's what I think has happened."

Nick drew a breath and laid it out: BR wanted to fire Nick and replace him with his squeeze, Jeannette, but his appearance on the Oprah show had made him the Captain's gold-haired boy, and that had made BR jealous. The threatening caller on the Larry King show had probably given BR the brainstorm to kill two birds with one stone: remove Nick and drum up some sympathy for tobacco by creating a martyr. BR, who'd come up from the mafia-murky world of vending machines, would have had the connections to hire people to do it. But, to judge from the 'Executed for Crimes Against Humanity' sign, the kidnappers had screwed up by dropping him off on the Mall, still alive. So BR and Jeannette contrived to pin the kidnapping on Nick by having Jeannette seduce him and get his fingerprints all over the boxes of "condoms" and plant them in the cabin on the Virginia lake, along with a few other compromising clues. Nick would go to jail, disgraced, and BR's suspicion would turn out to have been correct, so he'd look like a hero. Of course, the real loser in all this was tobacco. . . .

Nick finished. The Captain looked at him with lowered eyebrows, took a long breath, and said, "You sound like one of those people who thinks there were five gunmen on the Grassy Knoll in Dallas that day."

"I know," Nick said. "It'll probably sound that way in court, too."

"On the other hand," the Captain said, pulling himself up in bed, "preposterous though it sounds, elements of it have a certain," he sighed, "ring to them that make my liver twitchy." He frowned. "BR's been telling me since the week after the kidnapping that he thought you were involved."

"Oh?" Nick said.

"And I have it from my own man in there that he and that blond gal Jumelle—"

"Jeannette."

"—have been making whoopee on company time. So that fits in with this conspiracy theory of yours. I know BR for a jugular fellow. You know, he wanted us to go public that your friend Lorne Lutch had taken the money from us."

"Why?"

"So he'd look like a whore and there'd be no Rancho Canceroso foundation. He never wanted us to pay him off. One conversation we had, he said, 'There are better ways to deal with people like that.' I wondered what he meant. You know, when I hired him away from Allied Vending, we were up to our armpits in liability suits, and I told him I'd pay him a bonus for every one that didn't make it to trial. And three of the big ones didn't make it to trial, on account of, you re-member, they died from smoking in bed. BR made me pay him the bonuses even though those were accidents. Said a deal's a deal. Cost me plenty, too, though a hell of a lot less than it would have if we'd lost in court."

"Captain," Nick said, "I think there something's very *wrong* here."

"You don't think that he . . . no. Now, I don't doubt he mighta been a little jealous of my affection for you. And while it's true people in the vending machine business rub elbows with some rough in-dividuals, I shouldn't think . . . Good Lord, is this possible?" His head sank into his pillow. He put his hand over his eyes. "I'll need to have my man make inquiries."

"Your man? Who's that?"

"Best keep his identity private, for the time being."

The Captain opened his eyes again and removed his hand. "Now Nick, if these grotesqueries that you have revealed to me do turn out to be true, I don't suppose I need to elaborate for you what this is going to mean for our industry."

"Well, no, but . . ."

"Of course, that's not the *prime* consideration here. Assuming that you've been grievously wronged, we'll have to make amends to you. But let me cook you up some hypothetical soup. Suppose—just suppose—assuming we establish that what you're saying is true, which I don't doubt it is, that I fire BR's sorry ass—and that chippy of his, Jumelle—quietly, but with such extreme prejudice that he'll be lucky to get a job selling lottery tickets in Guam. And you were to plead guilty to these charges."

"Guilty?"

"Bear with me. Guilty with an explanation. That is, guilty to the sin of being young and impetuous, just like a lot of other people who've worked in Washington. Hell, you already *got* a reputation for impetuosity on account of telling everyone the President choked. For $450 an hour Carlinsky can damn well get you reduced time at some country club prison where they riot on account of the *coq au vin* was overcooked and the wine wasn't properly chilled."

"Uh—"

"Now here's the really good part. We open up a quiet little bank account in the Cayman Islands for you, say . . . five million dollars. What the hell, ten. Now even counting inflation and taxes, ten million dollars is *still* a lot of money, son. You wouldn't have to work for the rest of your life. You like to fish, don't you? Well, you could buy yourself a nice island somewhere and fish and be fed mangos by dusky women who don't wear clothes. That sounds pretty good to *me*. Tell you what, if you want to go on working for us, I'll put you in charge of the Hong Kong office. You'll be head of all American tobacco business in the Far East. Hell, that's where the future is, anyway. So many Asians, so little time. . . ."

Nick thought. "I like the part about firing BR and Jeannette. I don't know about the rest of it."

"Well, let's take it step by step. We'll start with BR, then see how you feel about taking early retirement."

"I—"

"You're in no shape to make the right decision. You're all wrapped around the axle. You look like you haven't slept in a week. Dark circles under your eyes. Fine tobacco spokesman you are," he murmured.

"All right," Nick said, "step by step."

"Knew you were a sensible fellow. Knew it the first day I met you at the Club. Do you remember? How I would love to wrap my lips around one of their mint juleps right now."

The head nurse was approaching with a stern look on her face. "I'll talk to you later," Nick said. "Get some rest."

"If I oink next time you see me, you'll know I been screwed again."

Nick turned to go. The Captain said after him, "Don't forget, tobacco takes care of its own."

26

The next day Nick was whistling *"C'est fumée! C'est fumée!"* in the midst of restoring his office after its deconstruction by the FBI when Gazelle stuck in her head and in her now customary paranoid whisper hissed: "Nick, *FBI!*"

"Show them right in," he said.

It was agents Monmaney and Allman. They clearly felt that they could dispense with the usual opening pleasantries now that Nick's ass belonged to them.

"Did you leave the city yesterday?" Monmaney barked.

"What," Nick said, going on with his cleanup, "and violate the terms of my bail?"

"You got into a cab outside this office. The driver drove evasively, breaking several traffic laws. For which he has been detained. And questioned."

"Picking on Muslims again, eh?"

Agent Monmaney clenched his fists.

"I'd say he drove quite normally, for a District cab driver."

"He says you told him that we planted something in his trunk."

"Well, you'll have noticed that his English is a little rough. He must have misunderstood me. I did ask him if he ever kept plants in his trunk."

"You're cocky this morning, Nick," Agent Allman said.

"Yes, I am," Nick grinned. "I feel *much* better."

"You bought a ticket to Winston-Salem, North Carolina."

"I did?"

"You want to add perjury to the list? You put it on your air travel card. We have the receipt. And you stayed at the Motel Eight in Winston-Salem. We have that receipt, too."

"Aha."

"What's that mean?"

"I lost my wallet yesterday. Someone must have used my credit cards to fly to Winston-Salem. I must say, odd choice for a travel destination. I'd have gone to someplace more fun. I only noticed it missing this morning. I called them in stolen." He smiled. "You'll be able to verify that."

"Slick, Nick. By the way, everything you say *will* be used against you."

"Are we under arrest again?"

"No," Agent Monmaney said. "For the time being."

"You know," Nick said, "I understand how you guys feel about me. But for what it's worth, I didn't kidnap myself. And you're going to find out that I didn't. So when you do, let's all have a drink together and say, Fuck was all *that* about?"

They regarded Nick dubiously. "You're expecting good news?"

"Oh yes," Nick said. "Very."

"Does it have anything to do with your visit to Winston-Salem?"

"Don't recall I said I *was* in Winston-Salem."

"Let's go," Agent Allman said.

"Say," Nick said, "why don't you let Akmal go. You can't blame him for being spooked. You guys *have* been kind of tough on those poor Muslims."

"Come on," Allman said to Monmaney.

"Ta ta," Nick said.

"Asshole," Monmaney said on the way out.

The visit by the Untouchables, along with his decision not to accept the Captain's hush money, had Nick's mood rising like a soufflé. He couldn't wait for the Captain. He walked to BR's office and, once again ignoring his secretary's remonstrations, went in. Jeannette was with him.

"Ah," Nick said, "teamwork. That's what it's all about, isn't it."

BR scowled. "What do you want, Nick? You're not even sup-

posed to be here."

"But I work here."

"You're on leave. Effective as of now."

"No," Nick smiled, "I don't think so. But I think *you're* about to go on a long leave. And so is Mata Hari over there. Don't forget your rubbers, Jeannette."

Jeannette said, "You can't prove a th—"

BR shushed her, indicating by pantomime that Nick might be wearing a wire. It was so deft that Nick wondered if this was the first time he'd performed it.

Nick wagged his finger at Jeannette. " 'Ooh, Nick, ooh. Here, take the condoms. I got the extra large. . . .' That'll make for fun in the courtroom. As for you, my wonderful, supportive boss, clear something up for me. I couldn't figure out why your rent-a-kidnappers let me live. But it occurred to me that maybe they screwed up. Am I getting warm?"

BR stared.

"So you and your dominatrix girlfriend cooked up the condoms-in-the-NicArrest-boxes scheme? *Very* neat."

"Nick," BR said in a forbearing voice, "you've been under a lot of stress. I think you ought to get some professional help."

"Yes," Nick said. "I have been under a great deal of stress. YOU ASSHOLES!!!"

BR and Jeannette started.

"Sorry," Nick said. "Stress. Well, see you round Cellblock C."

Nick closed the door behind him feeling much better. When he reached his office, Gazelle was sitting at her desk looking particularly woeful.

"Cheer up," said Nick. "Things are going our way."

"You didn't hear?"

"Hear what?"

"The Captain died this morning."

"What I don't understand," Carlinsky said, "is why you didn't tell me this before."

"I didn't *know* it before. And would you please stop saying that. It's very annoying."

"So, as you see it, BR had you kidnapped. The kidnapping failed. 243

Then he and Jeannette framed you by contriving to get your prints on the boxes of what you thought, in the dark, were condoms, but were actually the nicotine patch boxes."

"Right."

"You don't have any proof."

"No," Nick said, "I don't keep a video camera in my bedroom."

"And you shared this scenario with Mr. Boykin the night before he died."

"Yes. He was going to fire BR and Jeannette and then . . ."

"Don't hold back, please. It's very counterproductive."

"He's dead. Why does it matter what he was going to do?"

"Everything matters."

"He asked me to consider taking the fall, in order to spare the industry massive embarrassment. In return for which I'd be extremely well compensated. I decided I wasn't going to do that, and fight it all the way. Then he died."

"Was this conversation recorded?"

"No."

"Too bad. Not that it would have been admissible, but we could have gotten it into the press's hands. It would have caused such an uproar that it would have made it very difficult to empanel a jury. And we'd have ended up with a dumber one. You'll have gathered by now that I like a dumb jury. Dumber the better. Now, as to this matter of Mr. Boykin suggesting that BR may have had something to do with these tobacco liability litigants' deaths by smoke inhalation, *that*," he said, puckering, "is a very *full* can of worms."

"Yes. Nightcrawlers."

"Though again, we have no evidence."

"So, we'll start an investigation into their deaths," Nick said. "We'll feed the press, shake the bushes, the trees. Something'll drop out of them. It'll be great." Nick rubbed his hands together.

"Perhaps. But before we go pointing fingers at high places, you need to consider. It is a high-risk defense strategy. Because if there isn't something, and we've gone trampling on graves, alleging conspiracies that even Oliver Stone would reject, then we'll end up making everyone extremely mad, especially the judge, and you might end up serving a longer stretch of time than even the maximum. At sentencing time, he can decide to make you serve the term for each count consecutively, rather than simultaneously. He can also send you to a maximum security prison. And I'm not sure that's an experience you would enjoy. Of course, that's your decision. Myself, I like a good courtroom dust-up. But it's your ass, not mine. As it were."

Nick was considering all this, to the sound of steel doors clanging shut in his ears, when Carlinsky's secretary came over the speaker. "It's Mr. Rohrabacher, from the Academy of Tobacco Studies. He says it's extremely urgent. I told him you were with a client."

Carlinsky said to Nick, "I guess I should take that."

He picked up the phone. "Yes. Yes. Yes, he is here. I see. Have you told him? I see." He looked at Nick and arched his eyebrows. "Yes. All? Well, yes. We handle those. Of course. We're a large firm. I see. Let me speak with the managing partners and I'll have an answer for you by the end of the day."

Carlinsky hung up. He cleared his throat. "I'm afraid this is awkward. I'm informed that you are no longer with the Academy of Tobacco Studies."

This was a common phenomenon in Washington, finding out from a third party that you've just been fired. Usually, you hear about it on CNN, or over the phone from a reporter calling to confirm that the locks on your office were changed while you were out picking up your dry cleaning. Nick was not all that surprised, especially after receiving the frosty interoffice memo from BR informing him that he was not welcome at the Captain's funeral.

"Well, to hell with him. Let's fight him."

Carlinsky pursed his lips and furrowed his brows. "That might be awkward."

"I *know* you're expensive. But I'm sure we can work something out. You can attach my salary for the rest of my life."

"It's not that. It's a conflict of interest."

"*What* conflict of interest?"

"I can't defend one client by pitting him against another client."

"What 'another' client?"

"Our firm has just been asked to become legal counsel to the Academy of Tobacco Studies."

"You mean, just *now?*"

"Yes. Obviously, having the Academy of Tobacco Studies as a client would mean a considerable amount of business. What with all these smokers suing. But I guess I don't need to tell you that, do I?"

"No," Nick said, "you don't."

"If it were just my decision, it would be one thing. But I have a fiduciary responsibility to report the offer to the partners. On the other hand, who knows. Perhaps they'll decline."

"What I don't understand," Nick said, "is why you didn't tell me you were such a dick *before*."

"I assumed you knew," Carlinsky said.

Nick stepped off the elevators into the Academy's reception area. Carlton was waiting for him.

"Nicky," he said, blushing. "Could I have a word with you?"

"Okay," Nick said. "We can talk in my office."

"Uh, that's what I need to talk with you about." Carlton was whispering. "BR said—gee, Nicky, I feel like a real asshole having to tell you this."

"I think we're all feeling like that these days, Carlton."

"Yeah. Do you want me to bring your stuff to your apartment, or . . . ?"

"That would be fine. Do I get to say good-bye to people, or is this a Stalin thing, where I just disappear without a trace?"

Carlton blushed again. "If it was me . . ."

Jeannette clicked by, looking very smart in suede. *"Nick,"* she smiled. "Just leaving?" She looked at Carlton. "I told you I wanted those budget numbers *now*." She turned and walked off in the direction of BR's office.

Carlton said, "Our new executive VP. What a fuckin' headache, huh?"

TOBACCO LOBBY FIRES NICK NAYLOR

Rohrabacher Says He Is "Shocked"
By the FBI's Evidence Against Him

BY HEATHER HOLLOWAY
MOON CORRESPONDENT

The Mod Squad was no longer meeting at Bert's, but in a dark corner of the Serbian Prince restaurant in suburban Virginia. They deemed this a safe bet, since not many people went to Serbian restaurants anymore. It was so empty, in fact, that they wondered how it managed to stay open. Bobby Jay said that it was obviously a front for Serbian arms merchants. In any event, it was a suitable milieu for the Merchants of Death, for two reasons. The press wasn't likely to find them here; nor were the Muslims. The FBI, seeking revenge for Nick's escape in the taxi, seemed to have convinced Akmal that Nick was an agent provocateur working for the Israelis, and had provided him with his phone number, address, mother's maiden name, everything. What space was left on Nick's answering machine tape after all the calls from reporters was taken up with abuse and threats from a number of people with Middle Eastern accents.

"They cut off my medical insurance," Nick said into his black coffee. "Do you know how hard it is to get medical insurance when your previous place of employment was the Academy of Tobacco Studies?"

"Do you need health insurance if you're a federal prisoner?" Polly said. Polly, herself fleeing reporters, was in elegant mufti, sunglasses, and shawl. She looked like a cross between Jackie O and Mother Russia. And with the sunglasses, in this dark, she kept knocking things over.

"No," Bobby Jay said, stirring his coffee with his hook. "Prisons have their own doctors. Naturally, they're very highly qualified, all from Ivy League medical schools."

"Could we not talk about this," Nick said morosely.

"I'm sure it won't come to that," Polly said, touching his arm.

"That's what everyone's been telling me. Like, I might get really lucky and end up on a converted military base in a desert for ten years. It's a very consoling thought."

"Sounds a whole lot better to me than Lorton," Bobby Jay snorted. Lorton was the prison in Virginia where they sent the overflow hard cases from the D.C. jails. It enjoyed a reputation as a not particularly nourishing environment, especially for inmates of the Caucasian persuasion.

"You're not going to Lorton," Nick said, annoyed by the attempt   *247* at one-downmanship. "You're a handicapped Vietnam vet, it's a first offense. You'll get six months, suspended. So please, spare me the Ballad of Reading Gaol."

"Oh yeah? Then how come the lawyers tell me the prosecutor is just *itching* to put me away? First, I'm white, secondly, I work for the most hated lobby in America—"

"Whoa. The gun lobby is not the 'most hated lobby in America.' Do I need to remind you that I am personally responsible for the deaths of over half a million people each year, whereas you are barely responsible for thirty thousand—"

"Oh, Jesus," Polly said.

"I'm sorry," said Nick. "I'm not in a good mood right now."

"How odd," Polly said.

"The Captain's funeral is tomorrow. I've been told in no uncertain terms that I'm not welcome. And guess who's giving the eulogy." He shook his head. "BR."

As the sweat pooled inside his fake beard and fake nose, Nick reflected that it was a good thing the Captain had asked to be buried up in Roaring Gap, where it was a little less infernally hot than Winston-Salem. It was sweltering inside the Baptist church, and jam-packed. Nick's rubber nose felt like it was going to drop off and the pinched, elderly woman sitting next to him was already looking at him strangely.

There were reporters in the back, some from the national press. The Captain's passing, amidst the kidnapping scandal, was being played as The End of an Era. WHITHER TOBACCO?

BR had just taken the pulpit.

"Doak Boykin," he began, "strode the world of tobacco like the colossus he was. He would give you the shirt off his back. He was, truly, the salt of the earth."

God, who'd written this swill for him? (Jeannette.) Vilified in his autumnal years, his heart patched with parts from barnyard swine, and now eulogized by a Judas with a fondness for clichés. The man deserved better, even if he was a mass murderer.

"He was a man who believed in the Constitution of the United States of America, especially the parts about individual liberties and the right to the pursuit of happiness."

That was in the Declaration of Independence, but never mind. . . .

"I think everyone gathered here would agree that, these days, it takes courage to stand up to the politically correct and the sanctimonious, who are trying to destroy a perfectly legal American product."

A deft bit of self-praise. Murmurs of approval.

"And the Captain had that kind of courage, in spades. I also know that many of you agree that he would have been saddened by the recent events in our own backyard. If there was a silver lining to his far too premature parting, it was this—that he will not have to endure the slings and arrows of misfortune that his misguided, overambitious, and perhaps mentally ill protégé has brought down on our house."

The entire tobacco establishment, the heads of the Big Six—his new peers, now that he had completed his climb up from the world of vending machines—were all sitting in the front pews. And now he was distancing himself from Nick by making it clear that he had been the *Captain's* Frankenstein monster.

"Suh? *Suh?*"

It was the woman next to him, hissing: "Would you mind not growlin'? And there is something *very* wrong with your nose."

The Captain had been cremated—a brave choice, Nick thought, for a tobacco man; the press would have a good snigger over that—and his ashes scattered at the lake, from where he'd called Nick many times on his cellular while casting for one of the big ones.

The crowd along the shore for the scattering was deep, but Nick, being tall, was able to see from the rear. The Captain's family were all standing on the wooden pier: his wife Maylene and seven daughters, Andy, Tommie, Bobbie, Chris, Donnie, Scotty, and Dave, all in hats and dabbing at their eyes with lace hankies. The Captain's ashes were in a large silver cigarette box, a nice touch

The minister, a squat, pink man in robes, read what the program said had been the Captain's favorite Old Testament passage.

"And Nahar did go unto the place of Gunt, who had been unrighteous and split the tongue of Nahar's brother, Rehab, with a rock. And he did say to him, 'Thou boil and pestilence,' and did strike a flint on the rock, which madeth a spark, withthewhich he set fire to the hem of Gunt's tunic, and Gunt did flee, quickly, out of the land, for he *was* on fire. And Nahar said to his brother, Rehab, 'Now thou seeest that smoke and fire *are* good and have their purpose. And Rehab sayest, 'Yeth.' "

"A-men," said the assembled.

"And now," the minister said, "we commit his ashes to the deep . . ."

The man standing next to Nick said to his wife, "Ain't but four foot deep theah."

"Hush," his wife said.

". . . where they await in hopes of eternal resurrection. . . ."

As he spoke, the silver cigarette box with the Captain's ashes was passed from daughter to daughter, who each spooned out a little bit of old dad into the lake and passed it on to the next. It was very touching.

Nick felt a firm, gripping hand on his bicep. He spun around and saw a sheriff's deputy, young, meaty, and with a big semi-auto pistol handle protruding from its holster. Over the cop's shoulder, Nick saw the pinched, elderly woman pointing out Nick to someone.

"You Nick Naylor?"

"Uh . . ."

"Sir, we have been advised by the FBI to take you into custody. Would you come with me?" He tugged.

Shit, thought Nick. DISGRACED PROTÉGÉ ARRESTED AT MENTOR'S FUNERAL; NEW CHARGE IS ADDED TO LIST: BAIL VIOLATION.

He followed, awaiting the now-familiar snap of steel around his wrists.

Suddenly a man was at their side.

"Officer," he said in a commanding voice. He flashed a badge. "Raleigh FBI. Good work, deputy. I'll take it from here."

The deputy beamed and relaxed his grip, releasing Nick into the custody of—Gomez O'Neal.

27

Gomez played it all the way down to handcuffs, though it irked Nick that he did it in full view of the mourners. He even put his hand on top of Nick's head as he put him into the back seat of the car, just the way real cops do.

"I thought you might pull a stupid stunt like attending the funeral," Gomez said, "so I brought along a badge from my collection. How come you violated your bail for a second time?"

"I love North Carolina. Can we take off the handcuffs now? You put them on tight. I'm losing circulation."

"Maybe I ought to leave 'em on." A strange sense of humor, Gomez.

He drove for an hour, not saying much, in the opposite direction of Raleigh, then went onto back roads and pulled over at a roadside dive called Mudd's, where the menu offered hot fried catfish and iced tea. The catfish came on newspaper, the iced tea came in mason jars.

"The Captain told me he had a man at the Academy," Nick said. "I thought it was you."

"Our new *chairman*—" he pronounced the word with distaste "—has probably figured that out, too," Gomez said, wiping away the grease. "If he didn't know all along. Maybe that's why him and me seem to have this problem."

"I saw the Captain the night before he died."

"I *know* that. He called me at 11:45. The time of death was listed as 12:05 A.M. I told him he didn't sound too good." Gomez drank some tea and rattled the ice inside the jar. "He said to look after you if anything happened. Looks like we're there."

Nick leaned across the newspaper. "Did he mention anything to you about BR and those tobacco litigants who died?"

Gomez looked out the window. "Nice place." He stared at Nick. "I like you, kid. You got heart. But if you ever tell anyone—lawyer, prosecutor, judge, your two Mod Squad buddies, or even your kid— that this came from me . . . then you and I would have a problem, no matter what I promised the Captain. So, are we reading off the same sheet of music so far?"

"Yes," Nick said.

"All right, now let's see if we can stay on the ball. After Mrs. Cappozallo, who you'll recall was the third person with lung cancer who was suing us, died from smoke inhalation, I began to think that what we had here was some kind of pattern. So I made my inquiries. Do not ask how I made them, or who I made them to. It's only relevant that it turned out that BR was doing a little networking with his old connections from his vending machine days."

"Networking?"

"Setting up a squad to take care of these liability cases."

"A *death* squad?"

"What happened was, the Captain offered BR a bonus of a quarter million for every case that didn't come to court. Obviously, he didn't mean for BR to kill these people. He was just giving him some financial incentive to work his butt off with the lawyers who were fighting the cases. These cases were driving the industry crazy. Now BR, since he came up through vending machines—which is not Marquis of Queensberry—he decided to deal with it in his way, and before you know it, litigants are croaking of smoke inhalation, from dropping lit cigarettes on themselves in bed." Gomez shrugged. "In a way, you gotta hand it to him. It's kind of poetic justice. And as hits go, it's a piece of cake. Just sneak in, drop a lit cigarette on the pillow, and— suit dismissed."

"Can we prove it?"

"What's to prove? They're dead. The Captain's dead. BR is on top of the world. You're a yuppie dick facing ten to fifteen for a fucking publicity stunt. Who's going to believe you?" Gomez chuckled, "You're the guy who told the world the President was dead."

"Thank you for reminding me. Just when I'd forgotten."

"Use your head, kid. These people who did this are still out there. And they're good. I know they screwed up your case, but they sure as shit didn't screw up with those three litigants. You go telling the FBI about this, two things are going to happen. First, they're going to laugh their asses off. Second, *you're* going to wake up dead from smoke inhalation."

"So where does that leave us?"

"I'm okay. You're neck-deep in shit."

"That's helpful."

"Okay," Gomez sniffed, "here's what I can give you. Name and an address. I know they were both wearing makeup when they snatched you, but you will recognize him. When he's not killing people, he acts."

"Axe?"

"He's an *actor*. I guess he can't be that good, or he wouldn't be killing people for a living. It's amateur stuff, light opera, that kind of crap."

"Peter Lorre," Nick said.

"Yeah, him."

"I was kidnapped and tortured and nearly killed by a bad actor?"

"Bad actor, but a *good* killer. Before he did the three litigants he was—well, you probably don't need to know all that. But take my word for it, when you make your move, don't mess up."

"*My* move? What is my move?"

Gomez sat back in his seat and picked at a piece of stuck catfish with a toothpick. "That's up to you, kid."

"But I'm just a yuppie dick. What am I supposed to do, challenge him to a debate on hit men on the *Donahue* show? 'Men who kill other men, and the ones who get away, next, on *Donahue*'?"

"No." Gomez smiled enigmatically. "I'd expect you to be smarter than that." He slid a piece of paper across the table. There was a name and address printed on it.

"Can you memorize that?"

"Yeah."

"Then do it." Gomez took the slip of paper back, held it over the mason jar, and set it on fire. The ash sizzled onto the ice. "This will come in useful. 'Team B.' "

"Team B? The Presidential Foreign Intelligence Advisory Board?"

Gomez nodded. "Smart boy. I thought it sounded familiar. BR must have taken the name from that."

"But what's Team B?"

"Team B," Gomez said, "is the code name for his little special operation squad. Here's something else that will be useful: 'Team A.' "

"What's that?"

"Use your head, kid."

"Will you *stop* calling me that? I'm not Lauren Bacall and you're not Humphrey Bogart."

"Team A, obviously, is BR."

Nick thought. "I still don't get what I'm supposed to do."

"Well, Nick, the way things are going for you, you'll figure out something. Necessity is the motherfucker of invention."

In the car on the mostly quiet drive to the airport, Nick said, "Why are you doing this?"

Gomez thought. "I could tell you I was doing it for the Captain. But since I like you, I'm not going to bullshit you. I like my job at the Academy. I believe in cigarettes. I think we're overpopulated. The planet could use a break, you know what I mean? I'm glad we're getting into the Asian markets in a big way. I spent a lot of time working in Asia, Nam, Laos, Cambodia, Indonesia, China, and let me tell you, I'm not losing sleep over the idea of thinning out *those* hordes. Their food's good, though. I always liked the food."

"You're in this for *population control?*"

"Sure, but honestly? I like the hours, too. It's not too demanding. Most of what I do involves finding out stuff about people, and *that* I can do in my sleep. I like the hours, I like the pension plan, good medical, vacation. I like the whole package. But I do *not* like BR. And I like him even less now that he's got the chairmanship. And," he said, "I do not like this split-tail squeeze that he's just made executive vice president. Now I'm supposed to answer to her, and," he chuckled, "I have *never* answered to a woman before. So I'm anticipating problems, and at this stage of my life, I'm just looking to put in a few more years and take early retirement. And these two are complicating my plans."

"Split-tail? "Were you in the navy?" Nick asked.

"Do you *want* to know?"

254 "No," Nick said.

28

"I don't see why you can't say who told you about this," Polly said with an edge to her voice, owing to the headline in the day's *Moon*.

NAYLOR, GUN LOBBYIST, LIQUOR SPOKESWOMAN
BELONGED TO CLUB CALLED "THE MOD SQUAD":
AN ACRONYM FOR "MERCHANTS OF DEATH"

Three Spokesmen of the Yuppocalypse?

BY HEATHER HOLLOWAY
MOON CORRESPONDENT

Her boss was not at all thrilled by this deplorable revelation; nor was Stockton Drum, Bobby Jay's boss, who had so far been a brick, even proud that his boy was now down and dirty in the Second Amendment trenches. About the only person who was pleased, though he would not admit it, was Bert, whose restaurant had now been put on the Scandal Tours itinerary, a popular Washington tourist bus whose other stops included the Watergate, the Tidal Basin, and the hotel where the FBI had caught Mayor Barry smoking crack.

"Because," Nick said, "I want to live. And the person who told me this made it clear that that would no longer be an option if I revealed his identity."

"This stuff is so strong it's melting my hook," Bobby Jay said, wiping off the thick coating of coffee grounds.

"Would you *please* stop doing that," said Polly. A TV camera crew, hot on the heels of the morning's Mod Squad story, had shown up at her Sober Drivers 2000, shouting blunt questions at her during the Q and A. All she could do was to cast aspersions on the *Moon* for being owned by a Korean who said he was the Messiah. It was generally what people did whenever the *Moon,* a pretty good newspaper, published something true that they didn't like.

The strong Serbian coffee was not improving Polly's nerves. She was drumming her fingernails on the table. *C-c-c-clink, c-c-c-click.* "Then why don't you tell us where Ms. World Class Tits got *this.*"

"I would guess," Nick said mournfully, "that she got that from Jeannette."

"Oh?" Polly said, flaring. "And how did Jeannette know about the Mod Squad?"

Nick sighed. "You're not going to like it."

"My day *began* ruined, so you won't be spoiling it."

"She got it from you."

"What are you talking about?"

"You remember leaving a message on my machine congratulating me on the killer cheddar cheese the night I went on *Nightline*?"

"Yes," Polly said suspiciously.

"Well, uh, you, uh mentioned, uh the Mod Squad, and . . ."

"So I mentioned Mod Squad. People think that's a TV show in reruns."

"Yeah, but, uh . . ."

"Will you *stop* saying 'uh'? I've already maxed out my Prozac today, and I can't take any more. *Spit it out.*"

"Well, Jeannette was there in the apartment and we were, uh, she asked me what it meant and . . ."

It was good that Polly was wearing her Jackie O sunglasses, because Nick didn't want to see what kind of looks she was giving him.

"First," she finally said, "you tell us that you were fucking this slut. And now you tell us that you were fucking *us* at the same time."

"I'm not happy about this," Nick said.

"*You're* not happy about this?"

"I'm *really* unhappy about this."

"Oh, well then," Bobby Jay said, "in that case, no problem." He added, "Fornicator."

"Maybe I'll get religion after all this," Nick said.

"The Christian Prison Fellowship has chapters in most of the better penitentiaries."

"Asshole," Polly said, leaving.

They watched her go. Bobby Jay said, "Nicely done, son. Before you arrived tonight, she told me she was going to liquidate her savings to help you with your legal expenses."

"Why would she do that?"

Bobby Jay shook his head. "Boy, you're dumber than a mud box." Bobby Jay left.

"I'll get the check," Nick said, to no one in particular.

At first he didn't recognize the extraordinarily awful taste in his mouth, nor did he have a clue as to where he was. Wherever it was, it had a spectacular view of Washington. He was on the Arlington side, this much he did know. The dawning fact that he was surrounded by identical tombstones, and many thousands of them, suggested that he was somewhere in Arlington National Cemetery. Then he was able to identify the revolting layer of scum on his tongue. Slivovitz. The residue of glass after glass after glass of it. Yes, it was coming back now: he had ended the evening singing Serbian fighting songs shoulder to shoulder with the waiters and kitchen staff. Somehow he had driven himself to Arlington Cemetery, and had gotten himself over the fence. His ripped trousers and the acute pain in his right kneecap implied that this had not been smartly done.

But why Arlington?

That came back to him too. He had come here to kill himself.

He liked Arlington, sometimes came here on a nice day, just to stroll and check out who was who. There were over two hundred thousand people buried here, which was a lot of dead people, though it wasn't, it occurred to him uncomfortably, even half one year's smoking casualties. He remembered deciding not to kill himself at his apartment so his cleaning lady wouldn't have to find him. He remembered the speedometer hitting 110 mph and aiming for the concrete pillars of the overpass, but chickening out, just in time, when he remembered that the car had an airbag and he'd probably end up a quadraplegic for the rest of his life, and an extremely bitter one at that.

At which point he looked up and saw ARLINGTON NATIONAL CEME-TERY. Why not? There was no rope in the trunk, so he decided to hang himself with the jumper cables. There they were, by his feet.

He picked them up. They felt kind of rubbery. He didn't relish hanging himself with the equivalent of a bungee cord. He saw himself bouncing up and down, his head banging against the branch.

He considered. The Metro stopped at Arlington. He could clamp the jumper cables to the third rail. Seven hundred fifty volts should do the trick nicely. That would give the headline-writing bastards material.

His watch showed 4:23 A.M. The trains weren't running yet. He stood, wincing from the pain in his knee, and hobbled up the hill. He could see a flickering light not far off that turned out to be the eternal flame on President Kennedy's grave.

Who better to share his final moments with? One young victim to another, cut off in the prime of life. . . .

Whoa.

Hard to lie to yourself in a cemetery.

Let's be honest, kid—Gomez O'Neal seemed to be doing the voice-over for what was left of his conscience—*you're a washed-out, forty-year-old snake-oil vendor on the payroll, until recently, of people who sell death for a living. On the Karmic food chain, you're somewhere between a sea slug and eel shit. You've fucked up two careers, one marriage, and two good friendships. Just think what you could have accomplished if you'd lived to a ripe old age.*

So—a tragic career, happily cut short.

He stood at the fringe of the gravesite, apprehensive about being stopped by the park police.

NAYLOR ARRESTED WITH JUMPER CABLE AT JFK GRAVE

Claims His Car Battery Went Dead
Was Seeking "Inspiration" at Difficult Time

JUDGE ORDERS PSYCHIATRIC EXAMINATION

But there were no signs of police, so he walked closer to the flame, which glowed warmly in the predawn chill.

A rustle in the bushes. Movement. Oh God—did they let Dobermans patrol on the loose?

Remains at JFK Gravesite
Are Identified as Naylor's

For a man who wanted to die, he was awfully scared. He hobbled over to a bush opposite and crouched and hid.

A bum stumbled out of the bushes. Nick peered. He was layered with rags, and seemed enormous and hunched over, like an apparition out of a Grimm fairy tale. The bum coughed. A great, deep baritone volcano of a cough—one of our clients, for sure—and then spat in Nick's direction. It landed with a vile, liquidy *splat*.

His pulmonary ablutions done, the bum reached into his pockets and after much rummaging produced a bent cigarette stub. He stuck it in his mouth and rummaged for a match. The search went on for quite a while; he seemed to have about a hundred pockets in all those layers.

No match.

He walked over to the eternal flame, got down on his hands and knees, and lit his cigarette.

As epiphanies go, a mixed signal.

29

Moon Exclusive:
Naylor Says He Will Plead "Guilty"
To Charges in Self-Abduction Scheme

Absolves His "Mod Squad" Friends;
Says "Merchant of Death" Term
Was "Mine and Only Mine"

BY HEATHER HOLLOWAY

"The service here has improved," Polly said.

"Yes," Nick said. "The staff and I are all old friends now. They told me if I wanted to go over there and help them wipe out the remaining Bosnian Muslims, they'd be happy to arrange it. But I told them I needed to stay on the good side of Muslims. Lot of Muslims in the U.S. prison system."

Bobby Jay said, "Maybe the judge'll . . . he's *got* to give you something for pleading guilty."

"I wish you'd checked with us before you did this," Polly said, looking fraught.

"You weren't speaking to me."

"There might have been an easier way of getting us off the Mod Squad rap."

"It's a little late for alternative suggestions. Anyway, don't flatter yourself. Maybe I didn't just do it for you two."

"Then why," Polly said, "are you pleading guilty if you're not guilty? Assuming . . ."

"I am guilty," Nick said. "I'm just not guilty of that."

"Hell is that supposed to mean?" Bobby Jay said.

"Crimes against humanity. Maybe it's just a mid-life crisis. I don't know. I'm tired of lying for a living."

Polly and Bobby Jay stared. "You going soft on us?" Bobby Jay said.

"No, but let's be real. Who's going to believe *me* in court?"

"Got a point."

"And who's got a million and a half dollars for legal expenses? Do I want to work for a law firm for the rest of my life?"

"So," Bobby Jay said, "BR and Jeannette get a free ride after this world of hurt they dumped on you?"

"Well," Nick said, "*that* depends."

"On what?"

He grinned. "On whether *you've* gone soft."

"Vengeance is mine, saith the Lord. I *will* repay. Romans twelve, nineteen."

"What about you, Split-tail?" Nick said. "You want to be the designated driver?"

"Split-tail?" Polly said.

"I don't know if I'm cut out for this," Polly said. She and Nick were sitting in a rented sedan parked fifty yards from the Two-Penny Opera House, a converted warehouse in a part of lower Manhattan that was still some years away from having art galleries and coffee shops. Polly was chain-smoking, filling the car with so much smoke that Nick had to keep the windows open. It was steamy out, and it would have been nicer to have the air-conditioning on.

"You're doing fine," Nick said comfortingly. "But you shouldn't smoke like that. You're going to kill yourself."

Polly looked at him.

A snoring sound came from Bobby Jay in the back seat. He'd fallen asleep. Nick and Polly could hear the Bible tape playing on his Walkman.

"How can he *sleep*?" Polly said with annoyance.

"He was in Vietnam," Nick said, sipping coffee.

"But this person is a contract killer."

"So were the Vietcong," Nick said. He checked his watch. "They're running late tonight."

"It's the dress rehearsal," Polly said. "Maybe the director told them they all sucked and they're going to go through it again." She lit another cigarette. Nick groaned and rolled down the window. She said, "Why don't we just do it tonight and get it over with."

"Polly," Nick said, touching her arm, "just relax."

"Relax," she shuddered. "Two weeks following this . . . person around New York and you tell me, 'Relax.' "

"Do you want me to rub your neck?"

"Yes," Polly said. "There. Ah."

"What's going on?" Bobby Jay said from the back seat.

"Not much," Nick said. "They're running late."

"I'm glad opening night's tomorrow," Bobby Jay said. "I couldn't take another night of this. This town is not beloved of God."

"Why would anyone want to see *H.M.S. Pinafore* set in the twenty-seventh century aboard the Starship *Enterprise*?" Polly said.

"I don't know," Nick said, "but he's playing the right part. Dick Deadeye."

"Do you think he's any good?"

"How good an actor could he be if he has to kill people for a living?" Bobby Jay snorted.

The next night the three of them sat not in a sedan but in a rented panel truck. Polly was behind the wheel, tapping her feet nervously and chewing gum, as Nick had forbidden her to smoke until after the operation was over. She was dressed up as a New York City hooker, gold hot pants, heels, bustier, and so much makeup that her mother might not have recognized her; or, if she had, would have cried. Actually, Nick thought she looked kind of . . . good. For his part, he was once again sweltering underneath a disguise, a nylon stocking pulled down over his head. Bobby Jay was also uncomfortable, but having spent many a night lying in ambush in warmer places, was keeping cooler than Nick. He was doing a crossword puzzle with a tiny flashlight.

"They're coming out," Polly said, as the doors opened and opera-goers began to spill onto the trash-strewn sidewalks.

"Do they look uplifted?" Bobby Jay said.

"More like relieved," Nick said.

Bobby Jay checked his watch and went back to his crossword puzzle. "Three-letter word for air pollutant beginning with *E*."

"ETS," said Nick. "Environmental Tobacco Smoke."

"Fits."

About the time they estimated Peter Lorre would have removed his makeup and changed back into his regular clothes, Polly stepped out of the van, tugging down at her hot pants, which had ridden so high up in the car that half her southern hemispheres were on display. Very nice hemispheres, Nick observed. Bobby Jay chambered the round into the riot gun that he had borrowed from the SAFETY museum collection.

"That is a *large* bullet," Nick said.

"Brits use 'em on Irish Catholics." Bobby Jay grinned. "By regulation, they're supposed to aim at the legs. But this SAS major who came to lunch with me and Stockton told us"—he mimicked a British accent—" 'Sometimes we miss.' "

Nick winced at the thought of a hard-rubber projectile the size of a vibrator connecting with his tender vittles at five hundred feet per second.

Peter Lorre walked out the stage door and turned in their direction.

"He's alone, good." They'd observed, over two weeks, that the other actors didn't seem to gravitate toward him. Fine. Now they wouldn't have to follow him.

As Peter Lorre walked past the van, Nick opened the rear door just enough to give Bobby Jay aiming room.

On cue, Polly intersected with him on the sidewalk. "Got a match?" she said.

Peter Lorre looked her up and down. He smiled at her. "Don't you know smoking's bad for you?"

"Shoot that asshole," Nick hissed.

Bobby Jay took aim.

"Want to have some fun?" Polly asked him.

"I don't pay for fun."

"Tell you what," Polly said. "You look like such a stud, I'll do you free."

Peter Lorre said, "I don't sleep with whores."

"Too bad," Polly said, moving away, "you'll never know what you missed."

Bobby Jay fired. There was a loud shotgun blast and ten ounces of hard black rubber hit Peter Lorre in the solar plexus, knocking every every cubic centimeter of air out of his lungs. He went down onto his back. Nick and Bobby Jay jumped out of the van and dragged him into it, Bobby Jay looping his hook through his pants belt. Polly jumped into the driver's seat, pulled off her wig, and drove.

"This boy is *out*," said Bobby Jay, checking Lorre's vitals.

Nick gave him a kick in the ribs. "Now he's *really* out."

"I *thought* the point was not to kill him," Bobby Jay said.

"He'll live."

They cinched the plastic police bands tightly around his wrists behind him and put the black hood over his head.

They were under the river and into New Jersey before they heard him groan and start to shift around—painfully, Nick hoped. They waited another five minutes until they saw him lift up his head to try to take stock of his situation before they activated Phase Two. Satisfied that Peter Lorre was fully conscious, Nick pressed Play and the sound of their altered voices came over the speaker. They'd tested it several times to make sure that it would be audible in the rear of the van, where they had placed him, on the floor, right by the rear doors.

FIRST VOICE: Slow down, let's not get a speeding ticket.

SECOND VOICE: *That'd* be a fucking bummer.

FIRST VOICE: He still out?

SECOND VOICE: Yeah, he looks out.

FIRST VOICE: Well, if he moves, pop him with the .45.

SECOND VOICE: Hey, this is a rental. *I* don't wanna spend the rest of the night scrubbing blood out of the back.

FIRST VOICE: Is that an International House of Pancakes? I could really go for some bacon waffles.

SECOND VOICE: Bacon? You know what that does to your arteries?

FIRST VOICE: Frank, we gotta die of *something*.

SECOND VOICE: I want to be screwed to death. You pass an International House of Pussy, pull over.

FIRST VOICE: I got one of those cross-country ski machines. Twenty minutes on one of those and you sweat, let me tell you. You know who uses one of those things? Joey Two Stomachs.

SECOND VOICE: Get out of here.

FIRST VOICE: No, for real. He went to that Pritikin place, you know, where you eat crabgrass and they charge you ten thousand dollars a day. He's lost something like twenty-five pounds. And by the way, he doesn't want to be called Joey Two Stomachs anymore.

SECOND VOICE: Fucking *psychopath*. I could tell you stories.

FIRST VOICE: That's why I'm not calling him Joey Two Stomachs anymore.

SECOND VOICE: Sir Joey.

Laughter.

FIRST VOICE: How much further is it?

SECOND VOICE: Ten miles, about.

FIRST VOICE: I don't see why we gotta take him all the way out to some abandoned quarry in New Jersey when we could weigh him down and throw him in the fucking wetlands. No one is gonna *know*.

SECOND VOICE: I *told* you why. Because Team A said to take him to the quarry, and this is on his dime, okay?

FIRST VOICE: He's not gonna *know*.

SECOND VOICE: What's the fucking problem?

FIRST VOICE: I'm hungry. Maybe there's a McDonald's.

SECOND VOICE: We're not pulling into fucking McDonald's, all right?

FIRST VOICE: We'll do the drive-up.

SECOND VOICE: What if he comes to and starts moaning?

FIRST VOICE: I got my gun pointed right at his fucking heart. If he moans, it's going to be *his* problem, not ours.

SECOND VOICE: You got it silenced?

FIRST VOICE: *Yes* I got it silenced. Will you—Jesus. What am I, a fucking *amateur*?

SECOND VOICE: We'll be there before you know.

FIRST VOICE: Who is Team A, anyway?

SECOND VOICE: Some guy in Washington.

FIRST VOICE: Washington? Yeah? Is this one of those government subcontracts? This guy in the back important?

SECOND VOICE: Not anymore.

Laughter.

FIRST VOICE: So, who's Team A?

SECOND VOICE: Some lobbyist.

FIRST VOICE: Lobbyist? What's that?

SECOND VOICE: An asshole with an expense account.

FIRST VOICE: Yeah, well, you want my honest opinion about Washington? They're *all* assholes. I'm getting sick of this shit. Couple more of these and I'm out. I'm going to start a restaurant.

SECOND VOICE: You'll poison them to death instead of shooting them?

FIRST VOICE: No, I'm serious.

SECOND VOICE: I'll make a reservation.

They'd left in a few moments of silence.

FIRST VOICE: So is that why we're called "Team C"? Cause he's "Team A"?

SECOND VOICE: I guess so. It's a code. People in Washington like codes.

FIRST VOICE: Team C sounds like my kid's fruit drink. Why couldn't we be the Sons of Thunder?

SECOND VOICE: Okay, we're the Sons of Thunder. I think the turnoff is somewhere up—

FIRST VOICE: Look out for the truck!!!

Polly had been practicing bootleg turns all week. With the speedometer at just under forty, she turned the wheel slightly to the left and at the same time stepped down hard on the parking brake, whose locking mechanism had been disabled. The van spun 180 degrees. As it did, Peter Lorre was hurtled back through the rear doors, which had been loosely shut with a piece of duct tape. Out he went onto the deserted country road, landing with a thump.

The next snatch of dialogue was loudly amplified.

FIRST VOICE: Never mind him! Get the fuck out of here! Move it!

Off they sped.

"Did you *hear* that sound he made when he landed?" Nick said gleefully.

"Sounded squishy," Bobby Jay said.

"Do you think we killed him?" Polly asked.

Nick was looking back through binoculars. Peter Lorre was rolling himself over to the shoulder of the road. "Nope. Almost a shame."

"He's going to be sore tomorrow."

"I need a drink," Polly said.

"You know what I want?" Nick said.

"What's that?"

"A *cigarette*."

30

NEW HEAD OF TOBACCO LOBBY IS FOUND DEAD
OF SMOKE INHALATION AT HOME OF ASSOCIATE

Friends Say Rohrabacher Was "a Health Nut" and a Nonsmoker
Jeannette Dantine, ATS Exec VP, Is Sought by Police for Questioning

BY HEATHER HOLLOWAY
WASHINGTON SUN STAFF WRITER

Epilogue

"**G**ood evening, I'm Larry King. Our guest tonight, Nick Naylor, who has been here before on several occasions, but tonight is *not* going to tell us that there is no link between smoking and lung cancer. Right?"

"That's right, Larry."

"This book you've written, *Thank You for Smoking*. Curious title. What does it mean?"

"It's meant to be ironic, Larry. Though my former employers, the tobacco lobby, for whom I used to lie on shows like this, actually have signs printed that say that."

"This book you've written is very controversial. It's got a lot of people angry."

"Yes it has, Larry."

"Let's run down the list. Jeff Megall, head of the most powerful talent agency in Hollywood. He's called it 'Beneath comment.' "

"I'll take it as a compliment, Larry. As you may know, his former executive assistant, Jack Bein, has bought the movie rights to the book. He and Jeff had a falling out."

"Senator Ortolan K. Finisterre, very powerful man here in Washington, says that you wrote the book to quote clear your troubled conscience unquote."

"Actually, Larry, it was prison that pretty much cleared my conscience."

"So why the book?"

"Money, Larry. I wrote the book for money."

"That's refreshing to hear."

"My wife, Polly, and I are expecting a child and, well, you know, tuition and all. . . ."

"Congratulations. What about your other 'Mod Squad' friend—that stands for 'Merchant of Death,' right?"

"Right."

"Tell us what's become of Bobby Jay Bliss, the former gun lobby spokesman?"

"He's very big in the Christian Prison Fellowship organization. You know, the organization founded by Chuck Colson. He's happy. Still shoots. We see him. Of course, we don't call ourselves that anymore, since we now recognize the wickedness of our former ways."

"And Polly, does she work?"

"Yes, since becoming pregnant, she's gotten very interested in prenatal health issues. She's with the Fetal Alcohol Syndrome Foundation here in Washington. Fasfuff."

"You say in the book, which by the way, I recommend to our viewers, a very good book—"

"Thank you, Larry."

"—that you pleaded guilty even though you *didn't* kidnap yourself and cover yourself with nicotine patches. Question—Why?"

"Well, Larry, for two reasons. First, I was told that it would cost something like a million and a half dollars in legal fees to fight that, and I don't have that kind of money. Secondly, I came to the conclusion that I deserved to be put away for all the horrible things I did when I worked for the tobacco industry. By the way, if any of our viewers have lung cancer from smoking or anything, or have relatives who do, I'd like to apologize. And if any kids are listening, listen, don't smoke. It'll kill you. Also stains your teeth, which is totally uncool."

"Any idea, then, who did kidnap you?"

"None at all, Larry. I guess I'll go to my grave wondering."

"What was prison like?"

"Oh, not too bad. It was one of those minimum security places, Pleasanton, California, where they send insider traders and such. Mostly, it was boring. Really, really boring."

"And you were there for two and a half years?"

"Uh-huh. I did meet some interesting people. Lot of bankers."

"So what are you doing now that you've finished the book?"

"I'm working for an organization called Clean Lungs 2000, Larry. It's a very fine organization that, basically, tries to get people to stop smoking."

"Satisfying work?"

"Oh, very. And I'm learning things. For instance, did you know that smoking causes impotence?"

"No."

"It's a scientific fact, Larry. There's some very interesting research going on right now. Of course, the tobacco lobby doesn't want you to know that."

"In your book you depict your former boss, BR, Budd Rohrabacher, as a pretty devious person."

"May he rest in peace, he was a thorough swine, Larry."

"What about his assistant, Jeannette, the one the police suspect may have had something to do with his death by smoke inhalation."

"I understand from some former—from some people that she's probably in the Far East somewhere, working for an escort service that caters to particular tastes."

"Do you think that she killed him?"

"Who knows, Larry. These things do happen, of course. People get careless with cigarettes. Of course, the most careless thing you can do with any cigarette is to light it in the first place."

"The subtitle of the book—*Jujitsuing the Neo-Puritans*—what does that mean?"

"Well, as you know, jujitsu is the Japanese art of self-defense in which you use your opponent's weight and strength against him. That was really all I ever had to do. Though I certainly don't advocate smoking, there are some very sanctimonious people lined up on the nonsmoking side. So it was just a matter of giving them a little shove and putting my foot behind them. I was actually pretty good at it. It was the only thing I was ever really good at. Well, the Nazi war criminals were fairly normal, too. A lot of them were family types, you know, take the kids to the zoo on Sundays. Mondays, go back to exterminating people, invading countries, goose-stepping. The new head of the Academy of Tobacco Studies, for instance, is very big in the Boy Scouts, the Kiwanis, Rotary International, Elks. If you met him and didn't know what he did, you'd probably think, nice guy, regular sort."

"You dedicate the book to two people: Doak Boykin—'the Captain'—former chairman of the board of the tobacco lobby, and Lorne Lutch, the former Tumbleweed brand model."

"Fine people, Larry. I think they should be forgiven for their role in tobacco, because they were of a previous generation that didn't really know just how bad it was for you. And by the end of their lives, they both saw the light, as it were, and regretted their . . . well, they felt badly about it. I spoke to the Captain the night before he died and he told me as much. As for Lorne, who died a couple of years ago— BR actually sent me out there with a briefcase full of five hundred thousand dollars cash to bribe him to stop denouncing tobacco, and you know what he did—this is in the book—he kicked me right out of there."

"That's a lot of temptation, five hundred grand."

"It certainly was, Larry. Courageous man."

"We're going to take some calls. Winston-Salem, North Carolina, you're on Larry King."

"Larry, I want to say that I think that man is lower than the slime on a catfish's belly. And I apologize to the catfish."

"Nick, care to comment?"

"Not really, Larry."

"Emotional issue."